I0676032

Sylvanus
RISE OF THE DEMON

BOOK OF ALCE
BOOK ONE

R.P. O'RYAN

Contents

Prologue

Let me tell you a story...

My name was Armiger, then Eyu named me Ariel.

Eyu made me a scribe of the Domains; I've been mandated to chronicle the history of the lands, leaders, enemies, and wars.

I am of humble birth who, at one time, was a soldier for hire, bored with life. As unworthy as I was, Eyu chose me for the duties I now perform. It is not something I aspired or worked to achieve.

I scribe the history of the lands and conserve them in a repository of scrolls called the Historicals. Scholars come from all over to learn from the written volumes in my city.

The Historicals begin with my earliest recollections of how it all began, save those of my childhood.

Since I chronicle only what I or other credible sources experience, I begin with a story of a simple assault. A cog in the machinations of another that turned a simple incursion into a war, altering the road history was to take.

It started on a distant island called Ortet with a warrior of impeccable reputation. Her duty was to guard a cliffside village on the coast....

Chapter 1
THE LIGHT IN THE NIGHT

The bell's peal from Signal Hill wakes Geolufeoer with a jolt; it's the alarm. Her hands sweep the floor of her canvas shelter, frantic in the deep, pre-dawn gloom, and she finds the aduncus, aegis shield, and bow, but her armor and pollex blades are nowhere near. Heart at her throat, she grabs what she has and scrambles from her shelter, hands out, searching in the moonlight. She runs to the cliff edge, a few seconds away, but her right wing snags the supporting line of the tent, spinning Geolufeoer around and sending her aduncus twirling into the darkness.

"Skagget!"

In the moonlight, she makes out the honey-colored flight feather jutting akimbo from her wing. Repairs will have to wait. She locates the aduncus by the blade's reflection in the ghostly light. She grabs it, slips it over her right wrist, secures the aegis to her left arm, and the bow, with attached arrows, to the harness, then runs again. Jumping over the fallen tree trunk, she finishes her sprint to the cliff's edge and dives into the void.

Geolufeoer feels the tug of her wings on her back as she makes final adjustments to her aduncus. The wings catch the wind, and she rides the currents high above the cliffs. Then, disoriented from sleep and the confusing darkness, she rises into the sky. The cold night air is quick to stimulate her senses. The night sky is a diamond-studded umbrella. Geolufeoer has no trouble navigating over land, but the night sky envelops her like a glimmering mantle, and the ocean, a mirror of the sky, blurs the boundary between the two.

With a twist of her wrist, the blade of the aduncus flicks open; she then snaps her wings. She feels the sting of the broken feather up to her shoulder blade. It reminds her that she did not find the pollex blades.

"Skag—"

No, I will clean up my language.

She chuckles.

It is incredible what runs through your mind before battle.

The chill of the night and the anticipation of facing the enemy cut through her, and the curse escapes.

"Skagget!" She mumbles.

The armor would at least have kept me warm. Where are the rest of the Haloguardians?

A second bell sounds three times; this one has a higher pitch.

"Since when do the Solois attack at night?" She shouts. "Skagget!"

"Was that the neweguard I heard cursing?" A ferm's voice comes from the other skybournes flying above, and laughter follows from different points in the darkness.

Blakazfeoer, really. You were a neweguard a month before me. I thought you were my friend. Ugh! When will a recruit show up and become the neweguard?

"Keep alert; this is no time for raillery. The groundstay and skybourne Solois have been attacking the posts for the past three weeks." The coloner's voice booms in the darkness.

Twenty-three days of attacks with no reason or gains for them.

The attacks have been fast and brief, sometimes, without any interaction with the Haloguardian or groundstay guard.

"Have they found out what they are after?"

"We still don't know, neweguard, but it looks like ferms are singled out. Their leader, Sceagga, has also been spotted.

"Hey! Where's your armor... where are your pollex?"

The Coloner's voice, sharp and furious, cut through the rush of the wind. He banked close, his gaze easily picking out the exposed joints of her wings, details impossible to hide even in this dim light.

Ugh! He saw me.

"Sorry, sir," she shouted back against the wind, "I couldn't find them in time."

She hears raucous trumpeting and sees a swarm of dark shapes climbing above the forest. The Skybourne Solois rise from the weald's canopy. In the dim light, their soiled, frayed robes flap wildly as they fly, looking like tattered cloth in the wind.

"Ok, you seafowl, let's see if we can capture one. We need to find out what they're up to. Neweguard, keep to the rear. I don't want you fighting without your armor."

"But—"

"No buts! Stay to the rear. That's an order."

"Yes, sir,"

The attacking Solois fly straight towards the guard, but then they swerve and avoid the confrontation, flying wildly and executing mock attacks. Geolufeoer tries to keep track of them, but their attacks have no pattern or purpose. They remind her of stinger attacks when you get near their hive.

One Solois breaks from the group and heads for Blakazfeoer. He passes near Geolufeoer but ignores her. She can see the tattered feathers on his wings, begrimed by lack of care.

Don't they preen?

A second Solois suddenly veers and heads straight for Geolufeoer. His attack surprises her; she turns, spins, and dives, avoiding his extended hand by a feather's breadth.

Geolufeoer was well known for her speed. Born with wings shaped for high velocity and quick turns, her speed record still stands at the Campus Excercitatus, where she trained.

Now, someone born for a slow, stealthy flight is chasing her. For him, speed is not important. But she caught his stealth attack in time. She evades him with a spinning maneuver. The reflection of the moon and stars on the water confounds her, forcing her to fold her wings to see which way she will fall. However, the attacker continues his pursuit, so she dives towards the water.

Let's see how good you are.

She looks over her shoulder long enough to see Blakazfeoer swooping to evade her pursuer. Named for her black feathers, Blakazfeoer's wings seem to momentarily disappear in the darkness. As she turns, the Solois reaches out, and a dark line appears on Blakazfeoer's arm.

Why are we the only ones chased?

Geolufeoer slows down, letting the Solois get just within reach. Before reaching the water, she loops up and evades him.

Oh, that smell!

The Solois cannot turn fast enough, but reaches out before splashing into the water at the last moment. This time, Geolufeoer feels a sharp pain as something rakes her thigh.

Ouch! Too close.

She looks back and sees the Solois flapping across the ocean's surface like waterfowl do when they take to the air.

What's he doing?

She watches him for a moment as he tries to keep one arm out of the water while trying to take flight. He clears the water flying in a frenetic, almost desperate way.

"Oh no, you don't."

Geolufeoer immediately nocks an arrow. The Solois, a stealth flyer, begins his ascent with erratic, unpredictable movements—each beat of his wings shifts his body up, down, or sharply to the side. This evasive flight, coupled with the low light, confounds her aim. She looses the arrow. It sails wide. Nocking a second arrow, she shoots before the Solois manages to lose himself among the trees.

A single blast from a horn, and the Solois swarm turns and flees. Geolufeoer is angry and scared. With another arrow ready, she looks at the trees, trying to find movement. But the dark weald shrouds any movement.

"Flock, regroup."

The colonel's voice calls in the distance.

She takes one last look at the forest and returns to the flock.

Ten minutes later, the bell announces the end of the attack; her heart thumps hard against her breast as she begins to relax. She has never seen a battle. The incident has not only shaken off the night chill but has driven away all vestiges of her sleep.

The Solois, Busart, stumbles as he lands hard in the forest. Almost falling, he spins behind a tree and peers around the trunk.

She's still looking.

Busart tucks his wings hard against his back and slides back around the tree. He closes his eyes and gulps for air.

That was close, too close.

Busart cradles the hooked tool against his chest as if his life depended on it, which it does. He watches Geolufeoer flying in circles, searching the forest, until a voice, too far to understand, calls, and she flies away.

Ten minutes later, the bell sounds again, announcing everything is clear.

He peeks around the trunk and relaxes when he sees the haloguardian fly away. He looks at the wet tool in his hand.

If the sample is ruined, the master will kill me.

He proceeds to the meeting place, but the master is not there.

Did he see me fall in the water?

"Busart?" A voice calls from the brush.

Busart jumps and puffs a sigh of relief when he sees a skybourne solois emerge from his hiding place.

"Sisab, it's you. Did you get a sample?" Busart asks.

"Easy as plundering nests," Sisab says

He holds up the curved tool, its tip smeared with blood.

"And I didn't have to bathe for it," he mocks.

Busart looks at his tool and slowly shakes his head.

Sisab saw me.

"There you are."

They both turn as another solois staggers from the shadows. This one is a groundstay, a wingless solois. His face shows a dark wet smear in the moonlight, and his ripped hood dangles from his otherwise well-tailored robe.

He holds his arrow-impaled shoulder.

"Here it is, Master Hergian—" Sisab says.

He holds out his tool.

Busart sees the arrow on his master's shoulder.

"What happened?" Busart says.

"Stray arrows, the other came too close to my face. Pull this out for me," Hergian says.

Busart pulls the arrow. Hergian makes a grunting noise.

"I can wrap that for you," Busart says.

"Don't bother. I heal quickly," Hergian says. "Give me that."

Hergian takes the hook-shaped scoop from Sisab. He waggles his fingers, and a small globe of light appears, hovering over the tool. It was a simple trick, the first Sceagga had taught him, but it always impressed his minions.

Hergian pulls a small vial from a belt pouch; a thick, dark liquid churns inside. He dabs a small amount on his finger and touches the tool's tip. Immediately, a misty brume rises from the sample until it condenses to a solid lump.

"Nothing again."

Hergian says and tosses the tool to the ground.

As soon as Hergian turns to Busart, Sisab retrieves the tool. He might need it again.

"I'm beginning to tire of this."

"There must be one somewhere," Sisab says.

"The master believes there is, so there is," Hergian says.

He holds out his hand.

"Busart, let's see yours."

Busart hands him the tool, his trembling hand still wet.

"This is wet, Busart. You better hope the sample is good." Hergian says.

"Sorry, Master. I tried to keep it out of the water," Busart's voice trembles.

"Were there others?"

"No, Master, there were only two," Sisab says.

Hergian looks at the hook and sees a shred of blood-smeared flesh. Once again, he dabs it with the liquid. All the while, Busart looks on as his fate hangs on whether there is a reaction. Then, in the glow of the globe's light, a smile creeps over Hergian's face.

"It's turning blue! It's compatible with the master's blood. Well done, Busart," Hergian says, wrapping the hook with a piece of cloth.

Busart gives Sisab a priggish look. Sisab scowls back.

"Take me back to Master Sceagga; he will be pleased."

"To Master Sceagga.... himself?" Busart gulps.

"Yes, himself. You and Sisab will carry me back. We mustn't delay, or the sample will spoil; he'll want to see it himself; let's go!"

Busart and Sisab take to the air, carrying their master back.

Neither Sisab nor Busart had met the sortiarius, but from what they've heard, they hope Sceagga is in a good mood.

Geolufeoer speeds over the cliffs. She no longer looks for Solois; she's trying to spend her adrenaline-fueled energy.

"Guard, report."

She hears the coloner's shout and flies back to the flock.

"Nothing to report, coloner," says one of the guards.

"We didn't even get to use our blades," another says.

"Blakazfeoer, Geolufeoer, they were chasing you two. Did they say anything? Was there anything you noticed?" the coloner asks.

"Nothing, sir. But one did slash my arm with something," Blakazfeoer says.

"Same here, sir. Except he got my thigh." Geolufeoer says.

"You were slashed? You are excused then, go and take care of your wounds. For all we know, those weapons may be poisoned. Report tomorrow."

"Yes, sir," they both say.

As Geolufeoer flies back to her camp, a light low on the horizon catches her attention. It is farther than any local fishtanglers go with their pole lanterns at night.

"Coloner!" she shouts.

"Yes, Geolufeoer." He turns to her, hovering with powerful strokes of his wings.

"Isn't that fishtangler's boat out a little far?"

The coloner looks to the horizon.

"Your eyesight is good," he pauses for a milsec. "If he's tangling that far out, he will have thought to take supplies for the night."

He turns back to her.

"Either way, he's too far out to ask him; we would never find our way at night. Go back to your post."

"Yes, sir."

"And neweguard."

He calls back to her.

Ugh, neweguard again

"Yes, sir."

"Good work; you were the only one who noticed the fishtangler. I'll send someone out in the morning to check on him."

"Yes, sir, thank you, sir."

He hears the smile in her voice.

She will make a fine warrior.

"Now go and tend to your wound. The rest of you, keep watch; make sure they don't return."

"What are those outcasts up to?" The coloner grumbles.

The guards keep vigil around the cliffside village for the next few hours, ensuring the attackers don't return.

When he sees everything is quiet, the coloner dismisses them.

Back in her camp, Geolufeoer is still unable to relax. The trembling from the melee had subsided. But she is still restless. She cleaned her wound and waited to see if a poison manifested itself, but it had not.

Once again, she flies from her post to see if the mysterious light has moved; In the early light, it is still there.

I wonder if he is lost?

She decides on a short nap. The early morning attack had robbed several hours of her sleep.

Two hours later, within the calls of morning birds and chirrups of hopping insects, a sound, like the distant squawking of a horn, touches Geolufeoer in her slumber. Even though she barely hears it, her eyes snap open.

She stares at the roof of her lean-to for a few moments, wondering if it was real. Still, there's only the gentle flapping of the canvas in the ocean breeze, spreading its familiar smell around her. The voices and sounds of cooking utensils rising from the cliff-face, skybourne villagers below are the only sounds that do not come from nature. Then there is the heat radiating from the canvas.

"Skagget! I overslept. What time is it?"

She has tried eliminating the swear from her vocabulary, but it always returns.

She crawls out of her shelter and feels the grass.

It's dry.

The sun sits high above the horizon.

"Skag—" she catches herself this time.

I definitely overslept!

Geolufeoer stands and feels a sharp pain in her thigh. She looks down and sees the blood smear on her bind.

Looks like the bleeding stopped; I'll check it later.

The first thing she sees is the leather vest and pollex in the corner of the shelter.

I must have kicked them while I slept.

She straps the pollex on her wings, then dons the vest. She pulls at its bottom and stretches to make sure everything is comfortable. Her wings unfold and flap twice, creating a small vortex of leaves that scatter before her.

"Ouch!"

The broken feather twists wildly with the effort, sending the thorn-sharp pain to her shoulder.

"Skagget!"

A glance around the campsite assures her no one is around to hear the curse.

Forgot about the feather; what else can possibly go wrong?

She flexes her wing to the front and sees the broken, bright orange flight feather.

Should I pluck it?

She will grow a new one in about three weeks, but she will not be able to fly for a couple of hours until the bleeding stops. Then, it will turn into a mess if there is another attack.

"Bah, I'll splint it later after I check my leg."

Splinting the feather requires time, and it will have to be uninterrupted. Yelu ties the feather to another with a piece of thread.

That will keep it still for now.

She carefully tucks the tips of her vulpine ears beneath the tress of red hair and flinches. She learned the hard way that not only does the Haloguardian's braid keep the hair from getting in her face when she flies, but the intricate plaits also cover and protect the ears.

"That braid makes my head look like a red melopepon," she argued, and since it wasn't mandatory, she skipped it that first day.

Today, the tips of her ears still itch from the sunburn she received.

It is her fourteenth day on the watch. She is bored and tired, and her grey eyes are bloodshot from the wind and the sun.

Well, whatever it was, the alarm did not sound.

She flies around her post; there's nothing out of the ordinary.

Well, if the others see me, they'll know I'm alert...or at least awake and fully equipped this time.

She drops back to her camp, hoping one of the guards spotted her.

Who knows, the chief may have blown a horn himself to see who comes out.

It's time for her morning meal. She unfastens the bow from its harness and lays it down.

Lost two arrows last night. I have to replace them. But first breakfast.

She pulls her nosh bag from the shelter.

"I wonder what's for breakfast?"

She peeks inside a smaller bag and pretends surprise.

"Oh, look, dried fruit and fowl."

Her sarcasm is lost to the empty campsite.

After three weeks, even dried fish sounds good.

She gathers her meal, a water flask, the small leather case containing the pins, string, and wax to repair broken feathers, and a clean strip of cloth to bind her thigh.

Afterward, sitting on the log by her shelter, she spots something on the ground. It is a small carving. The mound of wooden figurines she had made during her free time is a measure of her boredom. They represent the parts of her culture she identifies with. A fishtangler carrying his catch over his shoulder; the hunter pulling his bowstring; the bernoz entering the cave for the winter. Another small pile of figurines, discarded for their flaws, lays to the side.

Geolufeoer was given her maturite name for the yellow feathers on her wings. However, she also carried a shock of bright red hair, and with her yellow wings, the trainees said she looked like she was on fire when she sped by.

She prides herself on being one of the few skybourne doyennes who made it through the rigorous training and testing of the Haloguardian.

Geolufeoer now wears leather armor, a fawn-colored leather vest with a golden wing over each breast. She also bears the mark of the Haloguardian between her shoulder blades, a brand placed where she cannot see it. Around her left bicep is the Haloguardian arm bracelet. It is made of long silver feathers that wrap around her arm with a black stone bearing a carving of two wings.

Geolufeoer completed her mandatory three-year cycle as a regular guard at nineteen, but she was not satisfied. She did not want to return to her village to become a denwyf and raise cildra. She knew she could do better, and the Haloguardian felt more rewarding to her at the time.

Then there was Gneisfeoer, the young Haloguardian with light brown hair and striped wings. It was his attention she was trying to gain; he was the one she was trying to impress.

However, in the end, it was Sextefeoer, the doyenne with six long flight feathers, who stole his heart. Just as in life, those clouds have wandered.

Because of her heartbreak, she decided to continue her training. Eventually, she became the youngest in the elite force at twenty-one years.

Geolufeoer gets up, walks to the cliff edge, watches the horizon, and wonders if the light will be there again tonight. It was farther than any of the local boats tangled at night; she flew up several times to look, and it had not moved, so she was sure it was not a star.

She walks back to the log again and sits.

"Three more days." She sighs, a little louder than intended, then looks around to make sure she is alone.

She picks up the carving she had been working on. Her fingers skitter over the small figure to feel for rough spots. It is a sitting groundstay with a fishtangler's pole. She ties a hair from the pole to the small fish she carved and sits the figurine on the log.

I'm getting better.

The distant rumble of thunder announces the dark band of clouds gathering on the horizon.

I'm so glad I didn't have to bivouac in the snow. But, of course, now it's going to rain.

With the season of snow behind her, she can shed some of the bulkier clothes. But now, the rains begin. She pulls her waxed robe from her pack and slips it on. It covers her head and torso but leaves the wings free.

She looks back at the clouds, calculating how long it will take the storm to reach her.

In the distance, against the rising wall of clouds, the bird-drovers are rising from their tall floating platforms to gather their flocks.

17

It looks far away, but it's bad weather if the drovers are bringing in the flocks.

Most young maritime Skybournes, at one time or another, tended the domesticated seabirds. Yelu was no exception.

A soft rustle of leaves raises a smile.

"Is that who I think it is?"

A shushing noise comes from the shrubbery as the culprits try to quiet each other.

"It sounds like a great bernoz from the weald. I better shoot it lest it eats me."

Suddenly there is a lot of squealing and rustling as two small skybourne pipios tumble from the bushes. They're in a confusion of arms, legs, and wings.

While young groundstays are called girls or boys, young skybourne girls are called pipios and boys duvos. The small pipio wears a bright green dress, while the older one wears blue.

"Well, it's Surnia and Pandion coming to check my work," Geolufeoer says. "Well then, come on, tell me what you think."

The two pipios start giggling; they run to Geolufeoer and wrap their arms around her waist. A lump rises to her throat.

Is this what it's like to have cildra?

She motions to a spot on the ground before her, and they sit.

They had befriended her on her first day on duty.

"So, tell me, which one do you like?"

She talks to Surnia, the younger one, whose hair is as white as the clouds.

"The hunter," she says, "I like the hunter."

Geolufeoer picks up the figurine of a man drawing a bow and looks it over carefully.

"I don't know; this could easily be one of my favorites."

The pipio pouts in disappointment.

"But, I guess someone should look after it."

Geolufeoer holds out the carving, and the little skybourne claps her hands excitedly. Then, she cradles the figurine in her hands.

"And which is your favorite?"

The older pipio, Pandion, is the other's sister. Her hair is light brown. The pipios had insisted on Geolufeoer braiding the Haloguardian's weave on their hair, so they both sported the braids. Geolufeoer picks a stray leaf from Pandion's braids and wonders if her color was also white when younger.

"I like the bernoz going into the cave."

"Ahhh, so you like the bernoz."

She picks up the carving of a heavyset creature walking into a cave.

"I think he had just had his fill of berries and honeyfly nectar. He must be going to his cave for the winter."

She hands her the carving.

"And what do I get in return?"

The pipios stand and give her another hug.

'Clannng!'

Geolufeoer hears the alarm. The feathers on her wings stand on end from fear and apprehension.

Another attack? It's only been a few hours!

The guard on the hill sounds the long bell. Its peal sweeps the treetops and spills over the cliffs losing itself in the distance.

The pipios are startled; immediately, Pandion holds her younger sister to her chest, wrapping her wings around her protectively.

"Go to your den, hurry!" Geolufeoer gently shoves them towards the cliff edge.

Pandion pulls Surnia towards the edge and jumps into the void.

'Clannng!'

The clangor pulses through the forest over and again.

"Skagget!"

She curses under her shuddering breath.

She straps the pollex blades to her wings and slides the aegis shield over her left forearm. Then, with trembling hand, she pulls the aduncus from her belt and slips her hand through the opening in the handle of the curved blade.

She takes another deep breath. Then, looking at her short war bow, a soup of jitters and apprehension kicks in. The bow makes it all real. Another deep breath.

She leans to pick it up, and the sting on her thigh reminds her of the last attack.

I can't let them get that close again.

Another deep breath.

I need to calm myself; I need to do better.

Think of something else...Yes, the pipios, think of the pipios; I have to protect the dens.

Geolufeoer runs to the cliff's edge and dives, her wings open, catching the swelling updraft that carries her high. A small band of Haloguardian soars into position over the weld. They come from the lookout stations along the cliffs. There she joins them.

Coloner Roanfeoer is a battle-hardened skybourne; Geolufeoer can almost count the encounters he has been in by his scars. He enjoys letting his sword cuts, arrow, and spear punctures show. He has a peculiar small round scar on his thigh, of which he is particularly proud. He slew five Solois with his aduncus while an arrow was lodged in his leg. She knows, though, that beneath all of his gruffness, he cares about his flock. So he has taken special care in training them to ensure they can survive any battle.

"Ok, neweguard, good! I see you're fully equipped. Here's your chance to prove yourself," the coloner says.

Even though she knows she is, she hates the word neweguard.

When will a new recruit show up?

Grating trumpet notes cause a flock of birds to explode from the forest canopy. It is followed by the Solois; there are too many to count.

"I have received word that some of the Solois killed in the south have been identified. They were over six hundred years old. That's a lot of time to practice fighting.

"Most of the ones you'll see will be puppa dolls, but among them will be Solois; be careful."

"Coloner, there are way more than last night. How many are there?" she asks.

"We estimate around one hundred and fifty in this swarm."

She looks around and sees only fifteen Haloguardian.

We are outnumbered by ten to one!

"Any chance of getting help?" she asks, trying to act calm, but the quaver in her voice is not convincing.

"The other flocks are busy with attacks on the southern shore, probably just a diversion. So we will have to defend the dens until they arrive."

"What are they after?"

"We don't know yet. But it looks like this attack is the real thing. The scout said he saw Sceagga leading them."

Sceagga?

Her stomach sinks.

Why would he lead an attack? What's so important about this place?.... Sceagga?

She recalls the history of the island nation of Ortet and the role Sceagga had in ruining their paradise, their utopia.

Over six hundred years have gone since the Battle of Merkoum, where Sceagga was defeated by a group of powerful sortiarius known as the Keepers. There has been no sign of him until recenly, and Geolufeoer will now face the leader of the armies whose barbarity changed Terraen's history forever.

"Coloner, It took the Keepers to defeat Sceagga the last time. What are we supposed to do?" Geolufeoer says.

"Think of the dens, Geolufeoer. We'll do what we have to."

I wonder if he's as powerful as they say.

"Is it true what they say? Can he throw firebolts, kill with a single touch, and control the dead?

"Those stories have been exaggerated with time," he says.

Her mind starts racing.

He is several hundred years old, and it took the Keepers to defeat him.

Geolufeoer can hear the raucous battle horn; they have been spotted and are now their target.

"Swalowe attack!" The coloner shouts.

The Haloguardian soar in formation, waiting for the Solois to get closer. The swalowe attack works perfectly with a large group, but with only fifteen?

Once the swarm is within range, the group flies down until they are a few feet off the ground. The Solois follow them to the edge of the cliff. Geolufeoer is one of the seven in the lead group. The ones in the rear spread their wings stiffly to the sides. They release a cloud of fine dust blocking the view of the Solois. Her group swoops down, out of sight, over the bluff's edge, just like the small cliff birds.

The rest clear the cliffs and head towards the open ocean, streaming the dust behind them with the Solois close.

Geolufeoer looks over her shoulder. When the last of the attackers pass over them, the seven swalowes turn and beat their wings furiously. They ride the currents upwards beneath the Solois stragglers.

Save for the night before, Geolufeoer has never been in actual battle, let alone killed anyone. She picks a young Solois in ragged clothes from the group. He seems to be flying blindly, just following the rest, his face expressionless. She draws the bow but can't release the arrow.

What of his family?

Then, a swarm of arrows passes her, and the young Solois is struck. He passes by Geolufeoer as he falls; he tries to slash her with his sword, his last dying attempt at completing his unknown mission. She blocks the sword as he plummets towards the water; his face is expressionless.

"Geolufeoer! Snap out of it!" shouts Blakazfeoer.

"They're no longer of the living."

That's right, no longer alive.

She snaps out of her trance; this time, the arrow flies, and her mark falls. Again, she sees the expressionless face and keeps repeating to herself.

Not of the living.

The Haloguardian shoot three volleys before passing behind the Solois and flying high above them. The Solois never notice that twenty-one have fallen. The Haloguardian turn and dive in formation to attack the stragglers of the group. Twenty more fall to the waters below. As they pass the group, the Solois battle horn sounds, and the rear half of the swarm dive with them as a unit.

"What just happened?" she shouts.

"I don't know…Pondflower!" The coloner shouts.

The seven go in different directions and loop up, like the petals of the pondflower in bloom. The Solois seem to be acting

23

with a single mind; however, they do not have the training of the Haloguardian, and they aren't quite as fast. Finally, as they rise to meet the Haloguardian, the coloner gives his last order.

"Shoot until they're close, then use the aduncus." He says. "May Eyu shelter you."

The Solois with the horn is the first hit.

At least the annoying noise is gone.

After that, Geolufeoer shoots arrow after arrow at the Solois, and thirty more fall to the water. The attackers do not attempt to dodge the arrows or even flinch.

The haloguardians secure their bows and open their aduncus when they're too close to reload.

A movement at the cliff edge catches Geolufeoer's attention. She sees a sortiarius standing with his arms up in the air. She flies higher to gain more time to observe him. He moves his arms and sees that the Solois change direction accordingly.

Skagget! It is true; he controls them.

"Neweguard! Hold your position," the coloner shouts.

"Coloner, it's Sceagga; he's controlling the Solois," she says, pointing at the sortiarius.

Roanfeoer looks at the cliff edge and sees what he is doing. "Get him!"

She breaks from the group and nocks an arrow on her bow. Sceagga sees her approaching and smiles.

Ahh, she fits the description. So, you're the one I've been looking for; come closer...closer.

When she is almost in range, he raises his hand. A brilliant ball of light forms in his palm, and he throws it like a stone.

The ball of light speeds at Geolufeoer faster than any beast or arrow has ever flown. Instinctively she dodges to the side, but the ball strikes her bow hand, burning it and splitting the bow.

Ow! What the?... What they say is true; he can throw fireballs!

The coloner calls to her. He saw the energy bolt and realized that any attack will be suicide.

"Geolufeoer, retreat!"

She realizes using the aduncus is out of the question; she veers away.

When she turns, she sees the pipios watching from the balcony. She motions to them to get inside. Sceagga catches the signal. He takes to the air to see what she is looking at, then looks back at Geolufeoer and smiles again.

Oh no!

Her eyes widen with fear. Sceagga flicks his wrist, and the five Solois pursuing her break away. They head straight for the balcony with swords drawn and a battle cry. One look at the howling knot, and the pipios disappear into their den, squealing with terror.

"NOOO!"

Geolufeoer forgets all about Sceagga and chases the Solois. She catches up to them; within seconds, she kills four. The fifth lands on the balcony and runs inside. She flies wildly towards the den, folds her wings, and pitches herself through the entrance. The pipio's mother is unconscious on the floor, pinning Surnia underneath. The Solois has Pandion by her leg, flapping wildly like a captured bird. The attacker drops his sword in the commotion and tries to grab it, but the struggling pipio keeps him off balance. Geolufeoer's momentum carries her through the portal; she lands hard on her wings and rolls into the Solois, knocking his legs out from under him.

"Let her go!" She bellows.

She viciously stabs the Solois as he tumbles over her, then spins, slashing him with the pollex as he falls. The wounds are fatal; his wings flap in death convulsions, then relax. Wasting no time, she stands, gathers the pipios covering their eyes, pushes them into one of the rooms, then unceremoniously drags the mother to them.

"She'll be fine; lock the door when I leave."

Pandion is holding Surnia to her chest, wings wrapped tightly around her. She looks back at Geolufeoer, tears streaming down her face. A sense of sadness fills the Haloguardian when she sees the blood-stained blue dress. The pipio nods while trying to control her sobs and closes the door.

Geolufeoer runs back to the balcony. She tries to discard the shattered bow, but the harness holds it fast. In five steps, she clears the room and dives off the balcony. The approaching sortiarius almost collides with Geolufeoer. Sceagga reaches for her; she parries and slashes his shoulder. The blow numbs his wing, and he falls. Geolufeoer could have finished him with the bow, but it's no use worrying about that now. After witnessing the fireball, she's no longer sure of the extent of his powers.

Can he kill with a touch?

Geolufeoer realizes he's after her.

Why me?

She speeds back towards the group with powerful flaps of her wings. The Haloguardian are all fighting at grips length with the Solois.

Sceagga's fall brings him within fifty paces of the rock-strewn base of the cliff. He regains his senses, swerves to avoid the rocks, and continues the chase.

Geolufeoer speeds back through the battle scene; she can see that the Haloguardian is starting to overpower the Solois easily. However, Geolufeoer notices that the blank stare and emotionless faces are fading. Life is returning to them.

They're not dead! Just spellbound by Sceagga.

A knot forms in her stomach.

Are they actually innocent?

"Whatever you are doing, keep it up," shouts the coloner as she passes. "They're no longer fighting back."

The coloner watches the two speed away into the gathering storm.

Geolufeoer keeps heading towards the open ocean and feels the heavy raindrops on her face. The churning clouds turn everything grey. Lightning shears the sky; its deafening thunder drums against her chest. Winds buffet them, but Sceagga continues his pursuit.

Let's see who's faster.

Geolufeoer goes faster. The raindrops feel like small pebbles, pummeling her face and shoulders. She looks back and is surprised to see that Sceagga is keeping up.

Impossible! Maybe he's using his powers.

Then she sees a figure advancing behind Sceagga.

More Solois?

She pushes herself to go faster, and so does the sortiarius. Between the gathering darkness and the rain, she can no longer see where she is headed. The wind tosses her about, disorienting her. Large drops keep pelting her face and arms; everything is dark grey, and the land is no longer visible. She looks over her shoulder once more, and lightning flashes across the skies, followed by the thunder's roar. This time she can make out the figure of the coloner taking aim at Sceagga with his bow. The light fades, throwing Geolufeoer into the grey darkness again.

A shriek tears through the gloom; she looks back as three lightning strikes light the skies and sees Sceagga plummeting towards the water. Roanfeoer waves for her to come back, then darkness once more. She swoops and turns towards Roanfeoer. Lightning flashes again, and she sees Roanfeoer waiting for her. In the darkness that follows, a ball of light speeds up towards the coloner. His body is strangely outlined by the illumination from below. The coloner looks down in puzzlement before it strikes; his body ignites, feathers, hair, and clothing incinerate with a bright flash, then falls like an ember into the water. Geolufeoer gasps; she has never seen anything like it before. She is momentarily blinded by the explosion.

Lightning strike? But it came from below!

A long series of lightning bolts light up the skies again; by the simultaneous sound of the thunder, she is now in the middle of the storm.

She looks at the waters below to see where Roanfeoer has fallen and sees Sceagga flying up at her. Her heart leaps to her throat.

He survived?

She turns to flee, but it is too late; he is already on her. Sceagga grabs her leg, pulls her down, and seizes her arm. Geolufeoer tries to reach the aduncus but loses the feeling in the limbs.

He is draining my energy.

Sceagga's eyes start to lose focus, and he looks like he is dying, perhaps from the arrowhead protruding from his chest.

Maybe using the energy bolts weakens him. If I can hold on longer—

He reaches up and grabs her forehead with his left hand. A sickly warmth courses through her head; she gags as it passes her throat and into her body. He releases her, and something moves inside her. She looks down, but nothing touches her.

She regains the feeling in her arm. Then, blindly, she reaches out and grips the sortiarius' water-laden robes, flicks open the aduncus, and drives the blade deep, next to the arrowhead. In the darkness, Sceagga coughs and takes a deep breath.

"You now carry the seed," he exhales.

Sceagga slips from her grasp and falls away.

When the skies light up again, he is floating on the waters below.

Geolufeoer does not know which way to go. She flies in a lazy circle, waiting for the next lightning to light up the land. The rain stops. She looks towards the horizon and sees the faint light above the water.

If that is the fishtangler's light, the land must be behind me.

Once again, she feels the strange sensation deep inside. She covers her stomach with her hands.

What did he do to me?

Then, a single lightning bolt pierces the clouds. The bolt strikes her forehead, travels down her body, and splits. One part bursts through her wings, shattering them; the other hammers into her womb. All goes numb. She feels herself falling; then, the cool waters wrap around her. Lightning lights up the skies, and steady rains begin. The clouds light above, and she sees the curious pattern that rain makes when you look up at it.

The rain is beautiful.

The sound of rain on the water brings a certain peace to her. There is no pain, no worries. She cannot remember anything; nothing is important. Sleep beckons; she closes her eyes and surrenders to the darkness.

The storm lasted three days. It isn't until the weather clears on the fourth that the rescuers can go out and look for *those lost in battle. The Lorica, the elite groundstay forces, is tasked with the grizzly job of gathering the bodies since it's easier for them to move around on the boats. They find the charred remains of Coloner Roanfeoer with the bodies of other Haloguardians who perished in the encounter, save for Geolufeoer and Sceagga. Witnesses say they saw the doyenne, the coloner, and the sortiarius in the waves. Yet, they only found the coloner's body.*

The Lorica in the boats encounter swarms of large carnivorous fish feeding on the bodies of the fallen Solois and Haloguardian. If the doyenne and Sceagga fell as far from land as reported, maybe the fish got to them first.

It is strange that most intact bodies only show minor injuries. Very few have wounds that would have proven fatal. They let the mystery fallow, though. The war is over after so many years, and a much-needed celebration will come first.

At the battle site, a ceremony takes place, and the Haloguardian erects a small monument with the names of the fallen heroes.

With the sortiarius gone, the compelling link is broken. The Solois flee into the weald. The rest are unaware of how they got there or what had transpired.

Chapter 2

THE RIVER SPIRIT

It is the end of summer when the leaves on the trees paint the forest in reds and yellows. The Taloosh are finishing their week-long walk, the migration toward the fishing grounds. This yearly trek has always been a part of the tribe's life. It all started when the great black rock was thrown from the heavens many generations ago, marking the place the spirits chose for them to live. Or so says the talekeeper of the Taloosh. Next to the great black rock, the shaman built his hut.

The River Spill ends in a series of falls before retiring into the ocean. Here, the large pink-fleshed fish leap over the stony falls, fighting the rocks and currents that leave their bodies in ruin, all to reach their breeding grounds. This is where the Taloosh goes to harvest the fish.

However, another large river must be crossed before reaching the River Spill. It is also large and powerful, but this river offers few fish.

Shaman Tiglit Leads the villagers. Behind him is his eldest son Tall Tree. Following is Tall Tree's wife, Red Bird, and their children Dancing Elk and Wrensong.

At five, this is Dancing Elk's first time walking the trek. His sister, Wrensong, is still too small to make the journey on foot, so she rides either in the dog travois or the papoose.

Though well marked, the path shows a year of neglect. Though the thorny brambles offer an abundance of red and black berries, their occasional reach across the path slows the group's progress.

Annoyed, as five-year-olds tend to get when tired, Dancing Elk rubs his arm from the most recent scratch.

"Father, why do we walk this far for the fish? Wouldn't it be easier if we lived at River Spill?"

"River Spill is only good to live this time of the year. There are few fish in the summer, and deer and elk are deeper in the forest. In the winter, it rains constantly, and the cold winds blow over the big water," Tall Tree says.

"So, why do we come?"

"The fish is more than plentiful now. We can catch enough in one week to feed the village through winter, which takes the pressure off the deer and elk from the hunting." Tall Tree says.

"Let's not forget, Dancing Elk, that our home was marked by the spirits when they dropped the black stone," Shaman Tiglit says.

"The black stone makes me feel strange when I get close to it," Dancing Elk says.

"What you feel is the spirit of the stone. How long have you felt it?" Tiglit asks.

"Two, maybe three days, before our walk," Dancing Elk says,

"Hmm. Do not let it bother you," Tiglit says.

His growth has been fast. Can he feel the spirits now? I must keep an eye on him.

Tall Tree calls White Eagle a young man who always does the climbing for him.

"Go to the high rock. Tell me if you can see the first river."

White Eagle nods and clambers up the rocky outcropping. He sees the waterway winding among the hillocks of reds, yellows, and tans.

The young man points and calls down to him.

"It's up ahead."

The trek continues until they reach the first river.

"The rains were heavy this summer. The river swells almost to the trees. If the water gets any higher, it will flood the area," Tiglit says.

"We have to cross to get to where the fish are jumping now," Tall Tree says. "It'll be two weeks before they reach this river. Even then, the harvest will be poor and take twice as long."

He turns to White Eagle again.

"We need to see if the river can be crossed," Tall Tree says.

Tall Tree points to a towering redwood.

"White Eagle, climb that tree. Tell me if there's a place to cross."

Once again, White Eagle does what he is told.

Tall Tree watches the young man clamber up the tree. He is strong for his age, and jumping from branch to branch seemed natural.

He will make a good warrior.

White Eagle didn't mind the climbing. As a matter of fact, he liked the challenge.

"If we're careful, we can use the rocks upstream to cross, it will take time, but it can be done." White Eagle shouts.

White Eagle leads the tribe upstream until they reach a series of flat rocks, barely showing over the turbulence.

"I will go first and take the crossing rope to the other side," Tall Tree says.

The warrior nimbly steps, hops, and wades across the river carrying the heavy rope. It was the leader's duty to do so. If the spirits did not wish for it, they wouldn't let him cross.

Once on the other side, he knows that the spirits have shown favor. So he secures the rope to a tree. Now the tribe will have something to hold on to when they cross.

"I'll go next," Dancing Elk says.

The boy grabs the rope. Then the roar of the rapids beckons a dare.

I've been waiting, brave one. Cross if you dare.

Dancing Elk's eyes widen.

Who said that? Someone is daring me.

He stares at the water.

"Just keep your eyes on Tall Tree," *Red Bird shouts over the roar.* "Don't look down, and don't stop."

"I am the son of Tall Tree; I do not fear the water." *Dancing Elk shouts.*

Red Bird looks at Tiglit. The shaman is frowning, staring at the water.

"What's he shouting?" *She asks.*

Dancing Elk starts to cross with a white knuckle grip on the rope.

Tiglit doesn't hear her; he just stares at the turbulence.

Did the water spirit call to him? It did; I heard it.

"Wait!" *Tiglit shouts.*

But the roar grows louder, drowning Tiglit's voice.

The frigid water washes over Dancing Elk's feet; he feels a tug on his ankles and gasps but retains his balance.

It is just cold water. I have to show that I'm brave.

After the initial shock, he ignores it and continues, keeping his eyes on his father.

The rocks farther across are not submerged, but the current constantly boils over them. Dancing Elk takes a deep breath and steps. The rushing water now slaps just above his ankles. The next rock is above the water, almost out of the reach of his stride. Hesitating, he looks at the span; it is wide but within his reach.

"I am the son of Tall Tree," *he repeats, though not as loud.*

He reaches with his step. The rock he's standing on moves, and his foot falls short. His leg goes deep to his knee. Something seizes his leg, and he goes into the water.

While all eyes are on Dancing Elk, Tiglit sees a mound of water rise, splashing up in an odd surge. To the shaman, it is definitely the river spirit.

It is Ijiraq!

The story of Ijiraq has always been part of tribal history. It is a primal naiad that seeks those with strong spiritual abilities. He takes over their bodies and uses them as a vessel so he can walk among men. He returns to the river when he tires of the land and drowns his vessel to become a spirit again.

Tiglit sensed the growth of Dancing Elk's spirit power and started training the boy to succeed him as shaman. Ijiraq sensed him, too, and now wants him.

The icy water is jarring; Dancing Elk fights to hold on.

He gulps for air and attempts to stand in the waist-deep water, but something keeps pulling his leg, and he goes under.

Tall Tree immediately jumps in after his son. He reaches Dancing Elk and, fighting the current, pushes him towards the shore.

The boy tries to stand, but the pull gets stronger. He falls again, and the river speaks once more.

I got you!

Fear grips Dancing Elk. He bobs out of the water, gasping for breath. He can't hear Red Bird's or Tiglit's shouts, only the river spirit.

You are mine.

He desperately tries to stand.

"Who…talks…to me?" He shouts between watery coughs.

Another pull, and he slips again. This time, his head strikes a rock, and he is swept away.

Tall Tree grabs Dancing Elk's leather shirt and drags his limp body towards the shore, jamming it among the rocks.

How dare you!

Tall Tree struggles against the current, but an odd wave rises out of the water. Tiglit watches in horror as the river envelopes the warrior with a thick watery blanket that does not fall and drags him under the water. Ijiraq claims Tall Tree.

The villagers only saw a strange wave rise, cover the warrior, and pull him under. But Tiglit knows otherwise.

"Get the boy, quickly. Get him out of the water," Tiglit shouts. They form a chain and pull Dancing Elk from the rocks. Red Bow, Tiglit's younger son, grabs the boy's arm and pulls.

"He is stuck; he won't move," Red Bow says.

Tiglit can see that the water around the boy is thick, like honey. Ijiraq is holding him.

"Pull harder, hurry!"

Red Bow pulls with all his strength, and Dancing Elk is pulled loose. The limp body is placed on the riverbank, where Tiglit and several others jostle, bump and pummel the small body until Dancing Elk coughs up water.

Red Bird hugs her son, sobbing with relief, but she looks at the river that took Tall Tree and wails.

"Go look for Tall Tree," Tiglit tells her. "I'll see to your son."

Red Bird and the others go searching for Tall Tree. Alone, the boy turns to the shaman.

"Grandfather, the river spirit spoke to me. It dared me to cross," Dancing Elk says. "Then it grabbed me."

The boy looks down at his leg. The reddish start of a bruise on his leg is shaped like a hand.

"I know, I heard it; it was Ijiraq," Tiglit says. "I tried to warn you, but you didn't hear me."

Coughing, Dancing Elk staggers to his feet.

"It seems your father angered the spirit," Tiglit says.

Dancing Elk looks across the river.

"Where's father?"

"Ijiraq wanted you but took him instead," Tiglit says.

"No! We have to get him back. Make it an offering."

"You cannot bargain with the river spirit. It goes after what it wants, and it wants you. Your father stopped him. This angered Ijiraq, so it took your father in retaliation."

"No, you can't have him. Give him back!"

Dancing Elk starts towards the river, but Tiglit holds him back.

"The others are searching for him, but you can't go near the river. If Ijiraq reaches you, he will take you too, look," Tiglit points.

Dancing Elk looks at the river. Its water laps on the shore, a hand reaching for him.

Come brave one, try again.

Dancing Elk back away.

"But, I need father. We need him. Who will lead us? Who will head our family?"

"I will lead the tribe until a leader is chosen. From now on, you will be my son."

Grandfather is right. I can never go near the river again.

Chapter 3

CALABAR, HERGIAN, AND MIZAR

The pacú is the energy in all living things. It manifests itself as either positive or negative. The positive energy, white or light pacú, creates, gives life, and keeps things in order. The negative, grey, or dark pacú destroys, takes life away, and causes chaos.

Six hundred years ago, a sortiarius named Calabar came upon the idea that the negative pacú could be used constructively. He experimented with and used it, which was strictly prohibited.

Calabar had been one of the Keepers, one of the Deccem. The Deccem were the ten powerful guardians of all living things. Some of the Keepers had the animal-like features of the species they represented. Others retained a human likeness, like Calabar, the twin midges, and the Decanus, the Grand Master of the Keepers, Eage.

The Keepers maintained and monitored nature's pacú from a monastery known as the Campus Exercitatus.

The Campus Exercitatus was a place of learning. Inside its high stone walls, those who wished to follow the ways of the pacú became sortiarius and studied. The few sortiarius that showed control over the pacú were trained to master and use it. Part of their training included creating and using the upashim, a concentrated energy sphere with tremendous destructive potential. It was used mainly to reduce stones to smaller manageable pieces for construction or clearing boulders from fields.

Calabar was able to incorporate the grey pacú into the upashim. Inflicted on another would cause physical illness, discord to their temperament, or death.

This activity not only disrupted the harmony of nature but, as a benefit to himself, Calabar was able to feed on it and become more powerful. The grey pacú had always been present but never used, disturbed, or consumed.

Calabar's actions woke the dark pacú, affecting Ortet's indigenes. Crime, once rare, became common. There was the failure of the crops, and some of Ortet's once gentle fauna became aggressive.

Once again, Calabar tried to reason with the Deccem. He tried to convince them of the benefits of the grey pacú.

"You can bend nature to your will. Make it the way it should be," Calabar said.

It became obvious that using the grey pacú not only made Calabar more powerful but twisted him. He no longer cared about keeping the balance in nature; he wanted to control it and be the one deciding what it should be.

He tried to explain this to the Deccem, but they were shocked. His meddling with the pacú was to stop, and word of his containment was mentioned. He was excused from the chamber while his future was discussed. When the Deccem adjourned, Calabar was gone. He fled before the Keepers could act. On his way, he stole a relic known as the Way Stone, a large white crystal.

The Way Stone allowed passage to a land called Terrae Exterus, but it required the pacú of two to activate it. Rarely used, The Way Stone could transport a Keeper to Terrae Exterus, where they would retrieve that unusual individual who could control the pacú and train them before they cause harm. But it had been years since it was used, so the theft went unnoticed.

Terrae and Terrae Exterus exist on parallel planes. However, the pacú on Terrae Exterus was unbalanced. More of the grey pacú influenced nature than the white pacú. Making it a place where you just didn't live but had to survive. Thus, an individual from that otherworld who could control the pacú could be immensely powerful. It was that abundance of the dark pacú that attracted Calabar.

Calabar wanted to cross to Terrae Exterus and feed on the grey pacú; he wanted that power. However, to use the Way Stone required another individual capable of controlling the pacú.

He wandered the country, looking for that individual. He picked up many followers along the way. His hair grew long and matted, he started to wear dark-colored robes, and his minions started to refer to him as Sceagga for his wild unkempt look.

Around that same time, a village was devastated by a flood borne of an unusually violent storm. A pair of boys, Hergian and Mizar, orphaned by the disaster, huddled under the rubble of a fallen hut.

"Mizar, I'm cold," Hergian says.

Hergian is the younger of the two. Mizar wraps his younger brother with a salvaged blanket, dirty and torn but warm.

"With this rain, everything is wet. I will try to dry the wood and start a fire," Mizar says.

He holds his hands over a stack of kindling. There is a wisp of smoke as the wood smolders then it's gone.

"Mother told you not to do that. She said it might attract the wrong attention." Hergian says.

"There is no food, and we are wet and freezing. Any attention would be welcomed now. But first, I must get the kindling dry," Mizar says.

Mizar sends his pacú to the bundle. His control of the life force was limited to creating heat and fire and making his hands glow, which he used as a candle in the dark. However, using the skill was exhausting. It was more so since they hadn't eaten in two days. His concern now was keeping warm. Twilight was quickly approaching, and the night before had been brutally cold.

"Help me. Give me your hand."

Mizar also knew he could tap into his brother's pacú to amplify his own.

He had taught his younger brother all he knew before the parents discovered their abilities and forbade the boys from practicing the skills.

An untrained girl, claiming to be a wonderworker, detonated while performing a skill, killing herself, her father, and her brother. After that, being capable of performing the skill was considered a punishment from the gods, penitence to make the unworthy whole again. It bore no logic to apply the burden on children. But then, logic was not a quality the primitives had.

Mizar merges his brother's pacú with his own. Threads of steam rise from the wood, then a small flame appears.

The small fire warms the boy's shelter. They have only one fish they found on the riverbank to share; it smells rank. Mizar places the fish on the fire. Immediately the stink permeates their shelter.

"If you eat that, you will most likely die an unpleasant death."

The boys start and turn towards the entrance of the shelter. A dark-robed figure looms on the threshold. Mizar scoots to the back of the shelter, pulling Hergian with him.

The stranger creates a small glowing orb which he releases. It slowly floats towards the fire and lands on the fish. The orb glows brightly, consuming the fish in its fire.

The stranger smiles at the boys and sends his pacú over them. They feel they can trust the stranger and relax.

"Here, I'll share this with you."

He produces dried meat and bread from a bundle he carries, and the boys eat greedily for the first time since the flood.

"Where are your parents?" The stranger asks.

"We haven't seen them since the river took our home," Mizar says.

"We were in the back room. The house tilted and fell into the water. When we opened the door, the front of the house was gone; they were gone," Hergian sobs.

"Well, if you boys like, you can come with me. I need someone to help me. In return, I can teach you how to use your powers."

"What powers?"

"What you were doing with the fire."

"The skill? That is forbidden wondermaking. A girl wondermaker died and killed her father and brother using the skill," Hergian says.

"Hmm. What would happen if you placed your hand in the fire?"

Hergian looks at the fire and then his hand.

"I would burn it," Hergian said.

"And you if spilled the coals inside a house?"

"I would burn the floor. Maybe the house?"

"Could someone die from the fire?"

"Why yes."

"Then why is making fire not forbidden?"

The boys look at each other and shrug. The logic made sense.

"I will teach you how to control the skill. Your ability should not be wasted," the stranger says. "Come with me, you both can become my assistants, and I will teach you how to use the skill."

Hergian pulls Mizar aside.

"Do you trust him?" Hergian asks. "I have never seen him before."

"I feel we can. Besides, he can protect us, knows how to find food, and teach us how to use the skill," Mizar says.

Mizar and Hergian decide that they will need someone's help if they are to survive. So they follow the stranger.

"Uh. What should we call you?" Mizar asks.

"You can call me…Sceagga."

Sceagga had found the means to activate the Way Stone. They just needed further training.

He honed their control of the pacú. Hergian and Mizar learned quickly. Sceagga grew fond of the boys and gave them extended lives. They would be unnaturally healthy and live for hundreds of years.

Stories of Sceagga reach the Campus. The Keepers are concerned that his experiments will destroy Ortet. They select three sortiarius to find Sceagga and bring him back.

After several weeks of following stories and rumors, they find Sceagga. The sortiarius try to convince him to return with them. Sceagga refuses; he will not be cloistered.

When they try to force him, Hergian and Mizar appear.

"Who are these children?"

"They are my acolytes," Sceagga says.

The boys look at their master, and Sceagga nods.

"Show them what you can do, Mizar," Hergian says.

The boy forms an energy sphere, the upashim, and without hesitation, hurls it at the sortiarius. The upashim strikes him in the chest, vaporizing his upper half. The concussion throws the one next to him against the wall, leaving him like a boneless heap. The remaining sortiarius is stunned.

He taught the upashim....to children?

Hergian forms his own upashim and hurls it. The sortiarius snaps out of his trance and tries to block it, but he is too late. Though not as powerful as his brother's, the finger-thin energy beam pierces the sortiarius's heart, killing him instantly.

"We must leave now. In case others are nearby," Sceagga says.

As they walk away, Hergian turns to his older brother.

"Some day, I will be as powerful as you."

"You should flatter yourself. Your upashim was like a spear," Mizar says, ruffling his brother's hair. "I don't think I can create one with such precision."

Hergian swells with pride and smiles at his older brother, his hero.

Sceagga and the boys travel the country with his followers preaching lies about the Keepers. He tells them the Keepers and their sortiarius want to control their lives. Many agree, join him, and become the Solois, the dedicated. Sceagga did not want to risk his followers unnecessarily, so he used puppa dolls for dangerous tasks. They were taken from the nearby villages and, compelled, turned into mindless minions until the mission was completed. If they survived, the compulsion would expire. They would be unaware of what happened, why their clothes were soiled or torn, or where their injuries came from.

The one sortiarius left behind by Sceagga survived. He was found by the locals and brought to the Campus. When the Keepers hear the story of Sceagga and the boys, they decide to take matters into their own hands and leave the Campus to find them.

Posters seeking information on Sceagga spread. He knows the Keepers are after him now, so Sceagga rushes the training of the boys. He needs to activate the Way Stone and escape to Terrae Exterus with them.

When near, Sceagga senses the combined pacú of the Keepers. So, he gathers a crowd, using the pacú to create 'curious feats of magic.'

When a sizeable number gathers in the town square of Merkoum, he compels them. They guard Sceagga while he wakes the Way Stone with the help of Mizar. The energy from the Stone is like a siren for the Keepers.

"What is that!" Katta, a Keeper resembling a spotted cat, says.

"It came from that direction," Golo and Nok speak in unison.

Golo and Nok are twins midges that forever look like little girls.

"Take me there," Eage says.

They each take one of Decanus's hands and lead him toward the energy source. Eage is blind. He has been sightless since he was young.

They track Sceagga to an abandoned storehouse. When the Keepers approach, the compelled crowd attacks them. He knows the Keepers will never harm the innocent. They will have to be contained, giving Sceagga time to finish the task.

While Mizar holds the stone and links it to his pacú, Sceagga jackets both boy and stone, adding his power.

Meanwhile, Hergian protects with a barrier, so they won't be disturbed.

The Keepers were aware of Sceagga's capabilities, so a compelled crowd was expected. The Keepers recruited their creatures for assistance. The compelled are swarmed by apes, wolves, large weasels, and many creeping creatures to restrain them. But no one is harmed.

When they find Sceagga and the boys, they see the Way Stone.

"Master Eage, they have the Way Stone!" Huanglong, the Keeper of reptiles, says.

"They must not cross to Terrae Exterus,' Eage says. "Stop them."

Apa, the gorilla-like simian Keeper, hurls the first upashim. The strike thunders like a hammer on metal, but Hergian's barrier holds. Golo and Nok throw theirs simultaneously. Hergian deflects them towards a wall, collapsing that section of the structure.

The most powerful of the Keepers, Grand Master Eage, throws his. It is too powerful for Hergian and pierces the barrier, striking the Way Stone.

The stone explodes, Sceagga, Mizar, and Hergian disappear, and when the dust and soot clear, all that remains are the splintered shards of the stone.

Golo picks up a crystal fragment.

"Did they get through?" Golo asks.

"I hope not," Eage answers.

Nok picks up another of the shards.

"Is the way stone is gone?"

"Yes, and maybe for the better," Eage replies.

On the opposite side of Ortet, Sceagga awakes, ears ringing from the explosion. He looks to his side and finds Hergian unconscious but alive. However, Mizar is nowhere in sight; he tries to sense him, but his pacú is gone.

"Hergian, wake up."

Sceagga shakes the boy.

Hergian's eyes open, and he looks around, hand to his head.

"Where are we? Did we cross?"

Sceagga shakes his head.

"No, we're still somewhere on Ortet."

He stands and turns, looking for his brother.

"Wher—where's Mizar? Do you see him? Mizar!" Hergian starts shouting.

"Hergian, stop!"

Sceagga grabs the boy by the shoulders.

"Look at me."

Sceagga's face is solemn.

"Mizar is gone. I felt his pacú dissipate. The Keepers killed him."

A little twist to the truth.

"No!...no." Hergian sobs.

Sceagga pulls the boy and holds him. Hergian cries.

"They saw him holding the stone and killed him," Sceagga says.

Sobbing, Hergian looks up at Sceagga.

"Master...father, I will kill the Keepers. I will make them pay."

Sceagga nods.

Yes, you may kill the Keepers. Maybe not all is lost.

Chapter 4
THE ANGELO

It is the seventh day of the third millennium, and since the beginning of the year, the people of Sylvanus still wait for the Promised One. They have kept a close eye on all the doyennes who are achilding. However, none shows the signs.

It has been a bizarre week for the weather. The torrential rains and tempestuous winds of the past three days proved it. Repair work must be done on the docks, seaside buildings, and boats anchored too close to the shore.

The sun had barely announced the day, but Koop and Chelle were already up and busy gathering their nets. Dislodged during the storm and washed ashore, a strange creature raveled in its mesh.

"Koop! Look at this giant bird."

Chelle rolls it over with his foot.

"By Eyu, it's a doyenne....with wings!" Chelle says.

"Are you still tanked from last night? A doyenne with—"

Koop turns to see what Chelle is talking about.

"It's a doyenne with wings!" Koop says.

"That's what I said."

"Don't touch it. Go and get the townmaster," Koop says.

"Why me?"

"Cause I'm older, your superior, and you run faster. Now hurry before anyone else sees her. There might be a reward."

"A reward?"

"Yes, a reward,"

Chelle nods furiously and runs into town while Koop covers his prize with a tarp.

Townmaster Rudo is upset at being roused at this hour. He wanted to ignore the knocking, but it turned into a frantic pounding. He decided to answer before the entire village awakened.

When Chelle tried to drag him into the street in his sleeping shirt. Rudo tried to argue with the man, to wait for a decent hour before taking to the street. But Chelle seemed so agitated and nervous that Rudo decided that it was best he followed Chelle, in case it was important. So he agreed to accompany him as long as he could grab a coat.

Now, Rudo finds himself following Chelle through the empty streets in the chilly gloom before morning.

"Chelle, I hope this is not some fabrication from a night of drinking, or you'll be spending the next week cleaning the city's sewage."

"Oh no, Townmaster, it is a doyenne with wings," Chelle whispers

"Wings? What kind of shindy were you up to last night?"

"None, I swear. Please, sir, keep your voice down. You may not want the attention." Chelle whispers.

"There's Koop now," Chelle points.

Koop is standing over a tarp, signaling them over.

"What is it?" Rudo asks.

"She's alive; she made a sound," Koop says.

"Let's see this winged doyenne," Rudo's voice is edged with anger.

Koop pulls the tarp off. Rudo takes one look, tries to back away too fast for his feet, and falls. He barely notices the hard stones under his sit-on.

"By Eyu! They're real. She's real."

Rudo is still sitting on the ground. His mind starts racing.

It's the year the Promised One is supposed to come, and she's got wings...the prophecy...the angelo, and I'll be the one who has her.

Rudo stands and brushes the sand from his clothes.

"Keep her wrapped and take her to my house."

"Your house?" Koop asks.

"My house. And I'll reward you if you tell no one," Rudo says.

The two fishers look at each other and nod furiously.

"Yes, Townmaster," they say in unison.

They walk their way to the townmaster's residence. Those who were getting ready for the day's chores cast a curious eye at the townmaster walking with two fishers carrying a suspicious bundle. But Rudo would give them a morning greeting and usher the two as if it was a normal event.

The townmaster has her moved to his residence. However, word gets out anyway, as it always does, when the fishers spend the tender from their windfall profits on ealu and talk too much.

The rumors disrupt the town's affairs. After all, winged folks are only found in childkeeper tales.

No one knows from where she came. The creature's wings are broken and burned, and her forehead is bruised. Her strange robes and the weapons she carried are not of this land. The answers will have to come from her. However, she remains a mystery because she uttered only that one groan, and after two weeks, she has yet to awaken.

The monakites are called for. With his curist, advisor, and praysayers, Dominant Saltes approaches the seaside town. The holy men wear robes, which at one time were brown and now show the wear from too many trips and the dust of too few washings.

The messenger, who delivered the somonen scroll, leads the way. The document's heading, 'This could be a matter of Holies,' was obviously meant to capture their attention, asking for their presence. However, the message made no sense.

The monachs arrive at dusk. Even though their transport beasts have a smooth gait, they are stiff from the long ride.

All roads to the city pass through the hills that surround it. The first thing they notice is the Mariner's Torch. The tall building houses a burning lamp, a beacon for ships at night. The surrounding town is a monotonous expanse of terra cotta roofs over drab-colored homes. As they near the town center, they find the whole village abuzz.

"What is going on?" Eophon, the monach's advisor, asks.

"The gossipry is about the unknown stranger. There are rumors that she is the bearer, and the folks are attributing several unexplained recoveries to her," the messenger says

"Hmm."

Eophon strokes his chin.

Rudo donned his best garments of red and blue to meet the guests at Central Hall.

"Welcome to Ka-Mer, Dominant; I'm so glad to see you here so soon."

The townmaster bows, sweeping the air with a white handkerchief and sending its perfumed aroma toward the travelers.

The dominant's group dismounts from their rides. The advisor looks at the frilled kerchief with contempt.

"I am the Dominant's Advisor, Eophon. This is the Dominant." He motions towards a young monach.

What Rudo can see from under the cowl is a young face. A long silky lock of sandy hair drapes over his cheek. He has the position of dominant because of his intelligence. However, some think that what he possesses in knowledge, he lacks in common sense.

"My pardons, Lord Dominant, it's just that you are so young."

The monach pulls his hood back, and Rudo gives a short gasp.

"Golden eyes!"

"Yes, we've noticed," Eophon says.

"Pardon my rudeness. I've heard of the golden-eyed scholars but not of monakites. Are you of the Saltes lineage from Lejandre?"

"No offense taken. Yes, I'm Tailon Saltes from Lejandre."

"It's an honor Lord Saltes."

"It's not the first time it has happened, nor will it be the last." The Dominant says.

"I will take you immediately to the doyenne in question."

"We have been to five different towns this month to look at supposed bearers of The Promised," Eophon says. "We are starting to tire of traveling from one end of Sylvanus to the other. We barely escaped a group of Wandrien raiders two weeks ago, we have yet to have a decent bath, and our behinds tire of traveling on these quoggen. All of this because of doyennes who enjoy wasting our time."

"Enough, Eophon, we have to assess every summons. Besides, we are the only ones in the area who can tell if she is the one."

"Yes, Dominant," Eophon sighs submissively.

The townmaster recuperates from his start but is somewhat surprised at the older monakite's submission to the younger.

Eophon is also intelligent in his own right; however, he has been a monach for a much shorter time.

"Do not worry, M'lords, I will care for all of your needs," the townmaster shakes the handkerchief vigorously.

Eophon rolls his eyes.

The townmaster, accompanied by his guards, leads the group through the streets of the Ka-Mer.

"Tell me, m'lord, why did you become a Monakite of Eyu? Don't the scholars of Lejandre usually become educators?"

"Yes, I broke with generations of scholars to become an Eyuist."

"Lord Dominant got tired of the daily routine. He wanted to travel, see Terrae for himself, and learn," Eophon says. "At least that's what he told us."

Tailon smiles and shakes his head.

"What is the condition of the doyenne?" Saltes asks.

"She still sleeps, Lord Dominant."

"Please, my name is Saltes."

"As you wish, Dominant Saltes, my name is Rudo."

"Very well, Townmaster Rudo, tell me about her. When is she due?"

"Due? No Dominant. We do not know if she's due. That is not why you were summoned."

"What?" Eophon growls.

Saltes raises his hand to quiet him.

"Tell me, Townmaster Rudo, why were we summoned during this critical time?"

"Well, first of all, Dominant Saltes, she has wings!"

"Wings? You summoned us because of the ceremonial outfit she has donned?" Eophon voice rises.

Once again, Saltes raises his hand.

"Townmaster Rudo? Saltes asks.

Rudo places his hand on Saltes' arm to ensure he gets his attention.

"No, Dominant, you don't understand," he says, trying to contain himself. "The doyenne has wings, real wings, sprouting from her back."

Dominant Saltes looks at Rudo, searching for signs of madness.

"You mean wings like a—"

"Bird! Yes, wings!" repeats Rudo. He is now flapping his kerchief.

"When the somonen arrived—" Eophon starts.

"I thought she was achilding and wearing a costume of sorts," Saltes says.

"No, like the Angelos in the Holy Scrolls."

Saltes looks deep into Rudo's eyes to see if there is some sort of waggery while the monakites murmur among themselves. There is none.

"Let's hurry," Saltes says. "Continue."

"She washed up on our shore two weeks ago; her clothing, footgear, and weapons are not of any of the tribes in the area. I have sent carriers far and wide trying to find anyone who would recognize her garments; none have," Rudo says.

"Weapons?" Eophon asks.

Eophon was a soldier who left the guard to join the order.

"Yes, she seems to be some sort of warrior."

"A doyenne warrior? With wings? Are you sure?"

"She carried a strange, curved sword, shield, and a bow that had somehow been shattered. Also, she wore a tightly woven robe that repels water. Under that, she had a thick leather vest, almost like body armor with a pattern of two wings tooled over the breasts, and a strange silver bracelet on her left arm."

"How curious," Saltes says. "Any battle wounds?"

"It looks like she received a blow to the head, and both of her wings are broken. Our curist died last year, so his apprentice did what he could to set the bones and keep the wound from infecting. We dare not attempt anything else."

"A head wound? And she has yet to awaken after two weeks," the curist Bandagee says.

He shakes his head.

"Not promising."

They reach the townmaster's house; guards stationed around the building keep the crowd of curious citizens at a distance. They pass through the barricade of soldiers and enter.

"Why the heavy guard?" Eophon asks.

"Last night, three munkyes stole into the house. They killed two of the servants before the commotion called the guard's attention. They were found in the doyenne's room; two were killed, and one escaped."

"Munkyes, assassins?"

"Not quite, Dominant. They seemed to be compelled, like a puppa doll. They were not of their own mind."

"Puppa dolls?" Eophon asks.

"They were trying to carry her away, but their actions didn't seem to be their own. Except for the one that escaped, their eyes were glassy and unseeing. They moved erratically and without concern for their safety. The third one seemed to have all his faculties. He might have been the leader," Rudo says.

"Who could possibly have such power?" Eophon asks. "What could they possibly want with her?"

"I don't know. The shocking part is that they were known members of our community, fishers. That is why the guards are present. If locals can be turned into munkyes, puppas, anyone can become munkye."

The servants are busy cleaning, cooking, and making sure everything is in order. Rudo's wife, Lenity, is supervising the whole presentation. First, they're introduced to Lenity and the staff and then escorted to the room where the doyenne rests.

The stranger, dressed in white, lays on a bed with her head completely swathed; only her face is visible. Many pillows support her bandaged wings, and a servant sits by the bed, watching over the patient.

"Those are her clothing and weapons." Rudo whispers.

Saltes, Eophon, and Bandagee look at the clothing. Then Saltes reaches out and feels the garment with his fingers.

"It's sioloc!"

"Shhh!" the servant admonishes them.

"It is of the finest quality." Lenity adds softly.

Lenity's curiosity is too great to stay behind with the servants.

"We can produce enough sioloc for only the richest of Sylvanus. Sioloc worms must be abundant where she comes from; if it can clothe an army," Rudo says.

"I know of no such place," Eophon says.

On the table by the bed, Saltes sees the silver bracelet and picks it up, turning it over in his hands.

"That is a magnificent piece of workmanship," Saltes says, scrutinizing it.

"I've checked with our artisans. They haven't been able to duplicate it."

"I wonder what it means."

"The bow looks like it was burned in half," Eophon says.

He is more interested in weapons.

"The bow, with an attached quiver, strange design; I wonder what the straps are for?"

"They kept the bow secured to her chest," Rudo answers. "At least that half of it."

"And how does the sword work?" He can't quite figure it out.

"It was on her right hand; the shield was on her left. Let me show you."

Rudo slips his hand through the opening in the sword, grips the crosspiece, and holds it up.

"Like this."

"She still could be from far away down the coast. There are areas there that we have yet to explore. There are tales of a half-

Sylvan half-snake from deep in the forests, and a gadabout from the north brought us the skull of a horned giant he found in a primitive grave," Saltes says.

The Dominant gazes out the window; he is not interested in the scenery nor aware of it.

"Wasn't there a bad storm just two weeks ago?" Eophon asks. "It lasted for three days, didn't it?

"Yes, there was," Rudo answers. "As a matter of fact, it was the day after the storm that she was found."

Bandagee goes up to the girl and lifts the bandage just high enough to see the head wound.

"This is a burn on her forehead."

The dominant turns.

"She probably fell into the water from one of the ships from a far-off village," Saltes says. "If you inquire on the matter, you will probably find a boat that caught fire and sank during the storm."

"With winged doyennes on board?" Rudo says.

He joins Saltes at the window.

"Dominant, if there were winged creatures anywhere near here, they would have been seen by now."

"Where else would she have come from?" Eophon asks.

"As the blessed monakite predicted, there will be visitors from another land," Rudo says.

"Yes, I'm familiar with monakite Eage's predictions," Saltes says. "I'm also familiar with his stories of the angelus, but it has been decided that his prophecies were metaphors and not a realistic or accurate account. Don't forget, you refer to predictions made many millennia ago by someone who is probably a myth."

"M'lord, will you look at her hair?" Rudo says.

"Why?"

"You will see."

Bandagee looks at Saltes, who nods. Then, carefully, the curist pulls the covering off her head. The red mass of hair spills out over her pillow. Bandagee stumbles back, startled, still gripping the bandages in his hands.

"M'lord, have you ever seen anyone with red hair?" Rudo asks.

"It... it's impossible! But, Eophon, are there any red-headed citizens you know of?"

"No, dominant...they don't exist."

"Sit her up, Saluk," Bandagee says.

"But master, she is badly hurt," she says.

"I need to see where the wings are attached," Bandagee says.

The servant gently moves the unconscious doyenne to a sitting position while the curist inspects her wings.

"They are real, and there is a strange mark between them."

They all gather to look once more.

"It looks like some sort of symbol," Bandagee says.

"That's not all, dominant; look at her eyes," Rudo says.

Bandagee looks over his shoulder at Saltes again; this time, he does not wait for the signal. Instead, they lean over as the curist gently lifts her eyelids.

They look at each other in wonderment.

"Lord Dominant," said Bandagee. "One is grey, and the other...blue."

The monakites back away, leaving the curist to continue the examination.

"This is a most unusual occurrence," Saltes says.

"It's an impossible occurrence, a winged red-haired doyenne with one eye grey and the other blue," Eophon says.

The monakite strokes his chin in thought, a habit persisting long after cutting his beard.

"I can only say that we will definitely have to stay and see who she is...what she is, and why is she here?" Tailon says.

"Maybe she's an angelo, a messenger from Eyu," Rudo says.

"If she was sent by Eyu, her presentation was less than inspiring," Tailon says.

"Agreed," Eophon says.

"Lord Dominant!" Bandagee calls. The curist is holding his hands over her abdomen.

"She is achilding! It is very recent, but a powerful signal comes from her, but...."

Bandagee labors with concentration.

"It's difficult to understand."

The monakites occupy the entire wing of Rudo's residence. Rudo and Lenity, of course, are delighted to have them in their home. It elevates their public stature. It places Rudo in the center of public attention and gives Lenity access to the highest circles in society. The town also prospers from the stranger, as hundreds of pilgrims are willing to pay premium hostel rates to visit the village in hopes of spotting the red-haired angelo.

The praysayers begin a vigil around the doyenne's bed. Their continuous drone fills the room, and when one tires, another steps in.

While cleaning the room a week later, Saluk finds the doyenne staring at her. Saluk yelps, startling the praysayers, then runs through the house, shouting the event. All rush to the room. They gather around the bed for the long-awaited occasion…then she speaks.

"Mandary ashiu?" She whispers.

"What?" Rudo asks her.

She turns to him.

"Mandary ashiu?" Where am I?

"I…I don't understand."

"She doesn't speak our tongue," Saltes says.

"Everyone speaks our language; where could she have come from?" Eophon whispers.

"Gondo ashiu?" Who are you?

She notices Saltes and gasps loudly when she sees his golden eyes.

Rudo fans himself furiously with the handkerchief, then leans over the bed.

"Where…do…you…come…from?"

"She doesn't understand us, Master Rudo," Bandagee says. "No…matter…how…slowly…you…talk."

Rudo throws up his hands, but he does not give up. He walks to her garments, still hanging on the wall.

"Who wears these clothes?" He asks, holding up the sioloc robe.

She takes her eyes away from Saltes and slowly turns her head toward him.

"Who uses these weapons?" He says, holding up the sword.

She sees her short sword in his hand.

"Ede aduncus mandi," that is my aduncus.

"Aduncus?" He says, pointing to her.

"Aduncus," she sighs.

Her eyes slowly close, and she drifts off to sleep again.

"She's an Aduncus," Rudo says, raising the weapon victoriously though keeping his voice down.

"I've never heard of the Aduncus," Eophon says.

"I wonder where they live," Saltes says.

Rudo walks to the window and looks out over the bay. He slowly caresses his cheek with the kerchief.

"Perhaps out there somewhere, there's a land we don't even know about."

"The land of the Aduncus," Saltes says softly.

Two more days pass before she wakes. Saluk helps her out of bed, supporting her while taking her first steps in weeks. She leans heavily on the servant and notices her flowing bedclothes for the first time. Her legs are weak from lack of use, and she gives a short cry when she tries to stretch her wings. The servant gives her a disapproving look and shakes her head.

"Vestirop ashiu?" Where are my clothes?

She holds up the folds of her gown between her fingers.

"Oh! Do you like it? I made it myself. I had to modify the back to accommodate your wings, though."

"Ishtonen?" What?

"I'm sorry, m'lady…I wish I could understand you."

She walks Geolufeoer towards the window.

"Here…the townmaster had this made for you."

She helps Geolufeoer sit on a special stool, looking out the window. Because of her large wings, sitting in an ordinary chair is out of the question. They modified a high chair to keep her wingtips from dragging on the floor. It has a narrow padded back support that fits comfortably between her wings.

Geolufeoer settles herself on the stool and finds it more comfortable than the benches they use in Ortet.

She still cannot remember how she got there; everything looks strange. The townmaster's house sits on top of a hill. From the window, she has a clear view of the city. Geolufeoer sees the homes neatly arranged along the winding streets leading towards the water. Each house has the same terracotta roof tiles giving a maze-like look to the city.

The town is large, but there are no cliffs for skybourne homes. Geolufeoer looks at the sky, and as far as she can see, there are no skybournes in the air, and only groundstays fill the streets.

She visited all of the coastal towns during her training, and this one was far bigger than any she had seen before. The designs of the homes are also different. They are sturdy but plain. Each is painted in drab colors. The streets are busier, though, rivaling the crowds of the Merkoum market after the harvest. Then there is also the question of the language.

What has happened to me? I can no longer understand speech.

The servant comes back and offers her some fruits and a drink. She says something Geolufeoer doesn't understand, holds up her hand as if telling her to wait, then leaves. Her stomach suddenly feels hollow. She has no idea how long she has been without solid food. The fruit is different and sweeter than any she has tasted. She starts nibbling at her meal as a proper doyenne would, but once she tastes it, she cannot eat fast enough. Luckily, the servant is out of the room because she would have frightened her.

Saluk comes back and smiles, pleased that she has eaten. She carries a different gown. The clothes came from Lenity's wardrobe; it has a white petticoat with a violet overdress and a black bodice that Saluk modified for Geolufeoer's wings. It seems somewhat overdressed for the house. She assumed she would be allowed to wear her uniform or something simple like Saluk's dress.

After being helped into the terribly uncomfortable gown, Saluk goes to the small table by the bed, opens an ornate box, and removes a hairbrush. Geolufeoer's red hair fascinates her. The servant combs all the tangles and braids her hair into a strange rope she winds around the doyenne's neck. A knock at the door is followed by the young sortiarius.

"Ah, she's up," Tailon says.

Saluk curtsies.

"Good morning, m'lord."

"Good morning, Saluk," he answers. "How is she doing this morning?"

"She walked around the room and discovered her wings were broken. She ate a bowl of food and let me brush her hair," Saluk says.

"Splendid! My, what a beautiful young doyenne. You have done an admirable job. It looks like she is starting to recover," Saltes says. "Now, if we could only talk to her."

He walks to Geolufeoer and takes her hand.

"How are you doing, young Aduncus?" he smiles.

Aduncus?

Once again, his eyes mesmerized her. It took her some time to get accustomed to them, and once she did, she noticed how handsome he was. She smiles and nods out of politeness.

"Don't worry, my dear," he says, patting her hand. "There's a sacerdos magike named Sakara who has the gift of languages. He should arrive soon. It's a shame that he doesn't have wings like you. He'll have to travel by quog." Saltes chuckles.

I wonder what he is trying to say.

She just nods and smiles back.

The servant brings a spyglass for her to look out the window. She marvels at the boats in the harbor, with dozens working on them like ants on a morsel. The largest Ortetan boat can carry three, maybe four, fishtanglers.

A strange yellowish cast washes over the city as dusk comes. When the servant returns, Geolufeoer motions that she wants to walk a bit.

Saluk helps her stand and walks around the room; then, she motions towards the door. Saluk is hesitant, then decides that there would be no harm. They go into the hallway and slowly walk to the end. She turns and walks back to the opposite end.

She runs her hand over the dark wood's artisanship, remembering her carvings.

I wonder how long it takes to make this by hand.

It has a vine-like design, simple yet sturdy. There is a window at the end of the hall, and she notices that the yellow light is brighter. When Geolufeoer reaches it, she leans on the sill and sees the Mariner's Torch on a small hillock by the water. She looks at the bright light at its peak, then at the harbor, where boats with small lamps on the deck are docked.

How curious. A light to help vessels find their way at night. What an excellent idea; these vessels must be able to travel far, then follow the light ba—.

Suddenly she remembers. A wave of dizziness comes over her, she sways, and Saluk rushes to support her.

The servant starts talking fast; Geolufeoer recovers and looks back at the light. A locked door opens in her mind, and a flood of memories sweeps over her; the Solois attack, the storm, Sceagga...he had grabbed her, and the faint light on the horizon. Somehow, she traveled to that light. Then she remembers the lightning bolt struck her. She touches her head and flinches; it is still sore. Then her hand goes to her abdomen;

it feels different. The servant sees this and starts chattering faster. Saluk takes her back to bed.

What did Sceagga say? Something about a seed, I now carried the seed…I think. What did he do to me? Where did he send me?

The next morning Saluk wakes her early. She says something to her and points to another dress draped over the stool; it's dark blue with a colored green stole. Geolufeoer rolls her eyes.

Functionality was not in the designer's mind when he made the dress. It would be challenging to make any defensive moves or run, never mind fly, in such an outfit. However, she decides not to argue. She likes the servant, and Saluk is proud of the stitchwork it took to make it fit; besides, Saluk wouldn't understand.

Geolufeoer is dressed, and her hair is brushed. By the time Saluk finishes, someone knocks at the door. The servant answers; it is the dominant. Saltes smiles; he gives her a courteous bow and enters the room. An older sortiarius with a kind face follows him. He takes a look at her and gasps upon seeing her wings and red hair.

"She really is an Angelos," he says.

"Yes, like we told you," Tailon answers.

"I thought you may have been exaggerating about the wings," he says.

"Or perhaps having light brown or reddish-brown hair," he says in amazement.

"No, the wings are real, and her hair is red."

"So, I see."

The old sortiarius reaches for the chair and sits down.

"Just like Eage said," he murmurs.

"Right, just like he said."

Saltes rolls his eyes.

Rudo, Eophon, and Bandagee follow; not to be left behind, Lenity sneaks inside and stands by the door.

"I would like you to meet Sakara," Tailon says.

He points to the old man.

She smiles and nods.

"Does she talk?" Sakara asks.

"Yes, she talked the first time she opened her eyes," Saltes answers.

"What did she say?"

"I believe she said she is an Aduncus."

"An Aduncus?"

What is it about my aduncus?

"Yes, she said she was an Aduncus," Rudo says.

Saltes looks at Sakara and shrugs.

Sakara pulls the chair closer to hers, then takes Geolufeoer's hand with his.

"Hello, my dear. My name is Sakara; what is yours?" He says slowly.

She smiles and nods.

"I can only link to her if she speaks: all I need is one word."

"I've heard her speak," Tailon says.

"We've all heard her speak," Eophon adds.

"My name is Sakara," repeats the old monakite.

He touches his chest and then points to her.

"Your name is...."

"Sakara..." he repeats, touching his chest once more. Then to her.

She suddenly realizes what he is after.

"Geolufeoer!" she burst out.

She feels a tingling sensation flowing through her hand and spattering into her head. It's like being splashed with cold water, the shock passes, but the wetness remains. Sakara closes

67

his eyes and leans back in his chair for a few moments. He feels a warm sensation flowing into his head, then he opens his eyes.

"Geolufeoer is a beautiful name," Sakara says.

"You understand me?"

"I am a sacerdos magike...a monach. I have some control over the pacú."

"Is a monach like a sortiarius?"

He thinks for a moment.

"Yes, sortiarius, same meaning, same thing. My ability is with languages. I can communicate with creatures. When one utters a sound, I can form a link and understand their language; that's what I've done with you."

"Can you see what I think? Can you read my thoughts?"

She looks concerned.

"Oh, no, my dear, I've only absorbed your language. Like a sponge that soaks up water, I soak up languages. That's all, nothing else."

She is relieved.

"Where am I?"

"In a town called Ka-Mer, in a land called Sylvanus. Have you heard of it?"

"No, I've never heard of such a town or land."

"You've never heard of Sylvanus?"

"No, I don't believe I am from Sylvanus."

"Hmm, why do you say that?"

Nothing is familiar: clothing, houses, boats, everything is different from where I live...or used to live. Besides, there are no skybournes."

"Skybournes?"

"That's what we, who have wings, are called...where I come from."

"So, there are more like you?"

"Oh, yes, about half of our people."

Sakara leans back in his chair. The others in the room are eager to find out what she has said.

"Well?" Tailon asks.

"She says she comes from another land."

"Another land. Where would that land be?"

"I don't think she knows."

"So, Aduncus is not a town; Aduncus is a land?"

Sakara turns to her once more.

"So, you're an Aduncus? Where is Aduncus?" he asks her.

She gives him a puzzled look.

"My aduncus is on the wall," she says, pointing to her short sword.

He turns and looks at the wall.

"Where?"

She gets up from the chair and slowly walks to the wall; she picks up her weapon, slips it over her wrist, and snaps it open. Everyone in the room takes a step back. Lenity gasps and covers her mouth.

"This is my aduncus."

Sakara chuckles.

"What's the matter?" Geolufeoer asks.

"Somehow, they got the idea that you came from a land called Aduncus."

She laughs, shakes her head, closes the blade, and puts it back. Immediately the others relax and murmur to each other.

"All of us skybournes carry the aduncus at one time or another, so you could say that it symbolizes the skybournes. I come from a land named Ortet. We are either skybourne or groundstays, but that is just who we are. We don't actually have a name for ourselves; I guess being called an Aduncus will suit us just fine."

"Aduncus, it is," Sakara chuckles once more.

"Tell me about Ortet, its folk, and how you made it here?"

Geolufeoer sits at the table in the room. There is a stack of parchment that Saluk had brought for drawing while waiting for Geolufeoer to awaken. Geolufeoer starts to tell him about her land and history.

"Ortetan folk are considered urbfolk or wealdfolk. The groundstays are the wingless Ortetans bound to walk the land. Some live in homes in the towns, the urbfolk, others live in villages in the weald, the wealdfolk.

"Most urbfolk are merchants or laborers working for others.

"The wealdfolk live outside the cities, alone or in small villages. They grow a few crops, hunt, and for the most part, keep to themselves.

"Either group can be skybourne or groundstay."

Geolufeoer starts to draw a thatched roofed home on the piece of parchment.

"Wealdfolk live wherever they can place a house. They build boats to fish in the lakes and oceans of Ortet.

"The skybourne, make their homes high up in the trees by the forest edge, colonize the cliffs on the mountains or bluffs above the ocean."

"I imagine that since you can fly, you have no need to travel by ship," Sakara says.

"Ship?"

"The large boats you see on the docks."

"Oh, you call those ships. Our crafts are small. Few skybourne ever go on them. Taking off or landing on our small boats is not easy. Falling into the water places us in an awkward position to get airborne again.

"In general, we herd bird flocks and harvest mountain fruits. The groundstays herd grasscutters, hunt, and grow vegetables. We trade the birds, eggs, and mountain fruit for meats, milk, and vegetables in the village markets. Marriage between the two groups is not rare, and the offspring are either winged or wingless."

"It sounds like paradise," Sakara says.

"Once it was. It is our belief that the entry of the energy that flows from our God, Eyu, is through Ortet. Through Ortet, Eyu breathes and gives life to the world."

"It sounds like one of Eage's adages," Sakara says.

"Huh, you've also heard of Eage?"

"He is part of our history," Sakara says.

"Ours too, how curious. Because of the constant exposure to this fountain of energy, many can manipulate it, like you do. We call them sortiarius."

"Ah, which we call monakites," Sakara says.

"A sortiarius can be either a groundstay or a skybourne. They wear light-colored robes and wander the countryside, healing the sick and energizing crops and livestock.

"We also have a select group of sortiarius who can control wild creatures. They bear the physical characteristic of the species with whom they link. For example, those who manipulate cattus are feline-looking.

"Cattus? Hmm, that would be our rotmoggie," Sakara says.

"Rotmoggie...yes. Those who manipulate birds look like birds. These sortiarius are eternal. They are called Keepers. They will live indefinitely if they do not suffer a fatal injury."

"So, Keepers really exist?"

"Oh, yes, I've trained under some."

"Then, they must be like a sacerdos magike."

"The same, but more powerful. They initially worked with the animals enlisting their help to assist the Terraens.

"The Keepers live in an area where they can teach without outside distractions in a walled-off compound called the

Campus Exercitatus. It has all Terrae's geological features: deep lakes, flowing rivers, mountains, deserts, and castle-like mansions. Here, the Keepers of the Species teach.

"However, because of Sceagga, their duties now include teaching the Ortetan military the fighting arts."

"Sceagga? Who is this Sceagga?" Sakara asks.

"Let me start from the beginning. Mind you, this happened over six hundred years ago. So, some of the stories might have commixed with myth.

"Ortet was the closest a land to paradise. That is until a sortiarius named Calabar started his experiments."

"I've heard that name before. He was considered a great monach," Sakara says.

"Really, well, he learned how to use the negative energy to alter the minds of others. The Keepers saw the danger in this. He wanted control over nature, bend it to his will."

"He learned to use the negative energy?"

"Yes, and when he used his powers to kill another, the Keepers sought to contain him. He was bringing a blight upon the folk of Terrae."

"This energy, positive or negative, what is it called in your land?"

"We call it pacú."

"Just as we do. Please continue."

"The Keepers went to look for Calabar. He was now an outlaw and had changed his name to Sceagga."

"So, Calabar became Sceagga?" Sakara asks.

"Uhuh."

"So that's why his name disappeared from our history," Sakara says.

"Yes, the Keepers also discovered that Sceagga had gathered dedicated followers, the Solois. They found Sceagga

in the village of Merkoum. When the Keepers confronted him, he sent an army of entranced villagers against the Keepers."

"The Solois?"

"No, the records show that they were ordinary villagers he had enthralled.

"During the battle, an explosion occurred. It was never revealed what caused it, but when it was over, Sceagga had disappeared.

"It was believed that he had perished in the explosion. But now, after six hundred years, he is back."

"Six hundred years! That's amazing!" Sakara says

"Yes, Sceagga was a Keeper, so he is eternal. We were never told what kind of Keeper, though. Nobody knows what he did for six hundred years, but he is back with an army."

"So, he was never captured?"

"No," Geolufeoer says.

"How did he convince the Solois?"

"Sceagga befriended the wealdfolk. The sortiarius appeared at their tribal gatherings wearing a flowing black robe. They named him Sceagga because of his long, tangled hair. He distorted the truth to get his results.

He told the wealdfolk, 'The urbfolk have joined the sortiarius and are gaining control over the lands. Soon, you will be forced to deal only with them. You toil here in the forest gathering wild fruits while they harvest the abundance of the stolen lands.'

'The Solois fell for his lies; they rallied their numbers to attack the rest of the Ortetans."

"He created the environment for a civil war," Sakara says.

"Yes, according to tales, the Wealdfolk attacked the Urbfolk. The Solois left the weald, destroying villages along the coast by land and air. The herald of their horns was a harbinger of terror, for it became synonymous with death.

Large villages close to the weald were next. The urbfolk were helpless, and their destruction would have been assured were it not for the Keeper's intervention."

"They intervened? In a war?"

" Yes, and they succeed."

"Yes, but the Keepers had to use the creatures trained to protect the Ortetans to control the enthralled. The Battle of Merkoum convinced the Keepers that a fighting force was necessary to protect the citizens."

"So, you never had a military force before?" Sakara asks.

"No, there was never a need for one. Conditions became so serious that all were obligated to serve in the militia for three sun-cycles."

"So, you were a part of the military force."

"Yes, I am...or was," Geolufeoer says.

"The best of the groundstay soldiers could enlist with the Lorica, the elite sword, bow, and sling guard who protect the land. The skybourne elite soldiers are known as the Salt Water Guardians or Haloguardian. They guard the coastal cliff villages overlooking the ocean and give air cover to the Lorica during ground battles."

"Did you become a member of the Haloguardian?"

"Yes, I did."

"So, you were one of the elites?"

Geolufeoer smiles.

"Yes, I was, but I was new to the guard. I had just become a Haloguardian."

"So, you encountered Sceagga in the attack?"

"Yes, it was a surprise. Six hundred years had passed. We thought the stories of Sceagga's abilities were a myth; they weren't. We were not ready when we encountered him."

Her eyes swell with the memory of Coloner Roanfeoer's.

Sakara gets an idea. He picks up a quill and a sheet of parchment and hands them to her.

"Show me your land."

She is an excellent illustrator and draws pictures of the cliffside homes and the Temple of Eyu. This arouses his curiosity since the folk of Sylvanus also called God by that name. She also drew sketches of Ortetan clothes, weapons, and boats. Sakara occasionally turns and translates the pertinent parts of the conversation for the others.

Finally, she whispers the question that has been burning in her mind.

"Who is the one with the golden eyes?"

Sakara turns and sees Saltes.

"Ahh, that is Tailon Saltes, the dominant of the monakites."

"Dominant? You mean he is the leader?"

"Yes."

"But he is so young."

"He is, but don't let that fool you. He is a brilliant scholar and has proven himself many times."

He sees that she is fidgeting in her clothes.

"You must find the clothing somewhat restrictive."

"They are almost unbearable, but the servant has worked so hard to make them fit me, and I didn't want to hurt her feelings."

Sakara chuckles again.

"Her name is Saluk; I'll make sure she makes you your chosen attire. Make a sketch; she will be happy to make the clothes for you."

"Thank you."

Finally, she speaks of her battle against Sceagga.

Sakara leans back in the chair once more, contemplating her story.

"What's bothering you, sortiarius?" she asks.

Sakara leans forward and looks at her gravely.

"Geolufeoer, have you ever taken a spouse?"

"Me? Oh no. We do not become denwyves until we leave the service. As Haloguardian, we are not allowed to spouse until we quit. Why?"

"Geolufeoer, do you know you are achilding," Sakara says.

"Achilding? What's that?"

"Achilding, with child."

Sakara concentrates for a moment, searching the skybourne's vocabulary.

"With cild," he says

"Me? No, you are mistaken. I have yet to select a doyen, let alone—"

She places her hands over her abdomen.

"Sceagga!" she murmurs. "He must of...How did he...How can it be possible?"

Tears spring from her eyes, and her voice starts to rise in a panic.

"That's all right, Geolufeoer; you are fine."

He pats her hand, and she calms down but continues sobbing.

"If he was as powerful as you state, he might have done it when he grabbed you," Sakara says.

"You mean...I carry...his child?" She says in between sobs.

"I don't know, but he may have been carrying some sort of life and was searching for a suitable place to put it. He found you."

"If not his, then who's?"

"According to the curist, the life force within you is very strong, strong enough to be the Promised One."

"Who is this Promised One?"

"Well, as the story goes, everything we knew about Terrae changed around six hundred years ago. Evil seeped into our world; the terraens did things we had not imagined. Then, the death of a terraen at the hand of a terraen occurred. The time it all started to concurs with your story of Sceagga." Sakara stares off, contemplating the thought.

"You mean that what Sceagga did affected your land as well?" She asks.

"The timing of the two events is too close. At that same time, a sortiarius called Eage started to have visions of things to come. Eage saw that the awaited birth by a 'strange stranger,' an angelos with hair like the sun, would come. He said she would bear the one who would become the right hand of Eyu. We believe he talked about the Promised One who would, through a stranger, guard the terraens from his own shadow."

"What does that mean?" Geolufeoer asks.

"There is a lot of speculation of what that part of the prophecy means. But he will be born during the first year of the third millennia after the seventh day."

"The third millennia from when?"

"'The third millennia' refers to how far back our written record goes. A Sacerdos Magike named Verus wrote, 'When the angelo walks among the Sylvan, the protector would soon follow.' Later he wrote, 'The bringer of the right hand of Eyu will be a strange stranger.' And, 'The number of years leading to the Promised One will be six times the number of steps leading to Eyu's temple.'"

"How many steps lead to Eyu's temple?

"The temple Verus referred to no longer stands. However, its ruins are considered a shrine to believers, and there are five hundred steps leading to it."

"That's...three thousand...three millennia."

Sakara takes a deep breath. "Yes...so, as you can see, all of the events preceding your arrival lead us to believe that you, Geolufeoer, are the bearer of the Promised One."

"But what are the signs? I mean, I am a stranger in this land, but there must be a lot of doyenne strangers."

"You come from a land that was, until now, unknown to us. Sylvanus has no winged citizens; to us, you are an angelos. Your hair color does not exist among us; you have one blue eye and one grey. You are, we believe, the strange stranger of the prophecy."

Geolufeoer slowly rises from the table, cradling her womb, and walks around the room. Though her pregnancy isn't noticeable, she can feel turmoil brewing inside, like a storm on the horizon.

"What else does the prophecy say?"

"It is somewhat confusing. It states that the Promised One will enter through the glowing gate," Sakara answers.

"A glowing gate? So, my child is not the Promised One?"

"As I said, the prophecy is confusing. But the two events are somehow linked."

She looks at all the eager faces around her, yearning for information.

"What are you going to do with me?"

Her voice has an edge of fright; she speaks the words almost in a whisper.

"If you fear for your safety, forget it. You have become a living treasure in Terrae. "You will not be restricted. But, for now, there will be a monach assigned to you. You are now the most important creature in the land."

"Monach?"

"A doyenne sortiarius."

"How will I understand her? Does she also have the power of languages?"

"I have discussed this matter with the dominant. Saltes believes, as do I, that if I am capable of learning your language, then I should be able to pass our language to you."

"I just want to go home." She sobs.

"We won't keep you from going; however, when the time comes, we will accompany you," Sakara says.

"If we can figure out where your home is."

The old sortiarius smiles at her, and she smiles back. All she can do is trust in the Sylvan and heal.

"I will make it so you can understand our language now."

Sakara reaches up and places his hand on Geolufeoer's head.

"Will I forget the Ortetan language?"

"No, Geolufeoer, you will add ours to yours."

She feels the warmth that Sakara felt when he absorbed her language. A wave of dizziness passes, and she blinks.

"Did it work?"

Everyone gasps.

"She spoke." Saluk whispers.

"M'lady, welcome to Ka-Mer." Rudo bows with flair.

Geolufeoer sobs; one significant obstacle has been removed from her path.

After that, there isn't a dry eye in the room.

The rainy season ends, and the warm weather is upon them. Tailon takes Geolufeoer on walks around the garden. At first, spectators line up outside the area around the house, shouting their petitions whenever the doyenne shows herself. So, Rudo erects tall screens around the property for her privacy.

The monakite has many questions, but the answers leave them more confounded than before.

"Yellow-feather, you say that the sortiarius and his army attacked the village you protected. So why did he need an army in the first place?"

Because of the difficulty pronouncing her name, Tailon started calling her Yellow-feather.

"Since the Deccem Magistrate had ordered his arrest, he wanted protection. Like the monachs that control the pacú, his powers wane when used. Fighting an entire army would weaken him and make him vulnerable."

"Opposing the Keepers does not seem enough of a motivation to join an army."

"No, it wasn't. So, he offered the Solois a life many times longer than the life of a normal being."

"Longer life—He can do that?"

"Apparently."

"Any idea why you were chosen?"

"No, but he did say that he had been looking for me; I don't know why, but if I carry the Promised One, why is its creator the foulest being ever?"

"Leave that to the scholars. Was it mentioned that while you were unconscious, munkye attacked the house?"

"Munkye? What's a munkye?"

"Generally, thieves or assassins. They tried to kidnap you. Two of Rudo's servants lost their lives in the attack."

"That's horrible."

" Do you have any idea—"

"Could it be that Sceagga has Solois here?"

Saltes sees her becoming upset.

"Well, whoever they were, they were killed by the guards."

At least two of them.

He hopes the small omission will keep her calm.

"We can leave that to the scholars also. But, for now, let's think about the location of Ortet."

She stops and turns to him.

"Wait, Dominant, you're a scholar."

"Yes, but these matters are discussed among many, not the decision of one," he says.

She lets out a sigh but is still bothered over the lives lost.

"When I saw the Mariner's Torch, it was towards the northwest. So, since the only unexplored part of the ocean lies towards the southeast, I believe that is where Ortet is located."

"Rudo summoned all the ship caputs and pilots in the area and questioned them. They all said that if they travel in that direction for more than two days, they will encounter the impenetrable coral reef called the Abuttals."

"The Abuttals?"

"Many ships blown off course have struck the reef and sunk. On a calm day, the reef's outcroppings protrude about four fingers above the water. But during storms, they are hidden by the waves. Accounts of those who had seen it make it too broad for an arrow to clear. This explains why no one has ever attempted to cross it," Tailon says.

"But, somehow, I did."

"The fact that you made it means that there must be some sort of passage, and the townmaster wants to find it."

"Rudo is looking for a passage? Why?"

"Rudo is always looking for a way to profit. He is now looking for volunteers to go and find a route through it, assuring them an island and trade wait on the other side. But no one is stepping up.

"There is a lot of superstition concerning the reef; most believe Eyu placed it there to imprison a monster," Tailon chuckles.

"Imprison a monster? That's ridiculous; I made it through, and in one piece."

Tailon shrugs.

"Well, apparently, that's not good enough. So Rudo now offers a princely reward to anyone who will travel to the rocky bar and look for a path; still, no one dares."

Several months pass, and a disproportionally large ship anchors at the port. An equally large caput steps off. He looks at the notice board, removes a faded parchment, and heads into town.

Townmaster Rudo is in his office, busy at his desk, sorting through the daily paperwork needed to run a village. He hears the floorboards of his office creak from the strain of a heavy burden. When Rudo looks up, a giant stoops under the doorframe and steps into his office. He wears a brown leather gherkin with a light-colored rough cloth undergarment. His pants are also of the same coarse fabric and tan in color. A baldric with red fringes holds a long knife at chest level with a golden coin sewn above the weapon, symbolizing a caput. He stops in front of Rudo's desk and sniffs the air.

Flowers?

"Townmaster?" his voice rumbles deep in his chest.

Rudo leans back to look at the caput's face.

"Yes, that's me."

"My name is Mayven. I am caput of the Scip Hudros, and I've come about the reward," he says, placing the parchment on the desk.

"The reward?" Rudo asks.

The townmaster looks at the notice.

"Oh yes, for finding the path through the reef. It's been so long that I've almost given up on it."

"Does it still stand?"

"Indeed, it does."

The townmaster stands, walks around his desk, and stretches his hand to the giant.

"My name is Rudo, by the way," he says, smiling.

He takes Mayven's hand and tries to shake it with little success.

Mayven is well over three strides tall; the townmaster barely reaches his belt. He recognizes Mayven as a Nauta, a good-natured seafolk.

"Coming into Ka-Mer, I heard of a bounty for the discovery of a passage through the reef."

"The post has been up for a while. You come here often?" Rudo asks.

"I'm from a town further down the coast, so I only stop at Ka-Mer to gather stores for my voyages up the coast,"

"How did you hear of the reward?"

"One of my crew saw it. So, when I stepped off the ship, I looked for the notice nailed to the common board at the docks," Mayven says.

The Nauta steps to the window and looks out over the bay.

"Well, Townmaster Rudo, I would like to undertake the expedition to find the passage through the reef."

Rudo contemplates the giant while rubbing his cheek with his kerchief.

"Many say that the reefs hold monsters at bay. Aren't you afraid of what may wait on the other side?"

"If there's an opening in the reef, the monsters would have found it by now."

Mayven is still looking through the window. He can see all the houses neatly arranged on the winding streets leading to the bay.

"I see the houses have a fresh coat of paint. Does the stranger in town have anything to do with it?"

"The people have been in a festive mood ever since her arrival. So, how about the monsters on the other side of the reef?" Rudo asks.

Mayven turns to Rudo.

"Well, logic tells you there is either no opening through the reef, or there is an opening but no monsters. Either way, there isn't enough danger to concern me. I will be more concerned with being blown on the reef and losing my ship than coming across any undiscovered creatures."

"Good, good."

Rudo's handkerchief flutters wildly.

The townmaster goes back to his chair.

"Besides, if your foreigner...Aduncus, I believe you call her, floated through the reef, then there must be a path."

"My theory, exactly," Rudo says. "When can you start?"

"I will need to take on enough stores for a prolonged voyage. Then, I'll be on my way once that's done."

"Splendid!"

"There is one thing, though," Mayven says. "If I should find this passage, I want to keep it a secret, known only to those I chose to tell."

"What?"

The handkerchief flutters to Rudo's lap.

"That is my condition."

"But…what will I get for my reward?"

"In return, I promise that all of my business with 'Urtet' will pass through Ka-Mer."

The caput struggles with the name.

The townmaster thinks about it for a moment. This time, Rudo holds the kerchief under his nose and sniffs deeply.

"Actually, I don't see why not. As long as we get the business, it doesn't matter who has the right to the passage."

The townmaster gives Mayven a sly smile.

"Besides, you are taking a chance against all those unknown monsters."

They both share in the laugh.

Rudo knows that if anyone can find the route, it is the Nauta. Not only is he a master sailor, but he is also of an amphibious race that is just as at home in the water as on the land. Nautas, are giants. Their average height is over four strides. However, they swim faster than most fish and catch them as a sport.

A handshake is all you need to seal a pact with a Nauta.

Six months have passed since Geolufeoer washed up on the shores of Ka-Mer. She is now a part of the community and is considered good fortune to be in her presence; therefore, she is a welcome sight wherever she goes.

Her wings have healed, molted. They are not only strong enough to fly again, but for reasons she doesn't understand, she is faster than before. Sakara said that it may be the influence of the Promised One in her womb.

Because of the difficulty pronouncing her name and Yellow-feather being a mouthful, Tailon nicknamed her Yelu, and the name stuck.

A member of the monakites known as the Watchers always accompanied Yelu. Thus, Watch Rewen becomes Yelu's permanent companion.

Rewen is a novice, a few years younger than the Aduncus. Rewen was an orphan from a Wandrien tribe; left for dead after a battle, a gadabout came across the child and took her to the nearest monastery, the Lea Abby, where she was raised.

The Lea Abbey is no ordinary monastery; it is the main abbey for the followers of Eyu. Located in Takamen territory, the Lea Abbey is where Regnant Dominant Debon rules over all monachs in Sylvanus. It did not take long for little Rewen to captivate the regnant's heart. She became the favorite with the monakites though her Wandrien nature kept everyone on their toes, and they were glad when she chose to become one of them.

She was heartbroken when ordered to leave the abbey, the only home she had known. However, the day she reported to Dominant Tailon Saltes, she forgot about the abbey.

As was the case with all that met him, his eyes fascinated her. This fascination made her into what Yelu said was a love-smitten doyenne.

"What are we looking for today?" Rewen asks.

"Spice-fruit, tartseed, eggs, and a few vegetables. Any news from Lea Abby?"

"Regnant Debon sends you his best and hopes to be here next summer to meet you."

"I think he just misses you. Dominant Saltes said you were Debon's favorite."

"I do miss the place, the mountains, the skank."

"Never knew anyone who missed those little horned beasts. Ahh, but all was forgotten when you met the Dominant."

"You're exaggerating."

"And you're a love-smitten doyenne."

That earns her a poke to the ribs. It did not take long for them to become inseparable; they always looked forward to the weekly trips to the market.

"We are here; make sure your hair is hidden."

An unfortunate side of her popularity is that crowds will gather if she is spotted.

Talea, the robemaker, was one of the first Sylvan to encounter the Aduncus when she first ventured into public. When he saw her wings, the tailor came upon the idea of making feathered robes for those who could afford them. Their use became the immediate fashion, and soon all citizens of means had to wear one of Talea's creations.

This annoyed Yelu. However, she realized she could lose herself in the sea of feathered capes. All she had to do was drape a short version of Talea's robe over her shoulders and hold her wings just right.

Rewen tucks a loose strand of red hair under Yelu's hood. With her hair and wings covered, she easily passes for a local.

They make their way through the crowd to one of their favorite kiosks.

"What do you think of these, Rewen?"

She holds up a braided string of dried spice fruit.

"They look too moist, m'lady. They'll spoil before long ...here, try these."

The young monakite holds up a different string.

"Ahhh, much better," she places them in the basket. "Look, ground tartseed."

"Honestly, you must have a blade-metal stomach to eat as much tartseed as you do."

"I didn't have a taste for it until I became a childing."

She rubs her growing womb and smiles.

"Many things change when you are with child," Rewen says.

There is a movement behind Rewen, and she crumples to the ground.

"Rewen!"

Yelu reaches for her, but a rough sack passes over her head and shoulders.

"Hey?"

She tries to struggle as she is dragged away.

"No!"

Automatically she reaches into the folds of her robes, snaps the aduncus open, and cuts through the bag. When she looks at her attackers, all, save one, have a blank stare.

Munkye!

The attacker to her right falls to the blade. She does not have time to secure the aduncus' strap, and it slips off her wrist. She spins and strikes the other with the joint of the wing. She is not wearing the pollex blades, but the blow is strong enough to knock him backward. Rewen's attacker rushes her and grabs her arm. The other attacker recuperates from the strike and grabs her from behind, pinning her wings."

"What do you—?" A gag cuts her short.

Wide-eyed terror starts to set. The crowd scatters in panic. She tries muscling out of the hold, but pain shoots through her right wing. Though healed, it is still tender. She starts to kick and struggle wildly. In the commotion, she catches a glimpse of Rewen staggering to her feet when someone breaks from the crowd, accidentally knocking her back to the ground. He draws a large blade. She does not know why they are attacking her, but she won't be able to stop him.

Skagget!

The stranger with the blade reaches her. Yelu shuts her eyes and waits for the blade. Then, to her surprise, he kills the attacker holding her arm. Once free, she immediately spins and, using the bend of her wing, strikes the attacker behind her. The blow catches him below the ear, killing him instantly.

What's going on? What do they want?

As the assailer collapses, she sees his leather arm guard. It is a cluster of snakes twisting into the shape of a trumpet.

Solois?

The expressionless face of the other tells her he was enthralled.

She jumps, rolls, retrieves the aduncus, and crouches into a fighting stance facing the stranger.

"I'm only here to help." He says.

He places the blade on the ground and holds up his hands.

The baby in her womb reacts, making her head spin. She steadies herself and rubs her belly with her free hand.

"M'lady, are you all right?" He asks.

"I'm fine. Who were they?"

She keeps a wary eye on him.

"I don't know. I'm here buying stores for my master's ship."

"He's telling the truth, Lady Yelu."

She recognizes the voice and turns to see one of the merchants helping Rewen to her feet.

"You know him, Trinker?"

"Yes, m'lady. His name is Pouke, and he works for master Mayven."

She relaxes a little and straightens up. The crowd gathers around the bodies; they recognize her but keep their distance.

"I owe you my life then."

"It was my pleasure." He looks at his blade. "May I?"

"Go ahead."

Pouke picks up his blade and tucks it into its sheath.

He bows and goes back to where Rewen is.

"Are you ok, m'lady?" Pouke asks.

"I think my head will throb for the rest of the day."

"Sorry for bumping into you."

"I saw what you did, young lord. I thank you in the name of the Watch."

"As I told lady Yelu, it was my pleasure. Will you be alright now?"

"Yes, they caught us by surprise, but I see the guards approaching now."

Yelu turns around.

"One of the bodies is gone! "

Pouke turns.

"You're right; I know they were dead, at least the one I ran with my blade."

"M'lady, are you alright?"

She turns and sees the guard; he looks pale with fright. She imagines what he might be thinking, munkyes attack his ward, and a stranger has to do the rescuing.

"There were three bodies; one is missing. Did you see them?"

"Sorry, m'lady, but no. I heard the screams and came, but I saw only two."

"I saw them," Pouke says.

"As did I," Rewen adds. "Yelu, you don't look well."

"Do you live far, m'lady? I'll accompany you to your home," Pouke asks.

"No, I'll be fine."

"As you wish, Lady Yelu. I must finish my dealings with Master Trinker."

Pouke bows again and turns to the merchant.

Yelu overhears the young Sylvan talking to Trinker about the supplies. She became interested in ships when she saw that the Sylvans used them for fishtangling, traveling, and carrying cargo. They would dock the vessel directly at the piers or row a smaller boat to them if they did not come to the dock.

"But, master Pouke, that is twice as many stores as Mayven normally buys," the shopkeeper says.

"Don't you worry, Lord Trinker. We will need all of it. He's not one to waste."

For the first time, she notices Pouke's features. He has very light-colored hair and sharp features. As young as he looks, he has a rugged appearance and shows signs of spending a lot of time working in the sun. His cheek is scarred, which adds to his intrigue, and carries one shoulder slightly lower than the other, probably an old injury.

"Where are you taking to with all of these supplies?" Trinker asks.

"Caput Mayven has accepted the townmaster's bounty to search for the passage through the Abuttals."

"You are going to look for Urtet?"

"Yes, I believe that's the name of it."

"Oh, luck and blessings with you, master Pouke," Trinker says. "I've heard bad things about the sea beyond the reef. They say the reef is there to keep evil beasts out of our waters, you know."

Yelu cannot help but interrupt the two.

"Lord Trinker, those are just rumors; I never saw any evil creature in those waters. And the name is Ortet."

The shopkeeper breaks into a beaming smile.

"Lady Yelu, I didn't mean to be disrespectful of your land."

"No offense taken, shopkeeper," she says. "I am very familiar with the waters around my land since I once guarded them."

"But, m'lady, the reefs are still too far from land for even the strongest Aduncus to fly to without the aid of a ship," Trinker says. "Surely, a creature of the reefs could remain hidden from your Urtetians."

"The proper term is Ortetan. But you are right, Trinker, though you'd think that sooner or later, one of those creatures would get washed up or become curious enough to look at the land side."

She notices Pouke's furtive glances at her and turns to him.

"So, Lord Pouke, how come I haven't heard of this adventure?"

"Master Mayven and Lord Rudo made the deal four days ago."

"When will you be sailing?"

"As soon as the stores are aboard the ship and the caput deems it ready."

"Where is your caput now?"

He shrugs.

"Aboard the ship, I suppose."

"Thank you, Lord Pouke; maybe we'll meet again," Yelu says.

She pulls the hood of her robe over her head and walks into the crowd. Hergian watches until she's out of sight.

Hidden by her robe, Yelu smiles.

Hmm, I must get to know him.

"He seems likable," Rewen says.

Yelu can see the curl on her lip.

"I just needed information."

"Oh, I see. What did you say? 'Maybe we'll meet again.' I guess you will need more information later, " Rewen says.

"Humph!"

Yelu picks up the pace and hurries through the market streets that lead downhill to the docks. The shorter Rewen tries to keep up.

"Yelu," Rewen gasps. "He was kind of cute, wasn't he?"

She sees the Aduncus smile.

"Sort of."

"Sort of? I saw the way you looked at him."

"Humph! I looked at him the way I look at everyone."

"And, the way he looked at you. Besides, you're blushing."

Yelu pulls the hood farther over her head.

"I looked at him the way you look at the Dominant."

For a moment, Rewen becomes silent, then changes the subject.

"What about shopping? Where are we off to now?"

The monakite is almost running.

"Are you blushing?"

"Humph! I'm getting hot from trying to keep up with you."

"I'm sure you are. We're off to meet Caput Mayven," the Aduncus says.

"Perhaps this visit should be discussed first with the Dominant," Watch Rewen says.

"I'm sure you would enjoy that."

"Humph!"

"You're blushing again."

"Alright, you win; I do find him to my liking. But you must admit that you were more than curious about Pouke."

"Yes, you are right. He is kind of cute."

They both start to giggle.

"But really, m'lady, you should discuss this with Tailon."

"So, we are on a first-name basis with the Dominant now."

"Stop it, m'lady. This is important."

"This affair will be of concern to me. Tailon can take part if he so wishes."

"It'll be a pleasure to see you again," Pouke shouts after her.

They turn and see him waving on the road above them.

"It's him again. Looks like you made an impression," Rewen says.

Yelu waves goodbye then turns back to Rewen, and they giggle.

"I wonder how they recognized us," Yelu says.

"It was strange. Like they were waiting for us."

"You don't think Trinker...."

"No, not Trinker. They must have followed us from home," Rewen says.

"One of them wore a Solois armband. How did he get here?"

"Solois? That wouldn't sense; maybe you just thought you saw it. Maybe Tailon—".

"I will tell Tailon when the time comes."

"Err...of course, but why are they here? How could they be here?"

"They're here because of me. Maybe when Sceagga was a Keeper, he visited Sylvanus long ago. In that case, he could have created some secret Solois group here. I can't explain the Solois otherwise."

"What are you planning on doing?"

"It is apparent that if the Solois are here, I'm no longer safe here," Yelu says.

"We can have additional guards."

"Where are they now?"

"They were still looking for the body. The guards never saw us leave," Rewen says.

"Once again, we are vulnerable. Things happen; we had a small army with us."

"It's not their fault Yelu."

"I'm not blaming them. But, it seems the Solois are now a part of the population. They can hide among the townsfolk, among the guards themselves."

"We can keep you—"

"Locked up! What kind of life is that?" She snaps at Rewen.

"Sorry, I didn't mean it that way."

Yelu stops, turns to Rewen, and places her arm around her shoulder.

"I'm sorry. I shouldn't bark at you like that. I'll discuss it with Tailon. Besides, they may have an army ready if they're already here."

"Why do they want you?" Rewen asks.

"As Tailon says, 'leave that to the scholars.'"

They both chuckle.

Yelu knows what she has to do. She hurries down the hill while Rewen runs to keep up.

"Lady...Yelu...he was...kind of brave...wasn't he?"

"Who?"

"Pouke." She gasps.

"Rewen, you're getting lazy. You have to do some exercise again."

"It's my head...It still throbs."

"Is that why you're out of breath?"

"Sort of."

It is a half-hour walk to the docks. Ka-Mer seems to be in a continuous festive state. Fairs and carnivals seem to spring spontaneously around town, and more travelers are expected when the time of birth nears.

The constant preparation, rebuilding, and repainting Ka-Mer is experiencing shows in the gaily-painted waterfront homes and stores.

Several ships are tied at the docks; any one of them can be Mayven's ship.

She looks at the buildings on the pier and finds the biggest and most attractive one. Guessing correctly, she knocks on the dockmaster's door.

"I'm looking for the whereabouts of Caput Mayven's ship," she asks the dockmaster.

"You are looking for the Scip Hudros. The one with the oversized plank. Actually, oversized everything," he says, motioning with his arms.

"Follow me."

He steps outside and points to a long ship at the end of the dock.

"That's the Scip Hudros."

"Thank you."

Yelu and Rewen walk to the ship. Yelu notices right away that not only is the gangplank oversized, but, as the dockmaster said, so is everything else on the vessel. Unlike other vessels, the wooden gunnels have been carefully carved in a wave pattern. There is a lamp on the side of the gangplank casting a soft glow. Still, a rope tied across it with red streamers dangling from it is an obvious sign that the ship is not receiving visitors.

"A very straightforward indication that the ship is closed to outsiders," Rewen says and starts to walk away.

"Of course, you would say that."

Yelu leaps, and with six wing beats, she's on the deck.

The monakite stomps her foot, frustrated; she does not know why she always does what the Aduncus doyenne wants. She lifts the rope, passes beneath it, hurries up the gangplank, and tries to hold her back.

"M'lady, the caput may not appreciate our visit," Rewen says.

"He might be interested in what I have to say."

She gently pulls her arm free.

"Hello, onboard! Caput Mayven!" She shouts.

Out from one of the cabin doors comes a mariner. Dwarfed by the size of the door, he is an older type but still shows a lot of life.

"M'ladies, did you not see that the plank was closed?" he asks.

"We've come to speak with the caput," Yelu says.

She purposely lifts her wings just enough for him to notice that it is not a part of a cape.

"The caput does not appreciate interrupt—"

His eyes grow a size when he notices her wings.

"What's your name, good fellow?"

"I would be Karp, m'lady."

He is unable to take his eyes off her wings.

"Well, Master Karp, tell your caput that there's a lady with wings," she says, stretching them to their full size.

Karp takes a step back, still gawking.

"And a monakite who wants to speak to him," she says with authority.

Watch Rewen places her hand on Yelu's arm.

"Just a lady with wings." She corrects.

"A lady with wings and a monakite? Hmmm."

Karp does not know why, but he feels that the caput will be very interested in talking to them.

"That is interesting; I'll see what he says."

Karp runs off to another section of the ship and disappears.
"M'lady, I've no desire to become entangled in this affair."
"But you already are, Watch Rewen."
The monakite stomps her foot again.
"Humph!"

The floorboards creak, and one of the large doors opens. The Aduncus is surprised when she sees the caput. He is immense. She recognizes him as a Nauta. She read about them; they are the largest intelligent beings, outside some large creatures living in the mountains to the north. However, those are the ogres and trolls.

Mayven is not wearing his outer coat; his inner shirt is clean and pressed, though, as if he has been expecting a visitor.

"A ship is not a place for a doyenne," the caput growls. "You may leave the way you came."

"Sorry, m'Lord, you must pardon the doyenne; she hasn't been herself lately," Watch Rewen says. "We'll be leaving right away."

She reaches for Yelu, but the Aduncus steps out of reach.

"I've come to have a word with the caput, are you Mayven?"

She ignores the warning and the monakite's embarrassed plea.

He eyes her carefully, wondering whether he should answer; he does.

"That I am."

Yelu pulls the hood down, allowing her red hair to spill out. Mayven's eyes widen at the sight. When she steps forward, the light from the ship's lamp catches her wings

"I am Yelu," she says.

"Ah, the red-haired angelo. You are the Aduncus they talk about. Welcome to the Scip Hudros," Mayven says. "Pardon my rudeness, m'Lady, but you must understand that there are those who would like to profit from my labor in this adventure."

He motions to his cabin.

"Would you like to talk in private?" Mayven asks.

The monakite grabs her arm again and whispers harshly.

"M'Lady!"

"You may wait out here if you like, Watch Rewen, or come in and listen," Yelu says.

"Humph!"

The monakite straightens her back and hustles inside the caput's cabin; Yelu follows.

The cabin is rather spacious. A table in the middle of the room has maps stretched out with crystal net floats and various navigating instruments weighing the corners. It reminds her of the room in Rudo's house.

There are four stools against the wall, one of them specially made for the Aduncus. Yelu raises an eyebrow when she sees it. Mayven takes the seats and places them in front of the table. The caput sits opposite them in an oversized chair.

"I've been waiting for three days hoping for this visit, m'lady," says the caput.

"Oh?"

"My men have been spreading word of the voyage, hoping it would reach your ears."

"If you wanted her to come, why is your ship closed to visitors?" Watch Rewen asks.

"It was only closed to those who weren't allowed," the caput answers.

"Why did you want me to come?"

"I'm curious about that, too," the monakite adds.

The caput leans back and eyes them both for a moment. Then, finally, he decides that she obviously is who she claims to be and can be trusted.

"I am sure that there is a passage through the reef. It will only be a matter of time before I find it. I have fished the waters around there for years and have never seen a ship on the other side. That tells me that your folks have yet to develop long-range vessels."

"Very good, Caput. All of our ships are designed for single-day use only."

"So, no one has ever attempted to cross the reefs before?"

"Two years ago, a group of Ortetans bundled several rafts together and tried to make it through the reefs. They were obsessed with legends of other lands.

"We found the wreckage of their craft and several bodies. Strangely enough, none of the dead showed signs of starvation or lack of water. They just died.

There was one survivor, though, who was delirious. Shortly before he died, he said they had found a path through the coral ring for the master. We assumed the master was a criminal monach trying to escape, but since there were no other survivors. But he was still causing trouble on Ortet, so it all became a mystery."

Yelu revised the story.

"However, if they did find a passage, why did the wrecked craft wind up on our shore? Anyway, that's how we found out about the reefs and the rumors of a passage."

"I see. From what the townmaster said, you were some sort of soldier from a warrior race."

"Yes and no. We had to develop an army because of the evil doings of monach. The Ortetans serve in the military for three years. In general, there is little difference between the Sylvans in this land and ours."

"Except the winged ones."

"Yes, except the winged ones," she smiles.

"What does all of this have to do with the doyenne?" Watch Rewen asks.

"I'm curious to find out also," Yelu says.

"As I said, I believe there is a passage through the reef. It would be nice to have eyes over the water to assist us."

"The doyenne is achilding. She couldn't possibly partake of such an expedition," the monakite says.

"We've been told by one of your crew—"

"Pouke," Rewen says.

Then turns and gives Yelu a sly smile.

"Yes...Pouke," she feels her face flush.

"Anyway, we were told that you are going to sail anyway. It seems you have plenty of good crew aboard. There is more, isn't there? Why don't you tell me the rest?"

The caput is surprised that she is so persuasive. He finds that he would have told her even if he did not want to.

"Pouke? He has only been a member of my crew for a short while. However, we have known each other for about one year on a business level. He would meet the ship out at sea, where I would give him a list of provisions. Pouke would acquire the stores for me, so I would just have to land, pick them up, and pay him. He was the one who told me about you and then suggested that I take him and you on the expedition."

"Why me?"

"I asked him that too. He said that if and when we cross the reef, we will need someone who knows the Aduncus and speaks their language. We must convince them not to attack the strange ship coming to their shores. It made sense to me."

"So, what you want is an ambactia representing the folk of Ortet aboard," Yelu says.

"Yes, you may say that. You are the only one I know who can speak their language," Mayven says. "And being a former member of their military, you may even be recognized. It will

101

be difficult to tell your folk of our goodwill if we can't speak the language while evading their arrows."

Yelu keeps to herself that Sakara can also speak the Ortetan language and just as easily act as ambactia. The ambassador's position could be her only chance to return to her homeland.

"M'lady, you couldn't possibly be considering taking part in this wild adventure, and…and think of the child."

Mayven picks up one of the netfloats and turns it over in his hands. The reflection from the green glass dances on the wooden walls. Yelu used to collect the ones that washed up on the shore in her youth and had a few in her home back on the island.

"You may bring whomever you wish to assist you. As a matter of fact, new quarters are being prepared for your group now."

"You have presumed that I would be interested in the trip."

"Why else did you come?"

Yelu smiles.

"It's not proper, Yelu. You may bear the child during the journey," Rewen says.

"Why would it matter where I bear? As long as I have you and the Watchers with me."

"But m'lady, you will be taking the Promised One from our land."

"The Promised One belongs to Ortet just as much as Sylvanus," Yelu says. "Don't forget, it was in Ortet that he was conceived."

"So, what they say is true. You are the bearer of the Promised One," Mayven says.

"So, I've been told."

"Maybe this was meant to be," Mayven says. "Maybe, Watch Rewen, it was intended for her to bear the child in her land."

"Caput, Mayven!"

"Watch Rewen; too many happenings of chance are coming together for this event. I would say that the final answer belongs to the doyenne. She and only she will know what the Promised One will want."

"Caput Mayven, it's not fair to place that burden on her. Of course, she wants to see her land again, except now is not the time to go."

"Watch Rewen; I think I know what the caput is saying. There have been many strange events since Sceagga placed his hands on me. Why did lightning strike me during that storm when skybournes are never struck by lightning? Why did I wash up on the shores of Ka-Mer when debris usually washes up on Ortet? The caput is right; there are too many coincidences. I believe I am being guided. To what ends, I do not know. Somehow, I feel our lands' future depends on what I decide tonight."

They all go silent; Watch Rewen thinks it over. Then, once again, she finds herself agreeing with the doyenne.

"Since you put it that way, I'll be there whether you decide to go or stay," the monakite says.

"Thank you, Rewen," Yelu pats her hand. "You better talk to Dominant Saltes then and get a group together."

For a moment, Rewen sees the corner of Yelu's lip curl up; she is smiling, though it does not show.

"I assure you that he won't be pleased. However, I'm sure he will see things my... our way."

Lucky for her, the lamplight in the room does not show her flushed cheeks.

"Thanks," Yelu says.

Chapter 5
THE SEARCH FOR THE PASSAGE

"That is a terrible idea!"

Saltes is shouting, pacing the room, looking for a reason.

"She...she could give birth at sea." He continues.

"Why would that matter?" Rewen says.

"Because she—"

"She will have all the help she needs on board," Rewen interrupts.

"Yes, but—"

"Why would it be any different in a room here than in a room on the ship?" Rewen says. "Besides, what would be the consequences if something happened here? If there would be another attempt by the munkyes?"

"Munkyes?"

"Uh..." Saltes tries to think of an answer.

"Just as I thought. At least on the ship, there would be more control over who comes in contact with Yelu," Rewen says. "Here, you have the entire town to worry about."

Rewen knows she's won and knows he will include himself. She has a hard time suppressing her smile.

Tailon looks out the window. He can see the Scip Hudros by the docks. He can't make out any details, but it is the largest ship in the harbor.

Nothing is ever easy.

As much as he would have liked it, Tailon knows that he can't confine the mother of the Promised One. That can have unforeseeable consequences. He does not care to dwell on them, especially if he is to go down in history as the one responsible. Of course, he will not be left out of the historical event either.

"Can I at least choose the company?"

"Definitely, but I will have to be included," Rewen says.

"Huh?"

"I'm the one Yelu trusts. Unless you believe you can tend to an achilding's needs," Rewen says.

Saltes sees her smirk and frowns.

"You had this whole thing planned, didn't you?"

"Oh! She's calling me now."

Rewen turns and heads for the door.

"I didn't hear—"

"Bye," she winks and closes the door.

Tailon sighs. Of course, if Rewen is going, he will go too. He realizes he looks forward to her company.

He finds attractive her wild nature and how she tries to keep it in check.

Am I having feelings...absurd!

He chooses Eophon, Bandagee, and Sakara as companions.

The group brings the vessel to full capacity. Still, the caput is happy to have them aboard.

Two days later, Rudo bids the travelers goodbye. He is pleased with the adventure because he won't lose whatever happens. If Mayven is successful, Ka-Mer will have new trading partners; if not, he will get the doyenne back.

The Scip Hudros cuts through the waters at a fast pace. Yelu walks the decks, watching the blowholes darting in and out of the bow wave like children playing in the surf. Above, the mainsail billows proudly. Mayven's family coat-of-arms, a half-man half-fish rising out of the ocean, is displayed on it.

Up ahead, Pouke rides a small catamaran called a tielog. Yelu watches skim ahead.

I wonder how the Sylvans court?

She hadn't been exposed to that part of Sylvanus' culture.

She thinks about what type of fathers they make and how everything might have been different if Gneisfeoer had chosen her, things young doyennes think about.

The gentle roll of the ship starts to make her queasy, so she lies down to let the nausea pass and falls asleep. She gets up late the next morning, now familiar with the movement.

Pouke invites her on his craft to help him search. The small tielog resembles two long boats held together with long braces. A section of heavy cloth, called a trampa, stretches across the poles. This is where you sit or walk on. Pouke's tielog has a bright yellow sail with a matching trampa.

The purpose of the tielogs is to scout ahead. It's more maneuverable than the ship and can move closer to the reef for inspection.

A small provisions barge is towed behind the ship with food and water for the tielog riders, so they need not board the ship for food or drink.

They scout ahead when the water becomes choppy since the waves will blear the reef. When the tielog hits a wave head-on, the sail's boom swings around and slaps Pouke on the shoulder. Pouke grunts loudly, releasing the tiller to cradle his shoulder and immediately grabbing it again.

"What? A seaman like you cries over a tap on the shoulder? Yelu says.

"Are you kidding? It almost took my shoulder off."

Yelu scoffs.

"I'll get Bandagee to wrap you up when we get back."

"Oh no, not Bandagee. He'll wrap me from head to toe."

They both laugh. Pouke always jokes around when he is with her.

Watch Rewen spends the morning following the tielog with the watch glass. Occasionally, she stomps her foot when

Pouke takes unnecessary risks. She finally decides it is less stressful to watch the outline of Sylvanus vanishing beneath the horizon.

"Frustrated with your ward, Rewen?"

She jumps.

"Dominant...I didn't hear you approaching."

Rewen feels her ears starting to warm.

"I think she likes Pouke," *Tailon says.*

"I think she gets careless when she's around him."

She likes the way the wind blows his hair back. He has a young but wizened face, which she finds incredibly attractive.

"The little craft looks like it would be fun. Maybe we should try it sometime?" *Tailon says.*

We?

She feels her heart skip a beat.

"Maybe—."

Her voice cracks. She clears her throat.

"Maybe we should."

She turns and gives him her best smile.

Now Saltes clears his throat.

"Yes...I'll see what the caput says."

With that, he turns and quickly walks away.

Did I scare him? I am so clumsy when he's around.

She bites her lip as he hurries away, then lifts the watch glass to see Yelu gliding while holding to the tielog's guideline.

"Humph!"

She stomps again.

Yelu finds that she now enjoys the ship's gentle roll, the smell of the ocean, and, of course, Pouke's company. In the evening, she practices fencing with Eophon, learning to use the Sylvan sword.

The next day she decides to walk the deck and watch the horizon. One hour after the noon meal, Pouke brings the tielog near the ship.

"Reef ahead, Caput!"

He then goes ahead to follow the reef.

"I want to see," Yelu says.

She leaps into the air and flies towards Pouke; she can see the dark reef below the surface and part of the coral ridge sticking out above it like small islands in a river of rock.

It is tricky landing on the moving tielog, but the yellow trampa makes an excellent target. Yelu levels off, folds her wings, and drops onto the canvas. When she does, Pouke smiles and, without hesitation, reaches out with his hand and spreads his fingers. She automatically does the same touching his fingertips in the Ortetan greeting. A glint in the distance catches her attention.

"What's that?"

"It must be fishtanglers."

"Fishtanglers?"

"This is a good fishing area; I'll tell the caput; he'll want to know."

Yelu looks again; the ship sits just above the horizon, not moving.

Fishtanglers? Well, as long as the caput knows...

There is something strange about the whole thing, though, something that tickles the edge of her mind but escapes her just the same.

"C'mon, let's find that pass."

Pouke shifts the sail sending the raft racing by the reef.

"At this speed, you won't find anything."

She takes to the air and soars over the tielog. She knows he is being playful and not serious about finding the path; however, she is.

Watch Rewen uses the watch glass to help Yelu and Pouke look for the pass; however, the whole area seems solid coral. Their wearisome search carries them until dark. The next day is just as fruitless as the day after.

Mayven is open to the idea of Rewen learning to use the tielog. Two tielogs would make the search quicker. So he approves it. Rewen learns how to pilot the tielogs. At first, she has little control over the craft and races across the water in erratic patterns like a surprised cucabug, much to the crew's amusement. However, it does not take her long to get the feel of the craft.

Mayven works out search grids. It places Yelu over the reef and Rewen on the tielog. For Watch Rewen, the swift craft is more of a toy; she becomes adept at it and is soon sailing better than the rest of the crew.

Yelu does the grids daily to keep her mind off the ever-increasing turmoil in her womb. The baby is growing active but is also going through a war of emotions souring her humour.

She continues her evening sword practice with Eophon. She tried to bring up her changing temperament with him, but he would just make a face and suggest she talks to Rewen or Bandagee.

Yelu talks to Bandagee about her moods, but he says it must be a part of the childbearing process. Rewen was of little help either since she had never been achilding herself and didn't know about Aduncus.

"Don't forget, at first, I thought you were going to lay an egg," Rewen says.

This always made Yelu laugh.

Two interesting side effects of her pregnancy were that she developed the ability to convince others to do what she wanted and tell if someone was honest.

She first noticed it when she became ill but still wanted to fly. Rewen wanted her to stay and rest that day, but she insisted on flying anyway. Then, Karp showed up at her cabin door. He said they would not be doing any searches that day because the caput was moving to another section of the reef. She saw through the lie, and Watch Rewen was at the bottom of it.

Yelu was furious because they made the caput stop the search for her benefit.

The doyenne spends a lot of time conversing with Pouke as they search the reef, Pouke on the outer edge, and Yelu on the inside. Her feelings for the young Sylvan grow, but something is off about him.

Blinded by her affection, she chooses not to see the obvious. Instead, she blocks all the warnings her subconscious feels, as the young often do when choosing their company.

The tedium of the search carries on to the second week. It reminds her of the days at her post and the long hours looking for anything out of the ordinary. Back then, she kept her mind entertained by the pipios visit and carving the wooden figurines. Now, the sword practice with Eophon or her discussions of Domain history with Sakara is her only escape.

Mayven moves the ship along as they complete each grid, but the scenery never changes. Like a long rocky road, the reef goes on towards the horizon. An occasional tall formation suggests that it was above the water long ago.

The air over the waters is warm. When it becomes uncomfortable, the skybourne flies high over the ship to get to the cooler air above. While soaring on an unusually warm day, she notices a speck on the horizon. She realizes that the fishtangler's vessel is still there. This is odd because there is no way to store the catch. Unless they sun dry the fish every day, usually done on reed mats on the shore, it will spoil.

I wonder if Pouke told Mayven about the fishtanglers?

Yelu flies to the ship and sees Tailon watching Rewen sailing back and forth along the coral barrier.

The only drawback to the tielog is that you get wet. This makes Rewen's robes heavy, and she constantly stumbles, so she gathers the robe between her legs and tucks it into her rope belt at the front. When Tailon spots her running back and forth on the craft, with her legs exposed, he shouts his objection though she is too far to hear.

"What's wrong, Tailon?" Yelu asks.

"Look at her! It's not proper to show her legs like that."

"Look around you; all on the ship wear half-cut femoralia."

"A ridiculous garment," he says with a wave of his hand. "What's the use of clothing that only cloaks down to the upper part of each leg."

"I believe you will see its use when you board the tielog. Mayven said you will be going with Rewen next."

"I am; I'll show them how a proper monakite ports himself. Femoralia, humph, useless."

"I believe you've grown fond of Rewen."

Tailon turns his head away.

"What are you saying?"

"You've grown protective of her."

"I have not."

"Sorry Dominant, but it's so obvious that everyone has noticed it. I just wanted to let you know."

She jumps into the air and starts to soar.

"Believe me, it's obvious. You are smitten."

Before he can reply, she flies away.

Now I forgot why I went there in the first place, hmm.

She heads back towards the reef.

Tailon thinks about what she said.

Have I become enamored with Rewen?

The next day he watches Rewen ride the tielog. He can almost feel his attraction for her growing steadily, but he still doesn't know how to express himself.

"She really enjoys the tielog," Yelu says.

He turns and sees that Yelu and Mayven have also been watching Rewen.

"I'm surprised. Rewen has a natural understanding of the little craft for someone who had never been in the sea." The caput says.

"If it weren't for her, I wouldn't have even set foot in the tielog," Saltes says.

Yelu sees the expression in his eyes as he watches her.

He's really hooked on her.

The caput is staring at the horizon as if calculating the location of the opening.

She remembers the question that had been nagging her.

"Caput?"

"Yes."

"How long do the fishtangler vessels stay out?"

"Fishtangler? What's a fishtangler?"

"Uh, those who…hunt for fish with nets or line and hook."

"Oh, you mean fishers?"

"Yes, fishers."

"What do you mean by stay out?" he asks.

"There is a fisher vessel just above the horizon; it seems to have been there for several weeks now."

"She's right, Caput; we saw it also," Saltes says.

"Really! Well, it could be that they've gone and come back," he said. "Have you seen it every day?" Mayven asks.

"I can't say I have. I saw it on our first day out, and I saw it again today." Yelu says.

"I've seen it several times." The Dominant ads.

"They could have taken their catch to shore and returned. But that would take three or four days. Hmm."

"I thought Pouke reported it to you," Yelu says.

"We told Pouke about it also," Saltes says.

"First, I've heard of it. So, Pouke knew?"

"Yes."

"Curious, I guess I know now."

He stares in the direction of the fisher's ship, a hardly noticeable speck above the horizon.

"Hmm."

Mayven turns and heads back to his cabin.

Pouke's tielog skims by the ship, and he waves. Yelu waves back and, for a few seconds, follows the tielog. But, once again, something about it bothers Yelu.

Yelu starts to take after-dinner walks on the deck with Pouke and Rewen. Sometimes, he would run the edge of his arm down her wing, a sign of affection. There are things about him that concern her, though, like why he never told Mayven about the fishtangler vessel. Also, whenever she is with him, she can feel a strange sensation from her unborn.

Today she gets out of her bunk, fighting that strange feeling that tells her something is wrong with Pouke. However, once again, she chooses to push it aside.

It's early morning, and Yelu and Rewen are on the ship's bow talking when Pouke approaches.

"There are some wave skippers following the ship. Come and see them," he says to Yelu.

"Sure, come, Rewen, let's look."

Pouke frowns.

"Sure, you too, Rewen."

Pouke is annoyed that Yelu is starting to bring Rewen along on their walks.

This changes everything. I need her alone.

By the second month of the voyage, the smallest effort on Yelu's part becomes an exhausting exercise. The monachs take over her duties in the morning to let her sleep late; however, the afternoon shift belongs to her.

Pouke has become less talkative. Yelu believes it's because of Rewen's presence.

Why would that matter?

Three days into the new month, they find an area of the reef that branches and juts into the ocean. The doyenne is as excited as the crew and joins the others to follow the channel. The branch it creates keeps its course towards the north. It slowly separates until the reef's outer edge is too wide for a stone's throw. The skybourne follows the branches until the inside fork opens to the inside of the reef.

Yelu marks the boundaries of the opening by shooting brightly colored arrows into the rocks. She then flies towards *the outside and calls the crew to the area. It is a peninsula of coral formed by a channel on each side. She follows it until it exits into the open ocean.*

She found the opening.

Chapter 6
THE PASSAGE

All this time, they searched for an opening that led straight through the reef. Instead, it's a canal that meanders south for two millisteps before turning north. It then continues for another millistep before opening to the ocean.

It is not that the opening is hidden; anyone would have thought it insane to take a ship into a narrow channel with no exit in sight. They would have to back out if they ran into a dead end.

With the passage found, the ship's crew takes over. They check the depth of the channel and replace the arrows with indicator flags, carefully marking the route. However, Mayven becomes impatient; he wants to navigate the channel before the day is done, and they are running out of daylight.

Yelu watches the crew from the ship's deck as they navigate the channel in their small boats and place the banners. From the vessel, the channel is almost invisible. No wonder it had remained hidden all this time.

She looks around for Pouke, but he is nowhere around. She has grown accustomed to his constant presence. However, now that the most significant event in the voyage is occurring, he has disappeared.

"So, where's Pouke now?" She asks Mayven.

The caput looks over the tielogs as they navigate the channel.

"That's a good question," he answers.

"He's not on the ship?"

"No, I saw him sail off a little while ago. I thought he was helping with the markers."

"He hasn't been around. I've been watching the crew since they started." Saltes says.

Mayven thinks for a few seconds and then calls his first mate.

"Karp!"

The old sailor looks up from the provisions barge.

"Yes, Caput."

"Have you seen Pouke?"

"Last we saw him, he took his tielog and headed to the northwest. Said he was running an errand."

"An errand? Hmmm."

"Caput, let me go above and have a look," she says.

Yelu leaps into the air and soars above the ship, looking in all directions.

"Yelu! Look in the direction of the fisher vessel," he shouts.

Why there?

She looks but cannot see it. Climbing higher, she can see a yellow speck by the fishtangler vessel.

"I see him!

Her voice sounds faint at that height.

"It's by the ship. I'll get him."

"Wait!" Mayven shouts.

However, she does not hear him. Yelu flies towards the ship.

"Watch Saltes, call Watch Eophon!" Mayven orders.

"What's wrong?" Saltes asks.

"I'm not sure. Something does not feel right. Just get Eophon."

Saltes runs below, and in less than one minute, he appears on the upper deck with the monach next to him. He finds Mayven pacing anxiously.

"What is it, Caput?" Eophon asks.

"Yelu has gone off to look for Pouke."

"So?"

"Something's not right; she may be in danger."

"Danger…? With Pouke? Why do you think she would be in danger if with Pouke?

"A gut feeling. Pouke is off where he's not supposed to be. The channel is why we are here, and he has gone to the fisher vessel. Something is off about it."

"Something about him was never right." Saltes hisses.

"We'll find her!" Eophon says.

"She's gone in that direction. Look for the fisher vessel." He says, pointing towards the horizon.

"There are no more tielogs," Saltes says.

"Karp!"

"Yes, Caput."

"We need a tielog now. Call one over and have the rider take the watchers wherever they need to go."

"Yes, Caput."

"Chibi!" Karp barks.

The driver of the nearest tielog waves in response, and Karp waves him over.

Saltes and Eophon climb into the tielog, with Chibi at the stern. Mayven watches them as they head northwest.

"Karp!"

"Yes, Caput?"

"Do we have enough markers to navigate the channel?"

"I think so."

"Bring in the barge and tielogs; we're going through."

Chapter 7
WRENSONG

Dancing Elk walked behind Shaman Tiglit with Wrensong close behind.

"Why do you carry grandfather's stick?" Wrensong asks.

"It's not a stick, it's Nenemehkia, and grandfather says that I must get used to it, and it to me," Dancing Elk says.

"But it is just a tree branch."

"It's more than that. It holds great power," Dancing Elk says.

"What kind of—"

"The power of thunder and lightning," Dancing Elk interrupts, waving his arms with flair.

"Wrensong, why don't you come with me," Red Bird says.

"But—"

"Grandfather is teaching your brother. He needs to concentrate, and he can't do that with you asking so many questions," Red Bird says.

"While he's busy, we can work on that leather pouch you want to make for him," Red Bird whispers.

Wrensong giggles excitedly and whispers back.

"It will be his gift when he becomes a warrior."

Red Bird nods and smiles. She takes the girl by the hand and leads her back to camp.

Wrensong looks back as she is led away. Dancing Elk smiles and waves at her, and she waves back.

Dancing Elk loves the eight-year-old, but his mother is right. He does need to concentrate on Tiglit's teachings.

"Can you feel the spirit flowing?" Tiglit asks

119

Tiglit has been asking the same question every day since he turned thirteen a week ago. That was when he first felt Nenemehkia's tingle. Today, the response from the staff was stronger.

"It feels like a blanket is covering my hand."

"Good," Tiglit says. "Nenemehkia is starting to trust you."

Dancing Elk looks at the staff. The reddish wood has been worn smooth from years of use. It is as straight as a branch can grow and strong enough to make it indestructible, or so it seems.

"Grandfather, how did Nenemehkia come to be? You told me you found it," Dancing Elk runs his hand over it. "It is yellow and red. It looks like it came from the tree we make our bows, a wazhazhe tree. Yet, it feels like it lives. Our bows don't feel like they live."

"You are right, Dancing Elk. It is made from wazhazhe wood. When I was made shaman, while I talked to the spirits during my fast, lightning struck the tree where I sat. Nenemehkia entered a branch and fell by my side."

"Will I get my own Nenemehkia?" The boy asks.

"No, Nenemehkia is Nenemehkia. There is only one. That is why she must get to know you."

"She?"

"She will be like the bear protecting her cubs. She will protect you when you can't protect yourself."

"If I take her, what will happen to you then?"

"When she determines that I can protect myself, she will let me go," Tiglit says.

Wrensong finished stitching her pouch and now needed the shell adornments.

She found Dancing Elk deep in conversation with Tiglit and pretended not to notice as she made her way to the river.

I'll stitch the shells on the pouch, then give it to him.

"Nenemehkia is a powerful weapon. Did you use it in battle?" Dancing Elk asks.

Tiglit takes the staff and cradles it in his hands.

"Nenemehkia will only help if she believes you cannot handle the condition. She is not an easy way out."

He lays Nenemehkia on the ground.

Suppose the situation can be resolved by other means. In that case, Nenemehkia will remain a bough of wood, a branch, fallen from a tree," Tiglit says.

A loud screech shatters the calm.

Dancing Elk turns, "what was that?"

He sees Red Bird running frantically towards the river.

"Wrensong!" she shouts.

He springs to his feet and runs towards the river, speeding past his mother.

"Wrensong!" he shouts.

He reaches the river and sees Wrensong crawling up the beach with only her feet and ankles in the water.

Red Bird arrives, panting. Then folds her arms as her concern turns to anger. Wrensong clawed at the sand, trying to crawl away from the water.

"Wrensong! You've scared everyone; just get up!"

But Dancing Elk sees she is trying to keep from being pulled in. Red Bird sees water lapping at her feet. Dancing Elk sees a pair of watery claws drawing her in.

"Let her go!" Dancing Elk shouts.

He runs to the river as the water pulls her waist-deep. Dancing Elk grabs his sister and lifts her high above his head. For a moment, the water clings to her like honey before falling off.

The other natives are starting to gather. All they see is Dancing Elk in knee-deep water. He flings Wrensong to the shore. The girl lands on the riverbank and quickly scrambles to her mother.

"Something grabbed me. It wouldn't let go," Wrensong said.

She clutches Red Bird's leather tunic.

White Eagle, leader of the warriors, looks at Dancing Elk, amused.

"I think he is stuck in the mud," he said.

The rest of the tribe laughs.

Dancing Elk struggles to get to shore. He feels the claws holding him now.

Tricked you. Now the toll will be paid.

As it did with his father, a strange wave rises, slapping him in the back and pushing him under the water.

The tribesmen are now laughing harder. All except Wrensong and Tiglit.

Dancing Elk rises out of the water, trying to break free. Now, his arm is also trapped. The water slowly creeps up his chest unnaturally. Still, those on the shore are too busy laughing to notice the oddity.

The clinging water slowly reaches his neck. Dancing Elk tries to rip it off, but his fingers find no resistance in the liquid.

So many generations have passed, and no one worthy of me.

A watery hand envelops Dancing Elk's head and covers his mouth. While the onlookers see Dancing Elk leaning forward with the current flowing over his back and head, Tiglit can see Ijiraq's hand and fingers wrapping around his face.

I will walk among your people. I'll become you.

Dancing Elk tries to shout, but Ijiraq's fingers fill his mouth, and the boy starts to drown. As a last effort, Dancing Elk holds up his hand.

Nenemehkia, help!

Tiglit is too dumbfounded to move. When the river spirit took Tall Tree, all he saw was water. Now, he can actually see Ijiraq, the river spirit. He sees its head and arms as it pushes the boy underwater and now sees the spirit as it stands behind Dancing Elk, waist-deep in the river, gripping the boy's head.

Suddenly Nenemehkia vibrates and leaps out of his hands. It flies as if thrown to the boy's waiting hand. Dancing Elk strikes out wildly at the water. Ijiraq roars and moves away from Dancing Elk, freeing him.

The river spirit pauses, realizing it has lost its prey; it charges Dancing Elk.

You will not escape.

Dancing Elk moves to knee-deep water, swinging Nenemehkia. He strikes the water again, and the watery figure backs away. He realizes that he might have, somehow, hurt Ijiraq.

Tiglit realizes what Ijiraq is doing. It is drawing Dancing Elk to deeper water.

"You took my father; now you want my sister."

Dancing Elk's shouts are muted by the rumbling water. Anger surges in the boy. He will make it pay for what it did.

Those on the shore can't make out his words but see him shouting at the river and swinging the staff like a lunatic.

Dancing Elk can see the Ijiraq's head bobbing in the waves. He tries to reach it, striking the river again and again. Each time, it moves a little farther into deeper water.

He screams at the river, tears mixing with his wet face.

"How does it feel?"

The onlookers murmur among each other.

Tiglit sees Ijiraq taunt the boy while moving to deeper water.

What's wrong, can't you catch me?

"Come and fight me now!" His rant continues. "I will kill you."

Tiglit runs into the water. He knows that if the boy slips and falls, Ijiraq will have him.

Tiglit is a few steps from Dancing Elk when the boy stumbles, falls, and goes under. Tiglit reaches into the water and grabs Dancing Elk's leather shirt. He pulls the boy's head out of the water. Syrup-like, the water clings to Dancing Elk's face. He opens his mouth, gasping for air, but there is only water. For an instant, his eyes widen as terror washes over him. In that instant, he releases Nenemehkia, and it floats with the current.

No! I will not be afraid.

Tiglit struggles to wrest him from Ijiraq's grip, but it's like pulling a heavy stone out of wet mud.

Dancing Elk pushes his fear aside and pulls free from Tiglit. He stretches his arm and again reaches out.

Nenemehkia, come!

The staff stops, then reverses its course, returning to Dancing Elk. He wraps his fingers around its familiar surface. Ignoring the watery mask, Dancing Elk drives the staff into the water like a spear.

Another loud roar from the river, and the water drops from the boy. Immediately, Dancing Elk strikes with Nenemehkia and makes contact with something solid. The roar changes to something resembling stone rubbing on stone. Ijiraq moves back, creating a hollow that momentarily leaves Dancing Elk in knee-deep water before the river fills the void.

You will pay.

Ijiraq's figure sinks into the river and disappears.

"Come, you coward!"

"Enough! Dancing Elk. He's gone; you have scared him away."

"It's not enough. I have to finish him," Dancing Elk sobs.

"Ijiraq is not of this world. You cannot kill him," Tiglit says.

"Then I'll hurt him."

Tiglit pulls the boy to the shore and walks him back to the camp. The onlookers part, letting them pass while giving him a curious look. All except Wrensong. She, too, had felt the hand of Ijiraq.

Chapter 8

POUKE

Yelu arrives at the fisher vessel and sees Pouke talking to one of the crew; there is a flurry of activity on the deck.

Strange? There are no nets, drying fish, and so much trash. Mayven always keeps his ship as clean as new.

She assumed that all caputs would do the same.

"Pouke?" she shouts.

He looks up.

"Yelu!" he says, surprised. "Come down; I want you to meet someone."

She descends onto the deck as Pouke finishes whispering to the other.

"Yelu, these are old friends of mine. I thought I recognized their ship yesterday and decided to visit."

"Really, you know them?" she asks.

Something is wrong, though; none seem interested in the fact that she just flew in, which always attracts attention. In fact, the crew looks somewhat lethargic.

The smell on the ship assaults her. The crew's clothing is soiled, and they reek from lack of bathing or what seems to be any kind of hygiene at all. She sees their faces slack and expressionless; only the caput seems sentient.

She approaches Pouke while keeping her distance from them. Without warning, an evil sensation assails her; she feels the entire ship painted with it, and Yelu's senses awaken. Her powers finally cut through Pouke's masquerade, and she sees the thin gnomish creature that was once a handsome Sylvan. His essence straff her senses, making her dizzy.

"Who?... What are you?" she asks.

A rope passes over her head and shoulders, pinning the wings to her side.

"What...?" then a gag cuts her short.

"Don't harm her," Pouke tells the caput. "Be extremely careful. The master will kill us if anything happens to the child."

"Yes, m'lord," he answers.

The caput still sees him as Pouke. He wears boots and heavy clothing that seems more at home in the forest than the sandals and loose-fitting femoralia Mayven's crew wears. He also wears an arm guard with golden snakes adorning the leather.

She immediately recognizes its design, and her eyes widen.

Solois!

Now all of the pieces fall into place, not telling the caput about the ship, the finger greeting the day they found the reef, the courting wing-touch, calling the fishers 'fishtanglers'. Those are all a part of the Ortetan, not Sylvan culture. There is only one thing that does not make sense.

How did they get here?

"I bet there are a lot of questions going through your head." Pouke chuckles.

"First, my name is not Pouke; my name is Hergian."

Hergian! Sceagga's disciple.

Shock creeps over her face.

"Oh, so you do remember," He says. "By the way, he is still alive. You almost killed him that night. But, nevertheless, he survived."

Yelu is dumbfounded and can't take her eyes off him.

"I can sense that you have broken through my illusion, a trick father taught me. But, as you can see, dealing with

127

negative energy does have its downside. My outward appearance is one of them, but it's easy to mask."

She shifts her head around until the gag slides off.

"Sceagga can't be alive!" she shouts. "I killed him; I saw him dead...in the waves."

"No, you saw him unconscious. I found him by chance; I sensed his presence when I got to the waters around the cliffs. I found him, stemmed the blood from his wounds, fed him off the battle wounded, and brought him back to the weald."

"Fed him?"

"Well, not feeding in the same sense as you think. Sceagga can drink one's energy. He can take it and use it to heal. Father would have died if it weren't for the abundance of wounded Solois and Haloguardian floating in the ocean. By the time we reached the shore, he had fed on so many wounded that he walked on his own."

"You call him father."

"For the past six hundred years, he raised me, trained me. To me, he is my father."

She shakes her head.

"He survived."

"Father is very powerful. If wounded, even mortally, he can heal himself...if he can add to his pacú. That was another lesson he taught me."

"That's why all the Solois on the raft were dead," she mumbles.

" So, you did find the raft. Well, think of it this way, if you're wounded, you need pacú to heal if you don't have enough to do the job, you die. If you can take someone else's pacú, then you have enough. If you're on a raft and need the extra pacú to survive those additional days, you take it from your crew.

"So yes, the raft was mine; it was one of two. Once I reached the reef, I needed four lives to continue. I hadn't counted on how long the ordeal would take; we ran out of food; what else could I do? The raft with the bodies was supposed to be found by the wavecutters; that way, suspicions wouldn't be raised."

"But wait, the wrecked raft happened long before Sceagga's attack. How could you be there and here? Unless—"

"Unless it wasn't my only trip," Hergian says. "How else could I have gotten my army of solois into the Sylvanus."

Struggling, Yelu is dragged to the storage room while Hergian walks next to them.

They stop by the door.

"The attack in the market," Yelu says.

"Yes, they were mine too. By the way, it took Mayven long enough to find the opening. Any longer, and I would have gone mad."

"You knew where it was all the time."

"Like I said, I've made the trip several times. I now know how much food it takes to make it. After all, the purpose of the trip is to bring Solois to Sylvanus."

Yelu looks down and mutters.

"Then, Sceagga still lives."

"Oh yes, very much so, and he longs to see you."

Yelu struggles again. The Solois hold her tighter.

"Be careful with her. I'll kill you if she's hurt," Hergian snaps at the caput.

He grabs Yelu's arm and draws a small amount of her pacú. Suddenly, her legs buckle as weakness overcomes her. They half-drag her into the storeroom.

"Sceagga was very angry with me for losing you. However, I did not know what he had done. Once he fully recuperated, he sent me to find you. I got ten Solois on two rafts to take me to the reef. The tide was going out, so it carried us through the channel. We rowed the rest of the way."

He stops and chuckles once more.

"Why did you need Mayven?"

" I needed to take you back to the Master and Mayven to get us there. The funny thing is that it was you who found me."

A movement in the water catches her attention. Hergian sees her eyes shift and turns.

"Ah, the Watch comes." He says.

She sees him bring his hand behind his back. A small glowing ball appears in his palm, like the one that incinerated the coloner that night.

"No!" she screams.

"No?" he says, turning to her.

He looks at the glowing sphere in his hand.

"Ah, I see you recognize this. It's called a upashim. It's pure, concentrated pacú."

He looks into her eyes, then smiles.

"Perhaps you're right," he says.

"They may be of more use to me alive. I may need to feed later, and a monakite's pacú is more powerful than a regular Sylvan."

He motions to the caput.

"Secure her in the storeroom and capture the others when they come on board!"

He turns back to her.

"Thank you," Hergian says, slipping the gag back over her mouth.

Chibi and the monakites approach the fishing vessel; they search for the doyenne in the air. However, she is nowhere to be seen.

"Do you see Yelu?" Saltes asks.

"No, I don't," Eophon answers.

"Watch Saltes! Isn't that her on the deck?" Chibi says.

Saltes looks where Chibi points and sees someone like her pushed into a storeroom.

"Isn't that Pouke over there? What's he doing?" Saltes asks.

The tielog pulls up to the vessel. Saltes and Eophon barely climb on board when the crew sets upon them. Eophon is the only one with any military experience. He fights with one crew, gets his sword in the struggle, and kills him. He takes two more down, but a group overpowers Saltes and puts a knife to his throat; Eophon surrenders. They bind the monakites and roughly shove them into the storeroom with Yelu.

Chibi sees what happened, turns the craft around, and speeds away.

Hergian watches him trying to escape when the caput arrives.

"Do you want me to send someone after him?"

"That won't be necessary." Hergian answers.

The sortiarius lifts his hand; a glowing ball grows from his palm, which he flings at the tielog. The upashim races at the small craft and strikes it with the power of a lightning bolt. Then, with a thunderclap, a fireball engulfs the craft leaving nothing but burning flotsam behind.

Chapter 9
RIPPENWAETER

Mayven hears the explosion; he turns and sees the dark cloud rising on the horizon. He leans over the railing and calls to his first mate.

"Karp!"

"Yes, Caput."

"Get everyone ready and take up anchors. We have to get going fast."

Karp looks at the horizon and sees the cloud of smoke slowly dissipating.

"How about them?"

"There is nothing we can do to help them. Their lives are in Eyu's hands now. We have to sail."

There is a gentle breeze, perfect for the speed they need. As the Scip Hudros nears the entrance, Mayven can make out the fisher vessel heading towards them. However, he must still pass the opening and turn around before entering the gap.

The Scip Hudros moves away from the reef and turns around. By the time the ship is in position, the fisher vessel is a mere half millistep behind them.

"Karp!" barks Mayven.

"Yes, sir!"

"Take down the banners as we pass them; let them find their own way."

"Yes, Caput," he gives a quick salute. It is the first time the caput has gotten one from him.

As the ship passes the banners, Karp knocks them over with his guide pole.

The fisher vessel nears the entrance while Hergian sails ahead on the tielog to lead the ship through the channel.

Dusk is coming fast. Mayven is hoping that what brought Yelu to the shores of Ka-Mer comes to his rescue now. But, he sees the sharp turn at the end of the coral peninsula and realizes that he is going too fast.

"Karp!" he barks again. "Use the guide poles to keep the ship off the rocks. The turn may be too tight."

"I'll get more men, sir," says the first mate.

"No time for it; make do with the ones you have."

"Yes, Caput."

Karp gets the three who are near him. Together they push against the reef deflecting the momentum of the ship. Unfortunately, the Scip Hudros is too heavy, and one of the poles snaps from the weight. When Karp replaces the pole, the ship starts to broadside the coral. Karp knows that he does not have enough men to push the vessel clear. His only choice is to guide the ship so that it strikes the coral with a glancing blow. They keep on pushing; the sound of the coral branches being crushed echoes through the hull. As those break off, the thicker, stronger ones come into play.

The caput keeps the ship from overcompensating and crashing into the opposite side. A board snaps below the water level, and the crew is on deck within a few moments to help with the poles.

Mayven shifts the sails, clears the turn and steers the ship towards the exit. The crew is busy keeping the ship in the center. They are not paying attention to the fisher vessel clearing the channel in the opposite direction. The fisher vessel is now only a flight's width of an arrow away from the Scip Hudros.

In the stores of the fishing vessel, Yelu hears the explosion; she struggles wildly, swinging her body from side to side to loosen the ropes.

"M'lady, you are going to hurt yourself," Saltes says.

"If they were going to kill us, they would have done it by now," Eophon adds.

She shifts violently until she can free one of her arms.

"Yelu, you will harm the child," Saltes says.

The doyenne pulls her gag off.

"We have to get out of here!"

"Calm down. They probably just want some sort of ransom for us," Saltes says calmly.

"No, he is not what he seems. He is Sceagga's disciple, he wants to turn me over to him, but he needs you to feed himself. He will kill both of you when he does."

They both look at each other and start struggling violently.

"I thought you said Sceagga was dead?" Eophon asks between breaths.

"I thought so too, but he's not, and he is worse than I thought. We have to get out now." She reaches for something under her robe.

She pulls out the aduncus ripping open the cloth of her robes.

"I thought you left that behind," Saltes says.

"I never leave it behind."

The sharp blade makes quick work of the ropes that bind her. Next, she frees the two monakites. She crosses the room and tries to open the heavy door, but it is locked.

"It's bolted shut. We have to find a way to force it...Skagget!"

"With a Skagget?" Saltes asks.

She gives him a blank stare.

"Never mind." She says.

I will have to be more careful with my language in the future...if I have one... it's funny what comes to mind when under stress.

Mayven can see Pouke's tielog in the channel guiding the ship. They will have no trouble catching them if they make it around the bend.

Though the larger Scip Hudros is a faster ship, it needs time to reach its maximum speed. On the other hand, the smaller maneuverable fisher vessel can reach its maximum in less time.

When the two ships cross, Pouke disappears behind the sail; Mayven tries to see what he is doing. However, it is getting dark, he is too far, and keeping the ship off the rocks is more important.

A small light illuminates the backside of the tielog's sail. The caput dares to take his eyes off the channel long enough to see what he's doing.

What's he up to?

It does not take long to get an answer. Pouke shoots a burning arrow into the mast of the Scip Hudros, and a volley of arrows follows.

The sortiarius could have used a upashim on the ship. However, destroying the tielog had drained too much of his pacú. Without replenishing himself, another energy ball will surely render him unconscious.

Mayven realizes that the burning arrow is guiding the bowmen on the other ship. Since the Scip Hudros is a cargo ship, it does not have weapons on board, save for the short swords that the crew carries.

"Karp!"

"Yes, Caput," the voice comes from the stern.

"Put out that flaming arrow; it's giving them a target."

"Right away, Caput."

Karp drops his pole and runs to the mainmast. He is halfway up when the next volley of arrows falls on the ship. One of them finds Karp's leg. There is no time to pull it out. Though a little slower, he keeps climbing until he reaches the burning arrow. He can smell the burning pitch when the thick smoke covers his face. He coughs uncontrollably, pulls out the burning shaft, and tosses it in the water. Another volley of arrows rains on the Scip Hudros. Two of them find Karp. He loses all feeling in his arms and falls back to the deck below, dead before he lands.

Mayven is in a rage. He would have taken the ship and rammed the fisher vessel if it were the open ocean. But instead, he will have to deal with them later; now, he concentrates on locating the banners in the waning light.

C'mon, where is it?

He hears a distant rumbling sound. He squints to his right and sees a thin line approaching fast on the horizon.

There you are.

"Garen!"

"Yes, Caput."

"You are first mate now. I will give you the order to open all sails in a few moments. When I do, I want it done as quickly as possible, no questions asked."

"Caput," he replies, "we're still in the channel."

"No questions asked," growls the caput. "Just do as I say."

"Yes, Caput."

"First, wrap one anchor in the spare canvas, then slowly lower it until it drags on the bottom."

"Sir?"

"No questions, Garen!"

"Yes, sir."

Garen takes a fleeting look at Karp's body, then gets to work. He wraps the anchor and lowers it until it barely drags on the bottom; the ship's joints complain as it slows down, straining its bracings.

Mayven looks back and sees the crew of the fisher vessel lowering their anchors to keep from crashing into the rear of the massive ship. Unlike the Scip Hudros' crew, those on the fisher vessel cannot think for themselves and drop all anchors.

"Lift the anchor, open all sails!" he shouts.

He draws the anchor; the wrappings keep it from lodging in the coral below. The sails drop, causing the ship to jump forward and list heavily to port as the wind catches them from the starboard side.

Those on the ship's stern hear the last volley of arrows fall to the water. Mayven is too busy now to look back. The ship is quickly accelerating, scraping the coral as it goes. The yards of the sails sweep dangerously close to the larger outcrops of the reef. Up ahead are the last two markers indicating the entrance, a mere arrow's flight away.

The fisher vessel finished clearing the corner and opened its sails when the Scip Hudros dropped its anchor, slowing the ship quickly. The caput knows the smaller fisher vessel will never survive a collision with the larger ship. He orders the crew to drag the anchor, but they are not of their own mind. They drop all the anchors, completely stopping the vessel.

The caput hears Pouke order the bowmen to shoot, but they are out of range. Then sees the Scip Hudros lift its anchor and open its sails. If the Scip Hudros clears the opening with full sail, they will be hard-pressed to catch it before it speeds away.

Pouke watches Scip Hudros.

What is Mayven doing?

The ship drops the anchor to slow down, raises it, and drops its sails to speed away.

He knows he can outrun us.

He is tempted to throw a small energy bolt to burn the Scip Hudros' sails. However, he has to keep the tielog from veering into the rocks, and the cargo vessel crew would quickly put the fire out anyway. The damage would be negligible to the ship, and the drain of his pacú will weaken him.

Caput Mayven has his eyes set on the open ocean ahead when he hears hurried steps coming from behind.

"Caput Mayven, your decks below are full of water."

"I know, Watch Rewen."

She holds on to the ropes securing the cargo, trying to avoid sliding off the ship.

"And how you pilot this ship makes me wonder about your abilities."

"Sorry for the inconvenience, Watch Rewen."

She looks at the mess on the deck.

"And your upper decks are full of arrows."

"I know, Watch Rewen."

"And I can't find Dominant Saltes, Eophon, or Yelu."

"I know, Watch Rewen."

"Do you know where they are?" she asks.

"Probably on the ship attacking us," he answers, signaling with his thumb.

"Back there."

She looks back and sees the ship closing in on them.

"What do they want?"

"Not sure, probably to kill us."

"Tailon, Eophon, and Yelu are on that ship?"

"I would say they are being held prisoners there unless he's killed them already."

"Skagget!"

"Skagget?" Mayven asks.

"Oh, sorry, something I picked up from Yelu."

"You may want to know what it means before tossing it around," the caput says, spinning the wheel.

"Are you sure they're on the ship?"

"Last time I saw any of them, they were heading towards it," Mayven answers.

"Skagget!" she murmurs and is gone.

"Caput!" Garen staggers to him. "Rogue wave."

The first mate points towards the approaching wave.

"Look closely, Garen, that's not a rogue wave," the caput says.

The ship is half a flight from the entrance now. Mayven eases the vessel closer to the edge scrapping the coral once more. He will need all the room he can get on the opposite side.

Garen looks intently at the wave, then notices that it is long, too long, and is not breaking up.

"By Eyu!" he cries. "It's a rippenwaeter!"

"That's right, First Mate Garen. The tide is going out, and the only way to come out is through this channel or over the top," Mayven says, concentrating on those last two flags.

Garen looks out the channel, estimates the time it will take to clear the opening, and then looks at the riptide.

"Are we going to make it?"

"Not by much," answers the caput. "Get the men to hold on to something solid."

"They already are; no choice," Garen says. Then he, too, is gone.

The Scip Hudros starts to slow. It's not much, but Mayven can tell. The current in the channel is shifting.

The caput on the fisher vessel is the only one who remotely knows how to pilot a ship. He knows more than the rest on board but lacks experience, and since Hergian compelled the crew, they are useless. The fisher vessel's caput does not know what the sortiarius has done to them. They can work without rest and will obey any order till death. However, they have lost all resourcefulness. Now, he has to tell them everything.

"Turn loose the sails!" he shouts.

The men work mechanically as they lower the sails to catch the wind. That maneuver with the anchors had cost him precious time; working them out of the stony bottom had been difficult.

He notices that the Scip Hudros has caught the wind and is speeding away. He thinks that the caput decided that he now has a clear passage out of the channel and tries to outdistance him. He only needs a couple of minutes. Once he clears the channel, he will make up the time and get close enough to use the grappling hooks on the bigger ship.

Hergian moved his tielog next to the ship and climbed back on board when it stopped in the channel. He leaves the small craft to its fate and runs to the caput startling him.

"What now, Hergian?" he grumbles.

The caput always refers to him by his real name.

"The wave is approaching fast from your right."

"The what?"

"The wave, the large wave that pushed us through the reef when we came."

"Here, you steer," the caput says. He hands the wheel over to Hergian. "Just point it straight at the back of the Hudros."

The caput goes to the main mast and climbs a short way to get a better look. Peering into the darkness, he can barely make out its foamy outline.

He's right; it's the rippenwaeter.

He recognizes its long profile.

"It's the rippenwaeter!" he shouts.

He jumps to the deck and runs to the wheel.

"You're right, it's the tide, but it's bigger today than when we came."

"Why?"

"Must be the season." He pushes Hergian out of the way and takes over the wheel.

"Is that bad? Even if it's bigger when we last rode it on the raft, it was pretty smooth."

"Well, when we came through, we waited for it to start before entering the channel. On the small raft, we pushed her away from the rocks. A ship this size has too much weight; we can't push her. If the wave catches us in the channel, it will throw us into the coral; we'll sink."

"Do you think Mayven knows?"

"Of course, he knows. That is why they made us slow down. They are now trying to race it to the entrance."

"Will we make it?"

The caput pauses for a minute and looks at the wave.

"No."

He sees Hergian turn to head back down.

"Where are you going? I'm going to need you up here."

"I'm going to feed."

The caput looks at him; the thought sends chills up his spine. He saw him feed when they crossed the reef the first time. He knows why he does it. Perhaps it is best to stay far away from Hergian at this time.

Hergian steps in front of the man guarding the store's door; he immediately picks up his sickening smell.

"Give me the keys,"

The guard reaches for his belt in slow motion to undo the loop that holds the keys.

"Hurry!" He says.

After fumbling some more, he pulls them out. For a fleeting moment, Hergian considers feeding on the guard. Still, he is so repulsed by his physical condition that the idea fades as soon as it comes.

The Scip Hudros clears the channel as the wave strikes. The surging water lifts and pushes it towards the reef wall. Mayven turns the wheel hard to starboard to face the rushing water and holds his position. Slowly, the Scip Hudros straightens and crawls away from the reef. The wind picks up, and the ship inches farther from the rocky wall. Mayven looks over his shoulder to the fisher vessel facing a bigger problem.

The guard is handing the keys to Hergian when the rippenwaeter sweeps over the reef wall striking the ship broadside. The vessel lists sharply; the wave lifts and pushes it against the rocks on the opposite side of the channel. Hergian and the guard fall and slide across the deck. The guard lets go of the keys. They drop to the floor, slide across the deck, and fall over the side through one of the drain holes.

"You fool!" Hergian shouts.

He gets to his feet and stumbles to the door. There is no time to wait. The sortiarius steadies himself, and a ball of energy appears in the palm of his hand. He lifts his hand, but the rushing water picks up the craft again, sending it back towards the curve.

The fishing vessel is now careening down the channel, back from where it came, hitting the rocks and coral. Pieces of wood *are starting to splinter off. The current begins to build, and the ship picks up speed.*

Hergian stumbles across the deck; he braces himself against the mast and hurls the ball. The energy drain is almost too much for him; he drops to his knees. The upashim strikes the door lock shattering the metal and wood as the ship rams the wall of the curve. With the bolt gone, the door to the storeroom swings open so hard that it breaks free of its hinges. It narrowly misses Hergian as it slides across the deck and into the channel.

Eophon is the first to fall through the opening. He slides across the deck, closely following the door. As he passes, Hergian reaches out and grabs his robe. The younger monakite struggles to his feet and swings, striking Hergian in the face; but Hergian holds fast. While holding Eophon's robe with one hand, he places the other on the monakite's head. Immediately, Eophon crumples to the deck. Saltes stumbles but does not fall. He staggers out of the hold with Yelu.

"NOOO!" shouts the doyenne.

Saltes looks up and sees Eophon collapse.

"What did he do?"

"He's killed him."

"What? So quickly?"

"He's as powerful as Sceagga, don't let him touch you," she shouts over the din surrounding them.

Energized, Hergian stands and lets go of Eophon's body. The ship starts to list further, and the dead monakite slides to the side amongst the garbage. The Dominant straightens himself; he looks at the trash and wonders how anyone can live in such squalor.

Yelu shoves him towards the side.

"Saltes! Snap out of it!"

He tries to take a step but quickly falls.

The ship shifts again when the tidal flow dislodges it from the rocks. The current through the channel grows, flushing the small vessel towards the bend. It is sinking fast, with the water washing across the starboard side.

"You have to get away from here," she shouts. "He needs me alive but wants to feed on you."

Saltes realizes that. Yelu helps him to the side of the ship.

"Look! There is a tielog there."

She points to a mast that seems to be keeping up with the ship.

"Try to get in it."

"You have to go," Saltes says. "You can't let him capture you, and you won't be able to jump on the tielog."

"Ok, may Eyu watch over you."

She leaps into the air and flies off the ship.

Saltes tries to lift his leg over the side but can't. With the ship now listing at a sharper angle, his feet slip. The Dominant falls and starts to slide towards the water. He reaches out and grabs a rope tangled in the railing. Another jolt and the ship lists even further. Saltes spins on the line so that now his face is against the deck. He turns his face up and sees the mast of the tielog still keeping up with the ship. Somewhere in the back of his mind, it registers as odd. He spins back around and sees Hergian working his way closer to him.

"Where are you going, Dominant Saltes?" Hergian mocks. "If you jump, you will surely drown. Come, I need to talk to you."

Saltes tries desperately to pull himself up the rope to the rail. Still, he can barely keep from sliding back because of his waterlogged robes and the slippery rope. Next, he tries to set his feet and climb. However, he slips on the wet deck every time the ship strikes the rocks.

144

Saltes makes one last effort; he pulls with all his might, reaches the railing, and grabs it. Hergian is still scrambling towards him. He climbs on the crates and other cargo that has not been washed away. His movements are strangely spider-like, entirely at odds with how a man moves. Saltes loops one leg over the rail and prepares to swing himself over the side when the ship strikes another outcropping on the side. He falls back on the deck and slides within Hergian's reach.

The sortiarius kneels and grabs the monakite's robe as he slides by. Saltes is stunned by the fall, although he has enough of his senses to see that Hergian grabbed him. The dominant waits for the inevitable.

"Just one second, Dominant Saltes, that's all I need."

He watches Hergian through fingers that close around his face, and then there is the sound of a loud crack, and Hergian's head snaps back; a second crack is followed by a loud screech.

Saltes starts to slide down, but something snags his hood.

"That's one second you're not going to have," shouts a familiar voice.

Hergian's disguise vanishes. Saltes watches the grotesque spider-like gnome holding his shoulder, blood spurting from what looks like a scar. The ship jolts again, and Hergian falls backward, slides down the deck, and plunges into the water. However, he stays put. Tailon looks up and sees Rewen standing over him with the broken pole in one hand and his hood in the other.

"Wake up, Tailon! I can't hold you much longer."

"Rewen?"

Did she just call me Tailon?

Saltes reaches up, grabs the railing, and pulls himself up.

"Hurry! The ship is about to go under." She says.

He looks around.

"Where's Pouke?"

145

"Swimming."

"Where's Yelu?"

"She's off the ship and heading for the Scip Hudros."

She helps the monakite over the railing. Then, they both leap into the waiting tielog tied to the vessel, bouncing recklessly against the rocks.

Rewen unties the craft and somehow turns it in the confines of the channel. The sail on the lighter craft catches the wind and slowly works its way against the current and past the fisher vessel. Rewen murmurs a prayer the entire time, hoping that the wind keeps up.

The two monakites turn towards the sound of splintering wood. In the moonlight, they see the fisher vessel's mast, reaching up like a skeletal hand pleading for help.

The fisher vessel slowly rolls; what remains of the mast is coming down on the tielog.

"Hold on!" Rewen shouts.

She turns the tielog back towards the bend. The mast chases them, scraping the rocks and trapping them between the mast and the rear half of the ship. The bend quickly approaches. Rewen angles the sail and catches the wind. The tielog lifts on one of its longboats and shoots past the vessel.

Saltes holds on to the side of the canvas with all his strength. He sees the vessel pass by faster than he cares for.

"We're going to crash into the bend!"

"Don't let go!"

When the tielog passes the vessel, it comes down hard behind it.

Saltes turns and sees the stern of the vessel speeding towards them.

"REWEN!"

"Stay down!"

The monakite spins the sail around, catching the wind once more. The craft jumps forward; she aims for the space between the bottom hull and the rocks. The hull boards pried loose by the jagged coral reach towards the tielog, ripping the rear of one of the longboats, but Rewen manages to keep the craft on course. The doomed vessel slowly passes them. She clears the ship's rear half, but now the fisher vessel starts to roll in the opposite direction. The tielog crawls painfully slow against the fast-moving water.

"Rewen, the mast; it's coming again!"

"The current is too strong. We're not going make it; jump to the rocks!" She says.

Saltes looks at the glass-sharp coral and sees a push-pole in the passing flotsam.

"Wait!"

He reaches into the water, grabs it, and braces the handle on the intact longboat and the opposite end on the dropping mast.

"What are you doing? We are being pushed down."

"Wait!"

The water starts to wash over the canvas.

"SALTES!"

"WAIT!"

"What are you—"

"HOLD ON!" He shouts.

The tielog reaches its critical point when the water is at their knees. Then, like a squeezed melopepon seed, it lunges forwards. Saltes falls back but keeps the pole pushing against the mast until they are as far as the pole will allow.

"Rewen, get close to the rocks; the ship is almost on us."

Rewen does as he says, while Saltes keeps the tielog off the rocks. The edge of the ship rolls into the water, barely missing the craft.

Carefully, in the growing darkness, Rewen works the tielog against the raging current murmuring a prayer, hoping the wind keeps.

The fisher vessel starts to tumble as the furious current dashes its remains into splinters. She catches a glimpse of Hergian's dark arm rising out of the water in a tangle of sail lines. It tumbles in the current and disappears with the sinking ship, flushed deep into the channel.

They can hear the cries for help from the surviving crew for a few minutes. Now that Hergian's control over them is gone, they have regained their wits. However, it is too late for them. The current shows them no mercy condemning them to the rocks and coral; one by one, the wails fade.

Rewen keeps the tielog in the center of the channel and heads for the entrance. Then, when they reach the open water, the ride turns into a gentle glide. The night drapes over them, and in the cool breeze, the terror of the channel begins to fade.

"You know, there is a lot to say about riding the tielogs at night…it makes you feel kind of secure…kind of free. It's kind of romantic, don't you think?" Rewen says, looking at the waxing stars.

Saltes is lying on his back, gasping, recuperating from the ordeal. He raises himself on one elbow and looks at her face in the moonlight. Her hood is down, and her hair is whipping behind her. She is the most attractive creature he has ever seen.

"What are you talking about, Rewen?"

She gives him a coltish look, which is lost in the night.

"Oh, nothing…nothing at all."

For now.

She is in no hurry to catch up to the Scip Hudros.

Chapter 10

GEOLUFEOER RETURNS

Pouke's revelations about his other identity devastate Yelu. He, with whom she had become enamored, not only deceived her but had also been a disciple, a son, of Sceagga. Worse, though, the evil sortiarius is still alive and wants to take the child she carries.

Three friends have perished because she decided to return to her land. She blames herself for everything that happened. Not because they were trying to protect her, but because she does not honestly believe she carries the Promised One. She had played on the emotions of the Sylvans to get a ride back to her homeland. The deaths of Eophon, Karp, Chibi, and the fishing vessel's crew weighed heavily on her. All had happened because of her.

Yelu withdraws to her cabin. For the next two days, her only companion is Rewen. Finally, on the third day, she emerges when she hears Garen's shout.

"Land ahead!"

Her spirits rise upon seeing the limestone cliffs rising out of the water and the sandy beaches below.

Her main concern is how to convince the Haloguardian of who she is. She will be approaching the island through the area she used to guard, so there might be someone who can remember her. She dons her uniform, though Rewen had to do some last-minute tailoring for her to fit her expanding girth into the leather armor.

Yelu is at the railing with Rewen when Mayven approaches with a large bulky cloth bag in his hand. He sees the doyenne and smiles at her. She really does not want to talk to him right now. She feels bad enough about Karp and the others; the caput's presence reminds her of it even more.

"Goodmorning, Yelu. Hello, Watch Rewen."

"Goodmorning, Caput Mayven," Yelu replies.

"Morning, Caput," Rewen says.

The caput stands next to them, looking at the island.

"It looks beautiful from here," the caput says. "You missed your home, didn't you?"

"Yes, but I wish I had arrived under different circumstances."

"You think all that happened was your fault, don't you?"

"It was because of me that they all died."

"No, it was because of Pouke… Hergian… that they died. If it hadn't been them, it would have been others," the caput says.

"As a matter of fact, we don't even know how many have died because of him."

A tear rolls down her eye.

"Still," Yelu sighs. "If I hadn't been on this ship—"

"He would still have been a part of my crew, and I may have been dead," Mayven says.

He reaches into the bag, pulls out a melon-sized crystal ball, and hands it to her.

"Have you ever seen one of these?"

Yelu turns it over in her hands.

"I've seen it before; it's beautiful; what is it?" Rewen asks.

"Can you tell us, Yelu?" the caput asks.

"Yes, it's a netfloat; our fishtanglers use them; why?"

"Of course, you're right. It is a netfloat. You see, Yelu, our fishers, use wooden ones. No one in Sylvanus uses crystal netfloats."

She looks at him and thinks for a moment.

"When did you find these?" she asks.

"I've had them for several years. I have three of them; you saw them in my chamber."

"Come to think of it...yes, that's where I saw them," Rewen says.

"Me too... so you knew all along about the channel."

"No, not exactly. The floats could have been able to ride the waves over the reef. However, I believed there had to be another civilization on the other side of the reef. Your passage to Sylvanus raised the possibility of a channel."

"Then what about the reward?"

"When I went to Ka-Mer to pick up stores for another trip to the reef, it wasn't my first time. So I had an idea, more or less, of where the opening would be. So when Pouke told me about you and mentioned that there was a reward standing for going out and doing what I had been doing, well, I couldn't pass it up," he chuckles. "I was going to get paid for something I was doing anyway."

He turns back towards the cliffs.

"Then Pouke asked to become a part of my crew, which would have facilitated the search by adding a crewmember to the Scip Hudros. He then suggested that I convince you to come along so that I could communicate with the folk of this land. It sounded like a reasonable idea to me. So I spread the word about the trip and let the pieces fall into place."

Mayven takes the viewing glass from his pocket and scans the cliffs. Several Aduncus are soaring near the Palisades.

He turns to Yelu.

"But, I did make a terrible mistake with Pouke. I did not take the time to check him out, especially when he did not tell me about the other ship. I thought it might have been an oversight since everyone's mind was on finding the passage. I counted my blessings for having all this help on my quest and never searched deeper. I excused his mistake since he had never been a part of a ship's crew. I always assumed he was a Sylvan. It never occurred to me that he might have been an Urtetan."

"Ortet—never mind, so because of your own personal interests, you both had to pay the price," the monakite says.

"I guess we both made our mistakes," Yelu says.

The caput places his immense arm around the Aduncus's shoulder.

"I'm still glad you came with us," Mayven says.

"Thanks, Caput."

"Aduncus on the horizon!"

Garen yells from the mast platform.

"He finally spotted them. It'll take him a while, but he'll make a fine first mate," Mayven chuckles.

"Well, time to do my job," she says.

"In the hands of Eyu."

"Thank you, Rewen."

She climbs on the railing and leaps into the air. The gust from her wings blows Rewen's hood back. Yelu flies towards the flock up ahead. There is a group of pipios and duvos playing; circle around the cliffside caves. The flock does not pay attention to her; she hopes it is not a swarm. They are not responding as a Haloguardian would, and this worries her. She flies closer and starts to circle; there is still no response. So, she swoops in closer, rises up high, and circles again.

The tolling of the alarm bell sounds in the distance. The flock dives and disappears into the cliffside caves. Mayven watches through the watch glass as the Haloguardian flock emerges from the forest, flying close to the ground. When they reach the cliff, at least twenty of them spill over the edge like a waterfall; they ride the air currents close to the waves. The other group rises into the air and comes in high. Again, it is the swalowe formation, but with a full complement this time.

Yelu watches as they approach.

I hope there are no neweguards; they might shoot first.

They come closer and gather speed. She waits until she can identify the coloner in charge. She looks down, and he is not there, then looks up and catches a gleam from his baldric. She raises the clenched fist of her left hand, showing the aegis and exposing the bracelet. Then she lifts the aduncus with her right. Both arms are in plain view while showing the design on the breastplates of her leather armor. She does a barrel roll to identify herself to both sides and then waits.

The group never slows. The ones coming from below begin to fly faster; those above dive. She can see their bows drawn, then catches the glint of an arrowhead. Instinctively, she blocks the arrow with her shield and returns her arm to the position.

There's the neweguard.

"Don't shoot!"

She hears the coloner's order.

The group rushes past her, then loops to her front while the other dives and swoops away to her rear at the last moment. She can feel the wind and hear the river-like sound created by the multitude of wings. Then they are gone. She looks up and sees the entire flock re-group above her. The coloner seems to be reprimanding one of the guards. He leaves the servience in charge, breaks away, and slowly circles down to her. When he passes by her, she is surprised by the golden color of his wings.

"Who are you, and why do you wear the Haloguardian uniform?"

"I am Geolufeoer of the North Shore Guard."

The coloner scowls at her.

"The North Shore Guard was disbanded months ago."

Geolufeoer? She died on the raid…six or eight months ago. Yelu stays at attention; she waits for permission to speak. Disbanded! That is not good.

153

The coloner looks her over carefully.

She has the right color hair. Not too many red-haired doyenne Haloguardian around, but the armor barely fits her.

The coloner remembers the North Shore battle. He had been in that flock as a servience. He had noticed her flaming red hair; it was hard to miss; however, he never became acquainted with her. After the battle with Sceagga, they promoted him from servience to coloner to replace Roanfeoer. The group was renamed the Palisades Guard.

Either way, there are others whose task is to make such decisions.

"What is that strange vessel out there?"

"That is the Scip Hudros; it's a cargo vessel from a land on the other side of the reef called Sylvanus."

"A cargo vessel?" he asks. "From a land called Sylvanus?"

Did she say the other side of the reef?

"Yes, their trade depends heavily on these large ships. Sylvanus is very large; they use the seas to transport their goods from one port to another."

That story is as wild as I have ever heard, but I'm stuck.

"Very well, I will go to the ship to talk to the fishtangler. You will stay here in the open. The Haloguardian will not hesitate to shoot you if you should try any trickery."

"Coloner...?"

"The name is Aureus, Coloner Aureus."

"Coloner Aureus, only one aboard can speak Ortetan."

"Nonsense, everyone speaks Ortetan."

"Trust me, Coloner Aureus, the folk of Sylvanus, do not."

"The one you are seeking goes by the name of Sakara. He is a sortiarius with the power to speak all languages."

This is almost too much for Aureus.

Other lands? Other languages?

"Is this sortiarius a skybourne?"

"No, he is not; there are no skybourne in Sylvanus," she answers.

"None?"

"No, I was the first and only one they had ever seen. They now refer to the Ortetans as the Aduncus."

"Aduncus?" repeats the coloner. "Why?"

"It will take a while to explain."

"You can do that later."

Aduncus...sounds nice...honorable... strong. I like it!

"Very well, I will summon this Sakara, but this ship must remain in place. If it attempts to come to shore, we will burn it."

"Understood, Coloner. I instructed the ship's caput to drop anchor. He will not move the ship until he is told, as per Haloguardian rules."

"Caput?" Aureus asks.

"Sorry, it's their word for ship's coloner."

A ship with its own coloner? Strange story; she does know her rules, though.

"Coloner Aureus?"

"Yes."

"I am with child; may I be allowed to rest on land."

She is starting to tire from the constant soaring. The coloner waves two guards over and instructs them to take her to the cliff edge where she can rest.

She sees a group of small faces peering at her from the safety of their homes as she nears the cliffside caves.

They must have been with the skybourne cildra I saw.

She smiles at them and cradles her womb; soon, she will have her own.

Yelu is happy to feel Ortet under her feet once more. She recognizes the area; it is the location of her last post. The first thing she does is shed the tight armor. She keeps the shield and *aduncus; after all, she is still a member of the Haloguardian. She looks around and sees the fallen log. A season had passed, and the trees' constant shed covered the ground with leaves.*

She moves the leaves with her foot and comes across the carving of the fishtangler with his catch. She picks up the figurine, a little soiled but not any worse for its time in the open.

"How did you know it was there?" the guard asks.

"I made it."

A twig snaps behind them, and the guards turn with their bows ready.

Two little pipios are standing in front of the bushes.

"See," says the older of the two, "I told you she'd come back."

Yelu gasps, and a knot rises in her throat.

"By Eyu, how much you have grown."

The pipios walk by the guards, keeping a wary eye on them, then run into Yelu's arms.

"Are these your pipios?" one of the guards asks.

"No, they are just my friends."

Tears roll down her cheeks, and she strokes their heads.

"Your hair," she says to the little one. "It's getting darker."

The little pipio has a cloth bag in her hand, which she hands to Yelu. She reaches inside and pulls out the carvings.

"You forgot these when you left."

The guard exchange looks.

Yelu shows the pipios the fishtangler.

"You missed one." She places them all back in the bag.

"I want you to keep these safe for me." She tells them.

A loud whistle sounds from somewhere over the cliff.

"That's mother. We have to go," the eldest says.

Then the eldest frowns at the guard.

"Just so you know, she saved us and our mother."

The smallest one takes Geolufeoer's hand.

"Will you come back?" the little skybourne asks.

Once again, a sob got catches in Yelu's throat.

"I don't know."

She kisses and hugs them both but cannot say goodbye.

They run to the cliff's edge and dive off.

Then she notices a stone pillar that stands where the pipios jumped. She walks to it under the watchful eyes of her guards. There is an inscription on one side of it, which reads:

In memory of the brave Haloguardian who gave their lives to keep our homes safe.

Coloner Roanfeoer

Asio

Scrowlfeoer

Craggefeoer

Geolufeoer

Albusfeoer

Dedicated by the skybourne of the Cliff Side Palisades.

They believe that I died in the attack. But, of course, why would they think otherwise? I've been gone for seven months. The Cliff Side Palisades? They renamed the place after the attack.

It was customary to give the locations of great battles names that were more attractive.

"We're told you claim to be Geolufeoer. What do you recall of the battle?"

One of the guards questions her in a half-mocking manner.

"Not very much," she says, ignoring his tone. "I was too busy trying to keep out of Sceagga's reach."

This changes his attitude.

"So, were you the one who killed Sceagga?"

"Coloner Roanfeoer shot him but didn't kill him. Sceagga threw an energy ball that set him adustus and burned him," she says.

"We were told that he was struck by lightning," says one of the guards.

"Have you ever heard of an Aduncus being struck by lightning?"

"An Aduncus?"

She stops and thinks about what she said.

"A skybourne," she corrects herself.

"No, but it doesn't mean it couldn't happen."

I guess it did happen to me.

"So Sceagga killed Coloner Roanfeoer, then left."

The guard is testing her.

"No, not exactly. Sceagga then came after me. He grabbed me, I stabbed him with my aduncus, and then he fell into the ocean. That's the last thing I remember."

The guard looks at her, thinking about her story.

"The bodies that were found, how badly wounded were they?"

She is trying to steer them away from the questioning.

"Not bad enough to have caused their death."

"Solois and Haloguardian?"

"That's right, why? What do you know about it?"

Just then, Coloner Aureus arrives with his squad.

"Everything is as you said," Aureus says.

They placed Sakara in a harness and carried him off the ship. He arrives with them, extremely excited.

"Yelu, you're all right? Watch Rewen was worried sick about you."

"Yelu?" the coloner asks.

"The folks of Sylvanus had trouble pronouncing my name. Yelu was the best they could do."

Sakara extricates himself from the harness.

"Everything is fine Watch Sakara," the doyenne says. "Look!"

She says, pointing to the small monument.

"Is that you?" he asks.

"Yes, as I thought, they believe I'm dead."

"How are you going to prove you are not?"

"By the brand," she says. "It's the only way."

"You seem to know a lot about the Haloguardian." Coloner Aureus says.

"I don't expect you to believe everything I say, coloner. But, if you did, I would wonder how you got your commission," Yelu says.

"You and I know that there is only one way for me to prove who I am, and that is to have my brand inspected by the Deccem Magistro."

Only a Haloguardian would know that.

The squad begins murmurings.

"Silence! You sound like a flock of eggbirds," the coloner says. "If you are who you say you are, you may be able to shed some light on a lot of what's been happening in the area."

"Oh?"

"But that will be best left for the Deccem," he says. "Will the boat be in need of stores?"

"They refer to it as a ship. So besides freshwater, they should be fine," Sakara answers.

"And there was a giant on board," the coloner says.

"He is what they call a Nauta. He is the ship's coloner, and he's friendly." Yelu says.

"Good." The coloner sounded relieved. "The guards will keep an eye on the...shiiep."

"Should we go to see the Deccem?" Yelu asks.

"I will accompany you. Lead the way. You should still remember where it is."

The doyenne smiles. Once again, she is being tested. She also knows he will keep testing her until he gets the verification from the Decanus.

"You don't mind if I take my time, do you?" she says, rubbing her abdomen.

"Take all the time you need." The coloner answers.

Sakara gets back in the harness and is lifted into the air. When she is ready, Yelu flies up and heads straight for the Campus Exercitatus.

At seventeen, she had spent one year at a training camp. Then came her two-year commission. She re-enlisted and made the cut for Haloguardian. The next phase of her education took her to the Campus Exercitatus for another four years of specialized training. The Deccem Magistro taught her science, math, history, and the fighting arts. This was a much higher level of education than she would have gotten otherwise.

The Magistro consists of ten sortiarius, each with a unique talent to teach their students. They are the superiors of the so-called Keepers of the Species who give their time to teach those who will protect the land.

Sakara has kept quiet but can no longer contain his curiosity.

"Yelu?" he asks.

"Yes, Watch Sakara."

"What is the brand?"

"The Haloguardian is given a special symbol by the Decanus, inscribed somewhere between the wings. Then it is logged into a scroll. Each Haloguard has one, and each is unique," Yelu says.

"So, it should prove your identity."

"Yes, it should remove all doubt."

The trip to the Campus Exercitatus takes several hours. They travel from the dry sea-side forest of the palisades, over the open savannas, and finally, the dense rainforest. The group stops several times for the benefit of the guards carrying Sakara. Then, they change the carriers and continue the flight.

After another hour, they make one last stop before reaching the campus. When they land, Sakara can see the valley down below. However, the ocean is no longer visible at ground level. He also notices that the forest is much denser in this part of Ortet.

"How are you doing? Watch Sakara."

She brings him a skin of water. He takes several gulps, then sighs loudly.

"I'm fine; all this excitement. I guess I'm not as young as I thought I was. You keep up a good pace."

"I'm trained for it," she says.

"This territory is so varied. You would have to travel Sylvanus for several weeks to pass through all the terrains we covered today."

The coloner listens to the conversation and then decides to join them.

"You don't do much flying Watch Sakara?" he says, trying another test.

"Oh, no, Coloner Aureus, this is my first time in the air. It is very...exhilarating...yes, that's how I would describe it. I usually travel at a more leisurely pace."

"Why do you push yourself, Geolufeoer?" the coloner asks.

She notices that he is using her proper name.

"I recognize this forest as Solois territory," she answers.

The coloner chuckles.

"A lot has changed since you left. The Haloguardian controls this area now. It was taken from the Solois when Sceagga disappeared."

"Is this true? I... we ran across his disciple on Sylvanus. He claimed that he had rescued Sceagga from the ocean."

"A cruel Sylvan, I might add," Sakara says.

"You met him too?" Aureus asks.

"He tried to kill us all," the monakite says.

"What was the disciple's name?" the coloner asks.

"He went by the name of Pouke, but we later found out it was Hergian," Yelu says.

The word almost catches in her throat.

Coloner Aureus goes silent.

"Hergian?" the guard asks.

"You've heard of him, haven't you?" she asks.

"We've had reports of the existence of a powerful sortiarius by that name. He was causing trouble back when Sceagga was at the height of his mischief." Aureus says.

"Believe me, Coloner Aureus, if Hergian still lives, he should not be underestimated," she says.

"You can't possibly believe that he survived the fall in the channel?" Sakara says.

"He was very resourceful to get to Sylvanus, Watch Sakara. He is very powerful, and we never stayed to look for the body."

She places her hands on the small of her back and stretches.

"If he were to appear here in Ortet, I wouldn't be surprised."

"M'lady, you are full of interesting information," the coloner says. "Let's continue our journey."

Knowing that the Solois no longer controls the area, Yelu takes the rest of the flight slower. Finally, they pass over the vast forests on the eastern part of the island and climb up to the plateau where the training camps are.

As the sun sets on the horizon behind them, its yellowed light colors the valley and hills in amber, making the campus walls look like they were dipped in honey.

They land at the compound gates; Sakara's eyes are wide with awe. He frees himself from the harness and runs his hand over the stone carvings. The stone structures on Sylvanus were crude compared with the architecture and workmanship before him. A sizeable hollow brass cylinder hangs next to the door, labored with intricate carvings of creatures. There is a mallet tethered to a stone pedestal next to it. The coloner picks up the mallet and strikes the cylinder. It emits a deep resonating gong.

They follow the sound of the bell, spreading across the valley, traveling back and forth, permeating all of its corners like ripples in a pond.

"What does the Haloguardian wish?"

The voice comes from behind; they didn't hear the sortiarius open the gate.

They all turn; an old Ortetan dressed in grey robes stands at the gate. A large key hangs by a gold-colored braided rope around his neck.

"Sortiarius," Coloner Aureus says. "It is important that we meet with the Deccem Magistro."

"And the Decanus," Yelu adds.

This takes even the coloner by surprise.

"The Deccem Magistro, yes, but the Decanus...? We'll have to see about the Decanus."

The sortiarius leads the group into a chamber.

"Wait here while I summon the Deccem."

They wait for a short while, which gives Sakara time to inspect the room. There is a large wall with a map of the Campus Exercitatus inlaid into it. In front of it are ten marble

163

busts. Seven were strange creatures, two looked like young girls, and one had a black cloth draped over it.

"Yelu?" asks Sakara. "What sort of creatures do these nine busts represent? Or is it ten?"

"Nine? There are supposed to be ten; those are the Keepers of the Species."

She says, walking over to them. She recognizes some of them, but Sakara is right; there are ten busts. One of them is covered with a very dusty dark cloth.

"That's strange; there are ten teachers."

She frowns at the two busts of the little girls.

"Except...I don't know which one is covered. Now that I think about it, I only studied under two of them; I never saw the other eight," she says. "It wouldn't be Eage, the blind one; he is the Decanus."

"Eage?" asked Sakara.

Could it be the same one?

"Yelu, remember I told you about the prophecy and the monakite who had them?"

"Yes, now that you mentioned it, his name was Eage. Of course, I didn't think much of it then, but—"

"Eage has only been Decanus for a couple hundred years. He is a new arrival compared to the others, but he's the most powerful. Unfortunately, we have yet to find someone to take over the position left vacant by him."

They all turn towards the old sortiarius, pointing at the covered statue. He appears again in their midst without being noticed.

"Who is he?" Yelu asks. "Why do you keep him covered?"

"He was a disgrace for the campus, a disgrace for the Keepers, and a disgrace to all of the sortiarius," he says.

He walks to the bust.

"The cause of all the disgrace that has befallen the Ortetans."

He lifts the cloth exposing the bust of a sortiarius who was, as the inscription below said, 'Keeper of the pacú.'

"Sceagga." Yelu hisses.

Her hands instinctively cradled her abdomen.

"You recognize Calabar? How curious."

"Calabar—Sceagga was the Keeper of the pacú?" Yelu asks.

"Yes," answers the old sortiarius. "A most effective teacher until he turned."

"There is a Keeper for the pacú?" asks Sakara.

The old sortiarius gives him a curious look.

"What do you...Who are you?"

"My name is Sakara, and I come from Sylvanus. A faraway land."

"Sylvanus?"

The old one stops to think.

"That explains it. Very nice land, I've heard."

They all look at each other.

"You've heard of Sylvanus?" Sakara asks.

"Of course," he says in a matter-of-fact tone.

He waves at them to follow.

"Most of the Deccem have visited Sylvanus. However, they refer to your land as 'the wild country.' I personally have never made the trip. That doesn't matter, though. Follow me; they wait."

They are led to another chamber; dark wood panels cover the walls, giving the room a warm feeling. However, as they enter the room, a sortiarius draws all of the heavy curtains, leaving the room's illumination to lamps and candles.

Yelu and Sakara exchange glances, each looking for an explanation from the other. A murmur comes from the center of the chamber, where ten large high-backed chairs are placed in a semicircle. Nine cowled sortiarius are already sitting there. The shapes within their hoods create strange shadows, and Sakara wishes he had been paying attention before the curtains were closed. One of the chairs remains empty.

The Haloguardian enters the hall, and Coloner Aureus stands at attention before the group.

The old sortiarius lights a wick and carries it to a sizeable open saucer made of bronze. He touches the inside of the bowl, and a soft flame flares inside, lighting the faces of the Deccem. Sakara is astounded; the Keepers have a strong resemblance to animals but retain the groundstay or skybourne characteristics.

Yelu starts to feel turmoil growing in her womb. She cradles her abdomen again.

"What does the Haloguardian wish of the Deccem?"

One of the Deccem asks. His face is covered in soft fur, and his forehead and cheeks are checked with spots. Dark markings surround his eyes, with a stain running from their inside corner to his black muzzle-like nose. Carved on his chair is the name 'Katta,' accompanied by a simulacrum of a large resting cat.

"We need to have a brand verified," says the coloner.

Katta steps down from his chair in a fluid movement; he pulls down his hood, exposing the spots that run down his neck.

"A brand? That is a most unusual request. Why would you need to have a brand verified?"

"This young doyenne claims to be Geolufeoer of the Palisades," Aureus says. "Our records show that she died in battle against the Solois."

Coloner Aureus tells what he knows of their arrival.

Another Keeper stands and walks around the group; her head moves with quick jerks and twitches, accounting for everyone in the room.

"Was a body found?" She asks.

She looks at Yelu through yellow eyes, foraging every feature. Satisfied, she returns to her chair. Fauken is carved on the chair, adorned by a bird of prey with outstretched wings.

"No, there wasn't; she disappeared during the battle and re-appeared this morning."

"We remember the aroint entry in the scroll, Keeper Katta."

Yelu turns and gasps at the sight of one of twin midges. They are a handspan below shoulder height and look like young girls. Their hair is sunrise yellow, and their green eyes gleam in the light from the flame.

She hops down from the chair and straightens her blue ankle-length robe. The word 'Nok' is carved on the backrest of her chair. A curious weasel-looking creature adorns it.

"Yes, we do," adds the other twin. "Nok, wasn't it during the end of last cold season that we placed that death notice?"

The other midge had 'Golo' with a snarling wolf on her chair. She wears an identical but green robe.

"Yes, it was Golo."

The midges look like groundstay children in all aspects. Yelu cannot help but smile at the sight of the small Keepers. They remind her of the pipios from the cliffs.

"You're smiling," Golo asks.

"Do we amuse you?" Nok asks.

"Oh no. Pardon me. It's just that you remind me of…friends," Yelu says.

"I see," Golo says

"Friends. Interesting," Nok says.

"Step forward, doyenne," says Katta.

Yelu approaches him.

"I see you are with child," he says. "Do you feel all right?"

"I'm not sure, Keeper Katta; the baby seems very active."

"A sign of good health, I'm sure," he says.

Katta, though, has a strange expression on his face.

"Noviciate!" Calls the Keeper.

A young groundstay in simple robes steps before the sortiarius and bows, "Yes, m'lord."

"Bring the kneeling cushion."

"Yes, m'lord."

The noviciate leaves and returns quickly with a large ornate cushion. He places the cushion in front of the sortiarius and waits.

"You may go."

The noviciate bows and leaves.

The twin midges rush out of the room. When they return, one carries a large scroll. Yelu imagines the roll would be too heavy for an average child to carry. The other has a large wooden stand for the scroll. They carry the scroll and stand with ease. Nok places the stand; Golo accommodates the manuscript on it, then fingers down the parchment while Nok watches over her shoulder.

"There!" Says Nok. "The annotation made on her death is in the five hundred and first Scroll of the Arointed."

"She had a peculiar brand," Golo says, looking at the drawing.

"A most peculiar brand," adds Nok. "That is why we remembered her."

All the sortiarius stand and gather around the scroll. There is a lot of murmuring between them.

"Kneel, my child," Katta says.

The doyenne kneels on the cushion facing the Haloguardian. Nok and Golo unlace the part of her robe tied under her arms, leaving a flap that can be lifted to expose the brand. Keeper Katta raises the cloth and looks at it. There is more murmuring among the Deccem as the three of them inspect the mark. Then he replaces the flap.

Nok and Golo retie the straps under her arm.

"Coloner...?"

"Coloner Aureus m'lord,"

"Coloner Aureus, it is the ruling of the Deccem Magistrate that this doyenne is who she claims," Katta says.

"Welcome home, Geolufeoer of the Palisade Guard."

The Haloguardian greet her by striking their shields with their aduncus.

"There is one more thing," Yelu says.

"What would that be?" Nok and Golo ask in unison.

"It is of great importance that I meet with the Decanus," she says.

"The Decanus does not receive visitors," the old sortiarius says.

Sakara steps forward.

"Are you a sortiarius?" he asks.

The old sortiarius is surprised by Sakara's question.

"Of course, all of the teachers and Keepers at the campus are."

Sakara grabs the old man's arm and pulls him to Yelu.

"This could be the most important event in the history of Terrae, and I'm not going to let you wave it away," says Sakara,

The old sortiarius is wide-eyed from shock; his authority has been challenged, and he is physically dragged around by the arm.

"This is...What are you talking about?"

Sakara takes the old man's hand and places it on Yelu's womb.

"This!" Sakara says.

"What are you doing?" He asks. "This is the most—"

The expression on the old man's face suddenly changes to one of surprise.

"By Eyu!" He says softly.

The old sortiarius looks at Katta.

"This is…most unusual."

Katta approaches Yelu, touches her, then withdraws his hand gasping.

"Where's the Decanus?" He asks.

"Right here!" Comes a voice from the entrance.

The blind groundstay, assisted by a younger sortiarius, enters the hall.

"Lord Decanus, the energy coming from this doyenne is incredible," Katta says.

"I know I felt it as soon as she arrived," Eage says.

Eage walks into the room, aided by his tutee, Bartolon. The Decanus continuously taps his walking staff on the floor. He goes directly to the vacant chair and sits; Bartolon remains at his side.

Fifteen years prior, a five-year-old boy appeared at the gates of the Campus Exercitatus. His parents were unknown, but because of the campus' isolated location, it is believed that the one who transported him there must have been a skybourne. Because, when the sacerdoyen answered the gong's summons and opened the gate, no one else was in sight.

He was named Bartolon. He had minimal control over the pacú; therefore, he would never be ranked among the Keepers. However, Bartolon impressed everyone with his highly analytical mind and his quick and penetrating ability for logical thinking.

Bartolon showed promise as an educator and would receive his training while assisting Decanus Eage.

"Who do we have here?" Eage asks.

Golo and Nok step forward.

"These are visitors from Sylvanus, Lord Eage," Nok says.

"They seem to have found a passage through the reef," Golo says.

"They crossed on a large boat," Nok says

"This is young Geolufeoer and Sortiarius Sakara."

"Come forward, my child," Eage says.

Yelu walks to his chair and bows her head.

"M'lord," she says softly.

The old sortiarius reaches out and touches her abdomen. The expression on his face changes, but he keeps in contact.

"What do you feel, m'lord," his helper asks.

"The energy in her is powerful. See for yourself, Bartolon."

Young Bartolon's powers are limited, but he immediately feels a sensation when touching her.

"It's so powerful," Bartolon says in a soft voice.

"Young Bartolon, what do you recall of your teachings on the brand?" Eage asks.

"The brand is placed on the individual where they cannot see it," Bartolon says.

"How is it placed there, and why?"

Eage constantly tests Bartolon on his studies.

"The sigil is made when the denotive necksquare is placed. The brand must be covered and not revealed to the wearer or the commonality because it might foretell the future," Bartolon says.

"Excellent, Bartolon."

Bartolon swells with pride. Now Eage turns to Yelu.

" Geolufeoer, has your state been troubling you?"

"Yes, lord Eage."

"I feel turmoil in your womb."

"It gets pretty bad at times."

"The creatures are restless," he says.

He then smiles.

"The little brothers argue as little brothers do."

"Brothers?"

"Why yes, my child, you carry twins."

A murmur rises in the room once again.

"I know what you are thinking," Eage speaks to the group. "The legend and the visions mention only the one."

"That's right, lord Decanus, the legend speaks of the coming of the Promised One. It did not bring up a brother. This could mean that she is not the bearer," Fauken says.

The Keeper walks around Yelu, eyeing her distrustfully.

"Touch her Fauken," Eage says.

"I don't need to touch—"

"Touch her."

The Decanus's voice changes; it is now a mandate.

Fauken reaches out and lays her hand on her shoulder. Her eyes widen, and the feathers on her head rise.

"There is great turmoil in her, like...like a whirlpool mixing trouble and...peace?" Fauken is confused.

"Did you feel the good?" Eage asks.

"Yes, very powerful...very, very powerful," the Keeper answers.

"She will see the right hand of Eyu come," Eage says. "But there is a brother. I do not know his role in our future or concerning the Promised One. Do not forget that I was the one who had the vision; I was the one who made the prediction. This young doyenne was in my vision."

Sakara finds himself in a state of awe. The necksquare, a piece of cloth, decides the brand. Not to mention Eage has been a part of Dominion's history for over a thousand years.

"Master Eage, how did a necksquare choose a brand for Yelu—Geolufurr."

Sakara trips over her name.

"Ah, you must be the monakite from Sylvanus," Eage smiles. "There's a blessing on the necksquare. When placed on the individual, it will read their pacú and mark them with the sigil."

"So all Ortetans bear the brand?"

"Oh, no. Only those commissioned as a Haloguardian or a Lorica are branded," Eage says. "If the necksquare does not produce a sigil, then that individual, for reasons determined by the necksquare, is not fit to be in the service."

Eage touches Bartolon's arm.

"Bartolon, look at the scroll and describe to me the brand," Eage says.

Bartolon goes to the scroll and looks at the sketch. His brow furrows when he sees it, then hurries to Eage's side and whispers to him.

Eage remains still, then, as if waking from sleep speaks.

"Geolufeoer, or is it Yelu? Within you is the right hand of Eyu. Having been placed in the scrolls of the arointed, your brand is no longer a matter of secrecy. Do you wish to know your brand?"

There's a murmur among the Keepers as they object to the ruling. In response, Eage holds up his hand.

"Is there a logic to your objections?" he asks them.

The Keepers look at each other. For all practical purposes, she has been dismissed and considered dead. So one by one, they all shake their heads.

"Geolufeoer?"

Yelu takes a long time to think.

Knowing the brand can change my future, actually, everyone's future. But what if knowing changes things for the better?

She takes a deep breath.

"Yes, I want to know."

"Golo, Nok, take her to the scroll," Eage says.

Even though Eage is blind, the twin midges bow to him and take Yelu to the scroll. Yelu looks at the sketch and is confused. The sketch is of a pair of wings. On the right is the skybourne's bird-like wing and on the left is the wing of a night mouse. She looks at the Keepers, but they offer no explanation.

"A very peculiar brand," says Golo.

"Very peculiar indeed," says Nok.

Eage turns to the group.

"Sakara, is it? So you came from Sylvanus; how did this come to be? I remember the land well; a most gentlefolk live there," Eage says.

Eage's question doesn't register with Sakara. His mind is still racing.

"Lord Eage, you are a part of Sylvanus history; how did you get there?" Sakara asks.

"Actually, I am a native of Sylvanus; I was discovered by Calabar and brought here by one of Huanlong's creatures."

"You were discovered by Calabar? What would he want from you?" Yelu asks.

"You mustn't forget, young one, Calabar was not always evil. He became Sceagga when he experimented with the negative side of the pacú and liked what he felt." Eage says.

"What are Huanlong's creatures?" Sakara asks.

"I am Huanlong."

The voice comes from the darker area of the room. Sakara sees a tall figure rise from a chair adorned with a winged snake-like creature. He slowly walks forward, a powerful being by the way he moves. His robes are scarlet in color, and as he steps into the torchlight, Huanlong's reptilian features become visible.

"I sent a creature called Perditor, my personal favorite. I summoned him from a different place to bring Eage to the Campus Exercitatus."

Sakara takes a step back at the sight of the Keeper. Though he poses no threat to him, he is still compelled to maintain his distance.

"What sort of creature is this Perditor," Sakara asks.

"A dragon, of course."

"An extraordinary fire-spitting reptile with intelligence and the power of speech," Eage says. "Though he does have one weakness, his fetish for hoarding treasure."

Huanlong walks around the group, circumspect of the newcomers, then stops in front of Sakara.

"Hmm, yes, he likes to sleep on top of an immense mound of collected items of great worth; gold, argentium, and precious stones," Huanlong says. "He is one of my favorite students."

"You said…a different place?" Sakara stammers.

"Yes, sortiarius, there is a place that few know about. It's another world, a more peaceful world under our care," Huanlong says. "It's called Terrae Exterus."

"I've never heard of such a place," Sakara says.

"Neither have I," Yelu says.

The Haloguardian exchange looks; they haven't heard of it either.

"We keep it a secret. So no one outside of the campus knows about it."

"Then why are you telling us this?" Aureus asks.

"Because it has recently been brought to our attention that Sceagga is not only alive, but he is looking for a way to reach the passageway," Huanlong says.

"Is this bad?" the doyenne asks. "If he were to go to another world, maybe our problems would end."

"No, young one, our problems would only worsen," Eage says. "You see, Terrae Exterus and its inhabitants are very delicate, but the pacú from there is extremely powerful. The pacú that flows into Ortet and from Ortet to Sylvanus comes directly from Terrae Exterus. Terrae Exterus acts like a filter to block most of the pacú's negative side. If Sceagga finds the Oriel portal, he will have access to dark powers beyond what we can imagine. He will have a chance at controlling all above and all below."

Yelu feels the hairs on her arms rise.

All above and all below?

The thought of Sceagga with such power makes her shiver uncontrollably.

"He would have control of all of creation?" Sakara asks.

"Yes, all above and all below," Eage repeats with a nod.

"That's inconceivable," Sakara says in a low voice.

Eage just nods.

"What is...the Oriel?" Sakara asks.

"There are two Oriels. They are portals through which Terrae Exterus can be entered," Eage answers.

"There used to be a third method, the Way Stone," Golo says.

"But it was destroyed in the battle at Merkhoum," Nok says.

"Way Stone? I have so many questions. Are these Oriels well guarded?" Sakara asks.

"They are well hidden. One of them is here on the campus, out of Sceagga's reach. But unfortunately, Sceagga knows the general area of the other one, as do the rest of us. Its exact location, though, is still unknown."

"What can be done?" asks Coloner Aureus.

"An Order of Prejudice will be issued for Sceagga. The order will become the primary mandate of both the Haloguardian and the Lorica."

"An Order of Prejudice! That is in the scrolls for hypothetical situations. It has never been used."

"That's right, Geolufeoer or Yelu if you prefer. There was never an argument found to justify such an order," the coloner says.

"That's because your studies never factored in Terrae Exterus," Golo says.

"Anyone who can acquire such power and attempt to use it against Eyu's creation will have justified the use of the Order," Nok adds.

Yelu still finds it hard to look at the twins as Keepers.

"What is this Order of Prejudice?" Sakara asks.

"It's the order to kill Sceagga on sight," Huanlong answers. "No questions, no hesitation."

"The Haloguardian and the Lorica will be sent on expeditionary missions to find the rogue sortiarius. Coloner, you will assign a group of your best to guard Yelu. If, as she says, Sceagga planted the offspring in her, he would want the child back. He may not know that there are twins, and we do not know his plans, but we know his actions were never random before." Huanlong says.

"The children in Yelu do bear great power, and thus they should be guarded," Eage adds.

The old sortiarius stands and walks over to her.

"My dear, for the good of both worlds, you must remain at the Campus Exercitatus."

This saddens Yelu. She is once again a prisoner. However, she expects it. She realized after her confrontation with Hergian that the child was important. Sceagga gave her the child, correction, children, and he will want them back.

"Yes, m'lord, I understand."

"Your friends on the ship may come and stay at the campus. Coloner, make the arrangements for their release."

The coloner bows and leads the Halo out of the room.

"I will have the speech facilitator go and give them the power of Ortetan speech."

"You have someone with that power?" Sakara asks.

"Oh yes, how else can the Keepers communicate with all their creatures."

"Decanus Eage, you said that Sceagga was looking for the entryway into that place called Terrae Exterus. Where is that passage?" Sakara asks.

"As I mentioned, one of the Oriels is here on the grounds. The campus was built around it. The other is in Sylvanus in the Crying Mountains," Eage says.

"The Crying Mountains? Little is known about that area. A few villages exist between Ka-Mer and the mountains. Still, those are mainly outposts for hunters, and there are stories of strange creatures that inhabit those forests." Sakara says.

"The Oriels were placed in almost inaccessible places on both worlds, with reason and origin lost to history.

As for Terrae Exterus, its inhabitants are not aware of our existence. We look different than they do. Though linked with ours, their creatures are completely different in form and manner, and they have no skybournes there." Eage says.

"What if one of them stumbles into our world?"

"It would cause all kinds of problems."

"The Oriel opens where it is sent, and it remains open until the traveler returns," Nok says.

"However, once the traveler leaves the area, the image of the Oriel dissipates," Golo adds.

"And an accidental traveler would most likely not know what happened. So they will be stranded unless they stumble back through the opening." Nok continues.

"It sounds like you have used it," Sakara says.

"Some of us have used it. Every so often, a sortiarius is born on Terrae Exterus with special abilities that we need on this side. Sometimes there may be a need of one of the creatures as in the case of Perditor." Eage says.

"We were from Terrae Exterus," says Golo. "Over there, we were referred to as shamana; it meant healer."

"Apa brought us," Nok says, motioning to another Keeper.

Sakara looks to see who they are looking at. A towering muscular sortiarius with ape-like features smiles and nods.

"Didn't your presence cause concern?"

"Terrae Exterus is still in an early stage of development; therefore, the Exterans are very primitive. The Oriel changes the ones who use it to match those on the opposite side. However, those changes are very superficial. For example, Apa's appearance changed, but his powers remained intact. No skybourne has ever crossed over, so we do not know how they would change." Eage says.

The old sortiarius stands, stretches his back, and then continues.

"Even though Apa's face changed, he remained the same size physically. Still, he was seen by one of the primitives and went down in their history as a hero in their culture."

Apa looks at the floor and shakes his head.

"They even spun tales about great feats I supposedly did."

"Amazing." Sakara murmurs. "So, you were sacerdoyennes in the other world, and when you came through the Oriel, you changed."

"Sacerdoyennes?" Nok asks Golo.

"Sacerdoyenne, I like the way it sounds," Golo says. "It's more...delicate."

The twin midges adopt the name, and it becomes a familiar term. In the same manner, all of the skybourne become the Aduncus.

"But that's enough about those events; what is important is that Sceagga knows of its existence, and he will try and leave the island to find it," Eage says.

"How is he going to do this?" Sakara asks.

"The same way you did."

Chapter 11

THE DECCEM

The fishtanglers are finishing their work for the day. They only have one net to bring in, then head back to the shore. Their catch is average; none of the fishtanglers go past 3 millistep this time of year, fearing that a turn in the weather will catch them too far out. The last net thought proves heavy, so much so that they must pull their boat to the source. They are surprised to find a creature with a grotesque face and long hairy spider-like limbs among the fish in the net. They cannot identify what it is, but it is wearing clothes.

"What do you make of it?" Ranick asks.

The other can see cuts and bruises covering his exposed skin.

"Whatever he is, he looks like he was dragged over the rocks," Tenk says.

"He may have fallen off the palisades and washed out to sea."

They start to lift him into the boat, and he moans.

"By Eyu, he's alive!" Tenk says.

"Quick, let's get him to shore and under some blankets," Ranick says.

Soon they have the creature stretched out on the beach and covered. Three other fishtanglers approach them.

"Get the curist quick," Tenk tells him.

"The curist? For an animal?"

"Animals don't wear clothes. So he might be a poor-born, deformed from birth," Ranick says.

The fishtangler leaves, running to town. The creature coughs up some water and starts to breathe easier.

"He seems to be resting now," Tenk says.

He groans and mumbles as the samaritans build a fire to warm him up. Ranick kneels by his side and starts to comfort him.

"You're all right now," he says. "We've sent for the curist."

The other fishtanglers move closer.

"It looks like you were out there for quite a while," Tenk says.

The creature reaches out to them with both hands and smiles.

"Thank you," croaks the stranger.

Ranick and Tenk look at each other.

"I told you," Ranick whispers. "He's a groundstay."

They each take hold of his oversized hands, smile back at him, and collapse. The other two stare wide-eyed as the creature transforms before their eyes into a normal-looking groundstay, stands, and grabs their shoulders. Then, they, too, collapse.

"Yes, thank you," Hergian repeats. "That was just what I needed."

The fishtangler returns with the curist, only to find his four companions dead.

It takes two days for the travelers of the Scip Hudros to arrive at the Campus Exercitatus. With the help of Spaecer, the speech facilitator, they can speak and understand the Ortetan language. Eage has Spaecer prepare an instructional sequence to teach all the beings on Terrae the Ortetan language.

This vast project takes several weeks to develop; Spaecer places a blessing on the songbirds of Ortet. The birds disperse and fly all over Terrae. Once there, they impart the common language by singing until all on Terrae hear them.

The monakites are more than eager to learn from the sortiarius hosts. They accompany their teachings with physical exercise in the form of different fighting arts such as archery, sling, staff, sword, and pike.

In preparation for a confrontation with Sceagga, they learn how to use the upashim. The ball of concentrated pacú that is thrown.

The energy comes from the one throwing it. Therefore, it will deplete the user's energy to the point where, if uncontrolled, it can render them unconscious or kill them. The sortiarius can use a donor to create the upashim. The donor can be willing or unwilling, and depending on the power of the energy ball, it can also kill the donor. The donor can be any living thing, animal, or vegetable.

Yelu is already familiar with the upashim, having witnessed it firsthand. However, none of the monakites had, and they soon find out that not all of them have the power to create or, for that matter, control the pacú.

Sakara was born with the gift of languages. Rewen also has the gift; not only can she sense the pacú in others, but she learns to create a bubble-like shield around her to repel the upashim. Bandagee, with his gift of healing, also has the ability.

The only one who is not gifted is Dominant Saltes, which surprised everyone. However, the biggest surprise is Yelu; she finds she can form a shield against the upashim. She also has the extraordinary ability to persuade all manners of creatures to do what she wishes them to do.

A week after the Sylvans' arrival, word reaches Eage of the fishtangler's death. He decides to meet with the travelers to listen to their opinion.

It is the group's first look inside the main building on the campus. The meeting occurs in a large dining hall around an immense oval table.

Mayven is fascinated by the rococo carvings on the chamber walls, depicting what seems to be historical events.

He marvels at the dark polished wood with dark swirls that the craftsman accentuated by how the panels were cut. He looks at the ornate work on the table's legs. Then runs his hands over the chairs, with flowering vines as the backrests and matching embroidered cushions.

"It's astounding by the amount of work that has gone into the walls and furniture," Mayven says.

"We place no time limit on the artisans. We only expect them to work on their projects regularly, if not daily. Some of these walls have taken years to finish." Eage says.

"And their compensation for their work?" Mayven asks.

"The Campus Exercitatus is a citadel of education. Because of our limited resources and the manner of education, entry into the facility is restricted to those we deem qualified to be here. On occasion, we will consider the admission of an artisan's son or daughter in exchange for a payment of 'sweat work.'"

"Such as the construction of these walls."

Mayven runs his hand over the delicate carvings on the doorframe.

"Exactly, however, bear in mind that the artisan's skill is also a factor in the value of the work."

"How about the other ones that are chosen? Who pays for them?" Sakara asks.

"Life-long service as sortiarius or one of the Keepers is payment enough."

The Deccem are present, as are those they preside over, the actual trainers.

Rewen and Tailon stop at the door and stare at the group, but they retain their composure. However, fear and panic paint Garen and the crew's faces when they see the Deccem for the first time. They start to back towards the door.

"Hold your stead," Mayven orders.

Wide-eyed, they stiffen in place. Though the Deccem resembles the species they represent, the trainers under them bear a more acute likeness.

"Sit," Mayven says.

The Scip Hudro's crew slowly sit, gawping at the Keepers.

Bartolon leans over and whispers in Eage's ear.

"I understand," he chuckles. "I remember my first time."

With that, Eage sends his pacú over to the crew, and they relax.

"I forgot. They have never seen a Keeper," Eage says.

Eage reaches out to Yelu, and she takes his hand.

"Young Yelu, do you have an opinion on what happened on that beach?" asks Eage.

"By the report from the curist and the description of the castaway from the surviving fishtangler, I would say Hergian is back."

There is a murmur in the room.

"But, I saw him drown in the channel," Rewen says.

"Hergian's body was never recovered. Besides, he had plenty of crew on which to feed. Enough to survive until he got to land," Yelu says.

"The description of the creature, what he was wearing, and how the fishtanglers died fits Pouk—Hergian," her throat tightens around the name.

She takes a deep breath to continue.

"The victims are similar to those found dead when he used them to cross the reef."

"So Sceagga's apprentice has returned," Huanlong says. "What can we expect?"

"I believe he has joined Sceagga by now. Hergian knows the location of the channel through the reef. I believe that Sceagga will try to reach the channel and cross it. I also believe that to do so, he will be building a craft similar in size to my Scip Hudros. Hergian had access to all parts of the vessel; he must have studied it." Mayven says.

"How about using one of the fishtangler's crafts? They are readily available." Katta asks.

"They are too small to carry the necessary supplies," Mayven replies.

"I believe that he will gather a small army for the expedition to the Oriel as soon as he reaches Sylvanus," Yelu says.

"He must be aware that we will be out looking for him, and like I said, he will need a larger ship to carry them all and enough stores for the voyage," Mayven says.

A single-horned Keeper with horse-like features addresses the Nauta.

"Do you have any suggestions?" asks Mix.

"Since ships the size of the Scip Hudros are not built here, they can be controlled. Therefore, I believe we should patrol the shores and control all construction of large vessels, at least until they are found." Mayven says.

"Mayven may be right," Sakara says. "If there aren't any ships available, Sceagga would have to make his own, a long, expensive process. On the other hand, this would give us more time to find him."

Mix shakes his quog-like mane. Except for the short horn in the middle of his forehead, he reminds Sakara of the riding beasts on Sylvanus. Mix is the Keeper of the monocerans and pike trainer.

"You would be depriving a large group of builders from practicing their craft. The fishtanglers are already talking about using the larger craft for fishing. Some even think of ferry passengers back and forth between the two lands."

"Sceagga and Hergian could easily be one of those passengers," the doyenne argues.

"You are asking us to control the Ortetans; that has never been done," Sparvo says.

He is one of the bird Keepers who, like Fauken, has a feathered head but is smaller.

"I believe sacrifices will have to be made until we can solve this problem. The problem will disappear if we can find Sceagga and Hergian," Yelu says.

Yelu persuades the group.

Was it her argument that convinced them or her innate power of persuasion? There is no way of telling now, but it does make sense. Eage wonders, or so he believes.

Chapter 12

THE UNKNOWN CHOSEN

Three months after her arrival on Ortet, Yelu gives birth to twins. She names the one with the brown hair Michael and the blond-haired child she names Lucero.

Even though she is no longer needed as a watcher, Rewen still accompanies Yelu daily. Rewen says that she is practicing for when she has a child.

It has been a month since their birth, and Yelu notices something different with the twins. Rewen offers a short hello to Yelu, then goes straight to the crib, or nest, as she refers to the wide, round cushion where the twins sleep. Since she thought Yelu laid eggs when they first met, she thought it appropriate to call the crib a nest.

"How are the duvos?" Rewen asks.

"They're sleeping through the night. It's been the most restful week I've had all month. I feel something different coming from them, though," Yelu says.

Rewen picks up Michael.

"How's little Michael?" she coos.

"I think Amita Rewen will spoil the two," Yelu says.

"Amita? That's a new one."

"It's from the old tongue. It refers to the sister of the mother," Yelu says.

"Well then, amita is going to spoil you—"

A sudden sensation washes over the two. It's like a sudden feeling of joy.

"Whoa, what was that? Did you feel it, Yelu?"

Yelu's eyes are wide.

"I did! They have...powers?"

"Have they done that before?" Rewen asks.

"No. This is the first time."

Yelu picks up Lucero. Again, the same occurs. The same sensation, but slightly different. Yelu and Rewen look at each other.

"I think we should take them to Eage," Rewen says.

"Let's get them ready."

A small academy was established to facilitate the training of local novices. Eage has been in the study hall with Bartolon since early morning. He lectures the novicite's on controlling the pacú while Bartolon assists those who show difficulties.

"I will conclude my class for the day now. Go to your duties now," Eage says.

When the class clears, Bartolon approaches Eage.

"Master Eage, you ended the lecture early today. Are you well?"

"Yelu and Rewen approach, I believe they have important news. Bring them to me, please," Eage says.

News?

"Yes, Master Eage," Bartolon says.

Eage settles in a chair and reaches out with his pacú; he smiles.

Bartolon escorts Yelu and Rewen, each holding one of the twins.

Before they can say anything, Eage reaches out.

"Hand me one of them," Eage says.

Rewen hands him Michael. Eage holds the baby and coos softly, then hands him back.

"Hmm, let's have the other,"

Rewen takes Michael back, and Yelu hands him Lucero.

"Interesting. They both have extraordinary powers, but they are each very different. I cannot tell if either is the Promised One," Eage says.

"I saw that you ended the lecture early. Is there anything wrong?"

They turn and see Tailon standing by the door.

Rewen rushes to him.

"Tailon, their powers have awakened!" Rewen says.

"They too?"

Tailon Saltes has always been a little nettled that everyone seems to have some control over the pacú except him.

"Don't worry, I'm sure our child will also have powers.," Rewen says.

Tailon frowns. He's not sure whether Rewen is pocking fun at him or not.

"Because of the twins' circumstances, their abilities must be carefully nurtured. I believe Bartolon should be in charge of their learning," Eage says.

A look of surprise comes over Bartolon's face.

"Me?"

"You are best suited for the task. I have little left to offer. You will receive the rest of your training by instructing the twins when they can comprehend. Prepare yourself and teach them well."

After his rescue, Rewen and Tailon become inseparable. Before the Watch traveled to the Campus Exercitatus, Rewen took Tailon on a nighttime tielog ride. It was there that Tailon proposed to Rewen.

Two weeks after Michael and Lucero are born, Rewen and Tailon are married, and their daughter Ewen is born three years later. The girl is an image of Rewen except for her eyes, which are golden like Tailon's.

The three grow within the walls of the campus. They eat on campus, study on campus, and cause tomfoolery on campus.

As his name implies, Lucero always brings light to a gloomy day. He is an exemplary child, always studious, helpful, and kind. His interest in the ways of the sacerdoyen makes him the top student at the monastery.

Michael always seems to be at the root of all mischief, and somehow he drags the other two with him.

His first serious prank came at the age of nine. Michael finds Lucero and Ewen taking a shortcut through one of the campus' training arenas.

"Luce, look what I found?"

Michael always referred to Lucero as Luce. He holds up a fist-sized bag.

"What is it?" Lucero asks.

"Michael, what are you up to?" Ewen adds.

Though five years younger, Ewen had more common sense than the other two combined.

"I don't know. Let's see what happens if I put it in this practice urn.

"Why?" Ewen asks.

"Uh oh, someone's coming. Run!"

They run and hide behind the wall.

"Luce, what's in the bag?" Ewen asks.

"Let's see," Michael says.

The keepers used the urns to train the novice monachs to aim and throw upashims, the explosive ball of energy.

The keeper and novice enter the arena. The keeper is busy explaining the technique. They stop, and the keeper points to the urn.

191

Michael starts to giggle.

"Michael, what is inside that bag?" Ewen's tone is now serious.

"What are you three up to."

The three jump. When they turn, Bartolon is standing behind them.

"Uh…we…we were watching the monachite train," Michael stammers.

The young monachite launches the upashim, and when it strikes the urn, the detonation is deafening. Bartolon is thrown back by the shockwave, as are the keeper and novice.

Michael peeks over the wall. He sees the keeper sitting on the ground, confused, and the young monach is sitting next to him, staring at his hands.

"Wow! I didn't know a upashim could do that," Michael says in his most innocent voice.

Bartolon gets up off the ground and dusts his robes.

"At that novicite's level," Bartolon says, "It can't."

The boys are taken, each by the ear, to Geolufeoer. But, to his credit, Michael takes ownership of the prank. Lucero and Ewen are absolved.

Yelu's anxiety multiplies in pace with Michael's growth.

"I don't know what to do. I'm afraid Sceagga's influence will take him over," Yelu says.

"Do not worry, Lady Yelu. He is just a young duvo. He'll outgrow it, you'll see," says Bartolon.

"I'm ashamed to say that I see him squandering his life. Don't you see it?" Yelu asks.

"Believe in him, Yelu. Another would not have taken the blame as he did. He did it spontaneously; I didn't have to ask him," Bartolon says. "He loves his brother and Ewen. That is not one of Sceagga's traits. I believe he is starting to understand his mistakes."

That still did not placate Yelu's ire. He was given three bathroom breaks a day, but all his teachings were in the confines of his room. It was a full month before Michael's feet felt the grass again.

Young Aduncus learn to fly at twelve years of age. Their wings are not strong enough to flap, though gliding for short distances is possible. That didn't stop ten-year-old Michael from climbing the roof of the Lough Building in front of Lake Lacustrali. Michael wanted to prove he could fly at ten.

"I'll be the first Aduncus to fly before twelve. I'll be faster than mother," Michael boasts from the rooftop.

"Stop it. You don't have to prove anything. You're already stronger than me. You're stronger than any other duvo our age. Come down," Lucero pleads.

Ewen hears the commotion and sees Lucero trying to talk him down.

"What's Michael doing now?" Ewen asks.

"Michael thinks he can fly."

Ewen looks up.

"He's too high," she tells Lucero.

"I know. He's going to kill himself."

"Michael, come down. You're too high; you'll break something," Ewen shouts.

Seeing Ewen below fans his courage.

"Just watch," he shouts.

Michael momentarily disappears from view, then moments later, he launches himself from the roof with a running start.

Michael beats his wings once, then twice.

"I think he's doing it!" Lucero says.

He beats it again, then a fourth time. Then his fifth only makes it halfway down.

"He's not," says Ewen.

His back muscles are no longer able to maintain his wingspread. Michael's wings fold back, and he spins like a wingnut seed into the lake.

That earned him another month of isolation, this time in the infirmary. Michael tore the flight muscles between his scapulae and spent the whole time face down with his wings supported.

After that, Michael flew with what Lucero called a lazy wing. Ewen said Michael flew with a limp, and Michael could never make sharp left turns.

At age twelve, Geolufeoer begins to teach the duvos to fly. Their lessons bring them closer together. Yelu teaches them the aerial tactics she learned as Haloguardian. Michale and Lucero spend more time playing flytag and sparring with sticks while airborne. Michael is self-conscious about his 'limp' and puts his energy into speed, but he can never best his mother at racing.

Michael does mature as he gets older. He leaves his childish manners behind and joins Lucero in his studies, succor for Yelu's peace of mind.

Bartolon likes to take long walks while tutoring the twins. Eage would always accompany them, offering his occasional nugget of wisdom. One day, during the outing, time stops; as the wind, the twittering birds, and even the insects' chirrups.

It is at this moment that Eyu makes his presence known to him.

"Eage."

"Who speaks?" Eage asks.

"I speak."

"Who are you?"

"Master Eage, who are you talking to?" Bartolon asks.

"To him," says Eage. "Whoever stands before me."

"There is no one here but us," Michael says.

The boys look around, but no one is there.

"Who speaks to me?" Eage asks.

"You know me."

"From where?"

"I'm always with you."

"My Lord!"

The sacerdoyen falls to his knees.

Bartolon feels a presence but cannot place it. So he follows Eage, slowly dropping to his knees and bowing his head.

The boys look around and see that Bartolon is also kneeling. Then a feeling of joy and peace enters their hearts. Immediately they know that they are in the presence of their God, and they too fall to their knees.

"What do you wish of me?" The blind sacerdoyen asks.

"I am pleased with the young ones," Eyu says. "I have gifts for the two."

"Yes, my Lord."

"To Michael, I give this blessed robe. Its powers will be in accordance with how he shapes his pacú," the voice says. "He is to use it to guide and protect my Sylvan children. He is to teach them my ways, for they have forgotten."

A spot of light appears in front of the sacerdoyen. It grows until it becomes blinding. Bartolon and the twins cover their eyes with their hands. Though blind, Eage can somehow feel its brightness. Then, the light dissipates, leaving behind a folded white robe on the ground.

"I have been mindful of Lucero since his birth and have always been aware of the goodness in his heart. To him, I give the Traduco Glass. This orb also yields great power, as he will learn. With it, he can guide and protect my children in Terrae Exterus, then teach them my ways, for they are still young and innocent."

The light reappears, and an egg-sized glass orb is left behind when it dissipates.

"Be aware, though, that the duvos were touched by evil. They will have to conquer it with their hearts. However, know that I have placed my hand on them. So, my favor will also accompany them to help them on their journey. This will be their test, for I will choose only one as my right hand. This is for only you to know, not them; keep it in your heart.

"The road they choose can be good or bad. It will determine how or what they will become. An evil one placed the seed; I touched it and added good. The duvos have the option of choosing, what to become, and how to use the gifts.

"As for you, Eage, you have served me well," his voice fades

Once again, the wind returns, as do the sounds of nature. Michael and Lucero immediately feel Eyu's departure. They go to the aid of Eage and help him to his feet.

"What just happened? Where did these come from?" Michael sees the items in front of the sacerdoyen.

"These are gifts. They come directly from Eyu," Eage says. "They are for you."

"For...What are they?" Lucero asks.

"The robe is for Michael; its power will develop as you develop your pacú," says Eage. "Use it wisely."

Michael picks up the white robe; he slips it over his head. It conforms perfectly to his body. He feels a surge of energy go through him.

Eage picks up the glass orb and, handing it to Lucero, says.

"This is the Traduco glass; it too bears great power. With it, you are to teach Eyu's children in Terrae Exterus. Let your wisdom be your guide when you use it."

Lucero takes the orb and holds it in his hand; its power flows through the sphere and into him, giving him a taste of its power.

Though they feel the gifts are powerful, they must learn how to use them.

Eage explains to them Eyu's revelation.

"I'm to go to Sylvanus?" Asks Michael.

"And I'm going to...Terra Exterus? Where's that?" Asks Lucero.

"Yes, it will be explained when we return to campus. However, for now, these are not things for others to hear," Eage says.

They walk back to the campus in silence, reflecting on the enormity of what just happened to them.

Bartolon's logical mind refuses to accept that something appeared out of nothingness. He starts to wonder if Eage planted the gifts to cement their beliefs. For the time being, he will go along with the illusion.

The deserted road has a few local farmers going back and forth carrying their goods on their backs or carts in the case of the wealthier ones. Every so often, one would stop them and ask for a blessing, be it for their health, family, or crops.

As they near the city, they encounter two travelers sitting by the side of the road. They look very poor and in need of a good meal.

"Bless my father, sacerdoyen," says the younger of the two.

He motions to his older companion with brown and black robes dirty from the road and long, grey, and matted hair. A soiled wrap beneath his hood hides his face.

Bartolon places his hand on the man's head; he feels a strange sensation he does not recognize.

His mind must be consumed by disease. He thinks.

197

"Blessings upon you, my friend," Bartolon says.

"Thank you, m'lord."

Eage then places his hand on the man. He feels the same sensation as Bartolon, but his interpretation is different.

There has been much evil in his life; his pacú is familiar, but there is a barrier I cannot penetrate, and the darkness I feel comes from behind it.

"Blessings upon you, traveler. Look to your future, for your past cannot be undone." Eage says.

"Thank you, holy one; I will heed your advice." says the elder. "And you, young apprentices, your blessings would also be appreciated."

Michael places his hand on the man's head. He feels a spiritual stench.

What sort of life has this man led? And there is more, more than I can sense.

"My blessings upon you, old father," Michael says.

The old man flinches as a searing heat passes through his head; stifling a gasp, he moves his head away from Michael's touch.

"Thank you, young sacerdoyen," the old man says.

Lucero approaches the man and places his hand on the man's head. The tingling sensation is not unpleasant. The spiritual aroma, though not sweet, is not altogether unpalatable.

"Blessings, old one," Lucero says.

The old man feels there is synonymy with his pacú. He smiles at the young Aduncus.

"Thank you, blessed one."

The sacermagi say goodbye and continue down the road. The travelers watch them disappear around a curve.

The older traveler pulls down his tattered hood and shakes his head. An ash cloud rises, exposing enough of his long-tangled hair to show the light grey streaks. He then pulls the dirty bandage off his face revealing robust features and fierce eyes. He stands and walks to the middle of the road looking in the direction the foursome followed.

"It's the fair-haired one," the elder says.

"Yes, I could feel it too, father," Hergian replies.

There are several arenas on campus. Here, the students practice their specialties and are tested to see if they merit the Keeper rank.

The two robed figures face each other; the doyenne Keeper is dressed in black, and the other doyenne is in the student's khaki. Potted trees and a small reflective pool adorn all the arenas, which is no different. However, they usually only allow Keepers and teachers to witness the testing. Today is different; two additional spectators have been allowed to watch, Lucero and Michael.

Neither of the combatants moves as they size each other, waiting for the first move. Finally, the black robe raises her arm and sends a upashim at the novice. The novice drops to one knee, and a shimmering translucent bubble rises around her. The sphere strikes the bubble shield and bounces wildly into the air. From within the shield, the novice touches the ground. A large planter, by the teacher, cracks as the roots of the small tree it holds jump from the pot into the ground.

The teacher immediately jumps to the side and sends what looks like a dagger of light flying by the novice's left. She ignores it from the safety of her bubble, but it is not until she hears it strike the water in the pool that she realizes she is not the target.

The water in the shape of a giant hand rises, grips the bubble, then runs down its sides, seeping underneath it. The water quickly fills the sphere.

"I think Ewen is in trouble," Michael whispers.

"Keeper Braedan can control water? I have never seen anyone control water," Lucero adds.

The Keepers Golo and Nok give them a terse look.

"Quiet, you two," Bartolon says.

"Sorry," Lucero whispers.

The novice remains kneeling as the water reaches her neck. Then, with a wave of her other hand, the bubble dissipates, dispersing the water. The watery limb rises once more. The novice knows she must distract the teacher to break her control over the water. A small tree branch reaches for the teacher, swinging its woody stem at her head. The teacher ducks under the attack, but the move fixes her to the ground. This is what the novice hopes for. The roots rise underneath the teacher and grip one of her legs. She drops an energy sphere on the offending stem, turning it into ash. Another sphere forms in her right hand. She raises it, but before launching it, more roots rise and wrap around her waist, pulling her to the ground.

"Ewen's got the upper hand," Michael says.

The Keepers scowl at him once more.

The novice races across the arena to where a small tree is. She touches it; suddenly, the tree grows to enormous proportions. The roots lift the teacher up, raising her off the ground. More roots wrap around her until only her arm is visible. Then the teacher makes a fist, and Ewen collapses, unconscious.

"What just happened?" Lucero asks.

"She's collapsed!" Michael shouts.

The roots wrapped around the teacher turn ashen and crumble. The teacher dusts off her robes and walks to Ewen. She lays her hand on the unconscious girl, who gasps loudly.

Braedan helps Ewen to a sitting position.

"Ohhh, my head. What happened?" Ewen asks.

"It's what I've been trying to tell you. You are leaving a connection between yourself and your opponent." Braedan says.

"You drew my pacú?"

"You have to sever the connection and kill the wood." The teacher reprimands her. "Outside of that."

She turns to the spectators.

"What did you think?"

"It was an excellent match, Braedan. You had her, Ewen!" Golo shouts.

"Now, you know. One mistake is all it takes." Nok adds.

The Keepers then turn to Lucero and Michael.

"That is a lesson you should also be mindful of," Golo says.

"When in battle, look for your enemy's faults," Nok adds.

"And be ready to take advantage of it," Golo says.

"But don't get complacent," Nok says.

"Victory is not assured until all is done," Golo says.

"Yes, Lady Golo," Michael says.

"Yes, Lady Nok," Lucero adds.

The boys always try to get on the Keeper's nerves, but they have a special bond and affection with the twin midges. Golo and Nok care for the boys deeply; however, they know them well enough not to fall for their rouse. The Keepers stand, kiss each of the boys, and walk away while discussing the bout.

"We will review the bout and practice the techniques," Bartolon says.

"Yes, Master Bartolon," they reply.

Chapter 13
THE MERCENARY BLESSED

The combined forces of the Lorica and the Haloguardian spend fifteen years searching the wealds of Ortet for Sceagga and Hergian. Once again, they start to encounter resistance. Though the opposing forces are not enthralled now. On the contrary, they are of free will and well trained.

The ground forces have to train harder to keep up with the enemy. They start to use flexible scale-like armor to protect themselves. On many occasions, they act as cover for the Aduncus when they fall in battle.

They follow many leads, and there are many sightings of Sceagga and Hergian, but when they get there, they are gone. Sometimes evidence points to their handiwork, sometimes a ruse. The leaders of the guard start to suspect that some of the sightings are a mere distraction to draw them away from something more significant; what it is, they do not know.

An attack on a nearby farmstead draws the guards of Merkoum. The coloner leaves Cepil, the neweguard, watching the town while investigating the disturbance. That night the neweguard decides to leave others to walk the wall's parapets and stay close to the campus gate; after all, it is the most crucial part of the city. A tramp, staggering drunkenly, catches Cepil's attention.

The poor and homeless have no place in Merkoum; there is a hospice for them on the outskirts of town, where they are fed and cared for.

The vagrant staggers to the front of the gate and stands with his back to the street. A glow comes from behind the figure.

"You, what are you doing there?" Cepil's voice booms.

He wants to make sure those on the other side of the gate hear him.

"Stop what you're doing and turn slowly!"

Cepil draws his sword.

The vagrant jumps slightly, and the glow disappears. He turns slowly towards the guard.

"What is the matter, m'lord?" he slurs.

"What are you doing by the gate?"

"Nothing, m'lord. I was cold, and the wall shielded me from the wind."

It is rather chilly.

"What was the light I saw?"

The guard on the other side of the gate opens the small window and looks through a grate.

"Is there something wrong?"

"Nothing, my masters," the vagrant says humbly. "I was going to show m'lord the small fire I made to keep me warm."

The vagrant holds out a glowing sphere.

"See."

He sees the confusion on the guard's face, and with a flick of the wrist, he hurls the sphere at him. The explosion kills him instantly. A second sphere comes from the darkness blowing out the grate on the window. The vagrant throws another sphere in the air, where it bursts into a brilliant flash, blinding the guards pacing on the wall. There is an outburst of cursing from the other side of the gate. More voices follow, but no one is there when bows are drawn. Only Cepil's charred body remains.

Two figures come to rest three blocks from the gate in a dark alley.

"Sorry, father, the gate was too heavily guarded," Hergian says.

"They must have added the extra guards recently," Sceagga says. "Don't worry, there will be other opportunities to get the young one. We will try a different approach then."

"Yes, m'lord."

"Let's go! Guards are approaching."

They blame Cepil's death on Hergian. However, no one could identify him or Sceagga. Soon, rumors begin to surface as to whether they are even alive despite the mysterious deaths of the four fishtanglers several years back and the guard's death.

Stories circulate describing the reports of the deaths as rumors created by the military to maintain control of the population. The Ortetans start to resent the continuous presence of the guards. Where there once was respect now, you have open defiance of prevailing laws. The origin of the stories belongs to Sceagga, of course.

The military turns barns and stockades meant for farm beasts into detention areas called prehensios for unruly citizens. Servience Plaitin Ruk of the Haloguardian always aspired to the next step up the ladder of command; he always wanted to be a coloner. When the civil unrest starts, they allow him to achieve his goal. They offer the charge of all the prehensios to him. Ruk jumps at the opportunity. He is soon traveling all over Ortet, keeping track of the prehensios and its prisoners. Some of the wards become familiar faces. An individual released from one location would soon appear in another. A pattern is starting to surface in Coloner's Plaitin Ruk's mind.

After many years of complaining to the government and fighting the guard, shipbuilders can now build large ships. Mayven, the only one allowed to use the channel, is asked to help design and build their vessels.

The Nauta prospers enormously from the exclusive rights to the route, and now he will help the shipbuilders. However, it is with the understanding that he will control the number of shippers. Since he is the only one with the experience and funds to design and build the ships, all parties agree to his conditions.

Mayven also designs the Haloguardian way stations. These are a series of tall towers on floating platforms constructed in the ocean. They serve as a resting place for the Haloguardian, who occasionally fly over to Sylvanus. The platform has store lockers with food and clothing for the traveling Aduncus. As part of the agreement, cargo ships rotate the stores at the stations.

Large signs placed on the platforms spell out the following warning.

KEEP OFF!

HALOGUARDIAN STATION NUMBER _#_

UNDER THE JURISDICTION OF THE CAMPUS EXERCITATUS

AUTHORIZED VESSELS ONLY

Six months after constructing the first location, a violent storm causes severe damage to the structure. A new structure is built, and it is bigger and reinforced. However, because of an oversight when ordering the new materials, the letters for the warning sign were missing. They tried to reconstruct it by *using as many pieces of the old sign as possible, but they did not find all of them, and the wordage now reads:*

KEEP OFF!

HALO STATION NUMBER #

UNDER THE JURISDICTION OF THE CAMPUS EXERCITATUS

AUTHORIZED VESSELS ONLY

In jest, those working on the stations start referring to the elite Aduncus guard as the Halo. Soon the merchants who sail by the stations also adopt the name. It does not take long for the Aduncus guard to become the Halo dropping the name Haloguardian in favor of the shortened form.

With the larger ships' launching, guarding the seas by day becomes another one of Halo's duties. The Aduncus use the stations as a home base for checking on vessels and their crew. Groundstay personnel is also assigned to the stations to patrol the area. They utilize the tielogs to rescue any in distress. They're kept in floating bunkers at the platforms. The seas do become a safer place for the Ortetans, but the unrest on the island does not stop.

As Lucero and Michael come of age, the preparations for their Maturite Ceremony are underway, a perfect time to cause disruption.

Twenty millisteps from the Port of Ortet is the city of Palisades, above Yelu's old home. Palisades blended with the original Cliffside Palisades into a large commercial center. Being the largest city on Ortet and the birthplace of Yelu makes it the obvious location for the ceremony.

Sceagga and Hergian take advantage of the citizen's displeasure with the campus guard occupation. Once again, he gathers those resentful of authority. They become the new Solois. The Solois gather Ortetans into a group with no other purpose outside of disrupting anything the Campus does.

Most of their demonstrations and gatherings are rather harmless. Halo and Lorica are usually present to ensure the crowds do not get out of control. The protests seem to spring up at different locations on the island. They keep the guard busy maintaining the peace.

On their fifteenth birthday, the twin's wing feathers change to their permanent coloration. Thus, it is determined that they have reached adulthood. The Maturite Ceremony plays an important part in Aduncus's life; it announces to the world that the individual is ready for the challenges and responsibilities society imposes on adults. It is a feast celebrated by family and close friends. However, the whole town is involved in the case of the twins.

It is time for the twins to start their devotion to the service of Eyu. Their journey to Sylvanus will begin in a few months.

At first, Yelu wanted Lucero to leave for Terrae Exterus from the Oriel on campus. However, Eage was concerned that Sceagga would find the Oriel in Sylvanus. Therefore he wanted Lucero to find it first, so it could be guarded. So Lucero will be crossing over from Sylvanus.

The festivities start early in the morning, are expansive, and turn into a town-wide celebration. After sixteen years, they still don't know if one of them is the Promised One, and the revelation is nowhere in sight. Many visitors come to partake in the momentous occasion. The guards have their job cut out, watching for troublemakers.

Michael and Lucero leave the confines of the campus and head toward the city. The flight to the town takes them several hours. The afternoon festivities are just getting started when they land on the rūnian.

All villages have rūnians where Aduncus visitors land. The skybourne walk, as a courtesy, when they are in the city, since flying around the inner city kicks up dust and creates what citizens call a common nuisance. Most rūnians are of simple design; a platform elevated one to one and a half piede or as high as a steep step. An ornamental banister, whose function mainly outlines the rūnian, surrounds the platform, usually made of wood. But, of course, larger cities use marble instead, as in the case of the City of Palisades.

After the ceremony, they head for the festivities to meet with Ewen. As planned, they find the doyenne waiting for them at the town's center, where the celebration is being held.

"Ewen," Lucero shouts.

"You boys are slow walkers. I left the temple after you," Ewen says.

"Mother had to give us the usual sermon about behaving," Michael says.

She holds out her two hands closed into fists.

"Here," she says.

She turns her hands over and opens them. There is a small seed in the palm of her hands. Immediately the seeds sprout, begin to grow, and flower. Then it dries and hardens, preserving the flowers. Ewen hands a flower to each.

"Happy birthday."

"They're perfect," Lucero says.

"You're always full of surprises. When did you learn this one?" Michael asks.

"It took me a week to figure out how to keep it from losing its color."

Michael inspects it closely.

"How long will it last?"

"They are pretty sturdy. So as long as you don't break them, they will keep."

She walks between them and hooks their arms.

"Michael, are you ready for the trip?"

"I don't think I'll ever be ready," he says. "I really don't want to leave Ortet. Will you come to Sylvanus to visit?"

"As soon as I finish my studies."

"How about me?" Lucero pouts.

"You might present a problem since you'll be going to Terrae Exterus."

She hugs him. As a soon-to-be Keeper and considered almost family, she was allowed the information.

"I don't think they'll allow me to go there just for a visit."

"Will they let you leave Ortet once you're a Keeper?" Michael asks.

"Actually, Keepers do a lot of traveling. So going to Sylvanus shouldn't be a problem."

Michael sees a young Aduncus ferm wandering in the street. She turns and smiles at him.

"Who is that?" He asks.

"Sorry, but even I haven't met all of the ferms in Palisades," Lucero answers.

"There's something about her," Ewen says.

"Yes, there is," Michael murmurs.

Michael is unable to take his eyes off her. He takes a step toward the stranger.

"You don't mind, do you?" Then walks to her without waiting for an answer.

Ewen is somewhat upset. He never abandons the group; none of them ever had. Whenever they are together, their time is sacred, and today, a day of such great importance, he wanders away.

"Michael, don't get lost," Lucero says.

"Don't worry, Lucero, meet me at the rūnian at dusk," Michael answers.

They watch him walk away with the doyenne.

"What was that all about?" Ewen asks.

"I have no idea, but he seems to have been possessed by her."

"I don't trust her; he has never done that. There is something about her that I find unsettling."

Lucero feigns surprise.

"Are you jealous?"

"Lucero, please, don't be silly."

She waves off the comment.

"When she came near, I felt something strange. I have never felt anything like that from another doyenne. It was...repulsive."

"You are really serious. That's odd...I felt the opposite. I found her incredibly attractive."

"Hmmm, curious. Keep an eye on Michael. I have to go; mother needs help with the celebration."

She kisses his cheek.

"Keep an eye on him." She repeats. "I'll see you later."

She leaves him wondering about what she said. Now, Lucero finds himself alone, heading towards the festivities. He sees the colorful tarps, food stands, and platforms with their performers. However, it now feels boring without Michael and Ewen. So Lucero decides to head back to the house.

When he turns, a smiling stranger approaches him. The middle-aged skybourne wears elegant clothes, fine jewelry, and fair hair like his.

"Ah, you must be one of the two responsible for this celebration?" the stranger asks.

Lucero immediately feels an odd sensation coming from the stranger, like standing in front of a hole. He can always sense someone's presence, but the one standing before him has none.

"Yes, I am Lucero...and, who may you be?"

"I am honored to meet you, m'lord," he said. "My name is Bullen; I am a sea caput."

"A sea caput?" he says, looking at his clothes. "Those are very expensive clothes; how can a fishtangler afford them?"

"No, no, I am the caput of a merchant ship sailing to Sylvanus tonight. I will carry some Ortetan crafts samples to see if I can start a trade business."

"A merchant's vessel? Tonight?"

Lucero stops to think for a moment.

"Not a fishtangler vessel but a merchant's vessel."

"That's right, a merchant's vessel."

"But the ban on shipbuilding had only been lifted for two months; how could you have built a ship so fast?"

"Even though it was unlawful to build the large ships, it was not illegal to prepare the separate parts for later assembly," the caput says. "In my line of business, you have to be fast if you want to succeed. Caput Mayven thought it was very creative on my part to have the ship ready for assembly, so I received the first contract."

"Caput Bullen, if I may be so bold to ask, could you possibly take my brother and me on your voyage?"

"Take you? Certainly, but...you are not talking about some sort of wild adventure, are you? Or are you running away from home?"

"Oh, no, Caput. In fact, we were to partake in such a voyage as soon as a ship was available. We just didn't know that any ships would be available so soon."

"Just where is it that you want to go?"

"My brother's is to go to Sylvanus to teach the folk of that land so that they don't forget the ways of Eyu. My destination is to cross the land and travel further north to the...villages on the foothills of Crying Mountains."

He catches himself; the presence of the Oriel is still a secret. But, in his excitement, he almost divulged the secret.

"To the Crying Mountains! I have never heard of them. Are you sure that place even exists?"

"Oh yes, it does, and from what I've heard, it is very different from Ortet. They are so big that you can always see snow in their heights."

"And where have you heard such tales?"

"From Caput Mayven. He has seen them himself."

"Caput Mayven has been to the Crying Mountains?"

"Well, not exactly; he says he saw them from the ship on one of his voyages to the north."

"Well, it sure sounds like some made-up adventure, but on the other hand, you two are set on going sooner or later."

"Like I said, I didn't think there would be a ship ready for another six months."

"Well, in that case, it would be an honor to have you two on board. I will have the crew make preparations for the journey. You find your brother and have him meet us on the Port of Ortet docks tonight. We will have to sail at midnight to arrive at the channel in time for the rippenwaeter."

"We will be there."

Lucero is excited. He thought their trip would have had to wait until later that year. But now, with Caput Bullen's ship, he will start the journey immediately.

"The name of the ship is the Fogbow. I will be waiting," says Bullen. "But understand that I have to leave at midnight whether or not you're there."

"I will be there, and thank you, Caput."

He looks around to see if anyone is near.

No one around will be bothered.

He does not waste time walking to the rūnian; he leaps into the air and looks for Michael.

For two hours, Lucero searches the town.

Where is he? It is getting too dark to see anything.

He goes back to the rūnian and waits until darkness falls.

Michael sits at the edge of the weald with the young Aduncus, Aliya. At first glance, Aliya is not outrageously beautiful. Still, something about her makes her irresistible. Of course, it helps that her tight-fitting bodice and bright red shorter than the usual skirt, visible when the wind blows her cape back, call Michael's attention. When he approached her, something happened. Now she is the most irresistible creature Michael has ever seen.

He was compelled to find out more about the ferm. So he asked her if she needed help, and, in no time, they walked hand-in-hand through the town.

"Thanks for the tour, Michael," she says. "By the way, who were the folks you were walking with earlier?" She asks.

"Folks? Oh, they are my brother and my best friend, Ewen."

"So, you're in town for the big ceremony?" she continues.

"Ceremony? uh...sort of."

He has a hard time concentrating.

"How about you?"

"I've never been to the Palisades before, so coming to the celebration was an excuse to come and see the town."

They sit to watch the sunset from the cliff-side edge of the weald.

"How far are we from town now?" she asks.

"About a half a millistep."

Aliya pulls a drinking skin from her belt and offers some to Michael. He raises an eyebrow.

"It's a fruit mixture, nothing exciting, really."

Michael tastes it. It is sweet and refreshing. He recognizes the fruit but has never had it in juice form.

"This is tanda fruit, isn't it?"

"Yes, it is," she says. "Do you like it?"

"It's refreshing; I've never had it this way before. It is usually very tart."

"We boil it first, then sweeten it." She says

She quickly changes the subject.

"The sunset is beautiful when you see it over the ocean."

"How can you not see it every day?" Michael asks.

"In the weald, you must fly up to the tallest tree to see the sunset. Even so, we can not see the ocean from where I live."

"Really, I have never lived that far from the sea. I couldn't imagine being in a place like that." Michael yawns.

"Am I that boring?" Aliya asks jokingly.

"I'm sorry; I've been up since sunrise. I must have really exhausted myself." He rubs his eyes.

"It's getting late. I have to go and meet my brother."

He tries to stand and finds himself extremely tired.

"Here, let me help you up."

She stands and starts to help him to his feet, but he rocks back and sits.

"I think if I close my eyes for a few minutes...."

He lays back on the grass; it is cool and smells fresh. He closes his eyes.

"I'll...I'll be fine."

Michael's eyes grow heavy. Finally, he draws a deep breath and falls asleep. She covers his body with branches and dried grass to ensure he is not disturbed. In six hours, he will awaken. The concoction of herbs in the juice will see to that.

Too bad, it is always the cute ones.

Aliya kisses him on the cheek, then flies back to the city and mingles with the crowd.

In the city, the young Aduncus swarm around her, trying to start conversations. Then, a large burly groundstay makes his way to her and slings his arm around her shoulder. He *gives the crowd an irate look, which causes their immediate dispersal.*

"Your manners are a disaster for my social life," she says.

"There was no one in that group that could be called 'your type,'" he answers.

They work their way to a less crowded area.

"Did you bring my package?" he says.

She slips from under his arm and pulls a pouch from her tunic.

"Here!" she hands it to him.

She is glad to get rid of the bundle.

"There's something else for you."

She also hands him a rolled parchment.

He takes the pouch and slips it into his robe. He feels a strange sensation as he stands next to Aliya; he has never given her a second look.

"Why are you staring at me?"

He clears his throat and unrolls the parchment. It is a map of Palisades City's streets and buildings with instructions on where to place the demonstrators and when to start the disturbance. This is the customary way Sceagga or his vassal, Hergian, works. He has been dealing with them for ten years now. He never knows why they want a demonstration to rise in a particular village at a specific time. Even though he suspects it is just a distraction to keep the authorities away from their real activities. He does not care why they ask for his work; all he cares about is the tender he receives for his services. They always pay very well.

The customary note, written by the sortiarius who employs him, is on the bottom. It is their personal touch, which means they are aware of his work.

Hake,

Many are the riches that will await you if all goes as planned; see that it does. As before, destroy this parchment when you have followed all instructions.

Be ready to travel when I summon you; I will need your services in Sylvanus.

Sceagga.

He never understood why they would sign their own name on the documents. Except to let him know he is trusted and that his own life will depend on his success.

"You're not going to count the tender?" she asks.

"What for? I trust the masters."

"Will everyone be in position on such short notice?" she asks.

"They will be ready."

"You start at midnight; the timing has to be perfect."

"You worry too much," Hake says, "I'll do my part."

"Good, I must go now."

Hake holds her arm.

"Why don't you stay a little while? There's still time."

"Why Hake, you've never acted this way," she says. "I didn't think you cared."

"I...I didn't think I did either," he says, letting her go.

"Bye, Hake," she says.

She leaps into the air and disappears into the night.

Hake stares into the dark sky for a few moments after she leaves, wondering why he had just asked her to stay, knowing she could not. But, for some reason, her face, smile, and scent linger in his mind, distracting him completely. He shakes his head.

Why would I ask her to stay? She is not of my liking anyway.

He opens the parchment and looks at the map once more.

I had better get to work.

He rolls it, tucks it into his purse, and heads back into the crowd, with Aliya lingering in the back of his mind.

Aliya flies to the other side of the city. She looks back over her shoulder.

"I'm sure glad Hake is a groundstay; he might have been chasing me all night."

Up ahead, between two buildings, she can make out a figure standing away from the crowd. Upon her approach, he ducks into the shadows. Like her, this one is dangerous. Luckily, he is on her side and technically her partner.

She lands on the street. There is so much commotion in the area that no one notices that she landed outside the rūnian. However, there is no need to take additional risks, so she quickly moves into the alleyway. The dark passage offers its own dangers, but she knows there is nothing to fear in this one. It has already been cleansed.

His presence is like a dark stain against her senses.

"Turmoil in the shadows," she whispers.

It's the code they use to identify each other in the dark.

She hears his movement and feels him standing next to her.

"It's been a long time Aliya," the dry voice says.

"Preparations for events like this take a long time," she answers.

There is a long pause, and then she hears Cerastes take a deep breath.

"I have your tender and your orders," she says.

He is starting to make her nervous.

"You know what to do?"

She shoves the heavy bag in the direction of his voice; he pulls it quickly from her grip.

"The same as always. Why do you ask?" He hisses.

"Good, I must go now."

"Now that our business is done, why don't you stay?"

Oh-oh!

Her mind is racing.

"What? You know what the master will do if we fail?" she says.

There is a pause; then, she hears him step away.

"I...I was just testing you. You may...must go," the voice sounds confused.

"Farengood!" she says.

Aliya leaps into the air and heads for the Port of Ortet.

That was too close.

Lucero cannot find Michael anywhere. It is late, and the time to get to the ship is drawing near. He returns and tells his mother and Eage about the merchant and the trip. She was not expecting him to leave this soon but knew that such an opportunity would not come again for a long time. She tells him to look for Michael again. He says he will but will have to go without him if the time to leave comes.

Lucero packs his clothing, places Ewen's flower in a small protective case in the bag with the glass orb, and is now ready to search for his brother. Eage bids his goodbyes and hands him a two-sectioned bracelet.

"Use this bracelet to find your way back to the cupula. It works together with the Glass. Without it, the Oriel will choose a random location. You can use the Glass and name a location. But without the bracelet, it won't be the cupula," Eage says.

Michael nods and slips on the bracelet.

Eage blesses him and walks him to the gate.

"Don't forget, if you use the Glass, do it wisely."

"Yes, Master Eage."

He flies over the ongoing celebration and realizes he will never see his brother from the air. After several passes, he gives up and goes towards the Port of Ortet. Along the way, he remembers Eage's words about the glass. He lands next to a field and pulls the glass from the pouch on his belt. He holds up the Glass in his hand.

"Michael!" he says.

A window opens before him with an image of the countryside as if witnessed by a bird. The image flies over the land and settles on the cliffside. It moves closer, but all that Lucero sees is a pile of brush.

Frustrated, he places the Glass back in its bag.

I should have practiced more with the Glass when I had the chance.

He takes to the air and flies to the dock. He is not too happy, though; he has never been away from his brother in all of his life.

Aliya arrives on the ship an hour after sunset; she knocks on the caput's cabin door as soon as she lands. Caput Bullen opens the door.

"Ah, there you are. How did your meeting go?" Bullen asks.

"As planned, he won't wake up until morning," she answers.

"Did you meet with Hake?" the caput asks.

"Yes, the currency was passed to him as you ordered."

"Good, then we should be ready to go shortly after midnight. How about Cerastes?"

"He too will be ready," she says. "Why do you keep a close eye on Hake if you trust him for your most sensitive work?"

"Soon, I will need him on the Sylvan side; I want to be sure he is as loyal as he seems."

Bullen walks to the door and calls out.

"Themer!"

Moments later, the first mate appears at the door. He is young-looking, but Aliya knows that his appearance is just a façade. After all, a sacerdoyen as powerful as he can have the appearance he chooses. Like Bullen, Themer will only show his true form when he wants to impress someone in a negative sense. For now, he chooses to look like a young man.

"Yes, Caput Bullen."

"Is the cabin ready for young Lucero?"

"Yes, Caput, and another ready for Michael, the twin," answers the first mate; his eyes drift to Aliya.

"Excellent, now we wait and see," Bullen says.

"Hello Aliya, it's very nice to see you," Themer says.

"Hello, Hergian. Why are you so nice today?"

Aliya lets his real name slip.

"Uh, I don't know?"

He smiles nervously.

"Aliya, always refer to him as Themer; we don't want any tongue slips during the voyage," Bullen says. "That'll be all, Themer."

"Yesss, sir," he says, trying to keep his eyes off Aliya; even so, he remains standing there.

Bullen closes the door on his face.

"Caput, may I respectfully request that you remove the blessing?"

The caput looks at her, then at the door where Themer had been standing, and starts to laugh.

"I guess it worked as planned," he says.

"You wouldn't believe how well," she says.

"Let's keep the blessing for now; it'll keep Lucero off-balance."

"Yes, m'lord," she sighs.

Bullen does not have to wait for long. Lucero arrives shortly before midnight with the sad news that he has been unable to find his brother. The young sacerdoyen, exhausted from the long day, is given a glass of tanda fruit juice by the first mate. He then takes Lucero to his cabin, who collapses in his bunk, sound asleep.

At midnight, a group of demonstrators appears spontaneously among the crowd with banners and signs denouncing everything from Halo's strict regulations to the campus's dealings with Mayven. Fires are set to buildings, and stores are broken into. The demonstrators are everywhere at once. Their only purpose is to attract the Halo and Lorica by causing as much damage as possible to property or the citizens.

Plaitin Ruk, also present at the celebration, quickly spots Hake leading the demonstrators. He gets the attention of the Magnus, Aureus, who is now in charge of the city's defenses. Ruk points out Hake and tells Aureus that Hake is probably at the root of the problem.

"What makes you think it's him?" the Magnus asks.

"I have seen him many times in and out of prison. I believe his actions are not random, hiding another purpose," Ruk says. "Every time he had been imprisoned for unrest, a crime of greater magnitude had been committed elsewhere."

"You think something else is going to happen?" Aureus asks.

"I'm almost certain."

Aureus calls one of his coloners over and orders the immediate arrest of Hake; he will be questioning the groundstay tonight.

He sends Coloner Garbo with five of his Halo guards.

The guards walk toward the demonstrators and stop in front of Hake.

"Citizen Hake, you are to come with us," the coloner says. "Will you come willingly?"

That is the required wording of arrest by the Halo. It offers citizens the opportunity to go willingly and receive a lighter sentence.

Today is different; Hake carries the direct orders from Sceagga, which Aliya passed on to him earlier that night. He used it to position all the demonstrators but forgot to destroy it after he was done.

It took Hake a long time to wipe from his mind the incredibly distracting attraction he had acquired for the ferm. Now that the effects of the blessing have almost worn, he does not see how he would consider relating to a mercenary like Aliya. However, thoughts of her still lingered.

Then realizes that the letter from Sceagga is still in his purse.

He reaches back and feels the folded parchment in his pouch. If the guards find the paper, they will discover that Sceagga is not only alive but behind all of the trouble for the last fifteen years.

In the back of the mob, a large groundstay stands with his face hidden under a cowl. He sees Hake reach back to the parchment showing through the bag's opening and recognizes it immediately.

Skagget! The fool still has his orders on him.

Cerastes moves closer to Hake; he will have to act quickly. Everything will be at risk if the parchment falls into the guard's hands. So he needs to create a distraction.

Garbo moves towards Hake for the arrest, but a voice sounds behind the demonstrators when he approaches him.

"They're attacking! Arm yourselves!"

A flash of steel flies by Hake's ear and strikes Garbo above his chest plate. The guard goes down.

The demonstrators pull their swords and strike first. The guards have never encountered violence from demonstrators, catching them by surprise. The next two guards go down under their swords. The Halo, whose training is better suited for the battlefield, reacts immediately with their aduncus and cuts down the revelers before they can do more harm.

Many rioters died that night, amongst them Hake. He died with a deep wound in his back. When they search his body, they find that his injury was not by an aduncus but by a Solois sword. A bag of tender and the remnants of a pouch strap on his belt give rise to suspicions. Whoever did it decided that Hake outlived his usefulness.

Chapter 14
DREAMS

Dancing Elk hears the sound of battle coming from the mist ahead. As the mist dissipates, he has an unfocused view of large, odd-looking birds flying over a battle scene, swooping, attacking a group of warriors. The warriors guard a mountain-sized stone dwelling against a mass of invaders from the land and the air. When the vision clears, he sees the birds are actually people, like him, but with wings sprouting from their backs.

His view changes, and he is now atop the stone dwelling, watching one of the winged people fighting against several winged people. The warrior uses a long curved knife. He swings it, twisting, turning, and fighting off his attackers. Then, he turns and shouts something. The view changes, and he sees who he is shouting to; a winged maiden with hair on fire.

Dancing Elk wakes with a start. That is the second time the fire-haired maiden has appeared in his dreams.

Dawn is starting to break. Dancing Elk can just make out his grandfather, mother, and sister asleep on the skins in the hut. He walks outside and sits where he's always sat for the past ten seasons, bow in hand, ready to protect the fishermen. Others are starting to stir to get an early start on the fishing. They gather their spears and gaffs or prepare the drying fires. The day before had been spent building the precarious platforms that extend over the river.

Dancing Elk sighs. He hated the trips to the river. Going in the water was not an option. So he would sit by its shore as the waters called him.

Come, young warrior, join your father.

224

Dancing Elk fingered the arrow. It angered him. he wished it were something tangible, something he could shoot at, something he could defeat.

"Father bested you," Dancing Elk murmured.

No one could hear him over the roar of the water. No one except the river spirit.

Did he? I still have him.

"But you didn't get me."

This was the only body of water big enough to swim in. Below the cascades is a pool of quiet water. This is where all the young learn how to swim. Dancing Elk never learned, and now he feared the water, not because of the spirit, but because he couldn't swim.

Long ago, he had gone to the Big Water with his father to gather clams. You couldn't live there. The water tasted strong; you couldn't drink it, and you had to use canoes for fishing. He saw the big black and white fish that swam there. Tall Tree called them *yáay*, and they were bigger than two canoes. *Yáay* was the guardian of the Big Water. *Yáay* never hunted the Taloosh, and the Taloosh never hunted *yáay*.

The river spirit did not live there, it would have been a good place to learn to swim, but he never got the chance.

So, he sits on the shore, bow in hand, guarding those fishing or playing in the water; he knows his arrows will never find the river spirit; they are for bears or lions.

You're a great warrior, Dancing Elk. Come and fight me.

The river spirit was relentless. Always challenging him, always taunting him.

"I hope you dry and the rubble of your bed be lost to the forest."

I've been here long before you came and will be here long after you're gone.

Tiglit had told him to ignore the spirit, but he could not let its taunts go unchallenged.

"Why do you want me? Why me?" Dancing Elk asks.

There is a toll to pay for fishing in my waters. You were the price.

"You have my father. Wasn't that enough?"

No, he wasn't. You were the price, and it hasn't been paid.

"Come, Tsálk, swim with me."

Dancing Elk's heart flits in his chest. It was beautiful Potwah. He is almost twenty, and soon she will be the one he will take as a spouse. He would have taken her as a spouse four years ago, but becoming the shaman came first. So he had to wait.

She had always called him Tsálk, squirrel, because he was always running around, full of energy. Maybe someday, he will tell her why he can never swim with her.

"He must keep guard, Potwah. You know that."

It was Tiglit. He, too, had been listening to the river spirit.

"We only saw a bear once. They no longer come here, Shaman," Potwah says.

"They don't beat a drum when they come. We must always be ready," Tiglit replies. "Go; Dancing Elk will watch over you."

"Bye, Tsálk. I'll bring you something to eat later."

Potwah tosses a smile at Dancing Elk and runs to join the others.

Tiglit had told him to keep his discourse with the river spirit from others. This river was the nearest that had the fish they sought. If others learned of the feud between Dancing Elk and the river spirit, they would refuse to come. They needed the fish to survive the winter.

"What did it mean when it said we had to pay a toll? Why don't we go to River Spill, like we used to?" Dancing Elk asks.

"The river spirit wanted you, but that day Tall Tree took you back and paid with his life. This angered the river spirit, so it used the flood to widen banks and push the crossing stones away. Now, the waters to the River Spill are too deep and strong."

How Dancing Elk hated the yearly trips to the river.

Chapter 15
THE VOYAGE OF THE FOGBOW

A burning arrow over the Palisade cliffs announces the beginning of the riots. The signal is meant to be noticeable. The Palisades guards also see the signal and, realizing there is trouble in the town above, leave the area to help where needed.

Caput Bullen orders his crew to lift anchor and sail for the open ocean. He watches the flames rise in the City of Palisades from the rear of his ship; he is not concerned about what the cost of his escape will be.

"How is our guest?"

Bullen does not have to look at Aliya standing behind him; he feels her presence.

"He is completely unconscious; it will be well into the day before he wakes."

"Good, to the reef, then, Themer."

"Yes, m'lord."

Under Themer's guidance, the Fogbow leaves the Port of Ortet under cover of darkness. It quietly slips away, becoming a part of the night.

It is almost noon when Michael wakes from his drugged sleep. He is somewhere on the cliffs overlooking the ocean. Brush and dried grass cover him, which he does not quite understand, and

Aliya is nowhere in sight. Michael calls her name several times, but there is no answer. It takes him a few minutes to orient himself before walking toward the town.

The tanda fruit narcotic has no residual effect, so he does not suspect it. He feels well-rested, though the extended sleep made him a little groggy. He walks that off after a few minutes.

The gentle sea breeze touching Lucero's face, lifts him out of sleep. He sits up in his bunk and finds a ferm opening the windows, letting the cool breeze and sunlight in. She wears a light cream-colored tunic, which for a moment, shows her figure when she stands against the light of the sun.

"Were you planning on sleeping the entire trip?" she asks.

He recognizes her as the one Michael was with the night before.

"I must have been exhausted."

He sits up and runs his fingers through his hair.

"Weren't you with Michael last night?"

"Oh, you knew him?"

"He's my brother."

"Oh, well, he met up with some friend, and I had to get ready for the voyage," she says. "Too bad, he was kind of cute."

"A friend? Was it a doyenne?"

"Uhhh, yeah. A doyenne."

"It must have been Ewen."

Lucero feels the gentle rocking of the ship.

"How long have we been sailing?"

"We left the harbor around midnight, and it's now midday, so it's been about twelve hours. You must be hungry; I'll bring you something from the galea."

"Galea?"

"Kitchen." She says as she walks out the door.

He changes his clothes and washes his face in the basin she provided. Aliya returns with a tray of bread, fruit, and cooked eggs. She sits with him and talks while he eats.

He finds that she has an attractive personality. She is not outrageously beautiful; however, how she dresses and carries herself makes her a striking figure.

"What are your duties on the ship?" He asks.

"I'm in charge of protecting the ship."

"Protecting? From what?"

"There has been a series of attacks on fishing vessels in the area. Caput Bullen thinks it would be wise to have us on board if whoever attacks the ships wants to try their luck with a larger vessel."

"You said us?"

"We are a group of retired Halo and Lorica guards hired by Bullen."

"How about the Halo outposts? Shouldn't they be protecting the ships?"

"They can't be everywhere at once," she shrugs. "They apparently were not present when the fishtanglers were attacked. The ocean is a vast place."

"Yes, but just because some fishtangler were attacked."

"Come with me."

She leads him to the deck. The wind is fresh and rich with the smell of the sea. He gets his first look at the ship. The crew is busy painting it, covering the dull grey color with bright yellows and greens. The design is similar to Scip Hudros, except this one is equipped with catapults on the deck.

"Look around. Do you see the Halo anywhere?"

She is right. There is not a single Halo anywhere.

"You can fly as high as you want. You won't see them anywhere; the ocean is too big."

"This is a dead area for the Halo."

One of the crew joins the conversation.

"We are at the outer boundary of the Halo's area of protection. Hi, my name is Themer; Caput Bullen's first mate."

"Pleased to meet you," Lucero says.

Lucero feels a strange sensation coming from the first mate; he, too, feels like he is not there.

"Tell me, why do we sail in these waters if they are so dangerous?"

"Frankly, because we can. With our security, we can afford to sail here, where the currents are strong and in our favor."

Lucero looks at the water spraying from the ship's bow and can tell they are moving fast.

"We'd lose almost a full day's travel if we took the safer route."

Caput Bullen must have thought of everything.

"Mother, do you have time for a question?"

"What bothers you?" Rewen says.

Rewen is helping with the clean-up after the ceremony while Eage keeps her company.

"Perhaps I should leave you two to your privacy."

"Oh no, on the contrary, Master Eage. I think I will need your advice."

"What is it then, Ewen?" Eage asks.

"Last night, I was with the twins when a stranger appeared and swept Michael away."

"Swept him away?"

"Yes, Master Eage."

"What was she like?"

"Well, that was the strange part. When she walked up to us, it felt like she was cloaked with another's pacú."

"Another's pacú?"

"It was awful. I can only describe it as a stench that could be felt."

"Interesting, and what did the twins feel?" Rewen asks.

"They were infatuated with her. She seemed to have gone after Michael, though. She stayed near Michael the whole time and kept me between Lucero and herself. It was really noticeable, but Lucero didn't see it that way. As a matter of fact, he thought she was attractive."

"Curious, you said you felt a spiritual revulsion to her, but the boys were attracted to her."

"Yes."

Eage walks over to Rewen and passes his hand over her.

"Tell me, Ewen, what you think of your mother now."

Ewen makes a foul face.

"Mother?... Master Eage, what did you do to her?"

"It's a special blessing meant to attract doyens."

"She placed a blessing on herself?"

"No, that is something that another has to do."

He waves his hand over Rewen once again, lifting the blessing. Ewen's eyes water; she runs to her mother and hugs her. Ewen keeps a hold of her mother's arm.

"Who would be capable of doing something like that?"

"Someone who has control over the pacú."

"A Keeper?"

"Perhaps."

"What are you saying?" Rewen asks.

"There is more to this underneath the surface."

"What about Michael?" Ewen asks.

"I think we better look for him."

"Who are you looking for?"

They all turn and see Michael standing at the door.

"Michael, are you alright?" Rewen asks.

"Sure, why?"

"What happened to the doyenne you were with last night?" Ewen asks.

"I don't know. I fell asleep on the cliffs; she was gone when I woke up. So it must have been my fascinating personality."

They all laugh.

Ewen walks to Michael and throws her arms around his neck.

"What's going on? You weren't jealous, were you?"

Ewen punches his shoulder.

"You wish. Why did you leave us?"

"I don't know. It was strange; it was something I had to do."

"Curious, very curious," Eage adds.

It is not until the middle of the next day that Lucero sees the first Halo. A group circles overhead while two break off the formation and land on the ship.

Themer summons Caput Bullen to the deck and waits for them. Lucero stands by out of curiosity.

"Welcome to my ship. I'm Caput Bullen," he says jovially.

"I'm Coloner Seez of the Halo guard, and this is Servience Bast," the Halo commander says. "I didn't know there were any ships this size besides the Scip Hudros, ready to sail."

"I was specially commissioned by Mayven himself to sail to Sylvanus."

"Mayven, eh?"

Themer appears somewhat nervous and moves closer.

"Yes, sir, and I carry a special passenger on my maiden voyage."

"Oh? Who may that be?"

"Lucero, come forward," the caput says, waving him over.

Lucero is surprised, but he smiles and walks over to them.

"Did you say Lucero?" the coloner asks.

"Yes, sir," Lucero answers.

The coloner looks closely at him.

"Where's your brother?"

"I couldn't find him on the night we sailed, so he will be coming on a later voyage."

The coloner grows suspicious.

Themer seems to be getting anxious and steps a little closer.

The servience leans over and whispers something to his ear; the coloner nods.

"Rumors have it that you carry a gift given to you by Eyu himself," Seez says.

"Yes, I do."

Lucero pulls a pouch from his belt.

"Would you like to see it?"

"Please," the coloner says.

Bullen has yet to see the Glass and is curious about its powers. He watches as Lucero pulls the orb from its bag. The transparent glass sphere reflects the sun as if it had been polished.

"What powers does it have?" Bast asks.

"I'm not sure yet," Lucero says.

He holds out the Glass.

"Which is your station?"

"We are at station number one."

With all the drama he can muster, Lucero holds up the Glass and says.

"Halo station number one."

Immediately a window appears in front of them. The aerial view travels swiftly over the waves until it arrives at the platform rising from the ocean. The coloner sees some of his crew cleaning up the station floors while others relax.

Lucero brings his arm down, and the image disappears.

"My pardons to have doubted your word, Caput Bullen."

"We've had sea rovers in this area. They set one of the waystations on fire. Since Mayven did not inform us of your ship—"

"Caput Mayven has had a lot on his mind lately," Bullen says.

"Yes, his business ventures keep him busy."

Seez turns to Lucero and bows.

"It's an honor to have met you, Lord Lucero."

Lucero returns the bow.

"Let's go," he says to the servience.

They leap to the air and join the rest of the group; the coloner waves down to them and leaves.

Bullen glances over to Aliya and is relieved. He looks at Themer, who shakes his head and then wanders away. Lucero is still holding the Traduco Glass in his hand.

"May I?"

Bullen motions to the sphere.

"Sure."

Lucero holds it out for him to take. Bullen is sure that he can probe the sphere with his pacú. As he reaches for it, his energy extends, touching the orb. There is a loud bang, and a discharge shoots from the sphere into Bullen's hand. The caput pulls his hand back in reaction to the sting.

"What happened?" Lucero asks.

Surprised by the sphere's reaction, he almost drops the glass. Immediately Bullen knows what happened. The Glass had repelled his attempt to probe it. His pacú is too foul for the glass.

"It must have been a clothes spark. Even though we are surrounded by water, the air is pretty dry."

Bullen rubs his hand on his coat.

"Let's try it now."

This time, he draws in his pacú, reaches out, and strokes the Glass. Again, he can feel the power but does not dare test it. He knows now that he will never be able to use the orb. However, if he can manipulate Lucero, he won't need to.

Meanwhile, the encounter with the Halo left Lucero a little concerned with Bullen's honesty.

Lucero looks out at the blue expanse before him, but he does not see the blowholes playing in the ship's wake or the small, winged fish flying out of their way. Instead, his mind is on the encounter with the Halo.

Why did Bullen have to bring up my name? The guards did not even ask for the travel authority. It is almost as if Bullen invited me to provide a passage for the ship.

He realizes the Fogbow's caput sidestepped the paperwork requirements.

Then he remembers his brother and pulls out the traduco glass again. This time he does not shout but merely mentions his name.

"Michael."

The window opens before him. The image travels over the waves and, in seconds, settles on Michael having a discussion with Rewen. They are walking down the street, he cannot hear what they are saying, but the conversation seems relaxed.

Hah! If he only knew, now I travel with his girlfriend.

Well, I am glad to see he is okay. He looks at the glass.

Hmm, I wonder why the traduco reacted to Bullen like that. But then, he was able to touch it later. So maybe it was a clothes spark after all.

Another thing bothering him is that Mayven had not mentioned to Coloner Seez anything about the Fogbow.

He was so proud of his ingenuity.

He stops to think.

Well, maybe I worry too much.

The next day, they reach the channel just before sundown. Lucero is on the deck with Bullen and Aliya, while Themer is looking out for rocky outcroppings at the bow.

"You look nervous, Lucero." Aliya remarks.

"I remember what mother told us about her passage through the channel."

"I heard the stories too; it was quite an adventure," Bullen chuckles.

"Aren't you concerned about the rippenwaeter coming when we're inside?"

"Look."

Bullen points to the current.

"The rippenwaeter is just finishing. By leaving at midnight, we arrive when it finishes, so the current has weakened and is in our favor."

When they enter the pass, the slight current makes sailing easier. Themer stands on the bow and points out to Bullen where the outcroppings are. Aliya flies overhead to ensure there are no other obstructions in the channel.

There are several spots where the ship scrapes the coral and grounds itself on the corner. However, the crew is quick to act and push the vessel off the rock with little damage to the structure.

Since Bullen had an inside spy working with Mayven, he had tidbits of information he occasionally tossed out for Lucero's benefit.

"Another project Mayven has been working on is widening the channel around this curve. It will be several months before the work is finished, but it will make the passage much safer."

I remember Mayven saying that.

When they emerge, Caput Bullen has the crew open all sails and set the course for Sylvanus at full speed. The seas are favorable, and with strong winds at their backs, they sight land late the next day. Bullen, Themer, and Aliya are on deck with Lucero looking at the forests and hills in the skyline.

"Is that the Mariner's Torch?" Lucero asks.

"Yes, the same one Yelu mentioned," Themer says.

"We will keep it to our left and sail until tomorrow. According to the charts, we should be at our destination between midmorning and midday tomorrow." Bullen adds.

Lucero watches the coastline.

"The wealds are so vast."

Around midday, Aliya leaves the ship and flies ahead. She tells him that she will prepare for their arrival at the port. Themer keeps busy doing simple tasks around the ship, always staying in sight.

By dusk, they arrive at a small town called Barbit 60 millisteps north of Ka-Mer. From the ocean, Ka-Mer is like a shining jewel. The brightly painted buildings splashed colors on the green background of the weald. However, Barbit is a different story. The small port city is drab and dirty compared to its sister down the coast. There are no bright colors, no flags or banners, and no new ships at the docks. It looks like an abandoned city the Sylvans forgot to leave.

Lucero spends the night on the ship. Early the next morning, he packs his traveling bag and is ready to leave. He leaves his room and finds the crew on deck, offloading the cargo. Aliya takes notes on a scroll while one crew calls out everything unloaded. Themer spots Lucero and waves him over.

"Morning, Themer. I see you are offloading already."

"There you are, Master Lucero," the first mate says. "I got good news for you."

A group of rough-looking groundstays with bags of gear board the ship. He recognizes most of them; it looks like they are back to continue the journey.

Bearers carrying the bulk of the heavy equipment follow them. The last one to board is an Aduncus. But, when he walks by Lucero, he feels like the Aduncus is not there.

"Where did he come from?"

Themer did not say anything for a moment.

"Him? He was a Halo who retired in Sylvanus. Many Aduncus have come over in search of other work or to retire. They use the way stations to get here."

There were five longboats secured on the deck. The bearers accommodated the equipment next to them.

"We have a group of hunters and trappers that want to go north to the mouth of the Big River. That is where you want to go. We can save you three weeks off your trip if you stay.

"They refer to the uncolonized wealds from here to the mountains as the Sylvan Forest. It is a dangerous place for those not familiar with it. The hunters can take you to the base of the mountains on their boats; that's as far as the river goes."

The news is almost too good; they have just saved him over a month's travel. Of course, flying, he could make the trip in a day or two. However, while carrying the heavy supplies he needs, he can only travel for less than an hour, then spend the nights in the wild. If he traveled by quoggen, it would take him weeks, and he would require a guide, which had not been provided since his trip was improvised.

"I can't believe it. I wondered how I would make the trip since I didn't have time to make plans."

"It's settled then. You can stow your gear again. We'll be ready to sail in a few hours."

"I'd like to go to shore and explore Barbit."

"Go ahead. Aliya!" He calls out.

"Yes, Themer."

"Master Lucero would like to see Barbit. So, take a break and go with him."

"Sure."

"Remember that we leave in a couple of hours."

"Right. I'll listen for the horn," Aliya says.

"Horn?" asks Lucero.

"The ship's bugler will sound the horn when it's time for the ship to depart," she says. "It warns any crew onshore that the ship will leave soon."

"That makes sense. By the way, where is Caput Bullen?" Aliya looks around.

"He went down to get his payment for the cargo and pay for fresh stores. He must still be bartering with the storekeeper. Let's go; we don't have much time."

Because of the Halo way stations, the Aduncus are no longer novel on Sylvanus. Even though they still draw curious glances from passersby, they do not create the attention Yelu had when she was there. Lucero is fascinated with all the different races he encounters in the marketplace. There are beings of all sizes and shapes, but the Aduncus are the only ones with wings.

The horn sounds in the distance.

"That's the ship's notice; we have to get back," Aliya says

"So soon?"

"It's been two hours. When you're done with your expedition, there will be plenty of time to sightsee."

"I guess, but this place is so fascinating."

"Wait 'till you see Ka-Mer."

"Can't we just fly back later?" Lucero asks.

"I want to be sure everything is stowed and ready for the voyage," Aliya says. "The caput is meticulous about having everything in order when he sails."

From the air, the city looks neglected. There were many abandoned buildings, and the homes on the outskirts were slowly being reclaimed by the forest.

"It looks like the people are abandoning the town," Lucero says.

"Barbit is no longer a center for commerce. You don't need a town the size of Ka-Mer as a stopover for hunters and wanderers," Aliya says.

Themer is on deck when they land.

"Not quite the Palisades, eh?" Themer comments.

"I can't believe a town could go into disrepair like that," Lucero says.

"When Ka-Mer got the attention, Barbit fell by the wayside," Aliya says.

"Maybe when you're done, you can explore Ka-Mer."

Themer looks up at the ship's banners blowing in the breeze. "With the winds blowing from the south, the trip to the Big River entrance should only take two days," Themer says. "Make yourself comfortable."

Themer and Aliya go back to their duties while Lucero roams the deck.

The trappers and hunters spend most of the trip gambling with a rune-toss game. Jorus, a tall thin Sylvan, seems to be winning all of the coins while Met, the short bearded one, loses his entire share.

One of them, Armiger, keeps to himself. He is well dressed. Though his clothes are definitely for traveling, they are of higher quality than what the others wear. Armiger avoids contact with the others, even though they call him by name to join them. However, he seems to have other things on his mind. The youngest of the group, Dag, enjoys putting out a line to catch fish. Kamir, who never lowers the hood of his robe, whittles. Fez, Mal, Argo, Blen, and Tully are losing their earnings with the runes. Teke, the mysterious Aduncus, spends most of his time high on the ship's mast in the observation nest.

For some reason, Kamir always seems to emanate darkness. His pacú seems tainted like another's pacú has mixed with his and soiled it.

Strange, maybe it's because of his past. I shouldn't trust him. I'll have to keep an eye on him.

When Lucero walks by Armiger, he gets a strong feeling of angst.

This one is different. His pacú is clean, yet, he's troubled.

He decides to approach him.

"Hello, hunter, I'm Lucero."

Armiger looks at his strange robes.

"Are you some sort of monakite?"

"Similar, I'm a sacerdoyen."

"Sacerdoyen? I've heard of your kind before."

He looks around him and sees the wings.

"You are from that island...Orset."

"Ortet," Lucero corrects him.

"Mmm, Ortet it is then," Armiger says. "I'm Armiger."

"Armiger, why are you coming on this trip?"

"Why do you ask?"

"It seems that you are troubled by something. Is this trip a distraction?"

"Well, you just answered your own question," the hunter says. "How could you tell?"

"Sacerdoyens have certain abilities; one of mine is to be able to sense the feelings of others."

He looks at Lucero.

"Curious."

"What?" Lucero asks.

"I seem to feel better when you are around."

"What bothers you?"

"Why are you on this trip?" Armiger ignores the question.

"I've been sent on a mission to teach…those on the eastern side," Lucero says.

"The eastern side? Of the Crying Mountains? I didn't know there were any Sylvans there." Armiger says.

"I've been told that several tribes are living there. They seem to be related to the Wandrien."

"Wandrien? Good luck. They are a bloodthirsty bunch."

"How about you? You seem to be better off than the rest. You really don't need the money, do you? So why are you going on this expedition?"

"Well, you have been sent on a mission. I have no mission, don't know where I'll be tomorrow, and feel like I'm wasting my life."

"And that is your torment?"

"Yes, I feel like I should be accomplishing something, except I don't know how to go about it."

He stops to think.

"Why am I telling you all of this?"

"Because it's another one of my gifts."

Armiger looks at him for another moment, shakes his head, and walks away. He needs more time to think.

Barbit was once Ka-Mer's rival for commerce. The Angry Maral was once the best inn and ealu house in Barbit. The sign above the door displayed a charging elk, casting steam from its nostrils. Only those that could afford it would lodge *there. However, when Yelu appeared in Ka-Mer, fortune shifted; now, Barbit is all but abandoned; a mere stopover for hunters and adventurers, and the faded sign on the Angry Maral showed it.*

Armiger had been drinking at the dockside inn and the ealu house, where most workers waited for jobs. He was in a foul mood. All week, Armiger had nightmares about his worthless life. After he left his father's farm many years ago to find fortune, Armiger worked hard and became well known as one of the best hunters. His pelts brought him lots of tender, and he accumulated the wealth he sought.

However, there was still a big hole in his life. He had watched the funeral of a monakite that had been a curist in the town. The poor old monach had spent all his life in poverty, giving his services to the Sylvan for free. Watching the funeral, he could not believe the number of folks showing up to mourn him. The town showed great sadness for his passing. Even before his passing, the citizens had cared for him and provided for his food and clothing. He never found himself in need. They had loved the old monach, and now he would be missed.

A month later, a wealthy trapper, who had been his partner, drowned when he fell into the river while fetching one of his traps. No one cared when he died because he had cared for no one. Armiger was the only one who went to his funeral. He had no family, so runes were thrown for his possessions, and everyone left happy for what they had won.

He realized that he, too, had acquired a fortune, and like his friend, he did not have anyone who cared for him. It was his fault because he had not cared for anyone else. Once dead, there will be no one to mourn his death; runes will be thrown for his possessions, and then he will be forgotten.

Armiger always felt there was more to his life. He knew he had been placed on Terrae for a purpose. Now, though, he realized that he had not done anything about it. Instead, he had squandered his life away.

The night before, a group of Sylvans had gotten off the ship that arrived during the night. They left the ship and made themselves comfortable in the inn. The following morning, Teke had walked in looking for a crew to go and find a passage to the Crying Mountains.

He is offering a lot of tender for the trouble.

Armiger was suspicious of the affair.

Why would he be offering to pay his own men? Unless they had contracted only to crew the ship as far as Sylvanus. Well, why not?

Armiger does not need the tender, but he does need the distraction. He is tired of wasting his life and tired of doing nothing. This trip will be different; perhaps it will ease his tormented dreams, or so he hopes.

Lucero wanders to where Aliya is finishing tallying the stores' list.

"What do you know of this Big River area?" he asks.

She looks up and smiles at him. Once again, he feels a strong attraction to the ferm.

"The Big River area is part of the unexplored territory of Sylvanus. The river originates in the eastern region, cuts a path through the mountains, and enters the Sylvan Forest, where it meanders until it flows into the ocean. The hunters *hired to go up the river will chart the area for future development."*

"Who will be paying for the expedition?"

"I hear Mayven is funding the expedition."

"Really, Mayven? He never spoke of it."

"I don't know much about it, but that's what I heard."

Once again, Mayven's name comes up when there's profit to be made.

Chapter 16
ARIEL

The *Fogbow* follows the coastline for the next two days. Finally, early morning of the third day, the ship clears a small peninsula, and the mouth of the Big River comes into view. Low ground and swamp surround the delta. It is a vast expanse with the foothills of the Crying Mountains as a backdrop.

Lucero is packed and ready to go. He watches the crew lower the rivercrafts and load all their equipment and supplies.

Aliya is busy most of the morning but takes time to talk with Lucero as they load his packs.

"Are you ready?" she asks.

"Ready and eager to start," he says. "Where's Caput Bullen?"

"He flew back to another entrance we saw on the way here," she says. "He wanted to see if there were other entrances to the river."

"I haven't seen him since we reached Sylvanus; too bad I wanted to thank him."

Lucero is disappointed.

"Don't worry, he is a busy fellow," she says. "He did make arrangements for you to have a guide."

"A guide?"

"Yes, he thought it would be best if someone familiar with the area and creatures of the land accompanied you."

Aliya turns towards the voyagers.

"Teke!" she calls.

The Aduncus trapper walks over. Teke is older than the other voyagers but looks the strongest except for Armiger.

"Teke, this is Lucero. As per your agreement with the caput, he will be your charge. Therefore, his safety will be in your hands."

The Aduncus bows low.

"An honor Lord Lucero."

"Aliya, this is not necessary," Lucero protests. "Now that I'm here, I have the means of finding my way around; I don't need a guide."

"He is more than a guide; he has spent many years trapping in the Sylvan Forest and knows the races and creatures in this area."

Once again, Themer materializes out of nowhere. "Besides, he is looking for a path through the Crying Mountains to explore the lands beyond," Themer says. "Isn't that where you're going?"

"I will be honored if you allow me to accompany you," Teke says.

Lucero expected to make the trip alone. He cannot look for the Oriel with someone following him. Once again, his senses tell him that Teke is not there.

"Well, it would be nice to have company, but you understand I will go towards the wailing caves; some tribes live near them."

When the wind blows through the caverns found in the area of the Oriel, they make an unearthly sound.

"Well, m'lord," Teke says. "The caverns in the mountains you seek are haunted by the sceadu, evil shades that dwell within. I am afraid you will have to go there alone. I would not go there for any amount of tender. You may be protected from them, but I'm not," Teke says. "But, I will point you in the right direction."

"Very well, then, I now have a traveling companion."

"Thank you, m'lord," Teke repeats his bow.

"Aliya, please tell the caput that I can't thank him enough for what he's done."

"I will, Lucero, and we might see each other again when you return."

"I will like that."

She leans over and kisses his cheek.

She catches him by surprise.

"This is for good luck."

"Uh...thanks,"

"Lucero, have a good trip. You're in good hands with Teke."

"Thanks, Themer, he will be a great help."

Lucero lowers himself into the rivercraft and sits in the middle, out of the hunters' way. He sees Aliya and the first mate wave as the craft pulls away.

They row the longboats towards the river. Lucero does not need to ride the boat onto the mainland, but he knows they would have to come to shore to pick him up once the trip starts.

This craft will surely capsize if he tries to land on it. There are five rivercrafts in the group. The first and last carry the food, while the three in the middle carry the equipment.

Once they enter the river, Teke identifies all the creatures he sees. He goes to great lengths to explain where they live, what they eat, and their habits. Progress is slow, as they are going against the current, so there is plenty of time to watch and study the local fauna.

"Have you gone this way before?" Lucero asks.

"No, no one has by rivercraft," the Aduncus answers. "I was curious about the river, so I flew over it yesterday. There is a small lake several millisteps upstream; the river continues from there."

They camp along the river's sandy shore that night. There are strange-sounding animals in the weald around them, and

Lucero notices that Jorus, Met, and Armiger are armed and guarding the perimeter.

"Why the guards?" Lucero asked.

"The creatures here are not like those in Ortet; they will attack us if they think we will make an easy meal," Teke explains.

"Aggressive creatures?" Lucero is baffled.

"Yes, on Ortet, since all the energy flows through there, their needs are provided. Therefore, most of their aggressiveness is gone. However, they are not taken care of here; the creatures must fend for themselves. Here they fight, kill, and eat each other," Teke says.

He pokes Lucero's chest with his finger.

"It will be for your own good that you remember that. You are a sacerdoyen; don't hesitate to use your powers to protect yourself."

Lucero has a hard time sleeping that night. He has many nightmares where he has to use upashims to kill beasts that attack him. Somehow though, he likes the feeling the power gives him.

At daybreak, they have a quick breakfast and continue their journey. By midmorning, they reach the small lake. Crossing the body of water is more comfortable since the current is negligible. The five rivercrafts break the single-file formation and travel side by side while the Sylvans chat. Teke chose to go in a different rivercraft because his was riding too low. As they pass the halfway point in the lake, there is a loud splash by the shore to their right, and they all go quiet.

Teke looks intensely at the water between the shore and the boats. The nose of a large creature breaks the surface with a loud hiss and a cloud of vapor one arrow's flight away from the boats; Teke gives the alarm.

"Krokewurm! To the river, hurry!"

Those guiding the rivercrafts start to paddle frantically, trying to make it to the mouth of the river on the opposite end. Those without paddles grab pots, pans, and whatever they can to help with the paddling.

The creature moves effortlessly through the water closing the distance to the boats. A second hiss and another cloud of vapor follow.

"Archers! Where are the archers?" Teke shouts.

The men with the pots and pans let go of the utensils and started stringing their bows. A complicated task on land becomes almost impossible in the confines of the rivercraft.

The first krokewurm disappears below the surface; the crew becomes more frantic in their paddling.

"Save us, master!" they shout.

Lucero's mind is racing.

They are asking for my help.

The boat with the heaviest equipment starts to fall behind. Jorus and Armiger are in that one because they are the strongest in the group.

Teke's rivercraft is just ahead of Lucero's; the Aduncus turns and waves for them to hurry.

"Master, help us!" Jorus calls.

Lucero does not know what to do, but then he notices something. The men are not calling for him; they are calling for Teke.

Why do they call for—?

There is an explosion behind him. The Krokewurm came up from the depths and struck the bottom of the last rivercraft, splitting it in half.

The creature surfaces next to one of the hunters. It has a long, broad head covered with pebble-like plates. Thorny scales protrude over its eyes; a row of teeth is visible, giving the animal a permanent, malevolent grin. He cannot see the animal's entire length; however, estimating the size in proportion to the head makes the creature over fifteen strides in length.

In horror, Lucero watches the beast lazily grab the screaming Jorus as it would a random, floating snack. Then, it tosses him in the air and swallows him with two loud snaps.

Lucero, who never witnessed an unnatural death, is horrified. There are three Sylvans left in the water. They are swimming frantically, trying to catch up to the closest rivercraft, but it makes no effort to slow down. The krokewurm swims lazily towards his next meal while the other reptile moves in. Lucero watches as the swimmer pounds the water furiously, trying to outdistance the krokewurm. The Sylvan tries to call the boat but chokes on the water. Lucero sees him turn to face the beast; it is at arm's length from him. The animal leisurely opens its mouth to grab the meal that has given up all hope of escape.

Lucero recognizes Armiger; he stops struggling and now waits, facing his death. The sacerdoyen calls on his energy and creates the upashim in his hand. He raises his arm to throw the sphere, but a strong emotion comes over him that causes him to hesitate.

He feels something familiar, something he had felt before. However, the krokewurm closes its mouth and quickly sinks. Lucero dissipates the energy sphere and waits, expecting the animal to pull Armiger under. Instead, he hears the hiss from the animal's snout coming from his left. He turns and sees the reptile surfacing and slowly swimming away. The second animal also loses interest in its prey and heads back to shore. Armiger does not move; he stays there, slowly treading the water.

"Armiger!" Lucero calls. The Sylvan does not answer.

"Turn around! Pick them up!" Lucero shouts.

"But master, they may return." The boatmen are terrified.

"Do as he says!" Teke shouts.

Armiger turns to see what is happening; Lucero shouts the orders at the rest of the crew. Finally, seeing that the beasts have lost interest in them, he orders the boatmen to comply and pick up the survivors.

It is said that when faced with certain death, an individual undergoes a complete transformation. Armiger weighed what he had done with his life with what he could have accomplished. Now, he realizes he was placed on Terrae for a higher reason, not to become a morsel.

When Armiger looked into the creature's mouth, thumb-sized teeth lined its jaws like tree saws with shreds of Jorus's tunic still clinging to them. He waited for the krokewurm to end his life. Instead, everything slowed to a standstill; the creature was frozen in place, its mouth open, its eye staring. He looked back and saw Lucero kneeling on the rivercraft, ready to throw a glowing sphere he held in his hand. The boats stopped, and the men stopped; he could swim to them, but he stayed for some reason, which did not make sense.

"Armiger," said the voice.

The Sylvan turned, but no one was there.

"Armiger," repeats the voice.

"Wh...who...calls me?" he stammered.

"Listen," the voice said. "Follow my path, do my will, and teach my children."

"Who are you?"

"You know who I am, look inside, and you will know me."

Armiger knew who it was but did not want to accept it; it was the one who gave him the life he was wasting. He was the one Armiger had given up on.

"Help."

His plea was not for salvation from the beast but for himself.

"I am calling on you to do my work. You will know where to go, what is needed, what to do, and when the time comes, your main responsibility will be revealed to you."

Armiger feels an enormous unwanted burden slide off his shoulders, replaced by a heavier yet more desirable one.

"From now on, you will be called Ariel, the aria for my song. Your lone voice will spread the melody of my way."

"Please forgive me."

"Because you have asked, your misdoings will be forgiven, you will be spared, for I have work that needs to be done, and I have chosen you to do it. However, I place a blessing on you that forever will be your burden. With time, it will be revealed to you."

Then, all returned to normal. Armiger heard the cries of the men once more and could smell the krokewurm in front of him.

Was that a dream? Is that what the last seconds of life are like?

Armiger held his breath, waiting for the end; however, the monster closed its jaws. His unmoving eyes stared as a reminder that such events were not normal. Then it sank beneath the surface. Then, the second krokewurm turned and slowly swam away.

Armiger is in shock; he does not hear those on the rivercraft call to him or feel them when they lift him out of the water; he lies staring at the slow-moving clouds.

The remaining rivercrafts make it into the river; they work their way upstream until they feel safe enough away from the lake to stop. Then, they take the survivors to the shore, where a campfire dries them off. A warm lunch settles nerves while Teke talks about the krokewurms.

"The larger reptiles like to live in the larger bodies of water, while the younger ones live in the rivers and streams that flow in or out of the lake. The younger animals pose no threat to us. So, you can relax now that we're back in the river," Teke says.

Lucero notices Armiger alone, deep in thought, staring at the flowing waters. He approaches the hunter and sits by him.

"How are you feeling?"

"I'm fine. It was probably the best thing to happen to me, sacerdoyen."

"Oh?"

"Up to now, I have just been working for myself to fund my personal entertainment. Then, this afternoon, as I looked down the throat of that animal, I realized that nothing I had done would have amounted to anything of importance. I would have died, and no one would have noticed or cared. Then He came to me."

"Who?"

He turns and looks at Lucero.

"Eyu."

"Eyu came to you?"

"Yes, as a voice."

He stands, stretches, and then looks at Lucero.

"He told me what I had to do; he has given me a second chance."

"Are you sure, Armiger?"

"Armiger? No, not Armiger anymore. He called me Ariel, the aria for his song, his message."

"You were very close to death, Armiger—"

"Ariel," he repeats.

"Ariel, you were very close to your death. Such experiences can place a lot of stress on you."

"You don't believe me," he says with a smile. "Why didn't you throw the light sphere at the creature?"

"The light sphere? The upashim? How did you know about the upashim?"

Armiger shrugs.

"How did you even see it? Your back was turned?"

"I saw you. Kneeling in the rivercraft, ready to throw the...upashim you had in your hand."

"Your back was turned," says Lucero.

"Yet I turned and saw you in the boat, upashim in hand, ready to attack. Then, I turned back. It was you that didn't see me."

"You didn't have time," Lucero argues.

"I was given the time," Ariel says.

Lucero stares at him.

The time to create the upashim and get it ready was not enough. Yet, he said he turned and saw me. Then there was that emotion I felt.

"I know if you had been killed back there, there would be those who would have cared, who would have missed you."

"I have been called to do more important things," Ariel says.

"You have done things of importance in your life, and I am sure you are now on a mission to do important things."

"It's not the same. I have been chosen; there are things I must do."

"Not everyone is chosen to do the work of Eyu," the sacerdoyen says.

"No, but when you are called to do it, you go," he says. "I've been called."

Ariel, as he now calls himself, picks up his gear.

Teke sees him leaving.

"Armiger, wait," Teke says.

"Ariel, the name is now Ariel."

"Ariel, we need you. With Jorus gone, we are shorthanded," Teke grabs his arm. "I will double your tender...triple it."

"Sorry, Teke, but I must go," Ariel says, gently pulling Teke's hand away.

Ariel waves to them and disappears into the weald.

Teke looks at his hand.

What was that strange sensation emanating from him?

They watch as the hunter, so sure of his calling, leaves on his journey.

Emotions start to build in Lucero's chest.

Why was he called? Why him? He is just a hunter. Why has He never called on me if I am the Promised One?

Lucero is having a hard time coping with that fact.

Eyu has called on the one Sylvan who has never done any good in his life.

Why?

Clouds of doubt start to gather over Lucero.

They continue their journey without the hunter. The men work hard at their paddles since, once again, they are going upstream. They camp that night with the Crying Mountains looming in the distance, a solid wall of rock from north to south that separates the Sylvan forests from an unknown land.

After dinner, Lucero sits by the river, looking at the faraway mountains.

"Magnificent, aren't they?"

Once again, Teke walks up to Lucero without his knowing.

"Teke, why can I feel everyone else's presence but not yours?" Lucero asks, a bit annoyed.

"Other sacerdoyen have said that I've been in the weald too long, and my soul is like an animal's. Perhaps since I come from Ortet, I do not throw an essence in this land."

Throw an essence? How odd that a hunter would use those terms.

Lucero knows something is different about Teke, and Teke does not seem to know what it is.

I can detect the pacú of any living being around me, including animals, something I was told is unusual. But Teke does not leave any kind of spiritual footprint.

"To answer your question, yes, they are magnificent," Lucero says. "This is the first time I see mountains. It's hard to imagine how big they are until you see them yourself."

"The caverns you seek are further to the north," Teke says.

"How far will you take me?"

"There are tales of a path through the mountains, somewhere near the gurges where the river flows," Teke says. "The walls of the gurges are too steep to climb, and the river flows too fast to navigate."

Lucero can see the chasm in the mountains cut by the river.

"I have an idea of where the path is so that the rest of the crew can pass," Teke says." That will be as far as I take you. From there on, you can fly; you will be on your own."

Teke is right; for the Sylvans to access the land on the other side, he will have to find a negotiable path.

"That will be more than I expected; thank you, Teke," Lucero says.

He walks back to the campfire while Lucero trails him with his pacú.

Does he purposely hide his pacú; he has to be some sort of sacerdoyen to have that capability. I wonder if he even knows that he possesses the ability.

Lucero learned, while on campus, about Ortetans and Sylvans. They could go their entire lives without knowing that they had sacerdoyen powers. Some knew they had it, but they would consider them gifts; however, they never developed them past that stage. Without proper training, their gifts are wasted.

If Teke knows he has the gift and is hiding his pacú on purpose, that would be the equivalent of someone trying to remain hidden from view. I do not know if I can trust him.

Well, soon enough, we will both go our own ways. So, he will no longer be of concern.

There is a lot of activity on the river's opposite shore during the night. Lucero can feel a group of large beasts wanting to cross the river. Their intent is to satisfy their hunger with the crew.

Lucero is up and standing by the shore, watching the other side. Though the moon is full, he cannot distinguish the shadows moving on the other shore. He feels darkness cross his pacú behind him. It is like a black cloud crossing the sky on a starry night. Though you cannot see it, you know it is there.

"Hello, Teke," Lucero says.

He feels a slight leak in the other's pacú as his surprise at being detected distracts him for a split second.

I knew it!

"Hello, m'lord."

Teke tries to act normal.

"What are those out there?" Lucero asks, changing the subject.

"They are barghest, m'lord, nighthounds. They are pack hunters and aren't afraid of attacking anything larger than they," Teke says. "Not that there are too many creatures larger. Luckily, they need particular conditions to breed, so there aren't too many of them, and their packs are never too large."

Barghest! Those creatures are not of normal birth; they are made.

"They seem to be hungry," Lucero says.

"They are always hungry, m'lord. But, lucky for us, the river flows too fast in this part, or else we would have to deal with them."

"I did notice the strong river current; how will we continue?"

"We will have to transfer our boats and gear on foot tomorrow. The river widens and deepens about three millisteps ahead; we'll put down there."

"Will we have enough crew to move all of the equipment?"

"We'll have to do with what we've got."

They break camp early the next morning and head east towards the slower waters. Lucero carries one of the food packs, while the other crewmembers handle much heavier weights. The terrain is rough, and there are places where they have to pass the boats over fallen trees and boulders that block their way; it is an exhausting journey.

It is midday when they arrive at the location, a sunny clearing by the river's edge. The ground is flat, and the trees are sparse. It would have been a perfect place to camp for the night. However, the travelers are less concerned with the site's looks than with getting on with the trip. The portage to the calmer waters is harder than expected. It was early, but the exertion made them hungry. All decide upon a meal of dried fruits and bread, washed down with river water.

Once rested, the hunters start packing the rivercrafts, ensuring the weight is properly distributed. Lucero hands the packs to them while Teke tells them where to put them.

"I guess my equipment didn't finish the journey," Lucero says.

Teke looks over the packs and equipment.

"It must have gone down with Jorus and Armiger's craft."

"Master Teke, we will be ready to leave in fifteen minutes," Argo says.

Come to think about it, Argo's pacú is like Kamir's and Dag's.

What is Teke to them? They treat him like their master.

Then Lucero feels it; he stops and faces the weald.

"What is it, m'lord," Kamir asks.

"Teke!" calls the sacerdoyen. "It's the barghest; they're coming."

Teke looks into the woods.

"Are you sure?" he asks.

Can he feel animals too?

"Positive."

"How far?"

"A little over a millistep."

"They must have gone further down the river and crossed."

Teke stirs the group into action.

"Finish loading! Hurry! Kamir, get the food on the boat. Mal and Argo get in the river and hold the boats ready; Blen and Tully, get your bows and cover our exit."

Two minutes later, the first animal breaks through the trees. They shoot it down immediately; however, there are eleven more beasts, and they all emerge at a full run. Another volley of arrows shoots down the next two, but they do not have time to reload.

Blen is closest to the tree line; he drops the bow and reaches for his long knife. Before he can draw it, a barghest leaps and lands on Blen, his weight crushing the hunter. It immediately begins tearing the body. A second barghest rushes in, wanting a share of the prize, and fights with the first.

Lucero becomes enraged at the beasts brawling over his companion. His upashim sends the beasts twisting in the air. But the energy sphere drains him; he feels the energy loss. He rushes to the wounded animal and draws its pacú before it dies.

Tully faces the onslaught with his long knife in hand; the first barghest comes bearing down on him at full speed. It leaps, but an energy bolt knocks it aside. The upashim incinerates the animal killing it instantly.

Tully turns and sees Lucero walking slowly as he generates thumbnail size upashim, which detonates once inside the beasts. The barghests keep coming out of the weald, but the upashims rain on them without mercy. With every step Lucero takes, the grass beneath his feet withers and dries as their energy is drawn. If a barghest survives the blasts, Lucero draws its pacú. A barghest, wounded by arrows, attempts to flee; however, the sacerdoyen flies to it and kills it with a touch.

Something deep inside Lucero awakens, and the more energy he draws and devastation he brings upon the barghest, the more exhilarating it becomes. The air around the campsite smells of charred hair and flesh. Lucero becomes voracious and seeks any living creature, drawing its pacú to quench his need.

Over and over, he throws the upashims and feeds until all the barghests are dead.

Spent, Lucero collapses to his knees and drops face down on the withered grass. He takes a deep breath; it smells like hay.

He rolls on his back and stares at the sky; inside, he still craves the nourishment that can only come from another being.

Slowly his hunger starts to fade, and he rises to a sitting position. Lucero looks at the voyagers, staring in awe, and for a moment, contemplates what it would be like to feed on one of them.

"M'lord, it's over; no more of them are left. You can stop now," Tully says.

Lucero looks down and realizes he is cradling a glowing sphere in his hand. He quickly reabsorbs it and stands.

The clearing looks like a battlefield. There are carcasses of animals everywhere, bushes on fire, and upturned trees.

Lucero looks down at his hands again.

What have I done?

He walks away in a daze.

I can't purge the craving for the pacú...

He shakes his head, ashamed, and disappears into the weald.

Teke looks for Lucero; he backtracks the trail they have come in on and finds him sitting on a rock by the river.

"Are you alright, m'lord?"

Lucero feels him coming; it is getting easier to find him now that he knows what to look for or notice missing.

"That should have never happened back there," Lucero says.

"M'lord, we would all be dead now if it hadn't happened. But, as it turned out, only one died."

"I lost control and enjoyed it." He wipes a tear with his robe.

"You didn't lose control," Teke says. *"You did exactly what was necessary to eliminate the threat, and then you stopped."*

"How come it didn't feel that way?"

"Because you have never used the energy before. The exhilaration comes with its use, then it dies off when you stop."

"How do you know that?" asks Lucero. *"How do you know what it feels like?"*

"To tell you the truth, you are not the first sacerdoyen I have guided through this land. I also guided a sacerdoyen called Katta and later Eage when they went to the mountains. They had a similar run-in with feral papios."

"Papios? What are papios?"

"A large ape trained to do battle," the hunter says. *"They had been the offspring of a battalion. Unfortunately, they had lost their trainer in battle. Without a trainer to guide them, they became feral. Papios are very dangerous beasts, like the barghest but with intelligence."*

"Intelligence?"

"Yes, the sacermagi had to kill a group of intelligent beasts or be killed by them."

"I see."

"They, too, felt the loss of the papio's lives and the shame that accompanied the deed."

Lucero is silent for a moment.

At least, barghests are not elevated to the level of an intelligent creature.

He takes a deep breath and stands up.

"Thanks, Teke."

He pats the guide on the shoulder as he walks by him. Once again, he gets a familiar sensation when he touches Teke but dismisses it.

Teke watches the sacerdoyen walk away.

Ah, yes. Lucero enjoyed using the upashim, and then he regretted it. He is now ready for the next step when he starts hungering for it.

Teke follows Lucero back to camp.

Lucero walks through the campsite. He sees the charred bodies and smoldering bushes. However, what impresses him the most is the path of dried grass.

Most of the upashim's energy came from it, but the most powerful blasts came from the energy he got from the barghest. Those were the ones that uprooted and toppled the surrounding trees.

If I had touched the hunters when using the energy spheres, I would have reduced them to dried shells.

The energy from the grass gave him a feeling of exhilaration. Still, the feeling he received from the fallen beasts had been greater.

I wonder what the energy from a person would feel like.

He quickly dismisses the thought.

What am I thinking?

He gets in the rivercraft and sits there, waiting for the last leg of the journey to start.

Teke is right; the width and depth of the river make the waters easier to navigate. As a result, they make good time and reach their last stop well before nightfall.

The loud roar of the river as it pours through the gurge between the mountains fills the campsite; the waterfalls in the chasm make river navigation impossible.

The sound of a woman weeping fills the background behind the waterfall's thunder; it is the wind as it rushes through the caverns in the mountains.

"That sound makes my hair stand on end," Lucero says.

"It's what gives the mountains its name. From here on, the hunters will carry the rivercrafts across the mountain path if I can find one." Teke says.

That afternoon Teke disappears. Lucero finds Kamir, Tully, Argo, and Fez sitting around the campfire, roasting the fish they had caught.

"Where's Teke?" Lucero asks.

"We don't know, M'lord. He said something about looking for the place where the wind howls. He said it sounded different from the wailing sound and thinks it may be the path he is looking for," Kamir says.

"Strange, he didn't mention it. I could have gone with him."

"He is very impulsive about such things. He gets an idea in his mind and goes for it." Argo says.

"You'll have to get used to it. Master Teke is always rambling about, poking his nose everywhere," Dag says.

His pacú is also…tainted.

Teke returns during the night. He is up early the next morning, getting the supplies organized and ready for their trip.

"Are you ready, m'lord?" Teke asks.

"Yes, I was just packing some things for the trip." Lucero answers.

Lucero sets up his chest pack. It is lighter now since the rest of his supplies were lost.

"As I said before, I'll point you in the direction of the mountain caverns. However, I will not go any further. That's as far as I took Katta and Eage, and it will have to do for you."

"Don't worry, I'll be fine."

I still do not know much about you. Best, I keep my search a secret.

Teke pulls the crew to the side and has a word with them; he dons a daypack across his chest and flies off towards the mountains with Lucero.

As they rise into the mountains, the air gets colder. Lucero pulls on the hood of his robe to protect his ears. Finally, they reach a rocky outcropping where Teke motions Lucero to set down. The wind has died down, but the air is still frigid.

The hunter points to the next peak across the range.

"Do you see the area where the shadows are?"

Lucero looks at the scree on the mountainside and sees dark patches amongst the fallen rock.

"Yes."

"Somewhere amongst the rubble, you will find the entrance to caverns; you might find the tribes you are looking for there. If not, keep following the foothills," Teke says. "Good luck."

Teke and Lucero wave at each other.

"Thanks, Teke. Maybe we'll see each other again."

"Maybe we will. I'll be getting back to my fellow travelers now. Good fortune in your search."

"To you as well," Lucero replies.

Teke leaps into the air, waves from above, and flies back towards the camp.

Lucero follows him as best as he can with his pacú. Soon, the emptiness he leaves dissolves into the background and melts with the pacú of other life forms.

Satisfied that Teke is gone, Lucero takes the glass from its bag and calls out, "Oriel!"

Immediately the image of the mountains appears before him. The scenery passes as the view follows a path between tall stone spires and under natural land bridges until it reveals a deep crag in the rock near the area Teke pointed out to him.

The view immediately descends into the darkness, following a route deeper into the mountain. Shafts of light piercing the chamber walls means it is near the side of the mountain. Finally, the view levels off and slows until it stands before a cupola. It is the Oriel, the entrance to Terrae Exterus.

The cupola is a large platform with intricately carved columns around the border that holds up a domed ceiling. A haze surrounding the Oriel with sparkling points of light gives a glowing magical appearance to the scene.

The Oriel is much more than what he imagined. Now, he must find it.

He places the glass back in its bag and flies to the path it showed him. From then on, he walks since the path winds through passages too narrow for his wings. He finds the spires and continues following the trail.

Somewhere in the back of his subconscious Lucero feels something wrong, and as he continues, the feeling grows stronger. Then, the feeling goes from bad to evil, and he starts to worry.

The rocks and shadows change in color; he feels that something wishing him harm surrounds him. He cannot see them, but he knows they are there, like when he encountered the barghest. He stops to get his bearings at a fork in the path. He recalls the view going to the left. He turns to go, but a giant hand reaches out and grabs him. The large fingers wrap around his chest, pinning his wings and arms. A giant stands, effortlessly lifting Lucero off the ground.

Just after dusk, Oing, the male ogre, had felt the strange urge to explore the other side of the mountain. His mate, Oid, also felt it. The ogres had never been to the other side of the mountains because the wailing sound unsettled them. But that night, something drove them to leave the village and cross the mountain. So, Oing and Oid gathered their sons, Ogam and Ojib, and started their trek over the mountain's snowy peak to hunt on the other side.

When they reach the trail, they settle in the rocks to rest; that's when Lucero stumbles across their path.

The stones around Lucero unfold as three more giants stand; a female and two young males, each armed with massive clubs.

"Who are you? What do you want?" gasps Lucero as he tries to struggle.

"This bird-natterfolc talks," the giant says.

The ogres and trolls refer to the people as natterfolc. Ogres only speak among themselves when utterly necessary. As a result, most of their communication consists of grunting and pointing. Ogres find human voices high-pitched. Since people socialize by talking, it becomes an annoying din that doesn't stop. So, they refer to people as natterfolc, chattering people.

"I'm not a bird-natterfolc."

"You have wings like bird; you talk like natterfolc," the giant says.

"What are you?" Lucero repeats.

"Bird-natterfolc wants to know who we are," the giant chuckles.

He brings Lucero up to his face.

The monster's face is broad with a wide, bulbous nose. His brow is thick, forming a hood over his eyes. The thick skin is leathery and has cracked and healed many times. The protruding lower jaw supports a pair of tusks that curve up as if trying to meet at the ridge of his nose. Strands of long reddish hair hang from his cheeks and the tip of his chin. Worst of all, his breath smells of rotting flesh.

He looks at the other creatures as they approach. They are thrice the size of a Sylvan, with disproportionably big hands.

"We are ogres."

"What do you want with me?"

The pressure on Lucero's chest does not let him breathe, and he sees flecks of light at the edge of his vision.

"Oid and my ogree are hungry; ogres eat bird-natterfolc."

The ogre reaches up with his other hand, grabs Lucero's head, and starts to pull. He realizes that the ogre will tear him into pieces to share with the rest. He feels the nails of the creature digging into his shoulder and neck.

The words of Teke come into his head. 'You did what was needed.'

He is right. I have to do it again.

Lucero draws in the ogre energy.

Without a grunt, the ogre topples to the ground; Lucero rolls out of his hand and lays on the ground gasping for air. The other ogres pause, confused.

"Oing?" The female grunts.

"Oing?" Repeats the older of the young.

Lucero rolls to his feet. The energy of the monster courses through his veins, and he likes it. It is an incredibly sweet, fulfilling sensation, and he wants more.

"Bird-natterfolc killed Oing," the female says. "Ogam...Ojib, kill the bird-natterfolc!"

Lucero forms a upashim in his hand and is ready to throw it. However, he feels the drain on the delicious sensation.

No, it is too good to waste.

He reabsorbs the upashim and replenishes the feeling. The two young ogres charge him, wildly swinging their clubs. The youngest is not as coordinated, and he strikes a boulder reducing it to gravel.

The ogre's pacú increased Lucero's speed tenfold. He easily sidesteps the younger ogre and grabs his massive arm as he stumbles past. It falls dead. His energy level rises again. The feeling is good; he wants more. His is a blur as he attacks the second youth in mid-swing; he, too, collapses. Oid sees her entire family killed in a matter of seconds. Oid turns to run, but she's too late. Lucero comes from behind and touches her shoulder; she falls on her second step.

A feeling of ecstasy flows through his entire being. He stands there and lets the feeling settle inside him.

Maybe if I do not use it, it will remain.

He looks around, disappointed that there is no more for him to consume.

I wonder if they were the sceadu Teke was scared of.

He takes a deep calming breath and continues following the trail without realizing he is being watched.

Teke eases himself from behind a boulder; he sees everything. The night before, Teke had used his pacú to persuade the ogres to cross the mountain, setting the ambush on the only path that meandered through the mountain.

Lucero had finally drunk the pacú of not only a living being but also an intelligent being, and now he craves more. Teke has found the right sacerdoyen. Now, he has to train him.

Lucero does not notice Teke's presence. His ecstasy distracts him for the moment. He probes for more dangers when the feeling settles into a more manageable state. He accepts the hunter's lack of presence as a part of his surroundings and does not detect him.

Lucero continues up the path until he finds the entrance to the cavern. He sends his pacú ahead and finds it devoid of life, so he enters.

Lucero follows the trail to the cavern's depths for the rest of the day; it is almost midnight when he reaches the Oriel.

The scene is more enchanting than the glass had shown him; a haze that seems to have points of light covers the entire area. The Oriel sits in the center of a pond illuminated by it. The water constantly ripples as if someone were walking in its shallows, but no one is there. Flagstones are present, affording a series of stepping stones for crossing.

Lucero crosses the pond and enters the Oriel. He takes the glass out of its bag and holds it up.

"Terrae Exterus!" he says.

There's a hiss, and a window shows a wooded countryside. Trees, heavy with moss and moisture, are everywhere. Lucero puts the glass back into its pouch, but the image remains. He twists the bracelet on his arm to activate it. When it's time to return, the bracelet will take him straight to the cupula. He steps off the Oriel and into the other world.

Teke emerges from the shadows in the chamber and quickly crosses the pond. Using his pacú, he places a wedge in the window to keep it open. He only has moments to make his move before the blockage collapses. When Lucero steps into the forest, he jumps into Terrae Exterus as the window closes behind him.

Caput Mayven has been away on a trip for the last two months supervising the re-building of a way station destroyed by fire. Coloner Seez decides to visit the reconstruction and say hello to Mayven, who he has known for many years.

"Mayven, how's my old friend?" he calls.

Mayven looks up and sees the Aduncus; he waves to him to come down.

"Coloner Seez, how are you doing?"

Mayven steps back to give the Aduncus room to land. Seez lands on the deck with a heavy thump.

"Greetings, I hadn't seen the damage and heard that you were almost done with your work. So, I wanted to see you before you left."

"You didn't see the damage?" Mayven asks.

"No, I've been on Ortet dealing with the aftermath of the twin's maturite celebration. Come to think about it, the platform caught fire around that same time. When that ship you commissioned came through here."

Mayven frowns.

"What ship is that?"

"If I remember the name correctly, it was the "Fogbow! Yes, Fogbow."

"Fogbow? I have never heard of such a ship."

"Sure you have; Yelu's boy was on it, Lucero."

"This is serious, Coloner Seez. Are you sure it was Lucero?"

"Of course, he even showed me the glass orb. He used it for me to see my station."

Mayven stops to think.

"Is there something wrong, Mayven?" The Aduncus asks.

"There is no Fogbow, nor are there any ships planned by that name."

"But Lucero was on board; who could have made that ship?"

"Only Sceagga," Mayven says.

"Sceagga? Are you sure? How about the boy?"

"Maybe he had him under his control, or Lucero didn't know it was him. Either way, I'll have to go back to talk with the Decanus."

"By Eyu! He was within my grasp."

"That doesn't matter now; if you didn't recognize him, he was disguised. Only a sacerdoyen could have seen through the guise. I'll leave right away."

"I'll accompany you. I will have to give a report," Seez says. "I'll go back to my station to let them know. I'll catch up with you later."

"I'll see you then," Mayven says.

Fifteen minutes later, the Nauta returns to his ship and heads back to Ortet.

The next day Seez catches up with the Hudros, and as soon as they dock the ship, Mayven and Seez rush to Eage. It takes him two days to make his way up to the town of Merkoum, then several more hours to get to the campus gates. Coloner Seez does not wish to go inside without Mayven, so he waits for him at the gates.

Both are old friends of the sacerdoyen, so no questions are asked as they enter the greeting chamber.

Eage enters the room, assisted by Bartolon. Michael, who has been visiting, is also with him.

"Greetings, Caput Mayven, Coloner Seez," Eage says. "You both seem rather upset."

"Greetings, Decanus, Bartolon. Michael, I'm glad you are here. This concerns you also," Mayven says.

The Decanus sits in his chair, and Bartolon takes his place on his right with Michael on his left.

"What brings you up here?" Eage asks.

"Decanus Eage, do you recall when Lucero left for Sylvanus?" Mayven asks.

"Yes, I do. It was sudden; he had found transport on a vessel constructed in an odd sort of way."

"From what Lucero said, a Caput Bullen had managed to build the separate parts of the ship and had them ready. As soon as the ban was lifted, he joined the pieces to have a fully functional ship in a portion of the time it takes to build a new one; he called it the Fogbow." Bartolon says.

"Caput Bullen?"

"I would have taken the voyage with him, but I became...somewhat distracted," Michael said.

"Bullen told Lucero that you were happy with his originality and had commissioned him to make the first trip to Sylvanus. Lucero left on the ship." Bartolon continues.

"He built it in parts? Then assembled it?" Mayven says. "That was extremely creative on his part."

Mayven ponders on the idea. He thinks the idea is worth researching for the future.

"However, I don't believe there is anyone capable of carrying on such a project here on Ortet."

"As we were saying, Decanus, we have reason to believe that the caput of the ship was not who he claimed to be," Mayven says.

"Oh?"

"Decanus, I do not know a Caput Bullen, and I do not know of any ship called the Fogbow."

Mayven starts pacing in front of Eage.

"We believe that Bullen is actually Sceagga and is now in Sylvanus."

"He took Lucero?" Michael asks.

"Lucero may not have known or recognized him," Mayven says. "Either way, Lucero may have crossed into Terrae Exterus by now. Most likely, Sceagga has found a way of following him there."

Eage contemplates this; the situation with Sceagga is now critical. Before, they had Sceagga contained with the hopes of capturing the rogue. Now, he may have escaped into the other world.

"Maybe we can go to Terrae Exterus to get him," Michael says.

"It's no use," says Eage. "We have spent almost twenty years looking for him on this island. How are we to find him in another world?"

"Is there anything we can do?" Bartolon asks.

"We go to Sylvanus and wait. Sooner or later, he will have to come back into Terrae." Eage says.

"The Scip Hudros is at your command, m'lord," Mayven says with a bow.

"Thank you, Caput Mayven. When can we leave?" Eage asks.

"Whenever you're ready."

"Good, Coloner Seez, we will need several Halo guards to help us watch and possibly confront the sortiarius," Eage says.

"I will gather the best, Decanus."

"We sail then, as soon as we get to your ship," Eage says.

"How about me?" Bartolon asks.

"You will be coming with us," Eage says.

"But I'm to start teaching the novices in two weeks," Bartolon says.

"I will need you in Sylvanus; this is more important," Eage says.

"Yes, m'lord."

Why me? This is not fair.

A swell of anger rises in Bartolon. All he ever wanted was to teach. The only ones he ever got to teach were the twins. Now his chance to teach at the campus has disappeared.

"You won't be leaving without me, though."

They all turn to find Yelu standing by the door to the chamber.

"I heard that Mayven had come for a visit; now I find that everyone is leaving."

"Mother! How long have you been there?"

"Long enough to hear that Sceagga has made it to the other world," she says, walking inside. "How did he get in?"

Michael tells her the story of Caput Bullen, Lucero, and the trip to Sylvanus.

She sits, distressed that the rogue sortiarius may be using her son like he used her.

"Do you think Lucero is alright?" she asks.

"I do not think Sceagga can harm him, but he may be able to persuade him to join him," Eage says.

This sends chills up her spine. Yelu knows the power her sons possess. If Sceagga can harness that kind of power, he will be capable of bringing Terrae to its knees.

"I may be the only one capable of controlling Lucero," Yelu says.

"What if he doesn't want to listen?" Eage asks.

"Why wouldn't he?" she asks.

"Who knows what Sceagga may have told him."

"Then I would be the only one capable of stopping him," Michael says.

The room goes quiet. Yelu is ready to object but knows he is right. The thought of the two most powerful creatures locked in mortal combat is terrifying.

"We have to talk to him. We have to get to him first," she says.

"At all cost," Eage adds.

After gathering their traveling clothes, they leave the Campus Exercitatus for their trek down the mountain. The Halo carries Eage and Bartolon down, but Mayven will have to walk. They would have no part in carrying him. Besides, there is not a harness big enough to fit him. Moreover, the number of Aduncus necessary to lift him made the whole thing ludicrous.

They arrive at the Scip Hudros and find the Halo guards waiting for them on the ship.

Coloner Seez has petitioned the local magnus for support. As a result, the magnus placed five guards under his command.

"You ought to try growing wings," Seez jokes with Mayven.

"believe me, the last thing you want to see, coloner, is me flying over your head." Mayven retorts.

The image conjured by the thought of Mayven flying sends all of the guards into hysterics.

The trip is blessed with smooth seas. Yelu has not traveled by ship since she returned from Sylvanus. When she sees the Halo Coloner, she goes to talk to him.

"Coloner Seez?" she asks.

"Yes, Lady Yelu," he says with a bow.

It is the first time she is referred to by that title, and she likes its sound.

"I have never seen you around before," she says.

"My duty station is with the first waystation going to Sylvanus."

"Is this your flock?"

"No, they were commissioned to him by the Magnus of Ortat," Mayven says.

"Caput Mayven, you should practice your pronunciation," says Yelu. "It's Orte-it."

"Forget it, M'lady. I'll stick with Ortat or spend the rest of the day nursing a cramped tongue," Mayven says. "As a matter of fact, you may find that the Sylvans pronounce it as Ortat."

"No thanks to you," she says.

"Well, maybe I had a little to do with it," the Nauta says.

Coloner Seez spots the armband.

"Lady Yelu, which group did you belong to when you were in the Halo?"

"I was with the Palisades Group," she says, touching her bracelet.

"The Palisades? There is someone you may like to meet," said Seez. "Officer Megafeoer."

A young Aduncus with extremely wide flight feathers comes forward.

"Megafeoer?" Yelu asks. "What is your lineage?"

"My father was Gneisfeoer of the Palisades Halo Guard, and my mother was Sextefeoer, who now serves as the advisor to the townmaster."

A lump catches in Yelu's throat.

The son of Gneisfeoer! Has it been that many years?

"I knew your father; we were in the same flock," she says. "How is he?"

"He died repelling a band of Solois that had tried to take over one of the way stations four years ago."

"I'm sorry to hear that," she says and means it. "How old are you, Megafeoer?"

"I'm twenty, m'lady, but may I ask your age? You do not look any older than I do. But, yet, you knew my father."

"I am thirty-eight," she says. "I, too, have noticed that I haven't aged since I was struck by lightning that night."

"Interesting; I must seek a lightning strike to see if it works for me," he chuckles.

A throat clears from behind.

"Oh, I forgot, two other guards are eager to meet you. They, too, are from the Palisades."

"Really, where..."

"Right here, Lady Eyu." Two voices come from behind.

Yelu turns to face two Aduncus ferms; one is slightly taller and older than the other.

"So, you two are from the Palisades?"

"Yes, m'lady." They answer together.

"What are your names?"

The ferms smile widely.

"Perhaps it would be better if we showed you."

"Showed me?"

The tall one reaches into her belt pouch, pulls out a small wrapped bundle, and hands it to her.

Yelu takes the bundle, opens it, and gasps. She looks down at a carving of a bear going into a cave. She stops, rummages through her memory, then looks up.

"Pa...Pandion?" Yelu chokes

The ferm's eyes swell with tears.

"Hello, Geolufeoer."

Yelu turns to the other, "Surnia."

Surnia holds out the carving of the hunter.

Yelu throws her arms around the two.

"You are so big."

The three hold each other for the next five minutes, with tears of happiness flowing freely.

Yelu strikes up a friendship with Megafeoer, and the four spend most of their free time talking about their past. Then, when they depart, the two promise to visit Yelu when their tour of duty allows.

The passing through the channel is much smoother than her last trip; timing the rippenwaeter is an art that Mayven perfected with experience. Yelu keeps on looking into the water, searching.

"You won't see much of the fishing vessel left."

Yelu jumps.

"Mayven, you startled me. I was just curious, you know?"

"Yes, I know how you felt. I had the channel cleared as soon as possible. The debris was shifting in the currents and becoming a danger."

"Did you find?... You know?"

"No, all that was left was the hull. It would have been nice to give Eophon a decent burial."

Yelu nods.

Two days later, they arrive at Ka-Mer, where they pick up stores for the lengthy trip. Mayven asks the dockmaster about the Fogbow, but the ship did not dock at this port. However, he does offer some hearsay information on a similar vessel heading north towards the port up the coast.

"Do you think it was headed for Barbit?"

"Yes," says the dockmaster. "Though I don't know why it would bypass Ka-Mer where the stores are cheaper."

"Unless you are trying to stay out of sight," Mayven says. "In Barbit, you can buy anything, including secrecy."

He returns to the ship and waits for the stores to be loaded. The next morning, they are on their way to Barbit, Mayven's hometown, and he knows it well.

By noon the next day, they reach the port. Mayven visits the dockmaster first, but he does not get any information. It is a good way to determine how much money a ship's caput is willing to pay for his privacy. So he goes to the Angry Maral; he will find information here. It is where seamen drink their ealu and look for work on passing ships. Mayven is familiar with the place since he often looked there for crew. As he looks around, he sees several Aduncus, a common sight on the land since some have decided to move here to live.

The owner recognizes him at once and hails him over.

"Caput Mayven, you have become too prosperous to be seen in Barbit."

"Hello, Spile; looks like you are doing fine without my help," Mayven says.

"This is the start of the fishing season; they hope to get picked up for work. Besides, I'm the only decent inn in town," Spile says.

He nods towards the group seated around the room.

"I guess you are not here to pick up a crew, are you?"

"No, I'm here for information," Mayven says on a serious note.

Spile leans across the counter.

"You know the house rules," he whispers. "No one talks. Everyone stays happy and healthy."

"All I want to know is whether a ship called the Fogbow stopped in Barbit."

"The Fogbow?"

Spile looks around the room.

"That was several months ago," he says. "It stopped one night and offloaded its crew. The next morning it rehired them, plus a few locals, then it was gone."

"Do you know where to?"

Spile raises an eyebrow. Mayven places several coins on the table and asks for a drink. The owner grabs a large flagon from under the counter, fills it with ealu, and then wipes the area in front of Mayven sweeping the coins into his waiting hand. He bends over, pretending to reach for something under the counter.

"What I heard was to take some trappers up to the mouth of Big River," he whispers.

He busied himself, cleaning some mugs.

"Big River? There's nothing around there except the Sylvan Forest," Mayven says.

"One trapper, an Aduncus, wanted to explore the other side of the mountains for possible colonization."

"Did you catch his name?" Mayven asks.

"Teke, I believed he was called."

Mayven lowers his flagon noisily on the counter.

"Thanks, Spile," says Mayven. "Have a keg of your best ealu ready for me; I'll have one of my crew pick it up later."

Mayven places some tender on the counter.

"Anytime, Caput, anytime."

The Nauta heads back to his ship and sends a crewmember for the keg. By the time they are ready, stiff southerly winds have developed. Not one to waste good fortune, Mayven immediately sets sail for the mouth of Big River.

Mayven's first mate Garen, now commands his ship. Once they are on course, he hands him the helm and calls the passengers to the dining area.

He meets with Eage, Bartolon, Yelu, Seez, and Megafeoer, who has become an important part of the group.

"I believe Sceagga had enough time to cross over to Terrae Exterus. If we find his ship, we may be able to assess the number that stands against us," Mayven says.

"That should be simple enough. His ship and crew should be somewhere near the Big River opening," Bartolon says.

"Finding his ship won't matter anymore; he can find recruits wherever he goes. Anyone he finds along the way can be convinced or controlled for his use," Yelu says

"There is the possibility that he found the Oriel. But, if we act quickly, we may be able to intercept him when he comes out," Bartolon says.

"So we just wait then," Mayven says.

"Well, it's not that easy," Eage says.

"Why? What's wrong with waiting?" Megafeoer asks.

"We don't know where he will return. He may come back anywhere in Sylvanus. He may even come back to Ortet." Eage says.

"So, we've wasted our trip," Mayven sighs.

"Not, necessarily," Eage says. "Terrae Exterus is a different place with different forces at play. If Sceagga causes a lot of grief or misery, we may be able to pick it up. The only thing is that we need to be near the Oriel to respond."

"So, you say we should sit and wait for a signal?" Bartolon asks.

"I always thought the valley in the foothills of the Crying Mountains would be a great place for a village," Eage says.

Bartolon sighs and shakes his head.

"You want to build a village in the valley?" Bartolon asks.

"Wait 'till you see it. It's a beautiful place. I always wanted to be a scēapherder. The valley would be perfect for raising scēap."

"I thought you were blind?"

"I am, Yelu, but not from birth. I was blinded when I was sixteen. However, I still remember what the valley looked like."

"But Master Eage, didn't we come to find Sceagga?" Michael asks.

"Sure, but what will you be doing while you wait?" Eage says.

"Yeah, but build a village?" Mayven asks.

"How long do you think it will be before Sceagga starts to torment the people of the other world? One week? One month? It may take him years. Eyu's mandate was to teach the Sylvans in his ways. The village would serve as a center for his teachings. It would also be the halfway point between Sylvanus and the unexplored territories on the other side of the mountains," Eage says.

"Well, I have been told of increasing activity from explorers. There seems to be a lot of interest in what's on the other side of the mountains," Mayven says.

"A wise investor might consider expanding his trade routes further to the east. Maybe establishing a trading post for explorers who wish to buy goods near the mountain route, instead of carrying them over the mountains."

Mayven thinks about it.

Of course, I will have to build more ships.

"Why that same investor might even think about a second trading post on the shores of the new land," Eage adds as an afterthought.

A second trading post? I could have control over both lands…I wonder. Mayven's mind starts to wander.

"I wouldn't try and establish anything in Terrae Exterus, though," Eage says, almost as a warning.

"Uh, how did you—" Mayven starts to say.

"So, it's a deal then, Caput Mayven?" Eage says.

No one in the room has any idea of what just happened. Mayven himself barely understands it. Still, he believes it would be beneficial for himself and the lands.

"Yes, yes, you've got a deal. I will bring you the supplies and all the scēap you want. I just hope Sceagga takes his time on the other side so I can establish my routes." Mayven says.

They all have a good laugh.

They travel all through the night and the next day. Michael has never seen so many trees before. One morning, he flies as high as possible to see if there is a break in the greenness, but it is too vast. The forest extends to the horizon. Only a series of large plateaus rise above the forest, breaking the monotony. He counts six of them, but there might be a seventh. In the distance beyond the plateaus, he thinks he sees blue. Perhaps the other side of Sylvanus or a lake; none can tell him.

Early the next day, they encounter flotsam debris lining the beaches. Mayven sends the Halo ahead to see what is going on. They returned within the hour to report to the caput.

"There is a shadow in the water ahead. We could not identify it, but it looks like a sunken ship," Coloner Seez says.

"Strange, we saw a lot of debris on the shore but no survivors waiting on the beaches or signs of life rafts," Mayven says.

"No one hailed us either. What do you think, Caput?"

"Maybe the ship was sunk on purpose," Mayven ponders.

"It takes a lot of tender to build a large ship; why sink it?"

"They must not need it anymore, or they're trying to cover their tracks," Mayven says.

"They didn't do a very good job," Megafeoer says.

"They probably didn't expect us so soon," Mayven says.

Yelu joins the conversation.

"Why didn't they take the ship back to Barbit? They could have sold it or passed it on to someone else." Megafeoer asks.

"Never underestimate Sceagga," Yelu says. "He knows exactly what he's doing. He will not risk it being discovered before his plan comes to fruition."

"So, what about his crew?" Seez asks.

"If hunters or trappers, they will have gone their own way. If they were enthralled, then they would be dead. If Solois, then somewhere out there, they await Sceagga's return."

They look out over the vast forest.

"We will never find them," Mayven says.

"I'm afraid that the contamination of Sylvanus has begun," Yelu says.

They spent the rest of the day looking for signs of survivors to no avail. Finally, it is late in the afternoon when they come across the scuttled ship.

Bartolon is on the deck with Eage and Yelu, describing what he sees of the ship. Mayven appears on deck in his light-colored shirt and pants that come up to his knees, giving the *appearance that he is in his undergarments. His legs are covered with small scales. Sparse, short hairs are interspersed among them. He raises a few eyebrows among the Halo guard, but his crew ignores his appearance.*

"Garen, lower the hook into the water."

"I'll let you know when it's ready to come up."

"Yes, Caput," Garen says.

Mayven dives and enters the water with a minimal splash.

They all rush to follow him, but they are too late. He had already disappeared into the depths.

"I can't see him," says Seez.

"You have to be quicker than that to see a Nauta in the water," Garen says.

He lowers the hook into the water and waits.

As they look into the depths, they occasionally catch a glimpse of Mayven's pale clothes as he streaks over the vessel's hull. The minutes pass, and the Nauta remains underwater.

"How long can he hold his breath?" Megafeoer asks.

"As long as he needs to," Garen answers.

Finally, Mayven surfaces, and with a few quick strokes, he is next to the ship. He dives deep once more.

"Stand back! He's coming on board," shouts Garen.

They all move back. With a watery explosion, Mayven vaults out of the water and lands heavily on the deck with a loud thud. Immediately one of the crew appears with an immense cloth toaille that he hands to the caput.

"There was nothing worth salvaging," he says.

He dries his hair, leaving it in a tousled state.

"I did see a curious opening on the bottom of the ship. It was built into the hull to flood the lower decks and sink the vessel."

"That means they intended to sink the ship from the beginning," Bartolon says.

"Was there any damage done to the ship itself?" Eage asks.

"No, everything is still intact," Mayven answers.

"That means all or most of his crew are out there," Bartolon says.

"It would make sense then. The crew doesn't need to get back. They'll just wait for his return," Yelu says.

"And, it looks like you've got yourself a new ship," Eage says.

Mayven thinks about it for a few moments.

"You are right, Master Eage," Mayven says

He ponders the idea.

"If done slowly enough, we can raise the ship with our crane as the water drains back out of the hole. It would then be a matter of finding a bung to seal the hole."

Mayven looks over the side of the ship, his mind working.

"This trip is becoming more profitable by the day."

They arrive at the entrance to the Big River as Mayven finishes dressing.

He anchors the ship, has Garen and several crew members prepare three rivercrafts, and load them with supplies.

As they lower the crafts into the water, Garen notices a group of men standing on the shore.

"Caput Mayven, we have company."

"What is it," Eage asks.

"It looks like three hunters waiting on the shore," Mayven says.

"Hunters? Could they be Sceagga's?" Yelu asks.

As the ship nears the shore, Eage sends his pacú to them.

"I think I recognize their pacú. These are not Sceagga's Solois. Describe them to me," Eage says.

"They dress like hunters, but they're wearing some sort of coned headwear," Garen says.

290

"Coned headwear? They are Calotes. They live in small forest settlements, so they must have a village nearby," Eage says.

"Should we be concerned?" Mayven asks.

"If you show no aggression, they will be open to trading. Also, the Calotes are familiar with the area, so we may be able to enter into an agreement with them to guide us to the Crying Mountains," Eage says.

Bartolon and Eage are taken to shore, where they meet with the clan's gaffer. Eage soon finds his way into the old Calote chief's good graces. So after bartering off a barrel of Mayven's good ealu, they form a compact with the village.

The next morning, Mayven has a new trading contract, and the group has Telum, a spear-wielding Calote guide. So the small group paddles up the river.

Michael has never seen such a forest. The immense trees are completely different from those on the island. On Ortet, the forest is dense, with understory vegetation. Here it is the opposite; you can see between the trees with little brush to block your view. Colorful birds dart through the canopy, their calls echoing over the river.

Telum finds the first campsite by the river; a hearth for a fire was there, among other telltale marks of previous users.

That night Michael sits with Yelu, Eage, and Bartolon, listening to the strange animal calls. Bartolon describes the creatures to Eage as part of his training. Telum describes his village and customs. He also tells them that the area they are in is called the Nurian Forest.

In the morning, Telum roasts several fish. After a quick breakfast, they are off once more, and an hour and a half later, they enter the lake. The travelers make good time as they cross the waters. However, when they reach a point past the center, they hear a loud explosive splash from the shore.

Michael looks at the water and can only see waves where the noise came from, and then the creature surfaces.

"What is that?" asks Michael.

"Krokewurm!" Telum shouts. The men start to paddle frantically.

"Hurry to the river, get to the river!" Garen yells.

The krokewurm approaches quickly and is almost at the last rivercraft when it sinks.

"What's it doing?" Eage asks.

"It went underwater," Michael answers.

"Not good," Eage says. "Bartolon, help me up."

Bartolon helps Eage to his feet and walks him towards the bow; the craft totters.

"Master, you'll tip us over," Garen says.

"Garen, stop paddling."

"But Master."

"Don't argue, and do it," Bartolon says.

Garen stops paddling and lets the craft drift to a stop. Eage stretches his arms and tilts his head.

They all go silent; Telum is sitting right behind Garen. He stares at the water surface, holding the spear, ready to spit anything near. The krokewurm surfaces about three strides from the boat.

"Let him come near," Eage says.

"But—."

"Let him come near."

Telum lowers his spear.

The krokewurm slowly swims to the boat. Telum's spear trembles under his white-knuckle grip. Garen does not dare move; the creature is longer and broader than the rivercraft. Garen's heart is beating so hard against his chest that he thinks all will hear. Eage reaches out and places his hand on its snout.

"This creature has been...cleansed? Maybe used, I can see through his eyes, I can see what he saw," Eage says.

"Did he see my brother come through here?" Michael asks.

"This creature is responsible for the death of one of the crew before he was touched."

Eage runs his hand over the krokewurm's forehead. The beast lids his eyes.

"I see one Sylvan in the water struggling to escape, but he stops and looks. After that, everything stops, the boats stop, the crew stops, and even the water flow stops. For it is Eyu that must be heard and nothing else."

The krokewurm opens its eyes once more.

"The Sylvan's name was Armiger and is now called Ariel. Ariel will carry the word of Eyu to those who can't hear his."

Eage lifts his hand from the beast; it slowly sinks beneath the water. Bartolon helps him sit.

"That is all I can say for now; that is all the creature saw," Eage says.

"Master Eage? You're smiling."

"Yes, Yelu, the creature has made a wish come true for me."

"What was it?"

"I was able to see through the krokewurms eyes. For the first time in my life, I have seen what an Aduncus looks like. I have seen all your faces and that of Lucero."

Yelu smiles.

"Master, may we leave?" Garen whispers.

"Do not worry, Garen. This creature will never hurt a Sylvan again. It has been blessed and will protect us instead."

"Still, Master Eage, if you don't mind."

"Of course, Garen. Let's continue," Eage says, smiling.

As they pass, the krokewurms sunning themselves on the lake shore ignore the rivercrafts. Still, Garen hurries the crews to the mouth of the river.

They paddle their way upstream and notice that the river widens for a short while, giving them a little relief from the strong current. However, as the river narrows again one hour later, the currents grow stronger. Telum directs them to the shore.

They find a place to camp for the night. Michael and Telum decide to walk by the river's edge. Upon their return, Telum talks with the rest of the crew.

"It looks like we're still on the right track, a millistep from here; there are signs of previous campers," Telum says.

"Anything fresh?" Garen asks.

"No, it has been a full season since it was used."

The next morning, they start early. The river's current becomes increasingly stronger as they enter a canyon. They make little progress, but it is better than attempting to travel by land.

As the sun gets closer to the horizon, they encounter a fallen tree blocking their passage.

"It looks like a tree is blocking the way," Garen points, "We'll have to carry the rivercrafts around it."

When they walk around its trunk, Bartolon notices strange burn marks.

"Master Eage, this tree was burned, but there are no signs of a fire anywhere."

Eage places his hands on the charred trunk. "The burn was caused by a upashim; the tree was deliberately felled to form a barrier or bridge."

"We have to keep moving," Garen says. "There's no place to set camp around here."

They return to the river and continue upstream. At dusk, they find a sandy beach. There are remnants of two campfires and burned fish bones, signs that the others had also been there. They settle for the night. Seez assigns guards to watch the perimeter of the campground. Not knowing how many of Sceagga's group consisted of followers or just trappers hired for the journey, they prepare in case Sceagga plans to ambush anyone following.

The night is uneventful. The Halo tire of the food rations, so they fly back to the cliffs by the ocean to find their favorite meal, eggs. They prepare breakfast.

In the morning, they can see the Crying Mountains rising over the forest. They will reach them by nightfall.

An hour later, they are on their way. The current keeps on getting stronger, slowing their progress. Around mid-morning, they paddle to shore and let the Halo fly ahead and scout the river. The Aduncus will see if the current diminishes up ahead. It does not take long for them to return with news that rapids are ahead. They will have to carry the equipment for about a millistep to skirt the whitewater.

For the crew, walking is a welcome change from paddling. They start their trek overland. Michael, Yelu, Eage, and Bartolon don their packs and walk ahead. An hour and a half later, they arrive, where they will place the rivercrafts back in the water.

Michael explores the area while Yelu and Eage prepare a meal for the crew. He feels something familiar about the whole area. However, Michael cannot quite place the sensation. He follows his senses until he comes across the corpses of dead animals. They have been dead for some time now, and the air is heavy with the musty smell of dried flesh. He returns to camp and goes directly to Eage.

"Master Eage!"

"Michael, you seem upset," Eage says.

Yelu sits with the blind sacerdoyen and Bartolon; she helps Eage to his feet.

"Master, I just found a group of large animals, all dead," Michael says. "Some look like they have upashim burn marks."

"Something else is upsetting you," Yelu says.

"Yes, mother, the whole area feels like...Lucero."

"Lucero, are you sure?" she asks.

"Come, I'll take you there."

As they walk, Eage can also feel Lucero's presence.

"Yes, I feel Lucero now; tell me, Bartolon, what do they look like?" Eage asks.

"They look like docgas," Bartolon says.

"Not the docgas that follows at your heel. These are very large, very muscular docgas," Yelu says.

"Are they as big as quoggen?" Eage asks.

"Yes, like a monstrous docgas," Michael says.

"Are they proportioned for their size with manes, or do they have a disproportionately large upper body and head."

"Definitely disproportionate," Michael says.

"What do you make of them, Bartolon?" Eage asks.

"They're barghest, nighthounds. Ravenous creatures whose only reason to live is annihilating any living creature it sees."

Eage prods the carcass with his staff.

"I believe in this case, Lucero did not have a choice. Once the group was spotted, the beasts would have worked themselves into a frenzy which would not have been satisfied until all were dead and consumed."

"Are these normal creatures?" Telum asks.

"No, the nighthounds do not develop on their own. They were created from the kratus of the Inulian Mountains," Bartolon says.

"The kratus are enormous, wild docgas. Normally they stay away from the Sylvans. These were not of normal birth," Michael says.

"You have both learned your lessons well," Eage says.

"I must assume that Lucero would have known that too," Yelu says.

"Therefore, he would also have known that they are not a natural occurrence but someone's creation. These barghest bear Sceagga's essence, but Michael would not know if he had never experienced his pacú. He might have believed that another was involved." Eage adds.

"Lucero may not have been aware that Sceagga was with him. Or else he wouldn't have gotten this far." Michael says.

"He knows that there are those that have the power here in Sylvanus. He may have thought that the creatures belonged to someone else."

Eage then grabs Michael by the arm and kneels next to the dead animal; the smell of stale flesh is overpowering. Eage pulls Michael down with him. He takes his arm and extends it over the carcass. Yelu and Bartolon watch while holding the corner of their robes over their nose and mouth.

"Forget the smell," says Eage. "Tell me, what can you feel?"

Michael concentrates on sensing the area over the animal. Then through the foul odor, he detects another worse smell.

"What is it?" Michael says. "It seems vaguely familiar."

"It took me a while to recognize it. Actually, when I sensed it last, it was masked. That is the odor of Sceagga's pacú. You sensed it almost two years ago when we encountered the two beggars on the roadside. The same day Eyu presented the gifts."

Michael stops to think about it. Eage is right; it was the day that Eyu had appeared. They were on that road, heading home when the two beggars asked for their blessing.

Bartolon frowns for a moment as he searches his memory. So one of the beggars was Sceagga?

"How could you remember that? It was so long ago," Michael says.

"His pacú was very peculiar and disguised," Eage answers.

Eage walks around the area for a few seconds, then stops. He taps his staff a few times on the ground.

"One of the crew perished here," he says.

Michael walks to where he is standing and feels the lingering pacú of the dead Sylvan.

"It seems Lucero may have saved the rest of them," Eage says.

"Still, there is still something wrong here," Michael says

"Yes, there is."

The old sacerdoyen takes a deep breath. Eage does not like what he will say; however, it is necessary.

"The upashims used here were definitely Lucero's," he says. "But they have been tainted with evil."

"What!" Yelu is shaken.

"Lucero drew the pacú of these beasts, and with it, Sceagga's pacú," Eage says.

"That means Sceagga created the beasts," Bartolon says.

"Yes, and in so doing, Sceagga has started to taint Lucero. He will be lost unless he is stopped."

"How can we find him, Master Eage?" Michael asks.

"As I told you before, we can't. So, we will have to wait until those on Terrae Exterus call for us or hope Lucero discovers what Sceagga is doing to him."

Eage starts to walk back to the camp.

"Come, Yelu, Bartolon," he extends his hand.

Yelu takes his hand and walks him back to the campground. Bartolon follows, mulling over what it all means. Michael remains in the area for a few more minutes, memorizing the different sensations. For some reason, he needs to do so.

The crew has hot vegetable and meat soup waiting for them. After eating, they place the crafts back on the river, eager to reach their final destination. They work their way upstream for most of the day. The river widens here, which makes the waters calmer. They continue paddling, without stopping, until they reach the waterfalls. The falls cascade through a narrow cleft in the mountains and empty into a small lake. The gurge is not navigable by boat, so anyone wanting to cross the mountains will have to do it on foot. The group lands on the shores of the lake and immediately sets about making camp.

Fish is plentiful in the small lake, and with little effort, the crew catches enough for the evening meal. Sitting around the campfire are Michael, Eage, Yelu, Bartolon, Garen, Telum, and the Halo members Caput Seez, Megafeoer, Clad, Meagle, Tan, and Nak. They discuss what they will do in the morning. Since Eage and Bartolon cannot fly, they will be carried by sling to the Valley of Sceapherders, as it is now called. Telum will lead those required to take the necessary supplies to the valley, where the sacerdoyen will establish their base. The rest of the crew will tend to the rivercrafts and wait for the return of the others.

This is as far as the crew will go. Garen will head back to the ship. Mayven will follow the coastline further north, then east, searching for a shorter route to the Crying Mountains.

The next morning, all are eager to start the trip. Clad and Meagle strap the harness to carry Eage. Tan and Nak will carry Bartolon. Megafeoer, Seez, Michael, and Yelu will carry enough provisions for a couple of days until Telum's group arrives with the rest of their food and equipment.

They take to the air and soon pass over the extensive forest, headed for the Crying Mountains.

The wind, rushing through the canyon pass and gurges, sounds like a woman's mourning wail. Up ahead, they can see the Valley of Sceapherders against a soaring wall of rock to the east, the Crying Mountains, which meanders north and south. The Nurian Forest to the west and south is the only entrance into the valley. A vast grassland borders the north of the Nurian Forest.

A spring, originating at the base of the mountains, feeds the stream that snakes across the valley. It is by this stream that they make camp. Leftover fish from the previous night becomes their lunch. They decide to spend the rest of the day clearing out the area to make the camp more comfortable and give the Halo a place to rest.

The temperature gets cooler as the sun drops behind the weald in the west. Finally, darkness comes; the campfire lights the surrounding trees and brush with a warm orange glow. Eage senses Michael's absence and reaches for Bartolon.

"Take me to Michael," Eage says.

Bartolon leads Eage outside the ring of light thrown by the fire, staring at the mountains. Michael holds his robes tightly around him; he senses Eage's approach.

"Can you feel him?" Eage asks.

"Yes, it's the same feeling I had back where the dead beasts were," answers Michael.

"The barghest."

"Yes, the barghest," he says. "Only this time, the feeling is strongly tainted."

"Yes, your brother has killed again. Only this time, his method was different."

"I have a feeling about what he may have done, but nothing to prove it," Eage says.

He is now standing next to him.

"I'll wait if you don't mind before I give you my opinion."

Michael turns to him.

"Is it as bad as with the barghest?"

"It's worse," he says.

"I was afraid of that," Michael says.

"What now?" Bartolon asks.

"In two days, the rest of the crew will arrive. Then we'll visit the site; I'll know for sure then," Eage says. "It's cold out here; let's get back to the fire."

They lead Eage back to the warmth of the fire, where they join the others. After two hours of tales, they turn in for the night.

Telum arrives with the rest of the crew two days later. A meal is prepared for them, and they sit to talk about their trek.

"Telum, what can you tell me about the grasslands north of the forest?" Michael asks.

"You are talking about the vast grassland called the Taluga Leah. The Taluga Leah is in the Taluga Region. It is home to the papios. Papios are giant apes domesticated by a curious group of beings known as the Sifaki, who use them to work the land, and in some cases, train them for battle."

Telum scratches a rough map of the region on the ground.

"We have no encounters with the Sifaki. They never venture into the Nurian Forest, nor we into the grasslands. So we have no contact with them," Telum says.

"Have you ever spoken with any of them?" Michael asks.

"No, the Sifaki have their own language; we don't know it. They can actually communicate with their papios, though. They have been observed having conversations with the papio."

Meagle and Megafeoer prepare the harness for Eage and leave on a short trip to the area where the cave's entrance to the Oriel is. This time Bartolon stays behind.

Following Eage's direction, they quickly find the path that leads to the cavern. They land at a favorable spot on the trail and start their ascent. It isn't too long until they come to the enormous bodies of the ogres. The smell is overpowering. Scavengers have ravished some of the cadavers, but for the most part, they are still intact.

"What kind of creatures are these?" Meagle asks.

"These are ogres," Yelu answers.

"How did you know?" Megafeoer asks.

"During my stay in Sylvanus, I studied the inhabitants of this land," she answers. "However, I remember that they live in somewhat primitive social groups. These wandered far from their tribe on the other side of the mountain."

"You are right, Yelu," Eage says. "They are far from their natural territory, from their tribe."

"Why?" asks Michael.

"To have them killed, perhaps."

The smell is worse than with the barghest. Flies and maggots are everywhere. Desiccation has not set in because cooler temperatures and rains kept the bodies moist. A cloud of flies rises as Michael's shadow passes over them.

"Can you sense it?" Eage asks.

"Yes, it's a lot clearer now, though more confusing," Michael says. "Lucero's essence is stronger, but the ogre's pacú are gone."

"What are you saying, Michael?" Yelu asks.

She talks through the sleeve of her cloak.

"Lucero's pacú level is higher than what I remember, and the pacú of the ogres has been ripped from them," Michael says.

Yelu's ability to sense the pacú is rather rudimentary. But she can always sense her duvos. She can feel that Lucero's pacú prints are intense here, while the ones by the nighthounds are almost too weak to feel.

"Master Eage, this is what Sceagga used to do, wasn't it?" Yelu says.

"Yes, this is the way he used to get his energy. These creatures were robbed of their pacú, but Sceagga did not do it. This is the work of Lucero."

"Why would Lucero start doing that?" Yelu asks.

"I don't know, but his transformation has started," Eage says.

"Master Eage, we have to get him back," Yelu says.

"I'm open to suggestions."

Yelu does not have any.

Chapter 17
THE TRIBAL PEOPLE

Upon entering Terrae Exterus, Lucero notices the difference in its feel. He senses the waves of negative energy around him, and they hum in tune with his own. Lucero looks at the surroundings and finds the trees, flowers, and even the songs of birds to be different. He looks at his hands and notices they have changed; they are darker and smaller now. Touching his hair, he notices that it is coarse. Then his fingers brush his ears. They are almost half the size and round. They do not even protrude through the hair. The Oriel has changed him; somehow, it deformed him.

Lucero hears voices and hides. He does not want to scare anyone if they see his misshapen form. He approaches the voices quietly; something else is different, but now is not the time. Lucero makes his way through the trees and finds a village. At first, they all seem like normal Sylvans going about their everyday business. Then he sees that they all have round ears, long coarse hair, and dark skin. He remembers that the Oriel changes travelers to match the land's inhabitants.

The village surrounds a long building made of logs. There is a path leading to the village. Between the entrance and the log house, a statue is carved from a tree trunk consisting of figures of different creatures, each standing on the other's shoulder. The first resembles the bernoz supporting the statue, and the last is some sort of bird with a large, broad bill. Unmistakably a bird of prey.

He wants to study the folk more before confronting them, something best done from a distance. Lucero leaps into the air to fly and find a better place to observe from. Instead, he falls face-first with a loud grunt on the trail. In seconds, he is surrounded by villagers pointing their long stone-head spears.

Lucero slowly gets to his feet and realizes that his wings are gone. Panic sweeps over him. He spins around, trying to see behind him. He tries to feel his back with his hands, but nothing is there. Lucero can feel them, but they are not visible. The villagers step back when he starts acting mad, turning in circles and grasping at his back.

An old villager pushes his way through the spear bearers. A man, slightly older than Lucero, accompanies him. The old man reaches into a pouch and pulls a round object on a stick. Then, with one hand, he shakes the object, which makes a rattling noise, and with the other, he holds a straight staff, made out of reddish wood, that he waves over Lucero's head.

The old man walks around him, chanting as if trying to scare away some unseen insect.

"Nenemehkia spirit of lightning and thunder, chase evil away!

Spirit of the ground, chase it away!

Spirit of the water, chase it away!

Chase it away, chase it away."

He repeats the chants three times as he slowly walks around Lucero. All the while shaking the rattle and waving the staff.

Lucero notices a strange sensation as the staff passes over him.

The old villager finally seems satisfied with his work. He stops in front of Lucero.

"Nenemehkia has cleansed your spirit. Who are you, wanderer?" asks the old man.

Lucero looks at him; he is obviously some sort of elder; he has strings of beads hanging around his neck and wrists and white markings painted on his face. The one who accompanies him is dressed similarly.

A novicite? or acolyte?

"My name is Lucero." He answers. "Who is Nenemehkia?"

"Nenemehkia is the spirit of lightning and thunder who lives in my staff," he says.

He motions with the red stick.

"Loo-se-ros? What does Loo-se-ros mean?" asks the old man.

"Loo-se...Uh, Bringer of light."

There is a murmuring among the men. Then one of them steps forward, pointing the spear.

"Why do you come to the Taloosh home?" he says.

The old man gently pushes the spear down and steps between the two.

"Let the visitor speak, White Eagle. "The elder says, "Why have you come?"

Lucero thinks about what answer he should give. Any story he can make up is just as farfetched as the truth.

"I was sent here by Eyu to teach the folk of this land."

Surprise comes over the acolyte's face.

"He is the one I have dreamt about," the acolyte whispers.

The old man raises his hand to quiet him.

"Who is this...Eyu?" the old man asks.

"He is the one who made all of the trees and the birds, all of the waters and fish."

The voice comes from amongst the trees. Immediately the warriors turn their spears towards it. From the forest emerges another old man, though not as old as the villager.

"Who are you?" the villager asks.

The warriors are getting nervous with all the strangers coming out of the forest.

"I am Qualut. I have followed my dreams for the last fourteen days; they brought me here."

The warriors start murmuring. The old man raises his hand and quiets them.

"Are you a shaman?"

The newcomer stops to think for a moment.

"Shaman? Yes, I'm Shaman Qualut."

"What sort of dreams did you have?" the old man asks.

"First, to whom do I talk?"

"You talk to Shaman Tiglit," he says.

"Health and long life to you, Shaman Tiglit," Qualut says.

The shaman nods in acceptance of the greeting.

"I have been dreaming of the coming of a great shaman. Every night, I dream of a small piece that fits the one before," Qualut says.

He approaches Tiglit.

"Last night, I dreamt he would come through a hole in the air that was not there before and would not be there after. Today, I saw him pass through the hole that closed behind him. Like a man leaving the river, there was no hole behind to say that he had gone through."

When he stops talking, he is face to face with Tiglit.

"That is what I saw," Qualut adds.

"You saw him step through the hole in the air?" Tiglit asks.

"Yes."

"Did anyone else step through the hole?" White Eagle asks.

"I did not see anyone else come through the hole," Qualut says.

"Come to the village Bringer of Light, you too, Shaman Qualut," Tiglit says. "We have many things to talk about."

The old shaman leads them through the village; there are smoky fires with large fish skinned and pressed flat and thin strips of other meats drying over them. Baskets of berries are also next to the fires. The women are busy working leather into garments while some men work on spears and longbows.

The ground in the village is muddy. The natives have thrown moss and grass into the mire to make it less slippery. Moss is not scarce in these parts; it hangs from all the trees, everything is wet, and there appears to be a constant overcast in the skies.

They pass all other dwellings until they come to a wooden structure separated from the others.

His hut is similar to, though smaller than, the longhouses. Next to the door, the main supports are intricately carved. The heavy timbers are carved with sharp-beaked birds, bernoz, and sea creatures Lucero had never seen before.

Next to the hut sits a large black stone. Its surface is smooth, though it has areas melted by considerable heat. Walking by the boulder, Lucero can feel a certain amount of energy radiated. It is almost pleasing but dark.

The interior walls are draped with skins in an untidy manner to ward off the cold. Lucero found it curious that all of the creativeness that went into carving the statues and the mainframe of the building was not present in its walls.

The shaman and the acolyte enter the dwelling. Qualut, Lucero, and White Eagle follow; however, the other warriors stay behind.

The inside is spacious, with few personal belongings and a complete lack of furniture. The open space is uncluttered, except for the support column also carved with animals. A hearth occupies the far end. The shaman's residence is a meeting place for the tribal elders. A stone circle in the hut's center looks like a reserved area for special occasions. He feels *the same dark energy from the shelter's walls that he got from the stone.*

The shaman's solitary hut in the village makes Lucero think that the shaman is the tribal chief.

As they move to the back of the hut, Lucero can see a woman and a young girl wrapped in blankets overlooking a large bundle on the floor. Tiglit approaches the woman and says something Lucero cannot hear, and then the bundle moves.

"Father..." a raucous fit of coughing follows.

Lucero moves closer, and Tiglit turns to face him.

"Who is he?" Lucero asks.

"He is Red Bow, my son," whispers Tiglit. "Nothing can be done for him; the disease takes his breath. So don't be concerned with him."

Tiglit tries to lead Lucero away, but he holds his ground.

"Let me have a look at him," he says.

He moves next to the bundle. He looks at the young girl and smiles.

"It's ok," Lucero says.

The girl moves aside. Lucero kneels and pulls back the blanket. He has never seen a creature in such poor condition. The young man is in his mid-teens, skeletal with sunken eyes and breath that smells like a dead rat. Lucero reaches out and places his hand on the boy's brow without thinking. Immediately he feels a discharge of tainted pacú coming from Red Bow, the same that happened with the ogres. The rush catches him by surprise.

Nevertheless, when the shadow pacú enters him, he finds pleasure in it. The boy takes a deep breath and falls into a deep sleep. Lucero feels that a great deal of energy has entered him. He is somehow satisfied. He does not know how but knows that the boy is now cured.

He stands and turns to Tiglit, who watches him with intense curiosity.

"What have you done?" the shaman asks.

"Red Bow will be fine now," Lucero says.

"What?"

"He has cured your son," Qualut says.

Shaman Tiglit turns to Lucero, looks into his eyes, and finds no deception. Dropping to his knees next to the boy, he gently pulls the blanket down. The boy is quietly sleeping without coughing or rattling in his lungs. As he looks at the youngster's face, he sees that the eyes are no longer sunken. He puts the blanket back in place and stands.

"Well?" White Eagle asks.

"I believe he has cured him," the shaman says.

"Then it is him," the acolyte whispers.

"Yes," Tiglit says.

"What about the raven from the dream? The one who can change his shape. Could one of them be the mischief-maker, the trickster that will lead him astray?" The acolyte asks.

"Dreams are not always certain. Of your dreams, only a part will come true. The rest will be like smoke in your eyes that hides the fire that it came from."

"I don't understand," he says.

"There are a lot of images in a dream. You must learn to choose what is important and throw away what is not; otherwise, like the smoke, it will keep you from seeing beyond the fire. The raven teaches his lessons with his mischief; remember that."

The acolyte stops to think about it.

Could the raven be playing tricks on me? He might be trying to hide the true meaning of the dream. Or, can he be showing his true self?

"There are important matters to discuss," says Tiglit. "Let us sit and talk."

The shaman leads them to an area near the hearth. The woman and girl quickly stand, pick up a stack of blankets piled by a wall, and place them on the floor for them to sit. When the woman puts the one in front of Lucero, she breaks down into tears. She grabs his hand and presses her forehead against it.

"The boy's mother is grateful," Tiglit mumbles and waves her off.

The girl smiles at Lucero and follows her mother.

As per tradition, only warriors can witness the elders' meeting. She gently pushes the acolyte ahead of her when she starts to leave.

"Wait!" Tiglit says. "He must stay."

The young man is surprised and proud to be of enough importance to be included in the meeting.

Tiglit sits on the blanket with him at his side. The others chose where to sit.

The warrior sits on the other side of Tiglit and remains quiet. Tiglit picks up a bone with a length of leather tied around it and places it on his blanket; it is the talking bone.

"I bring you to this meeting because the arrival of the Bringer of Light will change our tribe forever," Tiglit says.

The shaman places his hand on the acolyte's arm.

"This is Dancing Elk, my grandson; the folk of this tribe sees him as a messenger for the spirit world. When he becomes a warrior, the Taloosh will see him sit at my place."

White Eagle picks up the talking bone and sets it on his blanket.

"Hmm! He is not Tall Tree. Tall Tree did not dread the river," White Eagle says.

The words hit Dancing Elk like a hammer. He lowers his eyes, shamefaced in front of the stranger.

Tiglit takes the bone back and slaps it down on his blanket.

"Not now, White Eagle, that is a matter of the spirit world," Tiglit's eyes lock on the warrior's.

Lucero can hear Tiglit's anger, and so can White Eagle.

What is going on here?

The warrior goes quiet, and Tiglit continues.

"For many months, Dancing Elk has dreamt of events to come. Some showed him that our tribe would be chosen from all tribes to become important.

"Some showed him that a time of great dread would come past the time of importance. The raven was also present in the dreams. The raven likes to fool folk into thinking they know things. The raven is a trickster who sometimes uses mischief to help his folk. He can change his shape to walk among us to see how we react. You must not let the raven cloud your mind with doubt or needless questions."

Tiglit places his hand on Dancing Elk's shoulder.

"Dancing Elk dreamt that the one who would bring the light would come. But, in the dream, the raven warns him that one, who wants to rob the light, will follow. This is the one we must be aware of; this is the one we must find, or he will bring ruin to the spirit of Bringer of Light."

Dancing Elk picks up the bone from Tiglit's blanket and sets it on his own.

"Because it is raven who spoke, we might expect the one who follows to use deceit in ruining Bringer of Light's spirit, but we do not know what form this deceit will take."

Qualut picks up the bone and places it on his blanket.

"Dancing Elk speaks like a man; his mind is older than his body. We should give ear to his dreams."

At this, the acolyte swells with pride.

Dancing Elk takes back the bone.

"My dreams also showed a shadow being cast over Bringer of Light. A shadow that covered all of the tribes, including the Taloosh. But I also saw someone else chase the shadow to rescue Bringer of Light. Here, the dream was broken. Whether he succeeds was not clear."

Lucero has been watching the bone picked up by those who want to talk. He, too, has something to say, so he picks up the bone and sets it on his blanket.

"I do not know what a raven is or what he is supposed to do. I come from a place you cannot walk to. I was sent to teach the folk a message given to me by the creator, the same as the creator of your land. To help your folk in any way I can." Lucero says.

White Eagle picks up the bone.

"Why should we depend on a stranger to teach us or help us."

Lucero takes back the bone.

"An evil shaman, called Sceagga, wants to come to your land because this land acts like a fallen tree that blocks a stream, blocking the grey spirit from this land to my land. He wants to cross into your land, feed his spirit with grey spirit and become powerful. All this, he believes. So, I offer the help to fight the evil shaman to keep him from taking over your land."

White Eagle has a serious look; the warrior takes it as an insult that they would need help from a stranger to battle an enemy.

"Our warriors are strong and fierce."

He stands up and stamps the butt of his spear on the ground.

"We don't need your help," the warrior says.

Lucero holds out his hand and forms a small glowing ball the size of a pea that hovers over his palm.

Tiglit's eyes widen, and Dancing Elk scoots back. Then, with a flick of his hand, he throws the tiny upashim; the blast disintegrates the sharpened stone point on the spear.

The warrior lets go of the shaft, drops to his knees, and bows.

"My pardons for insulting you, Great Spirit," he says. "Forgive my ignorance."

"I am not the great spirit, and I am not angry with you. I just want you to understand how powerful the one who follows may be. Look at me." Lucero says.

The warrior looks up.

Lucero holds out his hand once more; a sphere the size of a man's head appears, lighting up the entire room.

"With this, I can destroy the tallest tree in your forest or rubble, the largest stone you can find. This is how powerful Shaman Sceagga can be."

Lucero dissipates the sphere. Through all of this, Qualut remains silent. However, Tiglit does notice that the other shaman is not impressed by the show of power.

"I want you to go and look for strangers, but do not confront them. If you see anyone suspicious, come back and tell us," Qualut says.

Shaman Tiglit offers Lucero and Qualut the evening meal. They accept it along with a corner of the hut to spend the night. Lucero is unable to sleep that night. The whole land seems to hum with the dark energy he yearns for but cannot touch.

He now believes that illness accompanies an imbalance of the pacú in their bodies. The inhabitants of Terrae Exterus absorb the energy from their surroundings.

Once inside a body, he can access it. He realizes that, unless the imbalance is great, as in the case of Red Bow, it does not affect them. They are not capable of manipulating or deriving any benefit from it.

Even the animal skins they use for insulating the dwellings feel as if they keep the energy sealed.

When he cured Red Bow, he savored his dark energy.

Then there is that curious boulder next to Tiglit's hut.

It seems to glow with energy. However, it is still unusable. Its pacú is palpable but untouchable.

The next morning, the tribe sets up two huts next to Tiglit's for Lucero and Qualut. Lucero knows that to gain the tribe's trust, he will have to live like them.

Tiglit sends his warriors to other villages to spread the word about Bringer of Light's arrival. Bringer of Light spends most of the morning arguing with Tiglit about his name. Finally, in the end, he mandates that he be referred to as Lucero.

Something else pops into Lucero's mind.

"Tiglit, what is the story behind the large black stone beside your home?"

"The stone was a gift from the heavenly spirit. When it was given to the Taloosh folk, we were told that it held great power, and we were to keep it safe from the demon spirit."

"Do you mean that the heavenly spirit came and gave it to you?"

"No, it was thrown down to the Taloosh from heaven."

Some sort of meteor that became another tribal belief?

The stone's shadow pacú is vast but unusable. It becomes a curiosity Lucero ponders whenever he walks by it.

Lucero joins the natives in their daily activities, like fishing, towards the end of summer. Lucero notices that an attractive girl seems to be always involved with Dancing Elk's shores. He also notices that Dancing Elk enjoys her presence.

He goes with them on their yearly trek to the river, where the large fish swim up the cascading currents to spawn. The fish can be jabbed with a spear when fighting the waterfalls.

They catch as many as possible and dry the meat for the winter. This takes the pressure off the deer and elk that supplies the meat for the rest of the year.

One day, while fishing, Lucero notices that while the others work or swim in the river, Dancing Elk will only venture to the sandy shore before returning to the grassy area to sit and watch the others. He talks to a girl sitting next to him. Dancing Elk seems content and happy. They both laugh at some comment he makes. The girl sees Lucero approaching and gets up.

"Bye Tsálk, I must go to my chores, and you must talk with Shaman Lucero," *she nods to Lucero and leaves.*

Lucero sits next to Dancing Elk.

"The girl is pretty. Who is she?"

Dancing Elk smiles.

"That's Potwah. One day she will be under my roof," *he says.*

"You mean, mate?"

"Mate is for animals. She will be my life partner."

Hmm, I see. We call our life partner denwyf."

"Mmm, den wiff?"

"Denwyf, one word," *Lucero says. Dancing Elk, she called you Tsálk?"*

Dancing Elk chuckles.

"When we were little, we played together all the time. Potwah said I ran and constantly jumped, like tsálk."

He looks up at the trees and, after a moment, points.

"That's tsálk."

Lucero looks to where he's pointing. A squirrel runs through the branches.

"Tsálk, eh," *Lucero chuckles.* "Well, I'll stick with Dancing Elk. So, why don't you swim with her or the others?" *Lucero asks.*

Dancing Elk looks embarrassed and starts to scratch the sand with a stick.

Because you're a coward.

Lucero hears the voice.

What...who was that?

He sends his pacú over the area, but no one is near. Lucero turns to Dancing Elk.

"Did you hear the voice?"

Dancing Elk nods. Lucero can tell he is embarrassed.

"You hear it, too?" Dancing Elk asks.

"Tell me about the voice. You can tell me. I can keep a secret."

Hmm, maybe all shamans can hear Ijiraq.

"It's a secret; the others don't know. When I was little, I fell into the river. Ijiraq, the river spirit, tried to take me. It was my father, Tall Tree, who rescued me.

"So, where is your father?"

"When my father rescued me, Ijiraq became angered. It altered the river so we couldn't cross and took my father. Tiglit said I drowned, and he and others brought me back. Since that day, Ijiraq has waited for me to take me back.

"Why does this, Ijiraq, wants you?"

Ijiraq says I must pay with my life so the Taloosh can fish here. My father died crossing the river, but it says it wasn't enough; it must be me. I can talk to the spirits, feel nature around me, and dream of things to come.

"And this is important to Ijiraq?"

"When someone with my ability comes along, it wants to take over the body and become that person to walk on land. It has been a long time since someone with my ability has come. It is ready to walk on land again."

"How often does this happen?"

317

"Ijiraq is ancient, but it has only happened a few times, and it has been a long time since it happened last, according to our storytellers."

Sounds like stories fabricated around accidental drownings? It's like a childkeeper tale to keep the children from going near the water. Yet, I did hear the voice.

"And now it's your turn?" Lucero asks.

"If the Taloosh knows about the spirit, they will never return, and we need the fish to survive the winter. Since I can't go in, I never learned to swim. Several seasons ago, Ijiraq tried to take Wrensong. It was a trick to lure me into the river. I managed to fight it off with Nenemehkia, but to the tribe, I had lost my mind."

"Wrensong?"

"My sister, you saw her in the hut, caring for Red Bow."

"The young girl?"

"Yes, her. I got Wrensong back, but in the process, I looked like I was afraid of the water. Truth be told, after almost drowning a second time, I am."

"So that's what White Eagle was talking about?"

"Because I can't go near the water, I will never be able to take the tribe to River Spill. That makes White Eagle angry." Dancing Elk sighs.

I've never heard of a spirit causing physical harm. Ijiraq's actions must have been misinterpreted.

"What is River Spill?"

"River Spill is where the river flows into the big water. We can catch enough fish at River Spill in two days to last the winter. But Ijiraq won't let me cross, so we have to spend weeks at the first river to catch enough fish."

"You said it wants you because you can talk to the spirits, sense nature, and dream of future things. In a way, I can do that too. Perhaps I can talk to Ijiraq."

"No, don't. Ijiraq is powerful. It will drown you," Dancing Elk says.

"I am powerful too. Maybe we can come to an agreement," Lucero says.

Lucero stands and heads for the shore. Dancing Elk also stands and grabs his arm.

"Shaman Lucero, don't. It's not worth it."

"What's going on?"

Tiglit comes upon the two.

"Grandfather, Lucero wants to talk to Ijiraq. It will kill him."

"Dancing Elk is right. Ijiraq is a powerful spirit. It has killed many," Tiglit says.

"You have already paid a heavy price. You believe I'm a powerful shaman; let me test my strength," Lucero says.

"A shaman must know his strength and worth," Tiglit says.

Dancing Elk looks at Tiglit. Tiglit nods, and Dancing Elk lets him go.

Lucero walks to the riverbank. He keeps his fists clenched, and his heart races.

I hope I'm doing the right thing.

Lucero steps into the shallows.

As the water laps his feet, he can feel Ijiraq.

Oh, what's this? Ijiraq is all dark pacú.

He calls to the spirit.

"Ijiraq! You have taken a life from this tribe. They have paid your price. They only want to go across the river to fish at River Spill."

They have fished my waters; they must pay the toll.

"You forced them by altering the river. Let the Taloosh cross. They will fish somewhere else."

You are a powerful one. I will take you instead.

"If this doesn't go as planned, we won't have fish for the winter," Tiglit says.

Dancing Elk absentmindedly nods.

Ijiraq seizes Lucero's ankles and tries to pull him in. however, Lucero had expected a move by the spirit and rooted himself with the pacú.

"I'm not here as an offering. The Taloosh have paid their price; let them cross."

You will pay the tribute, then they may pass; if they can.

The water creeps up to Lucero's knees. Lucero senses the spirit's power. Ijiraq is definitely stronger than Dancing Elk or Tiglit.

But you are not stronger than me.

"Ijiraq, I've come with good intentions. Let the Taloosh cross."

Having tasted Lucero's pacú, the river spirit wants more.

With your power, I will walk among men for generations.

The water rises to Lucero's neck.

"Ijiraq, I don't want to fight you."

Lucero is starting to worry.

Ijiraq is like an illness. I will treat it as one.

"Ijiraq, don't—"

The water rushes up, covering Lucero's face. A tinge of panic touches Lucero's mind.

Tall Tree's death was no accident. Ijiraq did kill him.

Lucero is dragged underwater, he struggles, but the water around him becomes thick and sticky. His limbs move in slow motion through the syrup.

Lucero pushes down the rising panic and replaces it with anger.

Very well. Now is my turn.

Lucero starts to draw Ijiraq's pacú. Ijiraq feels the sapping of his energy.

What's this? What are you doing?

Of course, Lucero can't answer.

Ijiraq tries to hold on tighter to Lucero. But he is still losing energy. Lucero can feel the panic rise in Ijiraq. It tries to release its grip on Lucero, but Lucero holds fast.

Let me go!

At the shore, Tiglit and Dancing Elk can hear Ijiraq's outcry. The waters in the river grow turbulent. All who were fishing or swimming run for the shore. Spears, clothing, and equipment are abandoned in the rush.

"The river is swelling. Everyone to high ground," White Eagle shouts, believing a flash flood is coming.

They all scramble up the hill. All except Tiglit and Dancing Elk, who watch the battle taking place in the river.

Lucero rises, standing in waist-deep water; he stretches his arms to the sides. He draws the spirit's pacú faster now.

So much pacú.

Lucero wants all of the pacú, but he wants to savor it, taste it.

"As you took the lives of others, I will take yours," Lucero shouts.

A loud wail rises from the river.

No, give me back. I'll allow the passage. Give me back.

But Lucero doesn't stop; he can't stop. The feeling is too exhilarant.

The waters crash against the rocks, boulders shift, and the waves carry the water high over the bank. Those near the water scramble higher up, away from the turbulence. In the center of the watery upheaval, Lucero stands unmoved. Ijiraq's cries grow weaker, then silent. The river grows calm and returns to normal. Lucero staggers out of the water. He is beyond tired, but it was worthwhile. He holds on to the feeling of ecstasy as long as he can.

"Are you all right, Shaman Lucero?" Dancing Elk asks.

Lucero doesn't answer. He's afraid that if he does, the rhapsody will fade.

"What happened to the river spirit?" Tiglit asks.

Lucero still doesn't answer. Trance-like, Lucero sits next to them and lets himself fall back on the sand. He lays there until the feeling subsides.

"It was an illness in the river. I drew it in," Lucero finally says.

Dancing Elk and Tiglit exchange looks.

Hidden from view, Qualut watches from the edge of the trees.

I should have thought of that. That pacú could have been mine.

"Now that the spirit is gone, you can lead the Taloosh to River Spill. You can learn to swim; I can teach you. We'll make it our secret," Lucero says, staring at the clouds.

"That would surprise everyone," Dancing Elk says.

The two become like brothers after that.

Dancing Elk shows Lucero how to skin and filet the pink flesh from the fish and prepare it for drying. Next, they show him how to make the glue to build their bows by boiling the skin to extract the sticky gelatin.

When the spawning is over, the tribe returns to their home. Their attention turns to hunting deer and elk. The animals live in the surrounding forest. However, the natives prefer to hunt away from the village. They often walk for many millisteps to avoid the local fauna.

There is a deep-seated belief that the spirits of their dead ancestors and the tribe's totem spirits sometimes occupy the animals to stay close to the clan.

White Eagle trains the young villagers to wrestle, hunt, and use the bow, spear, and knife they all seem to wear around their necks on a thong.

"The bow is good for hunting from a distance, but the cast is weak if the string gets wet. Then you use the thrower," he says, holding up an atlatl.

White Eagle places a long shaft on the atlatl and hurls the bolt. It impales a stump twenty-five paces away.

"The shaft of the thrower is longer, so it's harder to carry through thick brush, but the range is good, like the arrow. The spear is good if the animal you hunt turns on you. If a forest lion catches you by surprise and attacks you, you drive the end of the spear into the ground."

He jabs the butt end of the spear into the ground and crouches.

"You keep the head of the spear low, and at the last moment, you lift it."

He jerks the head of the spear up.

"The animal will impale itself."

The young villagers are in awe at White Eagle's cleverness.

After his lessons, the boys run into the forest with their small bows and spears, whooping and hollering to see what they can hunt.

White Eagle smiles and shakes his head.

I will have to teach them stealth next time.

The winter is long, cold, and wet. Snow is rare in this part of the land; it only falls in the deepest part of winter for a week or so. The skies are always overcast, and it rains in a constant drizzle the rest of the time, which keeps everything wet and the air damp.

Spring finally comes, and the sun finally breaks through the clouds. It is time for Lucero to visit the villages. As Lucero *walks among the huts to see who will go with him. He spots a small group of warriors with bows and spears ready; among them is Dancing Elk, dressed and painted as if for a special occasion.*

"What is happening?" Lucero asks.

"A xóots is entering the village at night; we are no longer safe," Tiglit says.

"A xóots?"

"Some call them bear," Tiglit says.

"Bear?"

"King of the forest, large hairy animal with a strong spirit, big claws to scratch trees, catch fish, catch deer and elk," Tiglit says.

"Sounds like a bernoz," Lucero says.

"Bernoz sounds like bear," Tiglit says.

"Yes, it does," Lucero says.

"This bear is consumed with an evil spirit. It does not act as bears do," Tiglit says. "It does not hunt, it does not scavenge, it only destroys."

"Is Dancing Elk going to hunt it?

"It's time for Dancing Elk to prove he can lead. To prove he is a warrior. He and four others will hunt the bear," Tiglit says.

Tiglit starts a chant while waving Nenemehkia over Dancing Elk's head. Next, he waves the staff over a spear and a long-bladed copper knife with a point on both ends.

"Dancing Elk will lead the hunters, they will help, but Dancing Elk must make the kill. He is now the hunter; it will be dangerous to hunt this unfamiliar creature. But he must do so with the spear or the knife to free its spirit," Tiglit says.

Lucero remembers being impressed at the sight of the bernoz back on Ortet. However, he could always fly away if they got too close. Facing one with a spear and knife seemed insane.

Lucero is surprised when he sees Dancing Elk stripped of his shirt covering; he has grown since he first arrived. He is no longer the skinny fellow he met on his first day. Now, he is lean, muscular, and as tall as Lucero.

Tiglit decorates Dancing Elk's chest and arms with paint. The men accompanying him are also painted and armed with bows, which Nenemehkia also hallowed. The hunters ask the tribe for their blessing in the hunt and bid their goodbyes, for they may fail to return.

After the brief ceremony, they head out to track the bear. Lucero can follow the group but cannot interfere in the hunt.

Half a mile into the woods, they come across a path that looks like a trail of destruction. The bear has been using the same trail to constantly circle the village. Whatever ailed the beast kept it in constant motion.

Blood bespattered the side of a tree where the bear had raked the bark with enough force to tear off one of its claws.

White Eagle uses his knife to pry the claw from the tree.

"What does it mean?" Lucero asks.

They look at the blood spread on the tree.

"The animal is not of its mind. I have never seen anything like this before," White Eagle says.

"The bear is circling the village, and the circle grows smaller. It won't be long before it attacks," Dancing Elk says.

Now that he points it out, Lucero notices the tracks circling the village in a closing spiral, almost entering the village in some places but driven to continue the spiral.

The bear is definitely driven by something.

They follow the tracks to the river, and there they find it. Its paw is stained and its brown fur matted with dried blood.

"There," White Eagle says. "He is the one."

White Eagle curls his finger into a hook and motions to the bear. Lucero looks and sees the tip of the paw with the raw flesh and bone exposed; it rubs on a root as the bear walks through the brush. The bear growls; it rakes the bush and tears it from the ground. Then, he rears, shakes his head, and renders the air with a growling screech. They all cover their ears.

"That is the cry of a demon," White Eagle says. "Is not the voice of a bear."

White Eagle motions to Dancing Elk; the hunter steps towards the bear. He is hesitant at first but straightens his back and firm the spear in his hand. The four warriors split into two groups, and they surround the bear.

"Brother xóots, I've come to release your tormented spirit," Dancing Elk shouts.

Lucero is startled.

I thought he was going to creep up on the bear.

The bear turns to Dancing Elk. Lucero sees that the bear's eyes are a dark red, with wisps of a dark mist seeping from its corners. Normally a bear would leave and avoid any confrontation. However, this bear sees the boy as something to exterminate.

Dancing Elk pauses, gawking at the sight of its eyes.

He is possessed!

The bear charges without hesitation.

"Wake up, hunter!" White Eagle shouts.

Immediately, arrows hit the bear from the sides; confused, the bear pauses and starts to spin, looking for the source of the pain. Dancing Elk snaps out of his trance as the bear rears and lunges at him. Dancing Elk has only enough time to thrusts his spear into the bear's chest. The animal swipes at him, raking his chest with his massive claws. The animal's momentum pushes him backward. Dancing Elk remembers his lessons on defending against an attacking forest lion and

326

pushes the butt-end of the spear into the ground. The animal ignores the spear. He is of one mind; to get to him. The bear impales himself, trying to reach Dancing Elk. Dancing Elk already has the long knife out. The bear is momentarily pinned with the spear, giving Dancing Elk enough time to roll out from underneath him. He stands, jumps on the animal's back, and drives the blade deep into his neck in one motion.

Blinded by rage, the bear twists, throwing the boy to the ground in front of him. He pounces on Dancing Elk but jams the spear deeper, piercing its heart. Blood streams down the spear shaft. The bear struggles for breath and finally accepts his fate, stops, and collapses. Several minutes later, his breathing stops.

Lucero approaches the animal; he has never been this close to a bernoz. He runs his hand over the coarse fur. Lucero can sense a dark, alien pacú he doesn't recognize. A tendril from the bear seems to wander into the forest. Then, when the bear's life vanishes, the tendril breaks free and follows an unseen trail like a snake fleeing into the brush.

What a strange pacú.

Lucero helps the others tie the bear to a pole. The animal is lifted and carried back to the village.

The group is proudly led by Dancing Elk; the deep wounds on his chest will forever be a badge of his bravery.

When they reach the village, Wrensong presents him with the leather pouch she proudly made.

"You made this for me? I will always keep it with me."

Dancing Elk hold up the pouch for all to see the gift. The tribe erupts with shouts of approval.

He crouches to hug Wrensong; however, dizziness from blood loss causes him to drop to his knees. Immediately Tiglit gives his mother, sister Wrensong, and Potwah permission to tend to his wounds. They lead him away to the family hut.

After such a victory, Lucero expected some sort of celebration. Instead, the group is solemn since the bear is one of the tribe's totems.

Dancing Elk doesn't want Lucero to help him heal; after all, he must prove himself to Potwah and the tribe. He doesn't allow Lucero into the hut. However, two days later, his wounds have not healed. Potwah and Wrensong keep a vigil next to him, cooling his brow and cleaning the wounds.

On the fourth day, Lucero notices that Potwah seems to be constantly crying. A sign that Dancing Elk is getting worse. So, one night, when exhaustion overwhelms them, they crawl to the corner of the hut to doze off.

As Wrensong's eyes close, a movement catches her attention. At first, she is terrified. She believes the Kushtaka, the Land Otter People, has come to claim Dancing Elk's soul. She grasps the bear-hunting knife and prepares to pounce on the specter. However, when he passes by the fire, she is relieved to see that it's Lucero.

Dancing Elk is unconscious, twitching with fits and bouts. Lucero places his hand on Dancing Elk's forehead. He senses a foul pacú in Dancing Elk, similar to the one from the bear. He draws it out, then sends ember-like pins of light, his own pacú, into the boy. Dancing Elk lets out a sigh of relief and enters a deep sleep. Lucero never noticed that Wrensong witnessed the healing.

The next day, Potwah's humour was brighter, no longer crying. Wrensong had cheered up, also.

Two weeks later, Dancing Elk is fully healed. He is no longer a boy; now, he is a warrior.

Dancing Elk joins the warriors in their practice to learn how to wrestle, wield the knife, and war club. Lucero enjoys watching their practice. He is particularly impressed by Dancing Elk's strength, speed, and ability to pick up the *instruction from White Eagle, the tribe's best fighter. The boy quickly learns the techniques in their mock fights and soon surpasses White Eagle.*

Lucero watches with the recuperating Red Bow by his side. Though too weak to join Dancing Elk, he is quick to comment on his techniques. Lucero wonders why Red Bow's recovery is taking longer.

When Red Bow recovers from his wasting ailment, he accompanies Lucero and Qualut wherever they go. He is an excellent hunter, usually rewarded with a kill when they go on a hunt.

It was a misty day when Dancing Elk, Lucero, and Qualut set out after elk. It does not take long for the young native to pick up the trail of a large bull. Soon, they follow him to a stand of trees by a stream. Dancing Elk shoots the elk and waits as the animal scarps through the thicket.

After a while, they follow the tracks to the animal. However, the elk is not dead yet, and as they approach, it tries to stand but collapses from blood loss. Dancing Elk takes out his stone knife and walks towards the animal, but Qualut holds him back.

"I feel Lucero should send the elk's spirit on its way."

Dancing Elk respects the wish of the shaman and steps back.

Lucero looks puzzled at Qualut, but the shaman nods at him.

"I feel that the elk needs your touch to send him on his journey," Qualut says.

"Why me?" Lucero asks.

"He has asked for the light," Qualut says.

Lucero doesn't fully understand; however, he does not want to offend them by not respecting tradition.

He quietly walks to the animal and touches him. Lucero draws in the animal's *pacú*. The strange essence of the bad energy fills him. Once again, he feels the exhilaration that comes from the dark *pacú*. It is a fraction of what he got from Ijiraq. Still, it reminds him that not only river spirits but all of the creatures of Terrae Exterus carry the tainted energy. It will not affect them as long as it maintains a balance. However, the elk's *pacú* was somehow different.

This pacú is so strong...no, not strong, but dense, yes dense.

Lucero does not question the strange *pacú*. Instead, he gives in to the overwhelming feeling; where it came from doesn't matter; he wants more, needs more.

Lucero doesn't move for a long moment as he rides the feeling until it diminishes.

The stained pacú on this side of the Oriel is so pure; it is more intense than what I got from the ogres. How would it be to taste another's pacú?

He helps process the elk and carries part of the meat. Dancing Elk will let the villagers know where the carcass is, and they will retrieve the rest.

Lucero walks back to the village in silence, deep in his thoughts. Dancing Elk is impressed by Lucero's ability to kill with a touch. Qualut, though, has only one thought.

Everything is going as planned.

Chapter 18
THE PERFODIUM

Summer has been warm and dry in the Valley of Sceapherders. The construction of a small school building and the sleeping quarters goes quickly. It is getting near the time of year when the leaves on the trees start to turn, and the air is brisk. Those who help with the construction assure them that the weather never turns severe in the valley. However, it is colder than they had ever experienced.

Mayven never found a favorable place to dock on the eastern side of the mountains, so he hires Calote villagers and others to build a road from the mouth of the Big River to the valley. Those not local come from far away to work on the project; some are the sons and grandsons of trappers who decided to stay and live in the wilds of the Nurian Forest.

Some come to the project out of curiosity, others out of a need for tender. Some say that a hermit, who roams the weald spreading the word of Eyu, sent them. But, wherever they come from, they are always welcome because there is a lot of work to be done.

Nak of the Halo helps Mayven map the area and the road's course, a task that took two months to accomplish.

Following his original idea of lifting the ship slowly from the bottom, Mayven raises and restores the Fogbow. He permanently seals the hole on the bottom of the hull, then uses the vessel to ferry supplies from Ka-Mer to the new port at the mouth of the Big River. The port is named Nak, after the guard that helped make it possible.

The construction of the road goes quickly. The massive rapids of the Nak Kil block the way to the valley. However, the creative workers build a massive stone bridge to cross it, finishing the link from the coast to the valley. The road is so successful that they continue south towards Barbit and Ka-Mer, creating a corridor to join all of the major Sylvan ports. The project will take several years to finish and employ hundreds of Sylvans.

Michael, Yelu, and Eage visit the Oriel occasionally. They watched the forests of Terrae Exterus from the cupola, but only once did they glimpse one of the natives. One day, Michael becomes curious about the Oriel's chamber and walks around the cupola's small pond.

The points of lights glisten around the cupola and over the lake; their luminescence creates shadows. The shadows on the opposite wall call Michael's attention, and he walks toward them. He finds a path by the side of the chamber that allows him to walk past the Oriel.

He notices something he has not seen before; another set of flagstones that wander into the darkness on the other side. When he entered the cupola, the view of Terrae Exterus appeared and blocked the view of the other side of the cavern.

Curious as always, he stands on the opposite side, turns, and faces the cavern's opposite side. Then, with the Oriel to his back, he sees an opening at the far side of the shaft. He walks to it and comes to a fist-sized opening on the wall. When he looks through it, he is surprised to find an opening to the outside.

The opening is in the thinnest part of the mountain, like a small window in a rock wall.

They deem the area a hallowed place to protect Terrae Exterus and keep the Oriel a secret. They seal the opening and cut a pathway through the ground-level rock to bypass the Oriel.

The opening is hewn into a stone archway. It is fifteen strides wide, enough to accommodate travelers and their carts, and twenty strides high, enough for three Aduncus to fly through it one over the other.

The bypass creates a shortcut to the other side of the Crying Mountains. Because of this, the small village is named Perfodium. The passage through the mountains means that fully supplied travelers now have access to the other side, and commerce takes another leap forward. Upon seeing the potential for opportunity in Perfodium Village, the Sylvans start to migrate into the area. Homes and businesses spring up around the village proper.

With the extra flow of tender and a steady supply of laborers, the monastery's construction starts around the Oriel.

The monachs hide the original opening to the Oriel, high in the mountain, with stone and brush. Then they destroy the path leading to it. Finally, the temple of Eyu, built at the site, conceals the entrance to the Oriel with a stone door.

The secret to opening the door becomes the property of the Perfodium Monachs, and invitations are sent to the original Monachs of the Watch to come and join the Perfodium Monastery. They are thrilled with the offer and become guardians of the monastery and temple.

It is a happy reunion for Yelu, Saltes, Rewen, Sakara, and Bandagee. They have not seen each other for many years. The Watch now has a central location to study and do its work. A vigil is set to watch for Sceagga or Lucero. However, two years passed, and there were no signs of them.

Finally, it is time for Rewen and Tailon to return. Ewen, who is completing her studies at the campus in Ortet, joins them. Then, with a promise of a comeback, they make the trip to Nak, where Mayven waits.

Lucero's long absence causes great concern for all. There should have been some sign from him. They also believe Sceagga has spent enough time in Terrae Exterus to become *more powerful than any sacermagi. Yet, there is only silence from the Oriel and the folk of Terrae Exterus.*

Chapter 19
RISE OF THE DEMON

Word of Lucero, the healer, spreads through the territory; villagers come from the surrounding tribes to cure their illnesses or cast away evil spirits. Even though the visitors bring prosperity to the Taloosh tribe, there is not enough food to cater to all. Lucero finds it odd that there is so much illness among these folk. Shaman Tiglit has to start turning them away.

"We should not turn our backs on their sick," Lucero says.

Then, during a tribal meeting, he has an idea.

"I know that the visitors are placing great pressure on the Taloosh. I can benefit everyone if I go to them," Lucero says.

"If he goes, he will not be protected from the raven," Qualut objects.

"Shaman Qualut, you are a guest of the Taloosh; the decision will be made by the Taloosh," Tiglit says.

Yes, let him go.

So, things go as Qualut planned.

The elders let him do it and decided that during the full moon, he could go and make his visits, teach the ways of Eyu, and heal those who were sick.

Once the decision is made, Tiglit notices that Qualut becomes absent, sometimes for weeks at a time. However, he is always there when it is time for Lucero to make his rounds.

Several miles away, Running Deer is closing in on the elk he has tracked for the last two hours. His companions Kenalt and White Crow are out of sight, making just enough soft noises to keep the animal heading in Running Deer's direction.

Qualut has been following the hunting party, waiting for the right moment to act. He curses himself more than once for successfully spreading the mystery illness.

Before, Qualut would go to a village at night and infect the folk while they slept. Then, he just waited for them to come to Lucero for treatment. But now, if Lucero goes to a village where Qualut has used the pacú to create the illness, he will detect it. So now he must go further away from the villages to find his victims. They must be away from their village hunting, fishing, or gathering. His success made his job that much more difficult.

His experiment with the bear had been successful. He had created a creature bent on destruction. It was something he didn't dare try in Terrae because that type of pacú remained tethered to the creator for a time after its making. A tether that Keepers could follow. However, there were no Keepers here in Terrae Exterus, and Lucero did not know about it.

Qualut follows Running Deer to where he waits to ambush the elk. The hunter crouches by a tree, listening to the animal's approaching footsteps. It will be crossing his path in front of the tree where he waits. Running Deer nocks his arrow and waits.

Qualut is now within twenty-five yards of Running Deer. He gathers the evil essence into one concentrated misty ball from the surrounding vegetation. The shaman has become impatient; he will now dispatch the same dense shadow pacú he had used on the elk, and Lucero will again ingest it.

He sends the misty cloud floating towards Running Deer; it strikes him and dissipates. The hunter sways as a flood of dizziness hits him. He shakes his head and regains his balance for a few moments. The elk enters the clearing in front of him, Running Deer raises his bow, draws the string, and then the world goes black.

Lucero visits the villages early in the morning. He waits for Qualut. The shaman returned late that night from wherever he had gone.

"I've been waiting for you; where did you go?" Lucero asks.

"I had to ask the spirits' advice on matters of the evil affliction that is attacking the villagers. Sometimes, they take a long time to answer," Qualut says.

"Did they answer?"

"Noting useful," Qualut says.

Lucero shrugs the whole thing off as some local custom or belief.

The first village they enter has a young girl who comes home sick from gathering berries. It does not take long for Lucero to absorb her shadow pacú. By just absorbing the shadow pacú, the people would heal. His appetite for the pacú seems insatiable; the more he consumes, the more he wants. It has given him strength beyond anything he experienced in Terrae, a strength he is yet to discover.

He finishes his work in the village and accepts food as payment. Though he is not hungry, he takes the offering because they are proud folk, and this is their way of paying a debt. It is all they can afford to give him, and pride is a big part of their lives.

They provide Lucero and Qualut with a place to spend the night. Qualut leads him to the next village in the morning, where he helps a group of older folk who became ill while fishing. He accepts a necklace from them as payment.

Lucero has enough time in the day for one more visit. He travels to a village where one of its hunters has been in a coma for three days. His companions brought him back unconscious, thinking the elk they were hunting had attacked him. Lucero inspects the patient and finds no external injuries. The blow that caused such a coma would have left signs of trauma on him. He places his hand on the man's chest to survey his life energy.

Lucero feels like he has fallen into a warm bath. The tainted pacú wraps around him, soothing and giving him immense pleasure.

I've felt this before. It's like the elk's pacú.

His hunger becomes uncontrollable; he gives himself in and absorbs it. It takes a while for him to absorb it all. While others have offered him sips of the sweet essence, this one gives him a full draft to imbibe. The young man opens his eyes and looks at Lucero when he is done.

"I felt evil spirits flowing into you; who are you?"

"I am Shaman Lucero," he answers.

He started to refer to himself as a shaman, which he decided had the same meaning as sacerdoyen.

"What is your name?"

"They call me Running Deer. You are the shaman from the Taloosh; I will offer my gratitude to Shaman Tiglit for sending you."

He tries to get up but is too weak and falls back on his mat.

"Rest and eat; Shaman Tiglit won't mind waiting for your gratitude," Lucero says with a smile.

Qualut has been waiting by the entrance to the hut. He felt the pacú passing from the warrior to Lucero. He, too, hungers for the shadow pacú Lucero consumes. However, feeding Lucero is more critical.

Too bad, it is a shame that energy must pass through a living creature before it becomes useful.

It is not the first time Qualut yearns for the negative energy in his surroundings.

Soon I will feed myself. As for Lucero, he will soon taste life.

Lucero kneels by the warrior and keeps his hand on his chest for a few moments longer. His pacú sweeps over the warrior; the negative essence is gone. However, Running Deer's essence is smooth and silky, promising a feast of pleasure if he can tap into it. Lucero pulls his hand away at the thought. The temptation is great, but the consequences would be disastrous for Running Deer. He stands, walks past Qualut, and out of the hut.

Qualut suppresses his smile.

Lucero sleeps uneasily that night. The temptation to take Running Deer's pacú was almost too great to resist. He realizes that a person's healthy pacú is more desirable than the tainted pacú.

I could have taken his pacú when he was in a coma, and no one would have known. Then, I could have announced that it was too late to help him.

Maybe if someone dies while they sleep, the blame will fall on something else.

He pushed the thoughts away.

What am I thinking? I am the Promised One—Or am I?

The episode with Armiger comes to mind.

What did he say his name was now? Ariel?

This troubles him more than his conflict with the pacú. First, Eage has a visit from Eyu, then Ariel, and maybe Michael has had a visit by now.

Why not me?

This makes Lucero angry. He wants to strike out but does not dare to do so. It is with these thoughts that the young shaman finally falls asleep.

When Lucero wakes in the morning, Qualut is gone. He thinks that he probably went to talk to the spirits once more.

He is probably conversing with Eyu.

The thought angers Lucero. He sulks back towards Taloosh village.

Maybe I should take a portion of their pacú that would be a just payment for my services.

He justifies it in his mind.

The trip to the village takes all morning and part of the afternoon. Lucero is within half an hour when Qualut comes running.

"Lucero, you must hurry!" he gasps. "The Taloosh are under attack!"

"Under attack? By whom?"

"A Kalama hunter was killed in their territory, and a Taloosh war club was found at the site."

Qualut is holding his side.

"They are blaming the Taloosh for the murder."

"The Taloosh would never do that," Lucero objects.

"Don't tell me; you have to go and stop them."

Lucero looks down the path; he can make it in fifteen minutes if he runs.

"Go ahead; I'll catch up." Qualut is doubled over.

Lucero runs down the path towards the village. When he disappears from view, Qualut straightens.

Good, it is time for the Promised One to feast.

Lucero runs down the trail wishing he had his wings. It has taken him a while to get used to the idea that he must walk everywhere. Now, what should take him three or four minutes, will take him thirty. As he gets near the village, he can hear the sounds of war cries. Then, when he runs around the last bend, he sees the smoke rising from the trees.

There are a lot of fighting sounds coming from the village. He runs inside and encounters a body sprawled on the ground, face down. He kneels over the body and places his hand on it; the pacú is gone. He rolls it over and sees the bloodied face of Red Bow.

"No!" he shouts.

Red Bow had been like a brother to him.

Anger swells inside. He stands and charges into the melee. Shaman Tiglit is on the ground covering his head as a Kalama warrior swings a wooden club at him. Lucero runs past him, and the warrior drops. Tiglit didn't see Lucero strike the warrior, yet he was dead. The old shaman stands and watches Lucero as he picks up speed. As he runs past a Kalama, the warrior drops. The attackers see what is happening and break the attack. They start to run for the forest cover, but they are not fast enough. In a matter of minutes, the Kalama are eliminated. The young shaman stops and assesses the damage he inflicted on the attackers. Only the ones, who fell wounded in battle, have survived.

Lucero feels the pacú of his victims flowing through him, like the lingering aroma of a delicious meal. However, his hunger is not satiated. He walks to Tiglit and checks his wounds. The old man has a gash on his forehead and arm. Lucero touches his head wound, and it immediately closes. With another touch, his arm heals. The Taloosh are gathering the Kalama that are still alive.

"Bring them to me," he tells them.

They push the wounded warriors towards the shaman and are made to kneel before him. Those who saw him kill the Kalama warriors covered their heads in fear.

341

"I have helped your folk with their illnesses, and this is how you show your gratitude," Lucero shouts.

"One of our hunters had been killed by a Taloosh; revenge was justified." Answers a warrior who seems to hold some rank over the others.

"Revenge does not account for the burning of an entire village," Lucero says.

"It is our way," the warrior answers.

"What proof do you have that it was a Taloosh," Lucero says.

"A Taloosh war club was found next to the body."

"Where is it?" Lucero asks.

"There."

The native points to a club that fell during the battle.

Lucero picks it up and feels a strange essence coming from the club; the feeling is vaguely familiar, but not Taloosh.

Lucero approaches the warrior.

"This was not wielded by a Taloosh."

He holds the club at arm's length.

"I know the spirit of the Taloosh; the spirit of this club is not Taloosh."

"Our shaman said the spirit was Taloosh," the warrior says.

"It is not Taloosh. I think it is a trick to take over the Taloosh. The Kalama will pay for what has happened," Lucero says.

Lucero walks in front of the Kalama and runs his hand over them. They drop dead as he touches them.

"Wait!" says Tiglit. "This is not our law."

But Tiglit is too late. All the Kalama lay dead.

"They killed Red Bow," Lucero says. "They have to pay."

"I know. I saw them kill him," Tiglit says. "But still, it is not our way."

"Maybe not, but it is my way."

With that, Lucero turns and walks towards the entrance of the village.

"Stop him!" Tiglit shouts.

Two warriors run after Lucero, grab his arms, and collapse. Tiglit is shocked; the shaman dedicated to healing the sick has changed into a monster. Lucero looks down at the Taloosh he just killed. When he killed the Kalamas, he hadn't taken the time to savor their pacú. Instead, he acted like a dog in a feeding frenzy, gulping as much food as possible before the others got to it.

Lucero grins; their pacú had been satisfying. When Lucero looks up, Dancing Elk stands before him holding Nenemehkia.

"You cannot go," the boy shouts, "The trickster is driving you."

"Step aside, Dancing Elk."

"I will not; I won't let you pass."

The boy defiantly points the Nenemehkia at Lucero. The sacerdoyen is fond of the boy; perhaps that's what saved his life. Even though the idea of another meal did cross his mind.

Lucero reaches out to move the staff aside, but the boy flips the staff, tapping Lucero's hand. The blow makes a loud sound, and Lucero's hand stings from the strike, much more than it should. He gives the wooden staff a curious look. He vaguely recalls Tiglit talking about Nenemehkia; however, he does not have the time to think about it now.

He leaps over Dancing Elk and runs into the forest, leaving the boy stunned.

Laughing Bear sits well hidden in the bushes. From his vantage point, he can see the whole front area of the settlement and the main path that leads to it. He will safeguard the perimeter of the Kalama village while the warriors go to seek vengeance on the Taloosh. Laughing Bear wants to go with the others, but they have decided that he is to stay.

Laughing Bear is small for his age; that is why they never choose him to go on hunts or, in this case, to join the war party. When he sees the smoke rising above the trees earlier, it assures him that the warriors have been victorious. However, now the skies are clear, and the warriors have not returned.

All is quiet; he scans the area to the south, as far as the trees allow him. He then looks north again and is startled at seeing someone standing in the middle of the path.

How did he get there?

He has a clear view fifty yards up the path; he should have seen him approaching. He recognizes the man as young Shaman Lucero from the Taloosh tribe. He knocks an arrow on his bow. Though the shaman has visited his tribe many times, he is still wary of him. Since the Kalamas are attacking the Taloosh, at this moment, all of the Taloosh are considered the enemy.

Lucero walks calmly into the village. Laughing Bear takes aim with his bow. The shaman makes a motion as if to start running, and he becomes a blur. The warrior puts down his bow to see where he went. He can barely follow the form of the shaman. He passes by a woman kneeling by a fire; she collapses. One of the elders is hanging fish to dry when the shaman passes him, and he too falls. The shaman picks up speed and becomes a mere shadow, everyone he passes dies. Laughing Bear gives up trying to aim. He just watches in horror as his entire tribe dies.

Laughing Bear is too shocked to do anything. He looks down at the bodies scattered about his village; all women, children, and elders are gone. His eyes have seen a demon kill his entire village in what it takes for a tree to fall.

The shaman goes back to the road. Something has changed about him; he looks larger, his skin is darker, and a long scaly tail sticks out from the bottom of his coverings. Lucero walks away without looking back. It is more than Laughing Bear can handle, and he passes out.

Lucero turns, and for an instant, he feels the pacú of a living creature.

Did I miss someone?

But the feeling is gone. He shrugs and continues. The next tribe is six miles away, and he is still hungry.

As Lucero walks down the path, a familiar shadow crosses within the range of his pacú. He stops and looks around; from the trees emerges Qualut. The old shaman looks different to him. He is now younger and bigger, and his skin has also changed into a darker tone.

"Are you going to try and stop me?" Lucero asks.

"On the contrary, Master," Qualut says, "I've come to help you."

"I don't need your help," Lucero says.

The young shaman continues to walk down the path.

"Of course not, m'lord, but I can save you time," Qualut says. "I know where all of the other tribes are located."

Lucero stops and turns; Qualut has his attention.

"What other tribes?" Lucero asks.

"The tribes we have visited are a small sample of the tribes found on this land."

"Why hadn't we visited them before?"

"Because some are more primitive, some are far away, and they do not interact with the ones in this area."

"And you know where they are?"

"Of course, I have traveled this land for a long time; I have seen them all." Qualut lies.

Lucero continues walking; Qualut takes this as an acceptance of his presence and falls in step next to him.

Laughing Bear wakes up; at first, he does not remember where he is. He stands and looks at the village below; seeing the bodies refreshes his memory. He realizes that if the warriors have not returned, he is probably the only one of his clan left.

What should I do next?

The demon shaman headed in the direction of the next tribe.

Am I the only one left?

He looks down the path where Lucero entered the village.

The only safe thing to do is to go from where he came. But that takes me to the Taloosh. Will they show me the same mercy as the demon?

He looks down the path, but the demon is long gone.

I have no choice.

He runs down the path towards the Taloosh.

As he nears, he becomes more cautious and blends into the bushes. Laughing Bear approaches the entrance and sees the bodies. Both Taloosh and Kalamas are strewn everywhere. The surviving Taloosh are carrying the bodies and setting them side by side. At the same time, the shaman makes incantations over the corpses.

Laughing Bear is shocked; he becomes careless and wanders into the Taloosh camp to look at the dead. He is spotted immediately, set upon by the Taloosh warriors, and captured.

They bring him to Shaman Tiglit.

"What have you done to my folk?" Laughing Bear shouts.

"This was not our work," Tiglit says.

"It was your demon who came to my tribe and killed all."

Tiglit is shocked to hear this.

"Why do you say that it was our demon?" Tiglit asks.

"When he came into our village, he was the shaman you call Lucero," Laughing Bear says.

"He went to your tribe?"

"Yes, and killed everyone," the warrior says.

"Believe me when I tell you that we did not send the shaman," Tiglit says.

"He is not a shaman; he is a demon," Laughing Bear spits.

"Because he killed your folk?" Dancing Elk asks.

"No, because when he left, he had a tail."

"A tail?"

"Yes, a tail, looked like the one on a water rat, but bigger."

"The influence of the evil one has won," Tiglit says.

"Where is he now?"

"I don't know; he kept on heading south."

"He must be following the route he used to take," Tiglit says.

"Dancing Elk!"

"Yes, Shaman."

"I remember that in your dream, the shadow was also cast over the Taloosh,"

"Yes, it was long and dark, darker than the others."

"I believe we must leave this land, or we will also perish," Tiglit says.

"Do you think this shadow is the demon?"

"Yes."

"What about the raven? Who is the one that corrupted him?"

Tiglit looks around the tribe and thinks about it.

"Good question," the shaman says. "The only one left is Qualut; he was never surprised by Shaman Lucero's magic. On the contrary, he always acted like he expected him to have this ability."

"You're right, and whenever Lucero visited the tribes, Qualut was always there, " Dancing Elk says.

"How about the Kalama warrior?"

"There is no more Kalama; he is Taloosh now," the shaman says.

The warriors release Laughing Bear.

"What is your name?" Tiglit asks.

"Laughing Bear."

"Laughing Bear, do you accept the Taloosh as your folk?"

Laughing Bear thinks about this. The shaman is right, his tribe no longer exists, and they offer him the chance to join their tribe.

"Yes, I do," he answers.

Tiglit then places his hands on the young warrior's shoulders.

"Welcome to our tribe."

Six months go by, and between Qualut and Lucero, they eliminate most of the tribes in the area. They work quickly, and most of the time, they can purge the entire population before an alarm is even sounded. Qualut does his feeding when Lucero cannot see him. He does not want him to know that he, too, can feed on another's pacú.

Qualut reveals to Lucero that he, too, can control the pacú. He starts to teach Lucero different ways to use it. He even reveals to him how he turned the bear's mind.

"That was you that made the bear go into a rage?" Lucero asks.

"Yes, it could become a useful weapon."

"Hmm."

On several occasions, hunters and gatherers spot them when they pass by in the distance. Stories of the forest demons spread. They refer to them as Sé-sxac, which means wild men.

Lucero stops wearing vestments save for the bracelet to access the Oriel and a strap for the Traduco Glass bag. His shape has changed to a large ape-like creature with long hair covering his body and a scaly tail. Because of the bracelet's influence, the arm that bears it remains human, smaller, and weaker than the other.

Qualut has also transformed and taken a similar appearance. However, he starts to wear concealing robes to keep his form hidden. He develops a large hump on his back, which becomes conspicuous. Though he has grown in height, he is still smaller than Lucero.

The tribes that come across the demon's grizzly work start to migrate towards the mountains to the south; others cross the big water to the west and travel far into the forest when they reach the opposite shore.

All tremble in fear at the mention of the name Sé-sxac. The name would later be corrupted to sasquatch and become a part of Terrae Exteran legend.

Lucero and Qualut have to get their fill hunting deer, elk, bear, and moose; whatever large animal crosses their path. They would often sustain injuries that would cripple or kill a normal human. But those wounds quickly heal, often within minutes. But the animal's pacú was like a tasteless meal that fills but does not satisfy. So they crave the sweetest essence of all, man.

It is early fall when they find themselves in front of the Taloosh village again. The weather has turned somewhat windy, the skies are heavy, and sporadic rain pelts them. For some long-forgotten reason, they had spared the Taloosh. However, now they long for their pacú. Like all the other tribes, the Taloosh abandoned their village to escape the Sé-sxac. This angers Lucero since he hoped to feed on them. Qualut also hoped to replenish his pacú and was equally disappointed. A strong gust blows Qualut's hood off his head, exposing his darkened naked skin. Lucero ponders what he sees. Qualut immediately replaces the hood and tries to divert unwanted attention.

"Gone, they are all gone," Qualut says. "We should have hunted the outer tribes first; then, it would have been too late for those close by to escape."

"Talking about what we should have done will not fill us," Lucero says. "We must find the tribes; you said you knew where they all were."

"But Master, we have visited them all," Qualut says.

"Most of the ones we visited were either abandoned or dead. Dead before we got to them." Lucero says.

The demon looks carefully at Qualut's face. He hadn't noticed before the changes that had gone on with his partner.

Qualut quickly turns to avoid his stare. He is starting to realize that he is losing control of Lucero. He is no longer naïve, no longer innocent.

"How is it that you have also changed like I have?" Lucero asks. "You have also been feeding on their pacú, haven't you?"

Lucero knocks the hood off Qualut's head with a quick sweep of his hand.

"Who are you? Why is it that you can feed on another's pacú?"

Qualut starts to back away.

"Master Lucero, you are powerful enough to return to your world and control it; no one is more powerful than you. So don't you think it's time to return to our homeland and rule?"

"Why is it that you call it our homeland?"

"But Master, what are you after if not to rule Terrae?" Qualut avoids the questions.

Lucero looks at Qualut in the eyes; he holds out his hand, showing a upashim glowing in his palm.

"Who are you?"

"I am your father," he answers. "I am Sceagga."

He opens his robes and throws them aside. Two large, leathery wings finally stretch after being cramped in a confined space; Qualut's hump.

"Sceagga? My father?"

"I was the one who planted the seed in your mother years ago," Sceagga says.

"How did you get here?" Lucero asks.

"I was the one you asked to take you to Sylvanus."

"Bullen?"

"Yes, then, I became your guide when you went to find the caves in the Crying Mountains."

"You became Teke?"

"Yes, then Qualut, to finish your training here," Sceagga says. "Come back with me; we can rule the lands of Terrae together."

"I am not interested in ruling the lands of Terrae; I want to get what I was denied. I am the Promised One, but others receive privileges over me. So I will take what is supposed to be mine; I will challenge Eyu and rule the universe."

Lucero steps closer to Sceagga.

"How is it you got your wings back?"

"Have you forgotten that you have them? Feel them; they are still there."

Lucero closes his eyes and tries to remember how they feel; yes, they are there.

"I need more nourishment from this land to challenge the creator. You have slowed me down; the abandoned villages were your doing, wasn't it?"

"I, too, need nourishment. I am like you," Sceagga argues. "I am your father."

Lucero opens his eye and looks at him.

"How dare you speak of my father. He died a hero. During the Palisades battle," Lucero growls.

"Did your father have powers he could pass to you? Did your mother? No, the powers you have came from me, from here."

Sceagga points to his heart.

Lucero scowls at him.

"If you are my father, why have you done this to me? Why have you turned me into this? You are no father. You just want to use me. Now that I think about it, you have been turning me into some tool, haven't you?"

Now Sceagga holds his hands up.

"Wait, Lucero, my son—"

"Don't call me son. If you were my father, where were you when I learned to tangle the pacú? Where were you when Michael got us in trouble? Where were you when I learned to fly?"

Sceagga starts to back away.

"There was an order of prejudice against me. I had to stay away."

"You are not my father, and you have taken pacú that was mine. But, I can take your pacú and retrieve what you have taken."

"Lucero listen, I can help you, I can fly, and I can find the tribes. I can show you how to get your wings back. We can still work together."

Lucero does not listen to what Sceagga says. Sceagga realizes this and takes to the air; Lucero's upashim narrowly misses him, exploding into the totem by the entrance. The tall pole tips and crashes to the ground. Sceagga flies over the treetops; Lucero runs, trying to keep up with him. However, with obstacles such as fallen trees, boulders, and streams, he begins to fall behind. Sceagga doubles back and goes towards the village.

Where is he going?

Lucero starts to feel his pacú draining away; the exertion of running at top speed is taking its toll. Finally, Sceagga drops to the ground at the base of a cliff.

Now you are mine.

Lucero breaks through the brush and finds himself facing a stone wall.

Where...?

There are no signs of Sceagga. Lucero sends his pacú forward, but nothing registers, not even the shadow of his hidden essence.

As he takes several steps forward, the air shimmers in front of him, then a window hisses open; he has stumbled on the Oriel's entryway.

The image of a valley shimmers before him. He wonders if he should continue the pursuit but has no idea where Sceagga has gone; He recalls that the bracelet will take him to the Oriel's cupula. However, it will open and close randomly without the bracelet; Sceagga could be anywhere but the Oriel.

I could use the Traduco Glass, but I am still unsure how it works. It couldn't find Michael that day.

I'll eventually have to return to Terrae to finish feeding. But now, I can't lose track of the tribes.

He steps back, and the Oriel hisses shut.

I'll have plenty of time to find Sceagga.

Lucero walks back to the village, wanders around the burned-down structures, and comes across Tiglit's shelter; the black stone sits where it has always been. Lucero sits in front of it, reaches out, and places his hands on it. He can feel the grey pacú swirling inside. It is strong, stronger than any creature in this world carries.

How can I harness this power?

Lucero tries to draw on the stone, but it will not yield its wealth.

Why can all of the creatures in this place absorb the pacú, but I can't? They don't even know how to use it.

Then a thought occurred.

Maybe if I don't try.

Lucero turns and leans on the stone. He starts to feel the dark energy soak into his back. It is a slow, steady trickle.

Ahh, it seeps slowly into the body over time; it's a natural process. But it's slow...too slow.

He stands back up.

I'll miss the Taloosh. The Taloosh first, and then I'll come back for the stone.

Lucero pulls the Traduco Glass from the pouch and holds it high.

"Show me the Taloosh!"

The air in front of him shimmers, and the window opens. The view floats over the trees near the ocean. Then he sees several Taloosh working hard in a clearing, hollowing out an enormous boat. It is long, narrow, and carved out of a single trunk of a large tree.

Why didn't it work when I called Michael?

Twenty-five yards away, he sees a second canoe. It is prepared just as big as the first. Tiglit chants and waves Nenemehkia over the craft, asking the tribe's totems for their blessings.

They are planning to escape across the big water. I'll lose if they finish the crafts before I reach them.

The view settles on Tiglit.

"I've found you," He growls.

Tiglit hears the words, looks up, and sees the face of the demon hovering over him. He produces a handful of powder from a pouch on his belt, which he tosses at the image. Somehow, the powder comes through the window. The dust stings his eyes and mouth immediately.

The demon drops the glass, coughing and gagging. Lucero rubs his eyes and stumbles for the stream, where he washes off the offensive dust.

How could he do that?

He estimates that the Taloosh must be a couple weeks' walk.

They're near the River Spill. Where we used to go fishing.

For the next week and a half, Lucero walks towards the north by day and tries to find his wings by night. Little by little, he starts to feel them again.

On the northernmost shore, Tiglit sits in his shelter. Day after day, he meditates on the tribe's totems, asking them for help.

While the men work hard to finish the canoe, Wrensong takes her basket to the seashore to search the water's edge for clams and seaweed. The shell-crusted rocks and boulders by the seashore are rough and sharp, and while reaching for a large cluster of mussels, Wrensong stumbles and cuts her leg on a rock.

Wrensong ignores the deep cut and keeps on foraging. When her basket is full, she walks back to camp, limping.

The next morning, Wrensong wakes feverish and can barely stand. Red Bird makes her stay in the hut while she tries to cure the wound. But an infection has started, and she doesn't know what else she can do.

Meanwhile, Dancing Elk knows he will have to get into the canoe they are building; there's no other choice, but he can feel the fear and turmoil deep in his stomach.

Potwah has not left his side since their escape towards the ocean shore began. They made their union when they fled the village; she is now his partner for life. Potwah looks at him and knows what he's thinking.

"You will have to face the water, Tsálk," Potwah says.

All the times Lucero offered to teach him to swim come to mind. He always found an excuse not to go. Now, he regrets not taking the time to learn.

"I know. I avoided Lucero when he offered to teach me. Now I have to face the water on my own."

"I'll be with you," Potwah says.

"Thank you," Dancing Elk says and means it.

It will take them several weeks to complete the canoes, and Lucero is on his way. Potwah tries to take him to the water, but he wants to be by Wrensong's side, another reason to avoid the water. Finally, one day she pulls him out of the hut and walks him to the water.

"We are doing this today," Potwah says

She holds his hand and pulls him into the shallows. The icy waters bring back memories of the day his father died. Potwah presses him to go further and manages to get him to his waist. He smiles at Potwah.

"Thank you," he says.

But going that far flails his nerves. The achievement is overshadowed by Wrensong's increasing illness and the dismal prospect of getting in the canoe. The darkness keeps growing in his mind.

The waters will be deeper than my waist.

Tiglit saw the demon's face in the hole in the air, and behind him, the burned longhouse and the black stone. So that means the demon was still in the village.

Perhaps with the totem's blessing, we might just make it.

Day after day, Tiglit asks the totems for help; all he gets in return is silence. Then he remembers something, Lucero was always talking about his God, the one he used to respect before he fell out of grace with Him. So Tiglit puts away his bones and charms. He starts to ask for Eyu's blessing. He continues his desperate petitions for the next four days. Tiglit fasts as an offering to Eyu; he refuses to sleep for fear of breaking any connection he may have made to the alien god. The more he asks for help, the more desperate he becomes. He feels that his entire tribe will perish like the others. He feels it is his responsibility to save the Taloosh, but he does not know how to do it. On the fifth day, desperation strikes him down to his soul. He feels lost and cries for the first time in years until sleep overtakes him.

Chapter 20
THE MAGUS CAIRN

Lucero is approaching the ocean; he can smell the salt in the air. He makes his wings tangible; however, they are weak from lack of use. Lucero will need a couple of days to make them strong and functional again. He stretches his wings; he has been doing this every half hour. It is a slightly painful process, like stretching a cramped limb. It takes some time to get used to their leathery texture; they remind him of the ones on those small mouse-like creatures that fly in the night.

What had Red Bow called them? The fur-hide bird?

The memory of the young warrior brings an ache of angst into his heart. He and Dancing Elk had been like brothers. Red Bow's death had been the catalyst that had pushed him over the edge and turned him into the uncaring beast he is now.

Dancing Elk had said that the trickster made me do it, and he was right; the trickster was Sceagga.

The path he has been following leads him to the river. All he has to do now is follow it to the ocean. Large fish splashing in the shallows satisfies his hunger but adds little to his pacú.

While feasting on a fish, his senses are assailed. It is like a loud bell suddenly pealing in a quiet room. The sound is not physical but spiritual. However, it is strong enough to knock him to his knees. He covers his ears, but it does not help. The initial toll fades, offering some relief; however, the following hum remains a constant reminder of its peal.

The loudness of the sound rouses Tiglit from his sleep. He looks outside his hut to see where the hum comes from. The men working on the long canoes, the women bent over the fires, the children playing, all act as if they had not heard it. He steps out of his hut. The hum gets more intense near the corner of his shelter. It is just outside the spot where he had fallen asleep. He looks closer and notices a shimmer in the air; it is like a small totem, the height of his knee and thick like his leg. He picks up a handful of stones and tosses them at the column; they pass through without effect. Dancing Elk also follows the hum to its source.

"Can you see it? It's like a stump of water." Tiglit says.

"I think Eyu has answered," Dancing Elk says.

The pasturelands outside Perfodium Village span a valley hemmed by a forested area to the northwest, the Taluga Region, a swamp surrounding a kil to the south, and the mountains to the east. Occasional flooding of the kil has made the pasturelands fertile.

Michael helps Eage tend the scēap on the pastureland. He is starting to enjoy the outings with the blind monach, and the scēap takes his mind off the village's everyday problems.

The weather is turning, and Michael dons his cold-weather robes. Soon, the rains will start, and the scēap will need to be moved towards the foothills.

Earlier that year, the herd was devastated by barghest from the weald to the northwest. When the pack started entering the village. Michael had to step in and kill them.

Later, several hunters from north of the mountains spoke of a black-robed Aduncus flying from a village. When the hunters reached the town, all the villagers were dead.

Eage and Michael go to investigate; Sceagga's essence stained the dead. He found that a disproportionate number of males were missing.

"A village this size with this many doyennes and children could not function if only a few males are present," he says.

"The Aduncus was seen heading towards the plains in the northwest. If it's Sceagga, it would explain the presence of the barghest," Michael says.

"Time will tell what else Sceagga left behind," Eage adds.

Once the barghest pack is gone, it is safe for the scēap to return to the valley. Eage hires the local youth to take care of the herd. However, with today's nice weather, Eage gives them the day off and enjoys the time in the pasture. The day is relaxing and uneventful, and at the end of the day, they start to bring back the herd.

"You know, Master Eage, the scēap do tend to grow on you," Michael says.

"Wait until winter is over. I will show you how to clip their lanin and turn it into cloth."

"Does it smell as strong as they do?"

"Oh heavens, no, the smell washes away, and the cloth can be either cool or warm, according to how you weave it."

"Sounds intriguing," Michael smiles.

Eage knows Michael can be sarcastic and chuckles.

"You'll like it; you'll see."

The spiritual assault catches them both by surprise. Michael's knees buckle, and he stumbles; only his staff keeps him from falling. Eage drops to his knees.

"What was that?" Michael asks.

He tries covering his ears, but it does not help.

"It feels like a magus cairn," Eage says.

"A what?"

"It's a beacon created by a sacerdoyen during a crisis."

"I've never heard of it," Michael said.

"I'm afraid its use is so rare that we may have overlooked it in your teachings."

"A magus cairn," Michael repeats. "When will it go away?"

"When the cairn is dissipated," Eage says.

"So, what does it mean? How is it dissipated?"

Michael is back on his feet, though the constant hum is strumming on his senses. He helps Eage back to his feet and dusts his robes.

"The magus cairn is a call for help. Somebody is in need, and that somebody is a sacerdoyen."

"Can you tell who it is?"

"Normally, yes, but this one is different, very rough. It may have been made unknowingly, by accident."

"You don't know whose it is?"

"No, I can't read the signature, but there is something curious about it."

"What's that?"

"It's not of Terrae, but of Terrae Exterus."

"Lucero?" Michael asks. "Could Lucero have created it?"

"No, it is not his signature, but whoever created it is in great need."

"Does that mean the outerworld is calling?"

"Yes, someone is in great peril, though I wasn't expecting a cairn from them."

"Does that mean Sceagga has started his disruption?"

"It is possible. But remember that Sceagga is back in Terrae."

"And there is word of recent attacks on more villages," Michael says.

"Yes, unfortunate, but too late for us to help. Some of the monachs are on their way there to offer whatever assistance they can," Eage says.

Eage grabs Michael's arm.

"Now is the time for you, Michael, to go to the outerworld, seek out the cairn, and see if your brother is well."

"Seek out the cairn? How should I do that?"

"Just follow your senses. Your robes will assist you."

"How about you?" Michael asks. "Aren't you coming?"

"Don't forget that I can't fly, and with a rogue monach on the loose, I need to stay around here," the old sacerdoyen says.

"I guess you're right. Still, I would have liked to have someone who knows what's happening."

"Don't worry, my son; you will know what to do when you get there. Besides, your brother is there; he will help you," Eage says.

I'll finally see Luce again.

"When should I go?"

""As soon as you get your robe. Let's get back to the village," says Eage.

They leave the scēap to fend for themselves; now, getting Michael on his way is critical.

On the way to the village, they spot a Sylvan walking on the road towards Perfodium. Soon their paths converge, and the three find themselves traveling the same trail. The stranger wears well-traveled robes. However, he is clean, and though he may be poor, he never asks the two for a hand out which is out of the ordinary.

"Do you have business in Perfodium Village?" Michael asks.

"Actually, I do. Are you from there?"

"Yes, we are," Michael answers.

Eage remains quiet, listening to the conversation.

"Do you happen to know if there is a metal worker in the village?" the stranger asks.

He notices that the younger is unusually large for his height and takes furtive looks at his massive shoulders.

"Yes, there is, and a fine one, too," Michael answers.

"Good, I'll need his services."

"Also, are you familiar with the citizens of the village?"

"With most," Michael says.

"I'm looking for a sacerdoyen named Eage,"

"He can be hard to find," Eage finally speaks.

He squeezes Michael's arm.

"Is your business with this Eage or the metal worker?"

"As a matter of fact, with both." The stranger says. "And of the utmost importance. If you know the master, I would appreciate being directed to him when we reach the village."

"Do you know Master Eage?" Michael asks.

"Never met him, but I've been sent to find him and seek his help in certain matters of great importance."

"If we are to help you, then by what name should we address you?" Eage asks.

"I go by the name of Ariel," he says.

"Ariel? The Hermit Scribe?" Eage asks.

"Yes, I guess I've been called that," he grins.

"I seemed to recall part of your story, as was told to me by a krokewurm," Eage says.

"A krokewurm? I encountered one a long time ago," Ariel says. "It almost turned unpleasant. But, I've never talked with a krokewurm?"

"Yes, it was somewhat of a surprise for me as well," Eage says.

"Luckily, our encounter ended with a mutual agreement," says Ariel.

"It was left with a message for me and a promise that they would leave the Sylvans alone in the future," Eage says. "If you are the Ariel I've been told of, then you may have traveled with an acquaintance, Lucero."

"Yes, I knew Lucero," Ariel says. "A good friend, though he seemed to have a lot on his mind."

"Oh?" Michael says.

"Did any other stranger travel with you?"

"As a matter of fact, yes, an Aduncus. I never really trusted him; he was called Teke. Something about him that made my skin prickle. He seemed very interested in Lucero; the two were always together," Ariel says. "Did you know Lucero? Who may you be?" Ariel asks.

"I'm Eage, the one you seek."

Ariel stops and looks at the two.

"Then you must be Michael," he says. "And I wager that those are your wings under that robe."

"Yes, they are. I didn't know I was that well known."

"So, you're his brother? There isn't any family resemblance," he says. "I was told I would find you two together."

"Been told by whom?" Eage asks.

"By Eyu, of course."

Ariel tells them about the last vision he had. He was to build a great sword whose design would be like no other.

"The blade is to be twenty knuckles in length."

"Twenty knuckles!" Michael says, "That's twice the length of the standard sword."

"Yes, and with a two-handed grip. The blade will have a slight upward curve and be made of this special metal."

Ariel pulled a large lump of silvery metal from his pack.

"Where did you get this?" Michael asks.

"It fell from the heavens in a great ball of fire," Ariel says. "I was told to take it to Perfodium Village and seek Master Eage's help processing it because no wood-driven fire would be able to smelt it."

Eage takes the heavy lump into his hands and turns it over, feeling its texture.

"Hmm. It's heavy for its size and smooth like a glaze. I can feel it emanate a strange pacú. No wood-driven fire? Hmm. I know a substance that takes time to ignite, but once it does, it will burn hotter than wood." says Eage.

"Good, then you two will help me."

"Yes, I will help you. But unfortunately, Michael is on a mission. He will be leaving us as soon as we reach the village."

"Too bad. I was looking forward to your company," Ariel says.

"There is great distress in a foreign land; Michael is going to help."

"I see. I had a vision of a land called Terrae Exterus. Is that it?" Ariel ponders.

"A vision? Then you've been informed," Eage says.

"Do you think it is a matter of Eyu?" Ariel asks.

"If a sacerdoyen from Terrae has been summoned to assist in Terrae Exterus, then it must be," Eage says.

"Interestingly, our summons seemed to coincide," Ariel says.

"Do you think they could be related?" Eage asks.

"If they both involve Eyu, then what do you think?"

"I see what you mean."

When they reach the village, Caput Mun Olar, of the Perfodium guard, meets them.

"Master Eage, Master Michael, an Aduncus courier, just brought news of another attack. It occurred yesterday in a village on the other side of Sylvanus," Mun Olar says.

"Hmm, it seems the attacks are moving farther away from Perfodium," Eage says.

"Do you think the attacker is purposely avoiding Perfodium?" Michael asks.

"The attacker could be preparing, gathering forces, for an attack," Ariel says.

"And you might be?" Mun Olar asks.

"I'm Ariel. I was summoned to Perfodium to seek Master Eage," Ariel says.

"Ariel? The Pilgrim?" Mun Olar asks.

"Yes, another label I bear," Ariel says.

"Master Eage, should I prepare for an assault?" Mun Olar asks.

"As Ariel said, whoever is doing the attacks seems to be gathering a small army. I believe we still have time. Their army will still need training. I will send a courier to Ortet for help. Perhaps they can spare a few Halo," Eage says.

"Very well. I will prepare as well," Mun Olar says.

With that, the caput bows and hurries away.

"Let's get home. Michael needs to be on his way. Ariel, you will be our guest; come."

They hurry to the village.

Yelu senses their arrival and waits in the garden. She greets and escorts them into the house. Yelu's day servant is still there and has a hot meal ready.

"We've been waiting for you, Master Eage," Yelu says. "We have some news that may be of importance."

"Oh? Does it have to do with that annoying hum?"

"No, but I was going to ask you about it also. Anyway, a hunter came down from the Crying Mountains today. He claims that he was hunting in the area of the attacked village. It was about two weeks ago, he said. He saw an Aduncus fly down into the village and kill all the ferms, children, and some menfolk. Then, those who survived followed him and abandoned the village."

"That's the same time the other hunters claim the Aduncus attacked the village," Michael says.

"Whoever it is, fed on the villager's pacú. There is always a bad element in any large village. They probably decided to follow the Aduncus." Eage says.

"It's like Sceagga and Hergian all over again," Yelu says.

"However, we haven't found any traces of either of them," Eage says.

Michael goes to his room and retrieves his robe. Yelu confronts him.

"Where are you going?"

"I need to leave for a short while."

Michael is evasive. Ever since Lucero left for Terrae Exterus, she has been nervous about Michael.

"How long will you be gone?"

"I'm not sure, mother," Michael answers.

Lucero has not returned. One look at Michael with the robe tells her Michael is going to Terrae Exterus to find him. Something has gone wrong.

"Michael, you know my gift. I can tell when you are being evasive. If you're going after Lucero, I'm coming with you," she says.

"Mother, I have to go alone; that's how we planned it. I have the robe and can fly faster. You won't be able to keep up." Michael says.

"I can still fly faster than you."

"Not while I wear the robes."

"Don't matter. I'm still going. Do you think I can just stay back here waiting? I can sense you. I can follow you even if I fall behind."

She gets her waybag and quickly puts in some clothes, weapons, and rover cakes.

Michael smiles.

I guess she hasn't forgotten her halo training.

They start for the door; Eage calls them aside for a moment.

"Michael, there is something you should know," Eage says. "Ariel, as scribe, you should hear this too."

He leads them to a separate room.

"Michael, take a seat. This will take but a moment," Eage says.

Michael sits.

"What is it, Master Eage?"

"First of all, you know that the work of Eyu is difficult to divine. However, he tells us just enough to keep us on course, and the rest is left to faith," Eage says.

"What are you getting at?" Michael asks.

"We have never told you about your father because the whole matter is complicated."

Yelu groans.

"I guess the time has come for you to know," Yelu says.

"Know what? What about my father? He died in the battle at the palisades....didn't he?"

"No, not exactly," Eage says.

"Let me help," Yelu says.

She places her hands on Michael's shoulders.

"What Master Eage is trying to tell you is that," she takes a deep breath. "You and your brother Lucero are Sceagga's offspring."

"WHAT!"

Michael stands, sending the chair to the floor. He is dumbfounded; the whole idea of it seems preposterous.

"How?"

"First of all, it's not what you think. It all happened during the battle against the Solois off the Cliff Side Palisades," Yelu says.

"You've told me of the battle," Michael says.

"Well, let me tell you the whole story."

The doyenne recounts what happened during the battle at the Palisades, her confrontation with Sceagga, and the lightning strike. When she is done, Michael sits again for a few moments.

"What does it all mean? I mean, how do we fit into it?" Michael asks.

"We don't know," Yelu says. "Perhaps your journey to Terrae Exterus will yield some answers."

"Let's try to find your brother. Answers will come when they come," Eage says.

"Ok, but I want the whole story when we get back."

She nods.

"I'll help Ariel on this project of his," Eage says.

"We'll be back as soon as possible to help," Yelu says.

"Have a safe trip," Ariel says.

They walk Michael and Yelu to the door. Eage hands Michael, a leather bracelet with an ornate golden band.

"Remember what I told you about the bracelet? Along with the robe, it will guide you back to the Oriel."

Yelu slips the leather strap of her waybag over her head, and Michael dons his robe, which shimmers with a radiant whiteness. With a wave, they jump into the air and disappear.

Their first order of business is to go to the Oriel's old entrance. It typically takes about fifteen minutes. However, with the robe, it only takes Michael two minutes. Yelu, on the other hand, takes five minutes longer.

She finds Michael waiting for him. Michael sees that she is starting to breathe heavily. She must have been flying at full speed to keep up.

He motions to the Oriel's entrance.

"If Sceagga has been in Terrae for the last three weeks, why are the outworlder asking for help?"

"You're right. Eage said that the cairn didn't have Lucero's signature. Maybe Sceagga went back," Yelu says.

"Maybe."

She doesn't know about yesterday's attack on the other side of Sylvanus.

"I will close this entrance. Whoever it is will have to go through the temple to use the Oriel," Michael says.

"Good idea."

Michael sends a series of upashims into the rocks high up the mountain, starting an avalanche and turning the entire mountainside to scree, thus covering the entrance.

He looks at his work.

Sceagga doesn't know about the temple entrance.

Michael realizes that his pacú has barely diminished.

Come to think about it, when I killed the barghest, the upashims barely lessened my pacú. It must be the robe.

"Let's go," he says.

Michael flies at a leisurely pace, so Yelu can keep up. This vexes her since she has always been proud of her speed. A few minutes later, they're at the doors of the Perfodium Temple.

Upon entering the temple, the Monachs of the Watch greet them. Eage's personal assistant, Bartolon, is the Keeper of The Oriel, a reward for his years of duty: since he has minimal control over the pacú. However, for Bartolon, it is like a punishment.

As Keeper of The Oriel, he must become one of the sequestered monakites. They are prohibited from interacting with others outside of a small chosen group. Bartolon has always been interested in teaching, so he does not understand why Eage made him the Keeper of The Oriel. He considers the promotion an insult.

"Greetings, Master Michael, Lady Yelu," the monach says. "I thought you were in the pastures tending the scēap with Master Eage?"

"Greetings Bartolon, the Exteraens have called. I have to go to them."

"I wonder if it's the same summons that Watch Sakara has been talking about all morning," he says. "I felt something, but nothing like what Sakara described."

"Yes, it probably is," Michael says.

They hurry to the back of the temple. The door to the secret passage is narrow and angled behind the altar, hidden from view. It is awkward to go through it with wings, but with the waybag, Yelu can barely fit, so she takes it off and carries it through the doorway.

"It must be wonderful to have the sacerdoyen's gift," the monach murmurs loud enough for the others to hear.

Maybe then, they would have considered someone else to do this.

"Believe me, it can be irritating at times. The constant hum of the cairn is starting to annoy me," Michael says.

"I, too, feel something. It does get to be annoying," Yelu says.

They follow Bartolon through a maze of passages. Only Bartolon and a few others know the path to the Oriel. Anyone else would become helplessly lost in the labyrinth. They enter *a chamber with many entrances. Bartolon chooses the one that is second from the right. The heavy stone door is identical to the other doors. Bartolon produces a key from the folds of his robes and unlocks it. From now on, it seems his entire existence will revolve around that key. He follows them inside, through a corridor, and into the Oriel's chamber.*

The cupola never fails to amaze him, with the mist of sparkling lights illuminating it and the pool of water that ripples continuously.

Michael steps onto the cupola, and immediately the window opens, showing the deep green forest on the other side.

"I'll visit the other side one of these days," Bartolon says.

"I hope it's for pleasure."

"Me too."

Michael turns to him and smiles. The monach places his hand on his shoulder.

"May Eyu watch over you."

"Thank you."

Michael twists the bracelet and steps off the cupola into Terrae Exterus.

As Yelu dons the waybag again, she watches Michael walk into the outerworld.

That's strange, he lost his wings, and his features have changed. I would never have recognized him. He looks like a rather rough groundstay.

She turns to the monach.

"Thank you, Watch Bartolon. We'll see you soon," Yelu says.

"I'll be here," his sarcasm is not for her.

Yelu takes a step forward, but the window closes.

"Wait, what happened?"

Bartolon looks just as shocked as she.

"I don't know; it closed fast. It was like you weren't allowed to go," Bartolon says.

Yelu steps towards the Oriel again. This time the window opens to an extensive grassland. The tall grass moves and parts. A group of large tan cat predators emerges, moving slowly, their eyes on Yelu. She takes another step towards the window.

"This place is different. Where's Michael?"

The animals charge with a barking growl, tails waving high, and throwing clouds of dust with each step.

"Lady Yelu, no!'

Bartolon grabs her arm and pulls her back as the cats pounce.

The window closes.

She stares at the Oriel for a few moments.

"What were those?"

"Some kind of panzoons. The window must have opened in the middle of a hunting group." Bartolon says.

"What if I'd step through and fly? Can I just go and look for my duvos?"

"No, Lady Yelu. Terrae Exterus is just as large as Terrae. You wouldn't know where to go. You could be thousands of millisteps from them. You could be on a different continent."

She glares at the Oriel for a few moments.

"I wonder what Eage knows about this."

"He might have some answers," Bartolon says.

Odd, he should have known about this.

"Thank you, Watch Bartolon," Yelu says.

She turns and rushes out of the chamber, mumbling to herself.

Bartolon holds out the key, looks at it and sighs heavily.

This will be the most exciting thing I'll see all day.

Having completed his duty, Bartolon places the key back in his robe and returns to the temple.

Yelu reaches the house and slams the door open. The servant cleaning the table jumps with a start and drops the dishes.

"Master Eage, why did the Oriel close before I could step through?"

"Yelu! Why are you here?" Eage asks.

"I couldn't get through."

"What do you mean?"

"Michael went through, then moments later, the window closed."

"I tried to go through, and it opened in a different location. I was almost a panzoon's dinner."

"What? a Panzoon? Did Michael activate the bracelet?"

"Yes, just like you told him."

"Hmm!"

Eage pauses to think.

"Maybe you both require a bracelet to go together. I assure you, I wasn't aware of this. Come to think of it, everyone that has gone through did have one. Maybe it is some sort of failsafe," Eage says.

He sits at the nearby table.

"Something to be aware of in the future," he says.

Yelu growls and throws her travel bag on the floor.

The servant jumps once more.

"That does me no good now," Yelu says and storms out of the room.

Michael looks back, expecting to see Yelu behind him.

"Mother?"

She was right behind me.

He searches the trees and brush to see if she has emerged somewhere else.

"Mother?"

There is no sign of her. Michael rotates the band until it clicks, opening the Oriel with a hiss to an empty cupola.

Humm, maybe she changed her mind.

When he rotates it back, the window disappears.

Michael doesn't feel like he has changed much; he can't see his wings, but he can still feel them.

He looks at his hands.

Still have five fingers. My skin is darker and...

He looks down.

The robes are still the same, and the leather bracelet is still on my wrist.

He looks around, frowning.

The hum is so loud now.

He covers his ears.

Hmm, rounded ears.

Michael decides to keep moving while adjusting to the environment. Walking through the forest, he comes upon the overgrown remnants of a forest trail. He loses it several times before finding it again, leading him to a deserted village. The first thing that catches his attention is a fallen statue of a series of animals standing on another's shoulder. The statue is very old, the wood is cracked, and the coloring added to the carved figures is faded. The animals depicted are similar to Terrae's.

There are fresh shavings on the ground. Michael sees a new figure recently carved, different from the others, sitting next to the fallen statue. It portrays an ape-like creature with bat wings and a rat's tail.

What type of creature is that?

As his senses acclimate, he notices that the hum comes from a single direction.

He slowly turns until he faces the northwest.

It's coming from there.

Without hesitation, Michael runs, following the invisible trail.

Lucero reaches the River Spill, but the tribe is not there. The annoying hum is getting louder and seems to come from farther south. He looks down the coast but cannot see anything. The breeze off the ocean feels good on his face. He stretches his wings and flaps them. The wind lifts him off the ground. He soars for a few seconds trying out his wings. They are strong enough to fly. His search will be easier now.

The first thing he wants to do, though, is to find the origin of the hum. For some strange reason, he is attracted to it. It is like a part of his life. So before looking for the Taloosh, he heads south, following the call of the beacon.

*Tiglit and Dancing Elk sit by the beacon next to the hut; it has
not disappeared or diminished. Potwah brings them food and
water, and the tribesmen decide to take down Tiglit's hut and
erect it around them. The shaman has been asking for help for
the last month and a half. His totems abandoned him, but he
got a response when he pleaded with the spirit called Eyu.
Tiglit and Dancing Elk still do not know what to make of it;
they ask many questions, but the small column of shimmering
light is the only answer they get from the spirit world.
Therefore, they will stay by the column until it reveals its
purpose.*

Around midmorning, a warrior comes running into his hut.
  "Shaman, the demon has been sighted."
  Tiglit's heart skips a beat.
  "Has he spotted us yet?" Tiglit asks.
  "No."
  "Are the canoes ready to ride?"
  "No," the warrior says. "But it won't matter."
  "What are you saying?"
  "The demon is flying; he will find us soon."
  *Tiglit desperation starts to grow. He does not know what
else to do. He stands up and walks to the entrance of his hut.*
  "He comes from that direction," the warrior says.

He points to the north along the shore. Tiglit looks in the direction that he is pointing. However, something else draws his attention. He looks up to the skies over the trees, he does not know what it is, but something else is approaching, something pure and cleansing.

"What is it, Shaman?" Dancing Elk asks.

"I don't know, but something approaches from that direction," he says, pointing. "It seems...full of hope, clean."

"What?"

Dancing Elk looks at the forest, sees nothing, and then looks back to the shaman. However, when he looks back, he sees a man in white robes standing by the edge of the trees. He is about fifty yards away, and by his strange clothes, the boy can tell that he is not from any of the tribes he knows. Dancing Elk nocks an arrow on his bow and takes aim.

"Another demon!" the boy cries.

But Tiglit pushes his bow down.

"That is not a demon," Tiglit says. "That is help."

As Michael approaches Tiglit, his clothes glow. He wears the Aduncus bracelet on his right arm, a gift from his mother that represents his Aduncus heritage. On his left wrist is the wristguard of metal and leather that Eage had given him.

"Who are you?" asks Tiglit.

"My name is Michael."

"Mi-cool? I have never heard a name like that. What kind of name is Mi-cool? What does it mean?" the shaman asks.

"It is an ancient name; it is sort of a question, it means 'Like God?'"

The boy touches Tiglit's arm as a reflexive action. Tiglit pats his arm.

"Why have you come?" Tiglit asks.

Dancing Elk moves to the side, just in case he needs a clear shot at the stranger. Without thinking, Michael sends his pacú out to the boy to read his emotions, and the boy feels it. Dancing Elk suddenly feels that the stranger is not a danger and lowers his bow.

"Your summons," Michael answers.

"You came because of the pillar of light?" Tiglit asks. "Where is it?"

Tiglit motioned for him to follow. They walk into the shaman's hut, and Michael immediately spots the beacon. He sends his pacú to the beacon and immediately absorbs its refreshing energy.

Dancing Elk watches as the cairn dissipates. He decides it's a matter of the spirit world, so the one called Mi-cool must be a shaman.

"Where do you come from?" Tiglit asks.

"A place called Terrae," Michael answers.

"Terrae?" Tiglit says. "The shaman called Lucero came from Terrae."

"The evil one!" the boy adds.

Tiglit raises his hand and motions him to relax.

Evil one?

"You knew Lucero?" Michael asks.

"He and another shaman called Qualut became a part of our tribe. Lucero helped with the sick and talked about the spirit called Eyu. But with the words of Qualut, Lucero became corrupted. The two started killing the members of the other tribes. Finally, he killed off all the tribes that did not escape. Now we are the only ones left, and he is coming after us," Tiglit says.

"Both Shaman Lucero and Shaman Qualut turned into demons. We don't know what has happened to Qualut, but we know that Lucero has been spotted heading in this direction," Dancing Elk says.

Michael has to sit down.

Is it my brother and not Sceagga that has caused the grief on the folk of Terrae Exterus? Has he become mightier than Sceagga himself? Maybe Lucero drove him from the outerworld. But why?

"Shaman? What is a shaman?" Michael asks.

"Holy man," Tiglit says. "Lucero told me once that they were called saa-ser-magoos and had the power of healing."

Michael buries his face in his hands.

It was him; it was Lucero. They refer to as a demon.

"What is wrong...Mi-cool?" Tiglit asks.

"I believe the one you call Qualut was an evil holy man from my land. His name is Sceagga; he came to get the energy necessary to take over your world, then ours." Michael says.

"Yes, Lucero spoke of this Sceagga. How would he get this energy?"

"The energy is all around your world. I do not know what happened; I do not know if Sceagga could get the energy he needed. I can feel the energy, though. It's all around, and it is sickening."

"This energy would give him power?"

"It can if he can absorb it. I can feel it, but I can't use it. I can't do anything with it."

"Lucero drew the bad spirits from those who were sick," Tiglit says. "Could this be the energy you talk about?"

Michael thinks about it for a moment.

"Is there anyone in your tribe that is sick?"

Tiglit knows what he is getting at.

"If this energy you talk about turned Lucero into a demon, why won't it do the same to you?"

He's right; what happened to Lucero can just as well happen to me.

"When the two shamans arrived, was there anything strange about them? Did they look different?" Michael asks.

"No, they were just like us. Why?" Tiglit asks.

"Do I look different to you?"

"You are not of the tribes I know. Your coverings are different. Those things around your arm and wrist are different, and so is your speech. There is no one in the land that dresses or talks like you; why?" Tiglit asks.

"The one you call Lucero was sent here to spread the word of Eyu. Somehow, he was tempted by Sceagga to feed on the evil energy in this land, which affected him. He became the demon...Lucero is my brother, and I have come to take him back."

Tiglit looks at him but sees no resemblance.

"The one called Qualut was also of my folk; I have just been told that he is our father."

"Now that you mention it, Qualut and Lucero looked very much like father and son, but you are completely different. Are you sure you are family?" Tiglit asks.

"I'm afraid so. I have to know how they got their energy. Do you have anyone that is sick?"

Tiglit is hesitant about exposing Michael to the evil spirits.

"I hope you know what you're doing," says Tiglit. "I do not wish to fight two demons."

He turns to Dancing Elk.

"Take him to your sister."

Dancing Elk feels trust in the stranger and is no longer wary of him. He takes Michael to his hut, with Tiglit trailing behind. There, the thirteen-year-old girl lays under several blankets. An older woman and a young woman tend to the girl. The older woman looks at Michael and runs out of the back of the hut, but the younger one, Potwah, moves back but stays.

"They fear all strangers now," Tiglit murmurs.

"What happened to the girl?" Michael asks.

"She was gathering clams; she fell and cut her leg badly," Dancing Elk says. "The evil spirits poisoned her cut; there is nothing the shaman can do."

Dancing Elk kneels, puts his hand on her forehead, and feels the fever. He whispers something to her that makes her smile. Then, she lifts her hand with great effort and holds it out. Her brother takes it in his. She labors to breathe and can barely keep her eyes open.

"Her name is Wrensong. Save for Potwah, my denwyf," Dancing Elk motions to Potwah, "Wrensong is the only family I have left."

"If you can save her, we will be in your debt," Potwah says.

Michael kneels next to the girl and lifts the blanket. He sees that the cut has started to ulcerate. Red streaks wander away from the wound; it is a bad infection; it will be only a matter of time before it kills her. He places his hand on her forehead; it is hot. He lets his pacú find the rank energy, which he draws out. Immediately he rushes out of the hut and throws the tainted pacú to the ground, where it pours from his hands like muddy water.

Tiglit raises an eyebrow at Michael's reaction and the vile puddle he has created.

"What is wrong?" Tiglit asks.

"The bad pacú is too repulsive to keep inside. I don't know how Lucero could do it."

"Pacú?"

Michael thinks for a moment.

"Spirit."

"Lucero enjoyed the bad spirit. I watched him feed on it," the shaman says.

"It's disgusting. I don't understand; Lucero is supposed to be the Promised One. He should be revolted by it."

Dancing Elk watches as Wrensong's wound heals. The girl smiles at him.

"Wrensong? How do you feel?" Potwah asks.

"The pain is gone. I feel strong again," Wrensong says.

Potwah looks at Dancing Elk.

"The mark on her leg is almost gone," Potwah says.

"Just like when Lucero healed you," Wrensong says.

"What do you mean? When did Lucero heal me?"

She tells him about Lucero sneaking into the hut when he was wounded by the bear and how points of light went from Lucero's hand into him.

"He healed me?"

Wrensong smiles and nods.

"You were healed and became stronger and faster after that," Potwah says.

"Lucero didn't want you to know," Wrensong says.

Dancing Elk shakes his head.

Everything is so confusing.

Dancing Elk gets up and leaves the hut.

A group had gathered around the hut.

"She is healed; the infection is gone!"

"What?" Tiglit says.

The shaman rushes inside and sees the girl getting up from the mat. She is still unsteady from her prolonged stay in bed. However, her leg is smooth and clean. All signs of the infection are gone, with only a small red line visible where the festering wound had been.

Potwah is in awe.

"She's clean." She says in a soft voice.

Michael returns to the hut; the wound's healing speed surprises him.

"Perhaps you were the one who should have come to us," Tiglit says.

"Me? No, I was told to teach the folk of Terrae of my land."
What is he trying to say?

"Shaman Michool," Dancing Elk says. "My life is yours."

The boy kneels in front of him; Michael can see a tear rolling down his cheek.

Michael places his hand on the boy's head; his pacú surprises him; it feels like Lucero. The boy feels Michael's but does not know what he feels.

A faraway cry interrupts them. A young warrior runs towards them, yelling, but he is too far to understand. White Eagle at the edge of the camp hears him and starts to beat on a hollow log, relaying the message.

"The demon approaches!" Dancing Elk says.

Michael reaches down and pulls him to his feet.

"We have to keep the demon away from the tribe. Especially away from you and the shaman," Michael says.

Michael sensed Tiglit and Dancing Elk's pacú. He realizes that they are sacermagi. If the demon seeks pacú, theirs holds more than the rest of the tribe combined. White Eagle joins the running warrior. They are both pointing down the beach. In the distance, Michael can see a colossal featherless bird approaching. He walks towards the edge of the camp; the two warriors run past him with terror on their faces.

Lucero lost the signal from the beacon. He was about to return to his search when he spotted the smoke in the distance.

Well, well, so that's where the hum was coming from.

He finally found the tribe and will now be able to feed. Lucero picks up the pace; he feels the hunger that comes in anticipation of a meal.

What is that?

A figure waits at the edge of the camp; his brilliant white robes shine like sunlight off the water. Lucero drops from the sky and lands fifty yards from the figure. He looks at Michael. He does not recognize his physical appearance, though. Lucero becomes weary of the stranger. He sends his pacú to him to see who he is. He feels the familiar essence, and his eyes widen.

"Michael! What are you doing here?"

Michael can hardly believe what he is looking at. It is Lucero's voice, but the creature it is coming from is a large, muscular, ape-like creature whose dark reddish skin is thick with coarse hair. His elongated lower jaw protrudes beyond his nose, armed with a row of sharp teeth. Spiraling ram's horns emerge in front of his ears, and his black eyes are horizontally elliptical, making his face goat-like. However, strangely enough, his left arm looks normal and out of place.

"Lucero, what happened to you? What have you done?"

"I have become even more powerful than that fool, Sceagga," he growls.

"What happened to Sceagga?" Michael asks.

He is trying to keep him talking.

"He was stealing the pacú, my pacú, from this world. He fled back to Terrae when I tried to take it back," Lucero says.

He shifts to get a better look at Michael.

"But don't worry, I will find him when I'm finished here. I will get it back."

Lucero starts to approach Michael. He walks by a bundle of spears the Taloosh have stacked. He picks out one of them, arming himself.

"Why do you want so much power? What are you going to do with it? Try to take over Terrae?"

"You are a fool, brother. Can you not feel how much power is here? Once I get it all, I'll return to Terrae and take the energy from there too."

"Lucero, you have to kill to get the power. What good is it to you if everyone is dead?"

"Dear brother, I don't care if everyone is dead; I don't care about Terrae or Terrae Exterus."

"Then, why do it?"

"I'm going to challenge Eyu, and when I defeat him, I will fashion my creation for my behest." Lucero hisses.

Michael's head reels; his brother has lost his mind and is now talking blasphemy. He realizes he is the only thing standing between Lucero and the rest of Eyu's creation. And does not believe he is strong enough to stop him.

Help me, Eyu!

Lucero takes another step forward.

"I won't let you do it!" Michael blurts out.

Lucero chuckles.

"Are you going to stop me?"

"Yes."

With that, Michael transforms as his wings become visible.

Potwah's eyes widen.

"It's the one from the storyteller," she says.

Dancing Elk and Tiglit gasp.

"It's like the legend," Tiglit says.

"The spirits are going to battle," Dancing Elk says.

Potwah rushes to Dancing Elk's side and wraps her arms around his.

"Your energy is the most powerful on Terrae Exterus now. I will start by feeding on you," Lucero taunts.

Lucero lunges at Michael and slashes him with his spear, but Michael's is too fast. He sidesteps the demon and strikes him with his fist on the side of the head; Lucero falls to the ground. Michael places himself between the demon and Dancing Elk.

Dancing Elk drops the bow. They are moving too fast to take a shot. He wrests his arm from Potwah's hold and takes Nenemehkia from Tiglit. He steps in front of the two to protect them. The demon springs into the air, and Michael follows. Once again, they face each other.

"Lucero, think of what you're doing," Michael pleads, "You are becoming worse than Sceagga."

"More powerful, you mean. Sceagga was a fool who tried to deceive me; I will deal with him when the time comes. Now get out of my way," Lucero snarls.

Lucero slashes Michael with his free hand, but Michael drops, and his arm passes over his head. Michael swings his fist upwards, striking Lucero with an uppercut. Lucero's head snaps back; the blow stuns him; he loses control and drops. Before hitting the ground, he regains his senses and flies up.

Blood mingles with his hairy chin, and he grins.

I see what you are doing.

"Not bad, brother. That one stung." Lucero mocks him.

He flies at Michael again. Michael spins at the last moment and swings his fist at him. However, Lucero expects the move and ducks under the attack on Michael's left side. Michael tries to turn, but his lazy wing does not cooperate. Lucero thrusts the spear as he passes, impaling Michael.

"You still fly with a limp, brother."

Michael's eyes go wide with surprise. Lucero had tricked him. What surprised him the most was that his own brother would hurt him.

"Luce..."

His eyes turn glassy, and Michael spins to the ground. A broken muckle of feathers and flesh.

Yes, now, I'm the most powerful being in both worlds.

He flies down to the body to touch it.

Michael quickly realized what Lucero had done. A flash of pain shoots through his midsection, then it's gone. A fire-like surge of power blazes through him. He becomes stronger. He tries to pull out the spear, but it is gone.

Did it go all the way through?

He looks for Lucero and finds him leaning over a body.

Who did he kill?

"Where's the pacú?" Lucero shouts. "He's just an empty shell."

The demon straightens, and Michael sees his own body on the ground.

Lucero looks at the Taloosh. They gathered to one side to watch the fight between the spirits. On the other side are Dancing Elk and Tiglit. They are helpless now.

No one can stop my feast now.

The demon can sense Michael's pacú and wants it, but it is completely inaccessible, like the grey pacú surrounding him.

I'll start with them.

The demon turns to Dancing Elk and the shaman. Dancing Elk crouches, ready to fight. Lucero leaps and, with two flaps, lands in front of Dancing Elk.

"Out of the way, boy. Let me have him. I'm fond of you; I don't want to hurt you."

Dancing Elk starts to walk in a crouch toward Lucero. He circles the staff.

"Nenemehkia, spirit of lightning, chase evil away!
Spirit of the ground, chase him away!
Spirit of the water, chase him away!
Chase him away, chase him away."

Lucero recalls the chant from the day he arrived.

"That did nothing then; it won't help you now," Lucero says.

Suddenly Dancing Elk feels the staff throb; it had never done that before.

Lucero sees a faint glow course the length of Nenemehkia and disappears.

What was that?

"I don't have time for this."

Lucero lunges at Dancing Elk. The boy thrusts the staff like a spear striking the demon in the chest. There is a loud crack, and Lucero is thrown, landing hard on his back.

Dancing Elk doesn't know what just happened, but he feels that Nenemehkia has come alive.

"The spirit of Nenemehkia has risen," Tiglit says. "Remember your training."

Tiglit steps back, pulling Potwah with him.

Lucero stands, trying to make sense of what just happened. He looks down and sees a scorch mark on his chest; the burn stings when he touches it.

"I don't know what you're playing at, but you die today," Lucero says.

With a driving rage, Lucero lunges at Dancing Elk. The boy spins the staff, and Lucero ducks and slashes Dancing Elk with his claws. Dancing Elk stumbles back, and Lucero is right there and reaches for the boy. Dancing Elk knows what will happen if the demon lays his hands on him. The boy turns, and Lucero misses. Dancing Elk's move flows to a strike to Lucero's side. Once again, there's a sharp retort, and Lucero is thrown to the side.

The demon rubs his side; it hurts to the touch.

The demon charges again and reaches for Dancing Elk. The boy spins Nenemehkia once more but misses when Lucero ducks. The demon drives his horns into Dancing Elk's midsection, throwing him back. Lucero stomps, but Dancing Elk rolls away from the attack, swinging the staff at the demon's leg. Lucero howls and falls to his knees giving Dancing Elk time to stand.

Lucero stands; his left leg is hurt but not broken. He grins a grimace at Dancing Elk

"Let's see Nenemehkia handle this."

It worked on Michael. Let's see if it'll work on him.

The demon beats his wings, throwing sand and stone at the warrior. The lunges behind the debris cloud and reaches for Dancing Elk with his right hand. Dancing Elk side steps to avoid the grab, but Lucero changes hands, grabbing Dancing Elk's shoulder with his left, his human hand.

"Got you!"

Lucero grins triumphantly when he sees Dancing Elk's startled look.

Dancing Elk gasps and waits for the inevitable. However, it doesn't come.

Lucero looks at the boy's shoulder and back at his face.

Where is his pacú?

Lucero tries to draw the pacú again but doesn't recognize it. He can't find it.

Something is wrong.

Dancing Elk sees the opportunity and raises the staff with force, striking Lucero's wrist above the bracelet. Once again, Nenemehkia makes a sharp sound, dislodging the bracelet from his arm. Dancing Elk brings the staff down on Lucero's shoulder in one motion. The sound of his collarbone breaking is loud. Lucero screeches and staggers back.

"Skagget!"

Lucero bends over his shoulder and feels the searing pain throbbing up his neck.

How can he do that? I must distract him.

"You will pay dearly for this, Tsálk; you, your denwyf, and your sister," Lucero says.

That's what Potwah called him. Lucero wants to get in his head, to strike that nerve. A brother's betrayal.

They both back away from each other. Dancing Elk can't believe that he once considered this demon his family.

At the same time, Lucero can't believe a tree branch can cause him so much harm.

Without the bracelet, Lucero's arm slowly transforms until it matches the other, but the collarbone is still broken. Unlike previous injuries, it doesn't mend quickly, and he feels the pain. He realizes he can't get close to Dancing Elk as long as he holds Nenemehkia.

As they start to circle each other, Lucero creates a upashim.

Michael had been trying to process why his lifeless body was on the ground all this time. His sightless eyes, lidded and clouded, stare at the sky; his arms and wings are motionless at his side. None of it seems real.

Nenemehkia's loud retort snaps Michael out of his trance. He sees Lucero is ready to throw the upashim and lunges at Dancing Elk. Something inside him tells him what to do. He does not understand how he will accomplish it or why he should do it. However, a higher authority has given a command, and he obeys.

Lucero sees a brilliantly white cloth fly past him. He cannot make out the shape, but he knows who it is.

There you are.

He sends the upashim to his brother instead. Michael deflects the bolt with one of his own, but it diverts towards Dancing Elk.

Dancing Elk sees the glowing ball closing in at a tremendous speed, too fast. The upashim hits the ground next to him. The explosion tosses Dancing Elk high in the air.

Lucero looks towards the hut and sees that Wrensong has joined Tiglit and Potwah.

He throws a second upashim at the gathered tribesmen on the opposite side of the camp. Michael chases the upashim, stopping it with his own. While Michael is occupied, Lucero lunges at Tiglit. The demon can sense that Dancing Elk and the shaman are sacermagi; he wants their pacú.

Nenemehkia, ripped from Dancing Elk's grip by the concussion, spins high through the air. Sensing its master, it shifts in direction, landing in front of Tiglit.

"What?"

Tiglit is somewhat confused.

The staff sought me out.

The shaman instinctively picks it up and holds it in front of him, his last defiant stand.

"Get Dancing Elk and Wrensong away from here," he tells Potwah.

Potwah nods and hurries to Dancing Elk, who has just rolled onto his elbow. Lucero's anger rises to the next level.

"First the boy, and now you?"

Well, the upashim worked last time.

Lucero throws the fiery sphere at the shaman. But Tiglit bats it into the forest, where it topples a hapless tree.

I see, then how about this.

Lucero bursts into a sprint, dashing towards the shaman. Tiglit sees the dirt fly as the demon charges over the open ground. Lucero creates another upashim and holds it. Then, the white form appears again, like a shining white cloth blown by the wind; it flies at Tiglit and strikes him in the chest.

Tiglit's body absorbs Michael. A feeling of ecstasy that takes his breath away. He suddenly understands all that is happening. He can see Terrae, its people, oceans, mountains, strange birds, and beasts in his mind. Michael's memories become his, and so does his mandate from Eyu.

Tiglit's clothing turns emerald green, and Nenemehkia shrinks several inches as if to become a proper size for the task.

Lucero sees the changes and pauses.

"What is this?" He mumbles.

"I was sent to protect the children of this land. This is why I'm here," Tiglit answers in Michael's voice.

"Michael?" the demon asks. "Tiglit is the Promised One?"

Michael does not answer.

Even though the body is that of the shaman, his voice, manners, and pacú are mixed with Michael's.

"What did you do?" Lucero asks.

Lucero feels a jump in the shaman's pacú; Tiglit's power increases; however, the dark energy is gone. Lucero becomes wary of the manifestation before him.

"I have joined Tiglit. We are now one," the shaman answers. "Do not press me into fighting you; there is still time for you to repent."

Tiglit has difficulty keeping up; he can feel Michael's power. It's like living one of the stories he told the children.

"Repent? I have nothing to repent. I'm just claiming what is rightfully mine," the demon answers.

"It's not yours to claim; it's Eyu's to give," Tiglit says.

Lucero growls, throws the energy sphere at Tiglit once more, and then lunges at Dancing Elk.

I'll get his pacú and heal.

Tiglit bats the upashim again; this time, he throws it back at Lucero.

What?

He dives onto his belly to avoid the sphere. Lucero feels the blow he received on his chest, side, and broken collarbone when he hits the ground. The upashim passes over him, gouges a furrow on the gravelly beach, and explodes.

He stands, gasping and flinching from the pain. He looks at the near-miss.

That was too close.

Lucero races for the downed warrior; he is a blur, but the shaman is faster.

The old man strikes Lucero's ribs with the staff and stands over Dancing Elk.

The strike from Nenemehkia sounds like a thunderclap, louder than before. It sends the demon sliding on the ground.

Lucero stands, cramping over the pain. Twice he was struck in the same place. Nenemehkia is now more powerful. It cannot kill him, though its strike may cripple him.

Tiglit charges and lashes out. Lucero spins to avoid it, but the staff catches Lucero right over his left horn, cracking it and sending him down again. Now his head throbs with pain. He realizes he cannot do anything against Michael without a proper weapon.

He darts back to Michael's body and withdraws the spear.

"I killed you once; I'll kill you again."

Let's see that limp again.

He lunges at Tiglit with the spear. Tiglit parries the jab, but Lucero ducks and attacks Tiglit's left side. The shaman changes direction and blocks the spear. It shatters from the staff's blow.

Lucero looks at the shattered wood in his hands.

How can this be? I'm the most powerful being.

"Lucero, Michael's body, is gone; there is no limp," Tiglit says. "As for you. You are banished from the lands. Whenever you bring violence to the righteous or the Promised One sees you, I will be summoned to exile you."

The demon does not know what Tiglit meant by being exiled, and he's not waiting to find out; now, he has to escape.

I must get to the Oriel. I'll return when things settle.

He glances to the right of Tiglit. Tribal members are gathered, watching the battle. To the left, he sees Wrensong and Potwah helping Dancing Elk to sit up.

"Don't try it," Tiglit warns.

Lucero feigns a move towards the group on the right; Tiglit reacts to block his way; instead, Lucero tosses a upashim at the shaman. Tiglit lifts the bacula, stopping the energy bolt, but it explodes in front of his face. The glare blinds him.

With a smirk, Lucero throws two upashim, one towards Dancing Elk and the other towards Potwah.

I told you, Tsálk.

The first upashim strikes Potwah on the chest. Its power is reduced because he has thrown too many, but the blow is still fatal. The second is different; it is a much slower dark grey orb, like concentrated smoke, not a ball of light.

Dancing Elk sees Potwah thrown back as if struck by a club.

"Nooo!"

Still sitting and somewhat numb, Dancing Elk struggles to move out of the way of the approaching smoky sphere. He knows the attempt is useless, but maybe if he can move enough, it'll only be a glancing blow. When the orb is mere paces from him, Wrensong jumps in front of it, protecting her brother. The orb strikes Wrensong, tossing her back.

"Wrensong!"

Dancing Elk looks for his bow, but it's out of reach. Anger boils inside of him. Lucero was a trusted friend. But now, he's hurt Potwah and Wrensong. He watches the demon fly away.

Dancing Elk staggers to his feet and goes to Wrensong. He looks at Potwah and sees a cloud of steam rising from her chest.

No!

"Wrensong, are you hurt?" Dancing Elk asks.

He looks at her. Something seems to crawl under her skin, from her neck to her face.

"I feel strange, brother. Like—'"

Wrensong's eyes turn a dark red, and dark grey wisps of mist seep from the corner of her eyes. She growls and rakes Dancing Elk's cheek with her nails. Wrensong reaches for his eyes. Dancing Elk grabs her wrists, but the girl fights him, scratching and biting Dancing Elk.

White Eagle sees what is happening and rushes to help Dancing Elk. Others come to his aid. Holding her is like holding a struggling animal. She growls, scratches, and bites at them until they manage to bind her with twine.

"Don't hurt her. Take her to a tent and leave her alone. I don't want anyone else hurt," Dancing Elk tells them.

He goes to Potwah; she looks like she is sleeping. Only the scorch mark on her tunic tells what happened. He holds her to his chest and sobs.

"Potwah, it's me. Wake up," he sobs.

Her body is limp. He tries to gather her, but her head and arms sag unnaturally.

"No, we're supposed to be together for life. You can't leave me now. I need you."

You will pay, demon!

Dancing Elk buries his face in her hair and weeps.

When the dancing spots of light clear from Tiglit's eyes, the demon, is gone.

The Oriel!

Tiglit speeds across the clearing. Regaining his senses, Dancing Elk sees a man dressed in a green covering run by.

Tiglit?

The shaman runs at incredible speed into the forest carrying the staff.

Dancing Elk glances at the villagers dragging away the struggling girl.

Gently, he lays Potwah's body back on the ground.

"Keep Wrensong safe," he shouts.

The demon will pay.

He picks up his bow and quiver, then runs after Tiglit.

He's running faster than a deer.

Dancing Elk knows he can't catch up with Tiglit, but he follows anyway.

Lucero drops into a clearing. He reaches for his bracelet and realizes it's gone.

"Skagget!"

He pulls the Traduco Glass from its pouch.

I need to get as far away as I can.

Lucero calls out a name he remembers from his studies of the Sylvan lands, the farthest on the top of the map. Then, when the window opens, he jumps through the Oriel.

As Tiglit nears the Oriel's window, he sees a wintry mountain scene. However, before he can reach it, the window closes. Tiglit nears the Oriel, and the window hisses open again; this time, it is a meadow with scēap browsing. Because of his union with Michael, he recognizes the valley.

The Valley of Scēapherders.

Lucero is gone.

He is sure that, eventually, he will meet his brother again, but for now, he is lost.

But first, I have a task to finish here.

Tiglit turns and heads back towards the village. He sees Dancing Elk emerging from the forest, panting and gulping from the run.

Tiglit's green robes are gone; he is dressed in Michael's white robes. Dancing Elk stops in front of him, gasping for air.

"What happened? Where's the demon?" he asks.

He takes a deep breath, then looks at Tiglit.

"What happened to your clothes?"

"I'm wearing them; why?"

The shaman was so busy fighting Lucero that he never noticed the change his clothes had gone through.

"You were dressed in long green robes. Now, your robes are white."

He looks at his outfit.

"Hmm."

He grabs Dancing Elk's arm.

"Here, help me over this rocky area. I'm not as young as I used to be."

"Shaman, I just saw you running like a deer through the woods; I could not catch up to you."

"Hmm, I can't remember all that happened, but that would explain how I got here. It was like a broken dream. Now Dancing Elk, what surprises me is that you are still alive."

"That first ball exploded at my feet, it threw me, but I was not hit. But then, Lucero threw a ball of light at Potwah; she's dea—". The words catch in a sob, then takes a deep breath.

"He threw another ball. It was like smoke. Wrensong jumped in front of me, and it hit her instead. She is now crazed... like the bear we had to hunt."

"Potwah is dead?"

He shakes his head.

"I didn't see a ball of smoke, but I thought you were hit by the ball of light. You were thrown almost a spear's cast; are you not hurt?"

"I may have broken the bones in my side," he says, rubbing his ribs.

"Lucero killed Potwah, and we treated him like family," Tiglit sighs. "I'll look at Wrensong and see what can be done."

Dancing Elk helps Tiglit across the rock-strewn hillside, leading him through the forest to the campsite.

The Taloosh are excited about the battle between the gods they just witnessed, each narration a slightly different version than the other. They gather around Tiglit and Dancing Elk; Potwah's body had already been taken away for preparation.

The villagers follow the two heroes to Michael's body but stay back as Dancing Elk and Tiglit approach the fallen god.

Tiglit kneels by Michael's body. The shaman must cleanse the body for the ceremony of passage before the others take it away. He straightens Michael's arms and wings. When he touches his head, a rush of memories floods the shaman's mind. He connects with Michael and all his thoughts. Everything that happened during the battle is absorbed. Between the tangle of memories and recollections, there is a message for Dancing Elk.

"Our land is safe from the demon, at least for now," Tiglit says.

"Was Michael the one who was supposed to come?" Dancing Elk asks.

"I don't know. Maybe he was."

Tiglit removes the wristguard and Aduncus bracelet from Michael's wrists.

"Why would Eyu send the other?" Dancing Elk asks.

"Sometimes figuring out a problem is the best teacher," Tiglit says. "Just telling you about Eyu would not be enough; you had to be shown. Lucero had a choice; he could have been the Promised One, but instead, he chose a different path."

Tiglit calls several members of the tribe to come closer.

"Take the body; he will receive the highest honor," Tiglit says.

"He was a brave warrior," Dancing Elk says. "I would have liked to know him better."

"Don't mourn his death; his spirit lives on and will keep guard overall," the shaman says. "You may see him again someday."

Dancing Elk thinks about it for a moment.

"What's going to happen to the demon Lucero?" He asks.

"He has gone into hiding in Terrae. Sooner or later, he will come out. You will need to be there to finish what was started here."

"Wait. You said, you."

"Dancing Elk, you are being asked to go to the other land," Tiglit says. "You are the Promised One."

"Me? But shaman, I'm barely a warrior."

"You are a warrior; you have proven yourself," the shaman says. "When the bear came to the village, you were the one who killed it. When others ran in fear from the demon, you stood like a tree in a storm. You are the great warrior of the Taloosh. The God Eyu has seen this and is asking you to go on a mission. You are the Promised One. You are the one who will keep us safe from Lucero."

"I can't go. I have to care for Wrensong," Dancing Elk says.

He does not like the idea. However, he is being asked. It is his choice.

Tiglit grabs the Dancing Elk's arm.

"You have the freedom to refuse. For now, you are to wear this."

He slips the bracelet over the Dancing Elk's wrist.

"This will allow your passage into the other world."

"But—"

"Like your knife, you wear it in case you need it," Tiglit says, then slips the Halo armband on his other wrist.

"How do you know this?"

"Michael passed this message to me."

He still does not understand all that Tiglit says. However, he will have to believe and trust in him for now. Other things worry him more, though.

"What of my sister?"

"I will personally care for Wrensong. The demon's curse has beset her mind," Tiglit says.

"I don't want to leave her. I already lost Potwah, and now this spirit, Eyu, wants me to leave Wrensong too, to leave all my family behind?" Dancing Elk shakes his head. "Why does he ask this of me?"

"As long as Lucero roams free, she will remain as she is, an animal. It is your duty to stop the demon and keep him from returning. Only then will the demon's stain over Wrensong will be cleansed."

"I'm not strong enough to kill the demon. I don't know how."

"I didn't say kill him. Lucero can't be killed. You have to confine him," Tiglit says.

"Confine him; how?"

"When the time comes, you will know. Have faith; Michael will be there when you need him most."

"Then why don't I wait for Lucero here? I can fight him when he comes back."

"You could do that; Lucero still wants the rest of the dark spirit, what he called dark pacú, from this side, so he will return. But how long will the demon take to come back?

Because he drank so much of the dark spirit, he is no longer affected by time; he is deathless. How long will Wrensong remain cursed? If he waits a lifetime to return if Wrensong spends her life as an animal, who will you blame?"

Dancing Elk sighs.

"There is nothing to stop you from coming back to visit," the shaman says.

It is a small ray of hope for Dancing Elk.

"So, Wrensong will remain a wild animal unless I defeat Lucero?"

Tiglit nods.

The shaman looks at the men that carry Michael's body away.

"We must prepare for Potwah and Michael's passing," Tiglit says. "You have a decision to make. Think it through."

The shaman and Dancing Elk follow them to the camp.

Chapter 21

DEPARTURE

The ceremony of death for Michael will be performed the next day. That night, Dancing Elk had a more focused dream, and he was now a part of it. The gathering of men is now immensely large, with a dark cloud over them. The numbers gathered would be greater than all of the known tribes combined. In the dream, he hears a new word. A word that represents this gathering of men, it is army. There is a purpose to this army; to kill, destroy, and conquer.

As the approaching army gets closer, Dancing Elk stands in the middle of a field, helpless, unable to move. He wants to move, to run, but his feet are deep in mud. As they get closer, he can make out the attackers. They wear strange clothes and carry dangerous-looking weapons. They see him and, with a deafening roar, charge. Dancing Elk doesn't understand why, but he is the reason for their rage. The attackers reach him, and the hacking starts.

Dancing Elk wakes with a yelp. Sticky sweat covers him; he must have been dreaming for a while. He gets up and makes his way to a nearby stream to wash. It is big enough to provide water for the tribe but not to fish. When he is done, he heads to Wrensong's hut.

As he enters the hut, he can hear a low guttural growl. Wrensong squats in the corner, and a foul smell permeates the enclosed area.

She needs washing.

It will take no less than five people to wash her. Four, sometimes more, to hold her down and one to do the washing.

Wrensong spots Dancing Elk and pounces. A harness of leather tethered by a simple knot to a woven rope snaps her back and restrains her. She snarls and rakes at the air, trying to reach him. He wants to hold her, talk to her and console her. But he might as well try to talk to a wild animal.

She could easily undo the knots, but she no longer knows how.

Like a tied dog, she no longer knows what holds her.

"There is no improvement, but she is not worse."

Dancing Elk turns. Tiglit is standing behind him.

He sighs and shakes his head.

"She doesn't even recognize me," Dancing Elk says.

"And she won't...How were your dreams?"

Tiglit has been keeping track of Dancing Elk's dreams, trying to determine their meaning.

"I had a strange one last night."

"How was it strange?" Tiglit asks.

"Before, the dreams were of people and creatures. They were going on long walks, like the ones we do. Last night, I saw a group of warriors, larger than all the tribes combined, crossing a valley to attack me. A dark cloud soared over them."

Two weeks after the battle,

Tiglit shakes his head and grabs Dancing Elk's arm.

"Have you made your decision," Tiglit asks.

"No. In truth, I have been trying not to think of it."

"Dancing Elk, you have to decide where to fight. Will Sceagga or the demon grow in power on the other side? If you wait for either of them, they may become too powerful. Who led the warriors, this army, you saw?"

"I did not see a leader," Dancing Elk says.

"Think of what would happen if that army came here to fight the Taloosh. Will the Taloosh survive?"

Dancing Elk's eyes widen.

"I, I hadn't—that can't happen, can it? Why would they come?"

"Who wants you dead? Lucero was not defeated; he retreated. He will try again when the time is in his favor. Sceagga? He was after the same power. He, too, will return. They both crossed before. What's to stop them from bringing an army next time?

"If you are on the other side, you might be able to gather men of like mind. They would know how to fight against the army. So where will you be of more use to your sister, family, and tribe?" Tiglit says.

Dancing Elk sighs.

"It will be best to keep the battle over there," Dancing Elk says. "But why must it be me? White Eagle would make a better leader. How does this concern me?"

"You are the warrior who saved the tribes. You have been chosen for this task. You ask how it concerns you. How Wrensong will spend her life depends on what you do and your success. You are not being forced to go; it is your choice. What will you do?"

Dancing Elk lowers his eyes and slowly shakes his head.

"I will go."

Immediately following the ceremony, there is a meeting of the elders to determine the next tribal leader. Dancing Elk is the obvious choice, being the son of Tall Tree and the grandson of Tiglit, and the one who stood against the demon. Up to now, White Eagle has been leading the tribe in Tall Tree's absence; this meeting will make the choice official.

The talking bone is passed around as the elders argue that a leader who cannot swim cannot take the rope across the river and can never get the tribe to River Spill. Their last trip to the river had not been very productive. They needed to cross it to get to River Spill and harvest the fish.

White Eagle takes the bone and argues that during the battle of the spirits, it was Dancing Elk who stood his ground and fought the demon. While the rest cowered in fear.

A gruff-looking elder takes the bone to his blanket. The deep voice of the elder, Growling Bear, rumbles through the hut.

"Still, we need the favor of the spirits to cross the first river."

White Eagle takes the bone.

"If you remember, I used to climb for Tall Tree."

"You were the best climber," Clear Sky comments.

Comments like this did not require the talking bone.

"Yes, I was the best climber, but I climbed for Tall Tree because Tall Tree's knees would grow weak in high places. Tall Tree feared heights."

There was murmuring among the elders.

"Despite this, Tall Tree was a good leader," White Eagle says. "He can have a good swimmer cross the first river."

Dancing Elk takes the bone next.

"Before we go any further, I would like to say that I've been having visions. I have been asked to choose between staying with the tribe or leaving. Even if I stay, I will not be able to lead the tribe as a leader should. White Eagle should be the next leader."

More murmuring.

Tiglit knows that the visions are preparing Dancing Elk for his next stage. He takes the bone.

"Two days after the spirits battled, Dancing Elk started having strange dreams. They were short visions, a blink, of events. Some were of a man with wings fighting giants. Others showed giants on beasts, larger than a hut. Then, after a week, he dreamt of a gathering of men marching together. I believe Dancing Elk is chosen for another task that does not involve the tribe. So I, too, believe White Eagle should lead."

There is much murmuring. Dancing Elk's dreams had always been true. So, after much deliberation, it was decided that White Eagle would become the new leader of the Taloosh.

Tiglit and Dancing Elk leave the meeting of the elders. Dancing Elk follows Tiglit to his hut, where the shaman picks up a bundle, a wristguard, and Nenemehkia.

"White Eagle has been chosen to lead our people. Now, it is time for you to go and help the people of the other land. Here, take this."

Tiglit hands Dancing Elk a bundle and the wristguard.

"What is this?"

He opens the bundle.

"Michael's robe and bracelet. This bracelet you will give to the one called Yellowfeather, the mother of Michael and Lucero."

Tiglit slips the wristguard on Dancing Elk.

"This will take you to the other land."

Dancing Elk looks at the bundle.

"What do I do with the robe?"

"You will give it to the blind shaman I told you about."

"You said his name was Eage, like an eagle?"

"Yes, he will release the robe."

"Release the robe?"

"Just go. It will all become clear. "

"Now?"

"Yes, now. Lucero has just left. He will need time to gather his warriors. It is time you need to prepare."

They walk through the forest until they come to a clearing. Tiglit grabs Dancing Elk's bracelet and twists it. A hiss comes, and the Oriel's window opens. Tiglit hands him Nenemehkia.

"Take Nenemehkia. She is yours now."

"But she chose you. She is yours. You need her protection," Dancing Elk says.

"She has chosen you as the next bearer. She has decided that I will no longer need her. So, I can no longer feel her presence."

Dancing Elk takes the staff in his hands. He feels a slight tingle that quickly fades.

"Nenemehkia is a her?"

"Yes, she is like a mother that will protect the bearer."

"I'll retell the story of the great warrior, Dancing Elk, that saved our tribe, so they don't forget," Tiglit says.

Dancing Elk nods and looks one last time at the forest around him. His heart is heavy. He is leaving everything he knows behind.

He sighs, then looks at the window and wonders about what awaits him on the other side. If it's the right decision.

Is this really the right choice? Should I step through?

END

Book 2: The Promised One

*A preview of Sylvanus: The Promised One, book 2 in the
Book of Alce series:*

Chapter 1: A Visitor from Terrae Exterus

*Dancing Elk closes his eyes and cautiously steps through the
Oriel's window. Shaman Tiglit told him it was his choice to
undertake this journey in pursuit of Lucero. It is his own
choice, but in reality, he has no choice. Not really.*

*He feels like a piece in someone else's game. Yes, he made
the right choice. But at what cost? How will I ever get back to
my home? He composes himself and takes a few deep breaths.
They are supposed to calm him, but this is too much stress for
simple breaths to relieve. Why am I bearing this
responsibility? What have I done to deserve this?*

*He did not summon Lucero or the spirit that banished him.
Yet, the demon blamed him, killed his mate, Potwah, and
corrupted his sister, Wrensong. Now, he's responsible for
saving his sister, his tribe, and both worlds.*

*I can still turn around and go home. Every fiber in his
being and instinct tells him to turn back. But then again, if he
does, his sister, Wrensong, will remain a feral animal trapped
inside a woman's body for the rest of her life.*

No, I'm a warrior, and warriors don't run from battle.

*He takes another deep breath and opens his eyes. He is
standing in a hut roofed by a cupula with smooth, neatly cut
square stones for a floor. It only has a supporting column on
each of its four corners holding the roof. What good is a hut
with no walls?*

Pins of light float around him, bespeckling the chamber. The lights are more concentrated around the floor of the hut, illuminating it. The structure sits in a large pool of water, like a small pond. Ripples in the water fade away from the hut, disturbed by the window's opening. The points of light illume a long flagstone path leading toward the pool's edge.

Is this the spirit world?

He turns back just in time to see Tiglit with the forest behind him before the window hisses close.

"No, wait!" he shouts. His voice echoes through the chamber.

He steps forwards, and the window opens into a massive desert canyon with towering walls and thorny plants. He steps back, and the window closes again.

I should have thought this through. There are so many questions to ask. There are things I still have to do back home. Though, nothing comes to mind.

Tiglit said he would care for Wrensong in his absence. Nevertheless, who in the tribe actually cares for her?

Maybe if I try again. Dancing Elk steps forwards, and once again, the window opens. This time, a frozen wasteland appears. Seconds later, frost starts to sprout on the stone floor. The icy wind buffets him, making him step back, and with a hiss, the window closes once more.

"NO!" he shouts. "Let me go back. I have to go back!" There is no response. The bundle and the staff slide from his hands. Nenemehkia clatters loudly on the floor. Dancing Elk reaches out and leans on one of the cupula's pillars. *What have I done?* He sees his hand on the pillar and gasps; *my hands...they are different. I've... I've changed; what did I do? Oh no. I will never be able to go home now.* The thought strafes him. Dancing Elk's stomach churns with anguish, and his legs weaken; he can feel the weight of his body. He drops to his knees and screams, slamming his fist on the stone floor, "LET ME GO BACK!" His words resile from the cavern walls, and the echo fades into the darkness.

He takes a deep breath, then another, and bringing his emotions under control, he slowly stands. *I decided to come here to help the tribe, to help Wrensong. It's the only way; I'm a warrior. I will see it through.* He turns, looking in all directions. *I'm inside a cavern.* Gathering the bundle and Nenemehkia, he approaches the stepping stones leading away from the cupula. *I have to see it through; no, I must see it through. Too much depends on it.*

The pins of light gather over the path, beckoning him and illuminating his way and the surroundings. *It all seems like one of his dreams. This place cannot possibly exist.*

The flagstones from the cupula vanish into the darkness, making the cavern seem endless. Dancing Elk takes another deep breath. *Ok, let's see where this goes.*

While crossing the water, Dancing Elk carefully chooses his steps on the slippery flagstones. On passing, he glances down at his image in the water and stops. Between the fading ripples, he sees the reflection of a stranger, a larger, more muscular stranger with long, smooth black hair, pointed ears, and dressed in a strange tunic.

Ijiraq! Surprised, he spins to face the water spirit. Stepping back off the stepping-stone, he loses his footing and, after some windmilling and balance-seeking twists, plunges into the knee-deep pool. Sitting in the water, he composes himself, looks around, and realizes he is alone.

Was that my imagination, or was it—? He reaches up and touches his ears. *My ears. They're pointed!* His mind races. *Did I die? Have I turned into a spirit creature?* Then he grabs a lock of his hair and looks at it. *My hair is so smooth.* Then he plucks his clothes. *What am I wearing?*

Finally, he feels the wetness on his skin. He takes a deep, shuddering breath. This water is cold! He gathers the bundle and staff from the water, wades towards stepping stones, and climbs back up.

He returns to the cupula, sheds his clothes, and removes the wet bracelet. He wrings the clothes and lines them out on the floor. They are a green lodin tunic and a kaki undershirt, both long-sleeved. A leather belt over the tunic held his knife. A knife on a belt. Interesting.

He is also wearing cream-colored braccae, similar to his deerskin pants, but these are of thick cloth. Instead of moccasins, he now wore ankle-high boots, like the ones he wore in winter, but without the thick lining.

He tries to wipe what he can of the wetness. How does this go? He dresses again.

Dancing Elk walks to where he placed the bracelet and picks it up. Without knowing it, he wanders near the window's activation area, and it hisses open. It is nighttime on the other side, so no light enters the cave.

Deep in the African jungle, a black forest leopard or panther, as some may call it, finally creeps up within a pounce of the bushpig rootling in the river's shallows.

It had been five days since his last meal, a young baboon, which was hardly worth his effort. If successful, the bushpig will last him a week, maybe two, if he can keep it away from the lions and hyenas.

His haunches twitch as his muscles tighten. It takes all his concentration to keep his tail from flailing with excitement. Then, with one explosive vault, it jumps at the hog.

When Dancing Elk inadvertently activated the window, it randomly opened to the slopes of Mount Kenya.

The panther's leap crosses it onto the cupula. The animal is startled when it finds itself in the cave. It crouches at the *edge of the window. The wave of dizziness passes quickly, but the points of light dazzle it. It leaps to the side to avoid the annoying lights and the creature in the middle of the room. The leopard walks along the pool's edge. Dancing Elk wandered away by then, and the bushpig was nowhere to be found.*

The pins of light are different and unsettling. In the leopard's mind, the pins of light aren't to be trusted, at least until tested. The leopard quietly glides off the edge and swims to the shore on the opposite side of the cavern.

Dancing Elk starts crossing the stepping stones. The only sounds are the dripping of his clothes and the clacking of his heels on the stones. These tall moccasins are too noisy.

A low huff in the darkness startles Dancing Elk. His reflexes take over as he spins and drops his pack. Ready to defend himself, he crouches with Nenemehkia firmly grasped in both hands. A rolling growl echoes off the smooth walls of the cave. A kallunguattuk? Roughly translated into 'a roar like thunder,' the Taloosh name for the mountain lion. Did I walk into its cave?

TO BE CONTINUED
In book two
SYLVANUS: THE PROMISED ONE

About the Author

When R.P. O'Ryan isn't building vast civilizations in his epic fantasy novels, he's perfecting the tiny, ancient art of bonsai.

He brings the discipline of martial arts to his characters and imbues his fantasy worlds with the strange beauty observed through nature photography and a keen interest in herpetology. He is currently hard at work on the next novel in the series, ensuring there are plenty more slimy, scaled, and slithery creatures to come.

www.ingramcontent.com/pod-product-compliance
Lightning Source LLC
Chambersburg PA
CBHW051934240626
47153CB00005B/1488